EST 1637

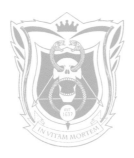

IN VITAM MORTEM

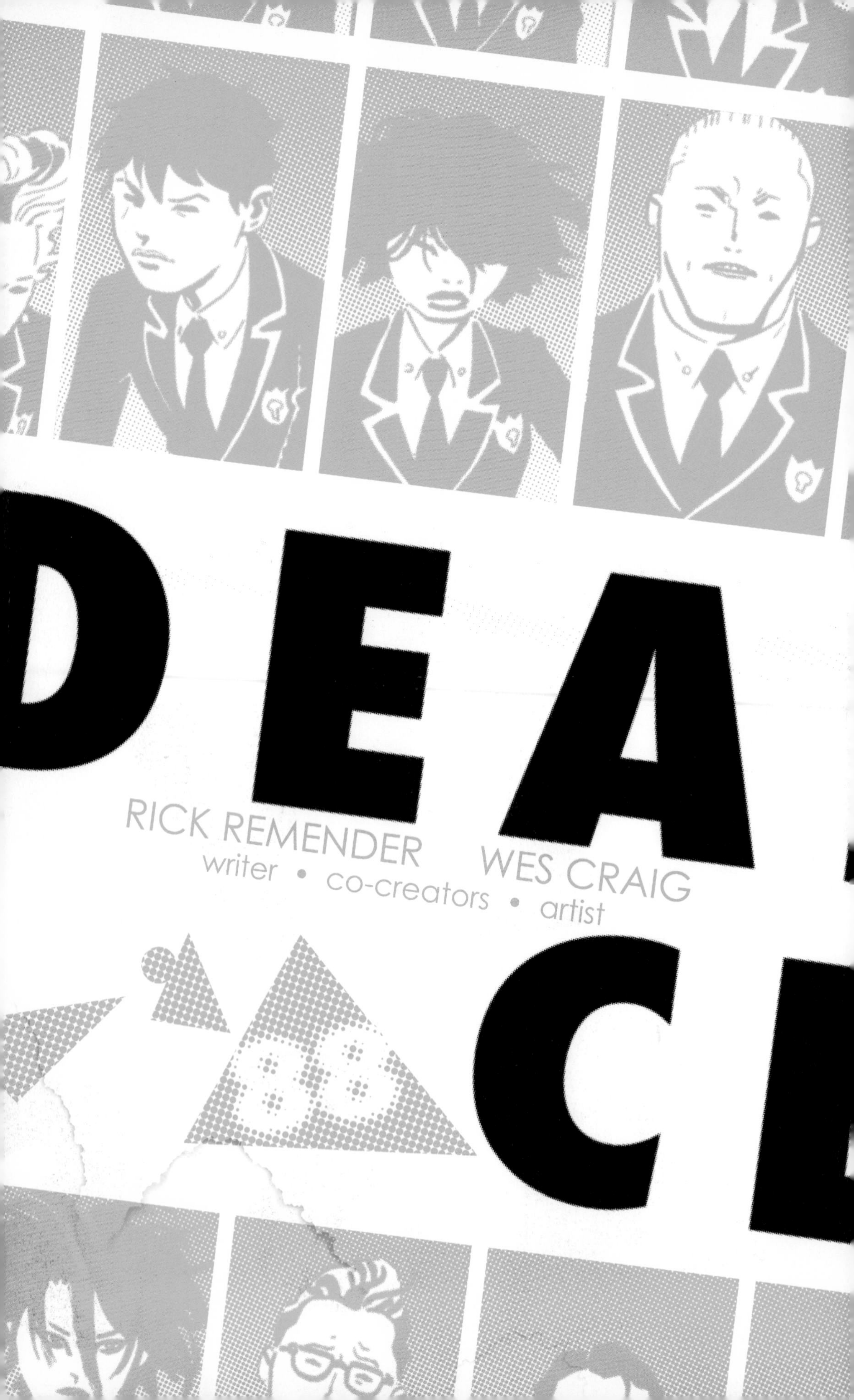
DEA
RICK REMENDER
writer • co-creators • artist
WES CRAIG
CL

DLY
ASS!

JORDAN BOYD
colorist

RUS WOOTON
letterer • logo design

SEBASTIAN GIRNER
editor

IMAGE COMICS, INC.

Robert Kirkman • Chief Operating Officer
Erik Larsen • Chief Financial Officer
Todd McFarlane • President
Marc Silvestri • Chief Executive Officer
Jim Valentino • Vice President

Eric Stephenson • Publisher/Chief Creative Officer
Corey Hart • Director of Sales
Jeff Boison • Director of Publishing Planning & Book Trade Sales
Chris Ross • Director of Digital Sales
Jeff Stang • Director of Specialty Sales
Kat Salazar • Director of PR & Marketing
Drew Gill • Art Director
Heather Doornink • Production Director
Nicole Lapalme • Controller

imagecomics.com

JEFF POWELL
collection design

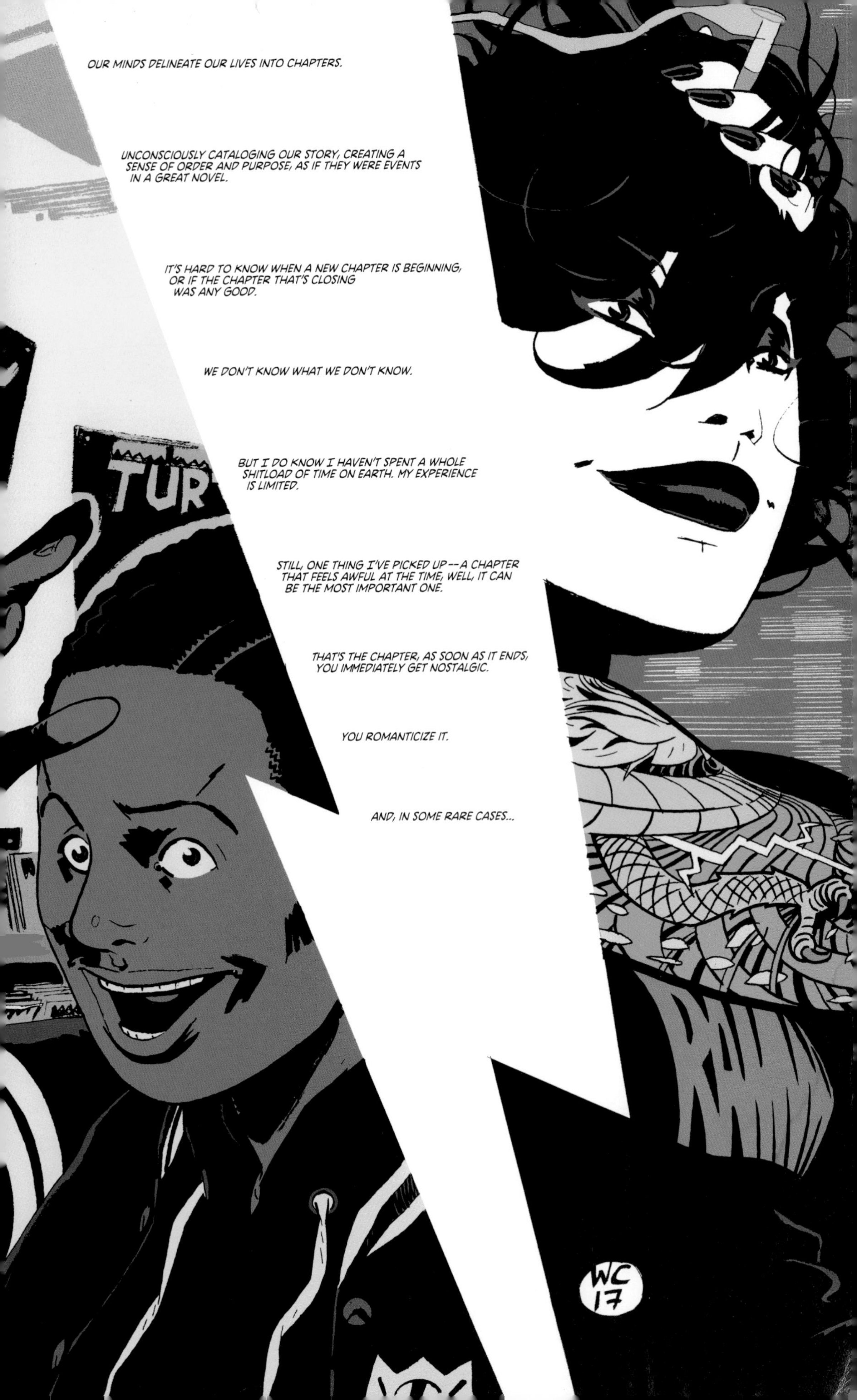
OUR MINDS DELINEATE OUR LIVES INTO CHAPTERS.
UNCONSCIOUSLY CATALOGING OUR STORY, CREATING A SENSE OF ORDER AND PURPOSE, AS IF THEY WERE EVENTS IN A GREAT NOVEL.
IT'S HARD TO KNOW WHEN A NEW CHAPTER IS BEGINNING, OR IF THE CHAPTER THAT'S CLOSING WAS ANY GOOD.
WE DON'T KNOW WHAT WE DON'T KNOW.
BUT I DO KNOW I HAVEN'T SPENT A WHOLE SHITLOAD OF TIME ON EARTH. MY EXPERIENCE IS LIMITED.
STILL, ONE THING I'VE PICKED UP--A CHAPTER THAT FEELS AWFUL AT THE TIME, WELL, IT CAN BE THE MOST IMPORTANT ONE.
THAT'S THE CHAPTER, AS SOON AS IT ENDS, YOU IMMEDIATELY GET NOSTALGIC.
YOU ROMANTICIZE IT.
AND, IN SOME RARE CASES...
TUR
WC 17

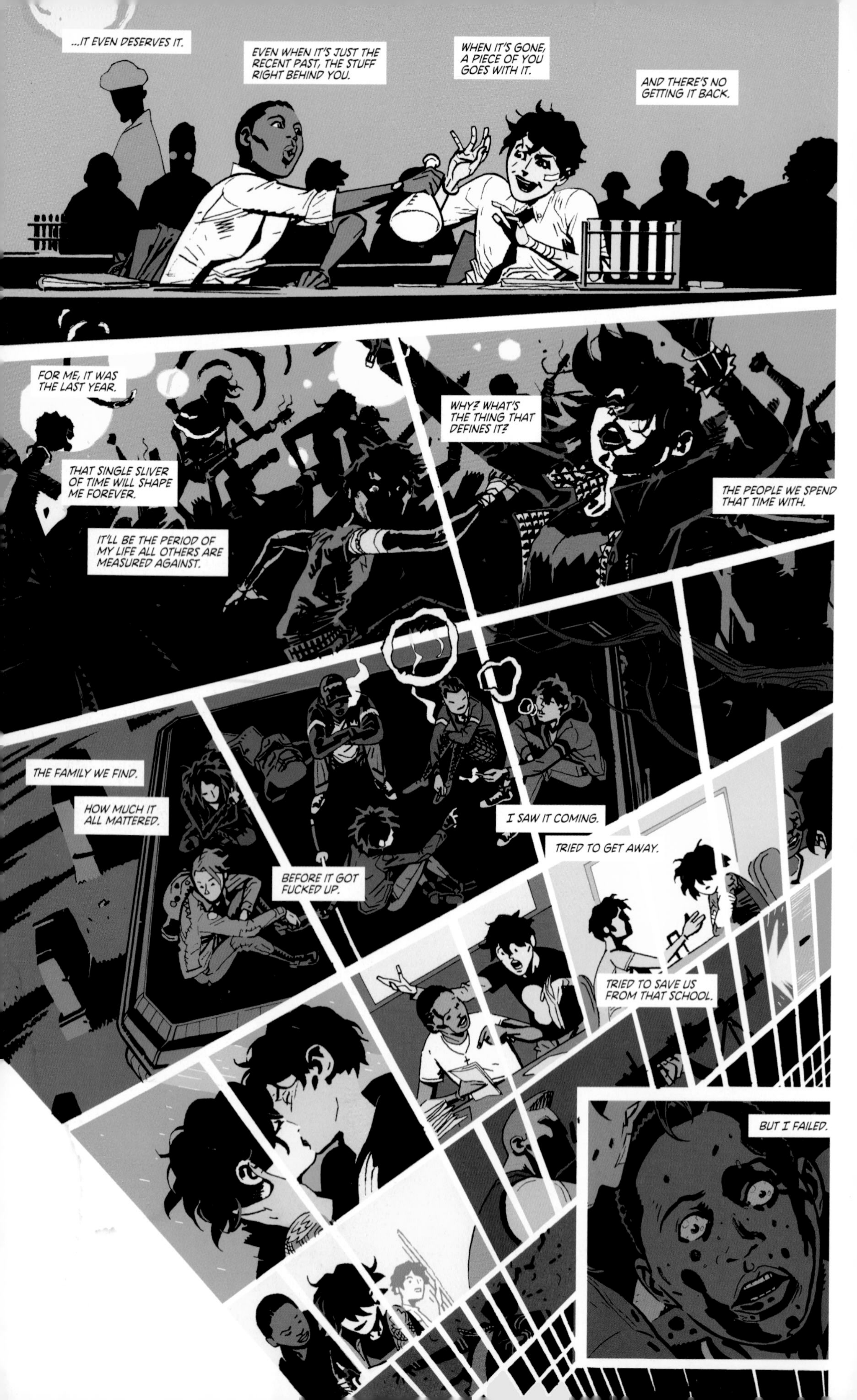
...IT EVEN DESERVES IT.
EVEN WHEN IT'S JUST THE RECENT PAST, THE STUFF RIGHT BEHIND YOU.
WHEN IT'S GONE, A PIECE OF YOU GOES WITH IT.
AND THERE'S NO GETTING IT BACK.
FOR ME, IT WAS THE LAST YEAR.
THAT SINGLE SLIVER OF TIME WILL SHAPE ME FOREVER.
IT'LL BE THE PERIOD OF MY LIFE ALL OTHERS ARE MEASURED AGAINST.
WHY? WHAT'S THE THING THAT DEFINES IT?
THE PEOPLE WE SPEND THAT TIME WITH.
THE FAMILY WE FIND.
HOW MUCH IT ALL MATTERED.
BEFORE IT GOT FUCKED UP.
I SAW IT COMING.
TRIED TO GET AWAY.
TRIED TO SAVE US FROM THAT SCHOOL.
BUT I FAILED.

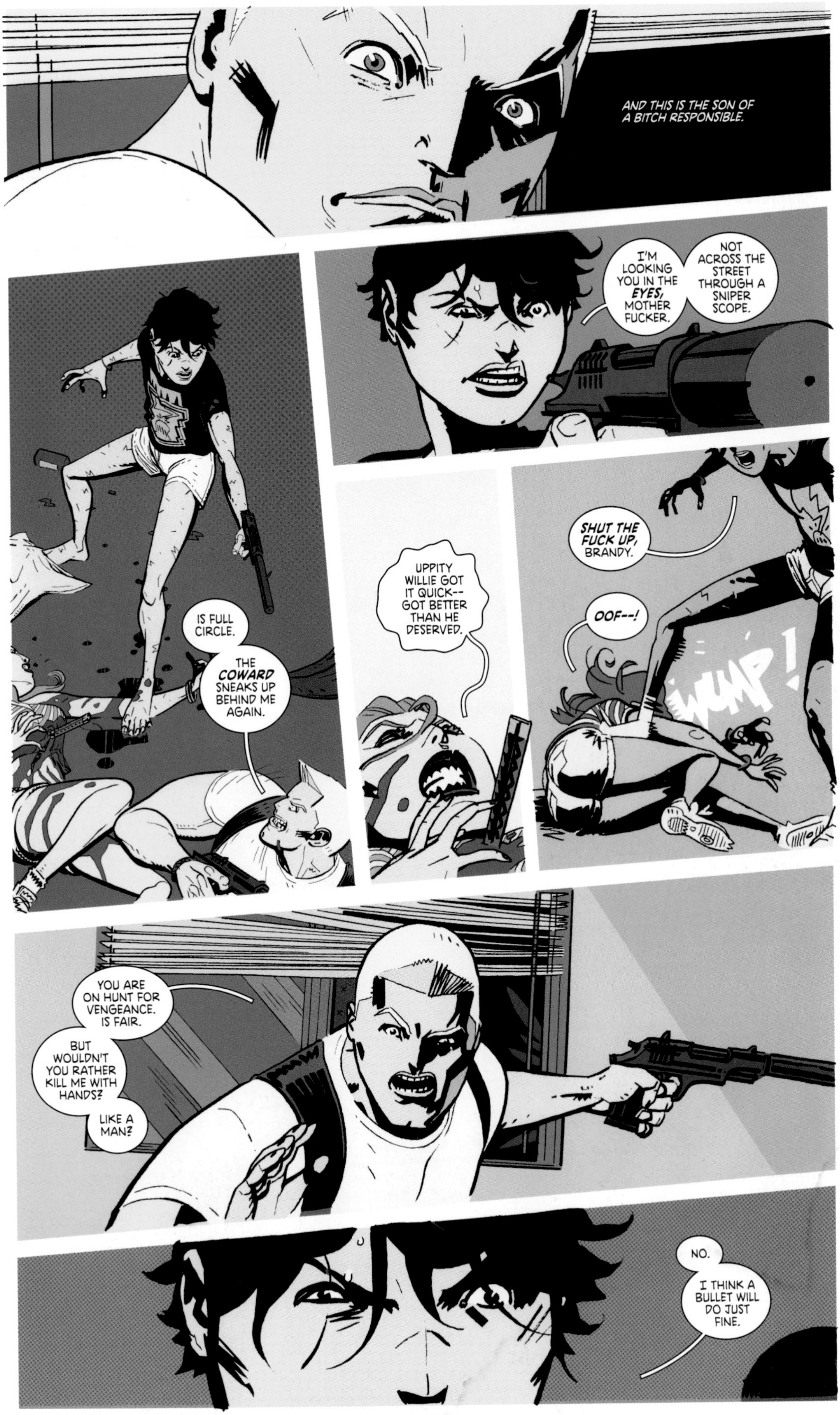
AND THIS IS THE SON OF A BITCH RESPONSIBLE.
I'M LOOKING YOU IN THE EYES, MOTHER FUCKER.
NOT ACROSS THE STREET THROUGH A SNIPER SCOPE.
IS FULL CIRCLE.
THE COWARD SNEAKS UP BEHIND ME AGAIN.
UPPITY WILLIE GOT IT QUICK-- GOT BETTER THAN HE DESERVED.
SHUT THE FUCK UP, BRANDY.
OOF--!
WUMP!
YOU ARE ON HUNT FOR VENGEANCE. IS FAIR.
BUT WOULDN'T YOU RATHER KILL ME WITH HANDS?
LIKE A MAN?
NO.
I THINK A BULLET WILL DO JUST FINE.

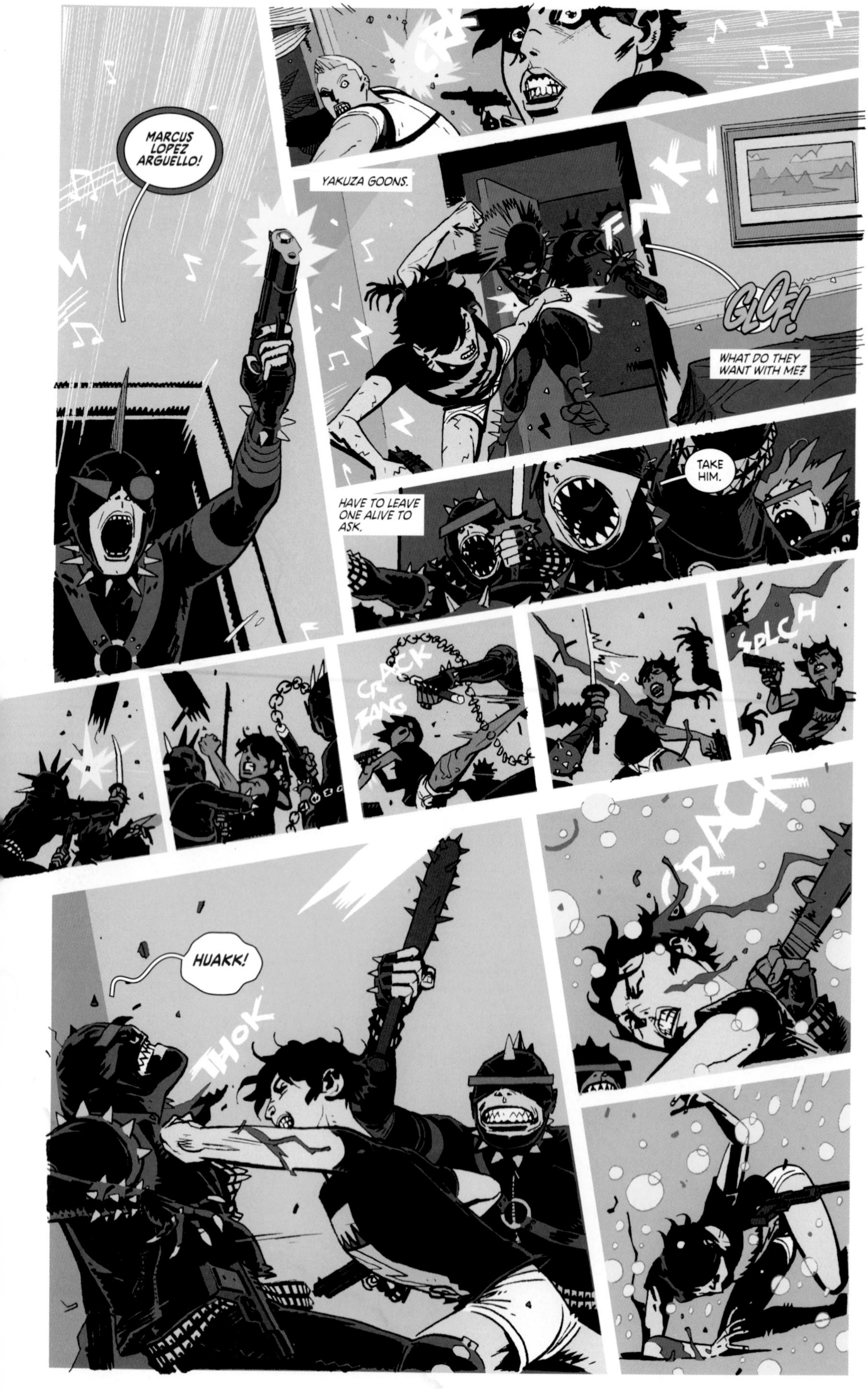
MARCUS LOPEZ ARGUELLO!
YAKUZA GOONS.
FNK!
GLOF!
WHAT DO THEY WANT WITH ME?
TAKE HIM.
HAVE TO LEAVE ONE ALIVE TO ASK.
CRACK
BANG
SP
SPLCH
HUAKK!
THOK
CRACK

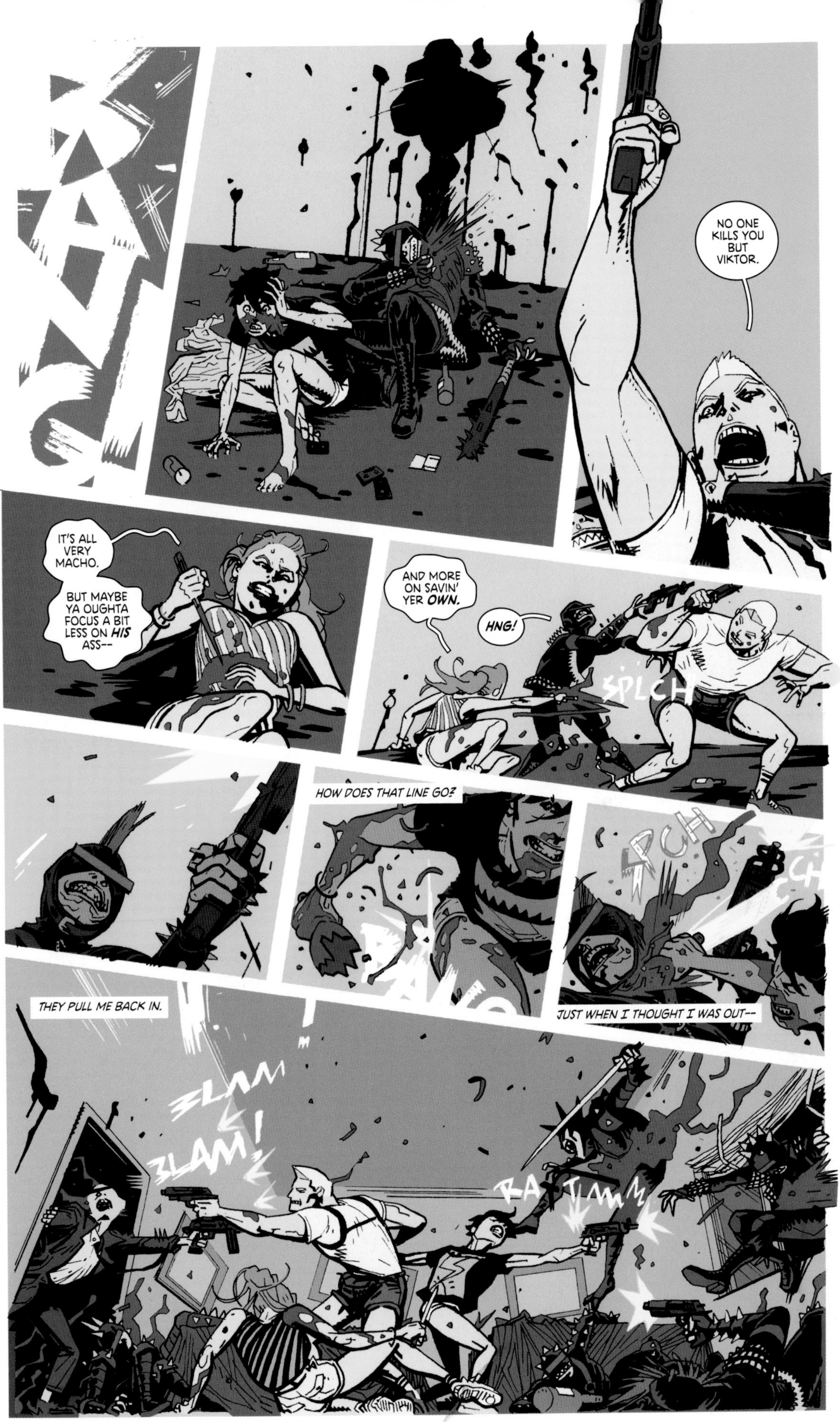
NO ONE KILLS YOU BUT VIKTOR.
IT'S ALL VERY MACHO.
BUT MAYBE YA OUGHTA FOCUS A BIT LESS ON *HIS* ASS--
AND MORE ON SAVIN' YER *OWN.*
HNG!
SPLCH
HOW DOES THAT LINE GO?
PCH
JUST WHEN I THOUGHT I WAS OUT--
THEY PULL ME BACK IN.
BLAM
BLAM!

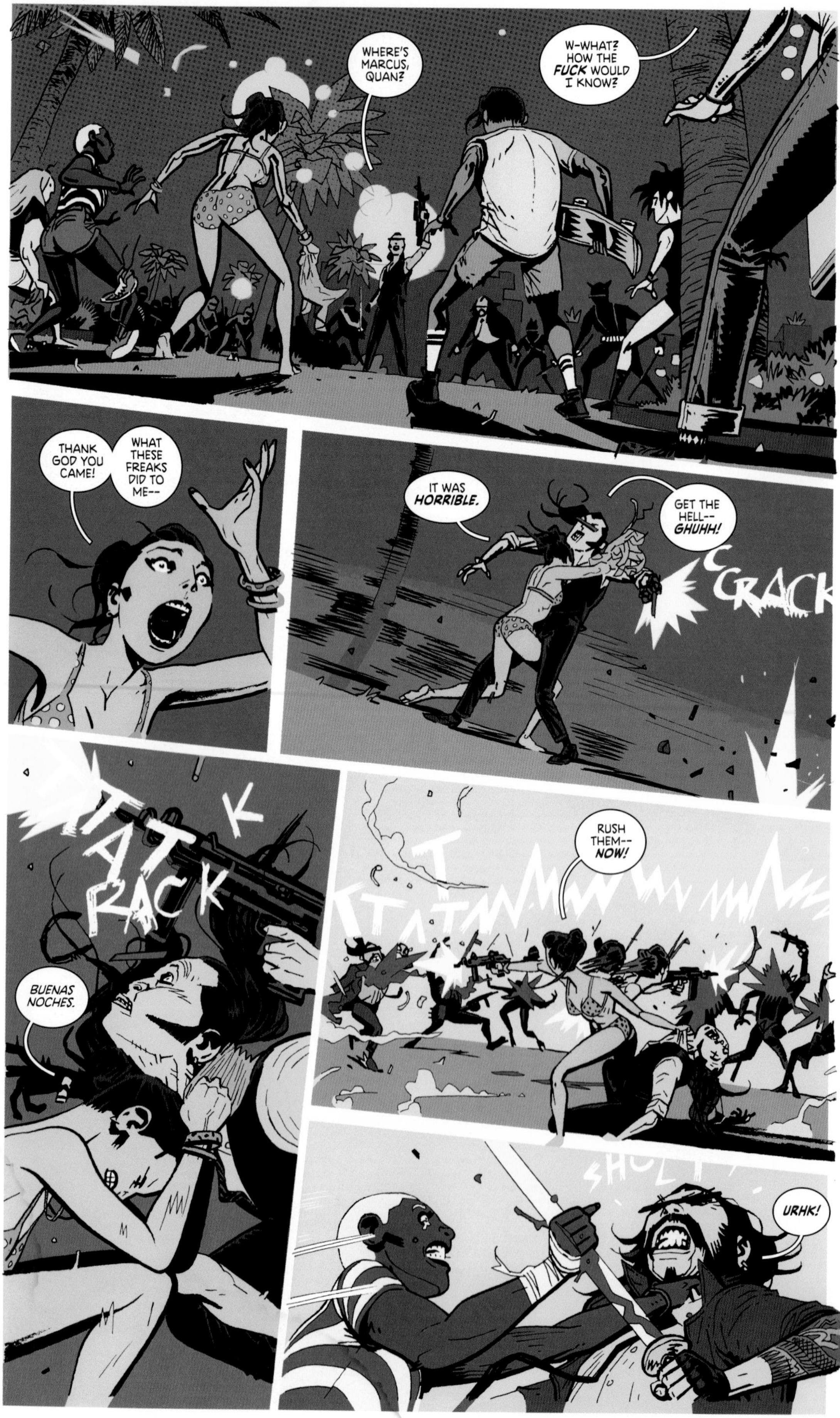
WHERE'S MARCUS, QUAN?
W-WHAT? HOW THE FUCK WOULD I KNOW?
THANK GOD YOU CAME!
WHAT THESE FREAKS DID TO ME--
IT WAS HORRIBLE.
GET THE HELL-- GHUHH!
CCRACK
TAT RACK K
BUENAS NOCHES.
RUSH THEM-- NOW!
URHK!

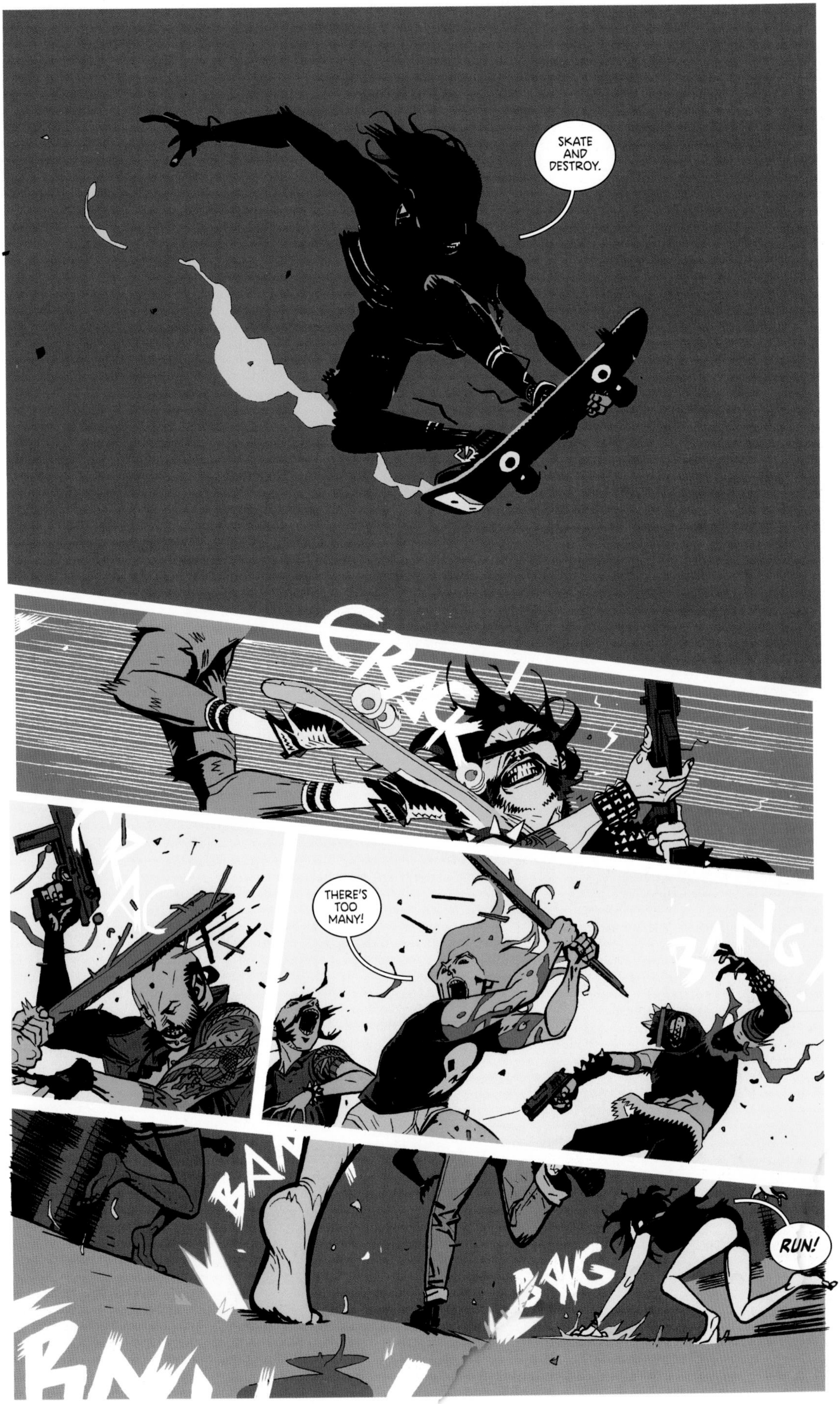
SKATE AND DESTROY.
CRACK!
THERE'S TOO MANY!
BANG!
BANG
RUN!

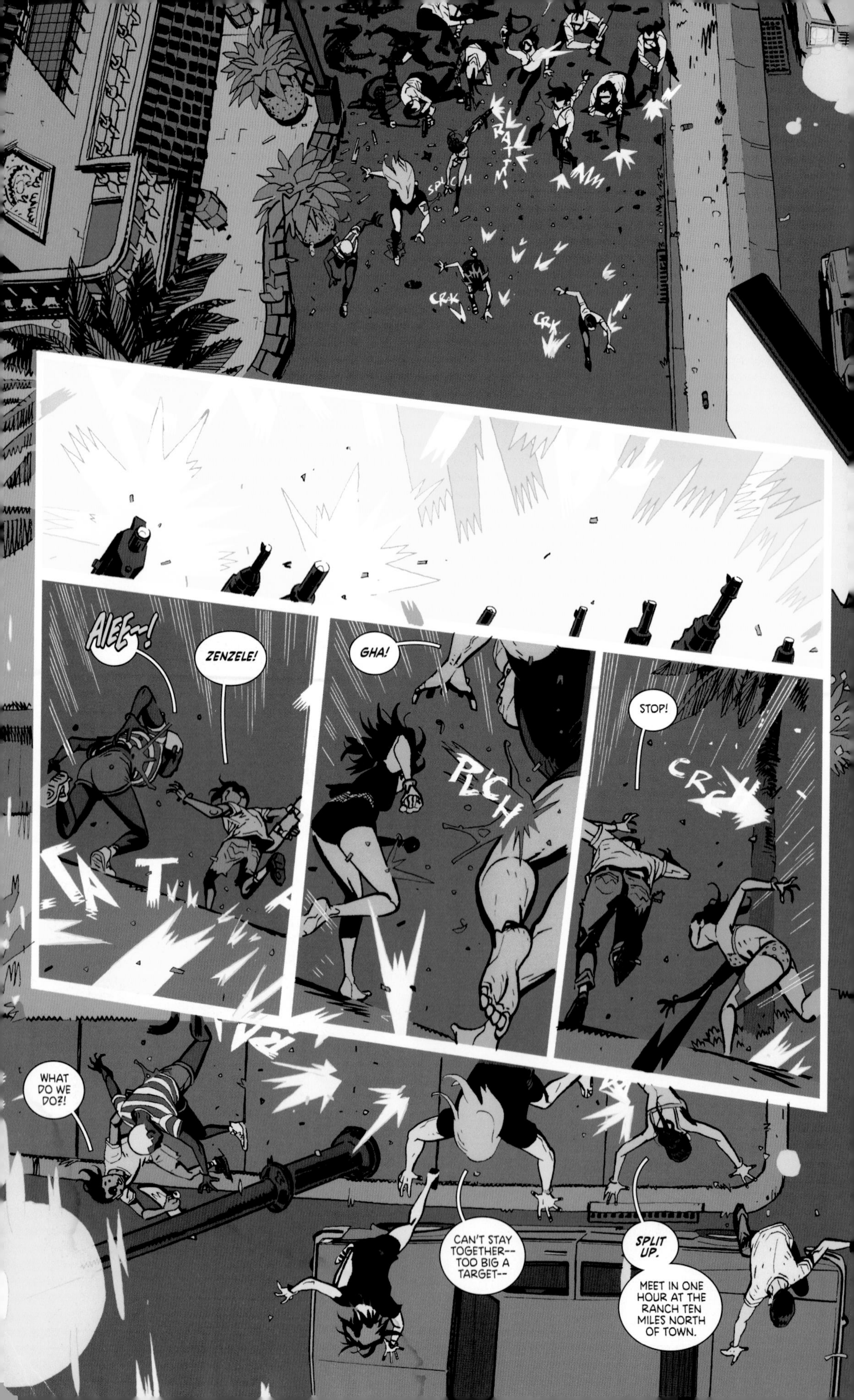

SPLCH
CRK
CRK
AIEE--!
ZENZELE!
GHA!
PLCH
STOP!
WHAT DO WE DO?!
CAN'T STAY TOGETHER-- TOO BIG A TARGET--
SPLIT UP.
MEET IN ONE HOUR AT THE RANCH TEN MILES NORTH OF TOWN.

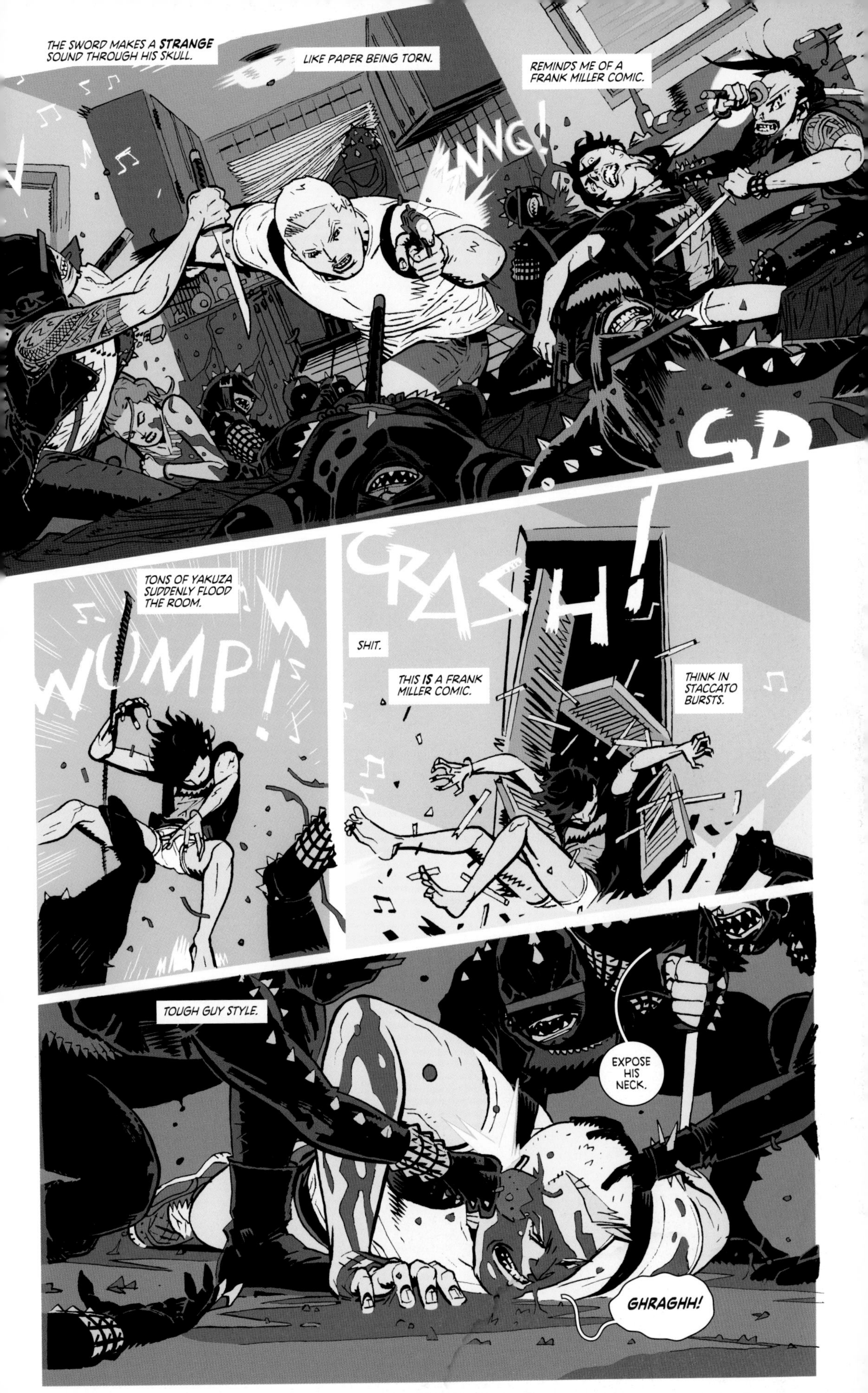
THE SWORD MAKES A **STRANGE** SOUND THROUGH HIS SKULL.
LIKE PAPER BEING TORN.
REMINDS ME OF A FRANK MILLER COMIC.
NNG!
TONS OF YAKUZA SUDDENLY FLOOD THE ROOM.
WOMP!
CRASH!
SHIT.
THIS **IS** A FRANK MILLER COMIC.
THINK IN STACCATO BURSTS.
TOUGH GUY STYLE.
EXPOSE HIS NECK.
GHRAGHH!

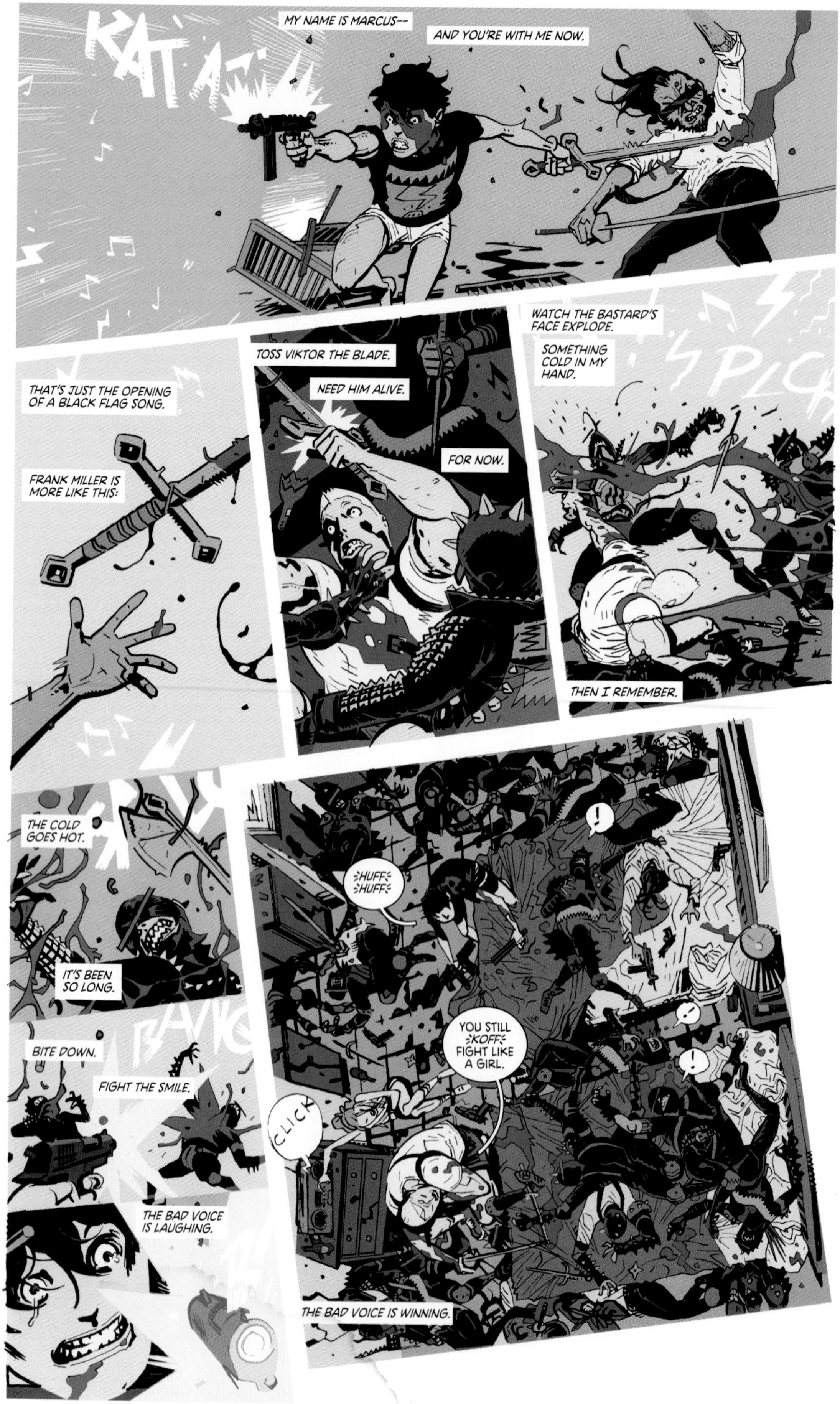
KAT A
MY NAME IS MARCUS--
AND YOU'RE WITH ME NOW.
THAT'S JUST THE OPENING OF A BLACK FLAG SONG.
FRANK MILLER IS MORE LIKE THIS:
TOSS VIKTOR THE BLADE.
NEED HIM ALIVE.
FOR NOW.
WATCH THE BASTARD'S FACE EXPLODE.
SOMETHING COLD IN MY HAND.
SPLCH
THEN I REMEMBER.
THE COLD GOES HOT.
IT'S BEEN SO LONG.
BITE DOWN.
FIGHT THE SMILE.
THE BAD VOICE IS LAUGHING.
HUFF HUFF
!
YOU STILL KOFF FIGHT LIKE A GIRL.
!
!
CLICK
THE BAD VOICE IS WINNING.

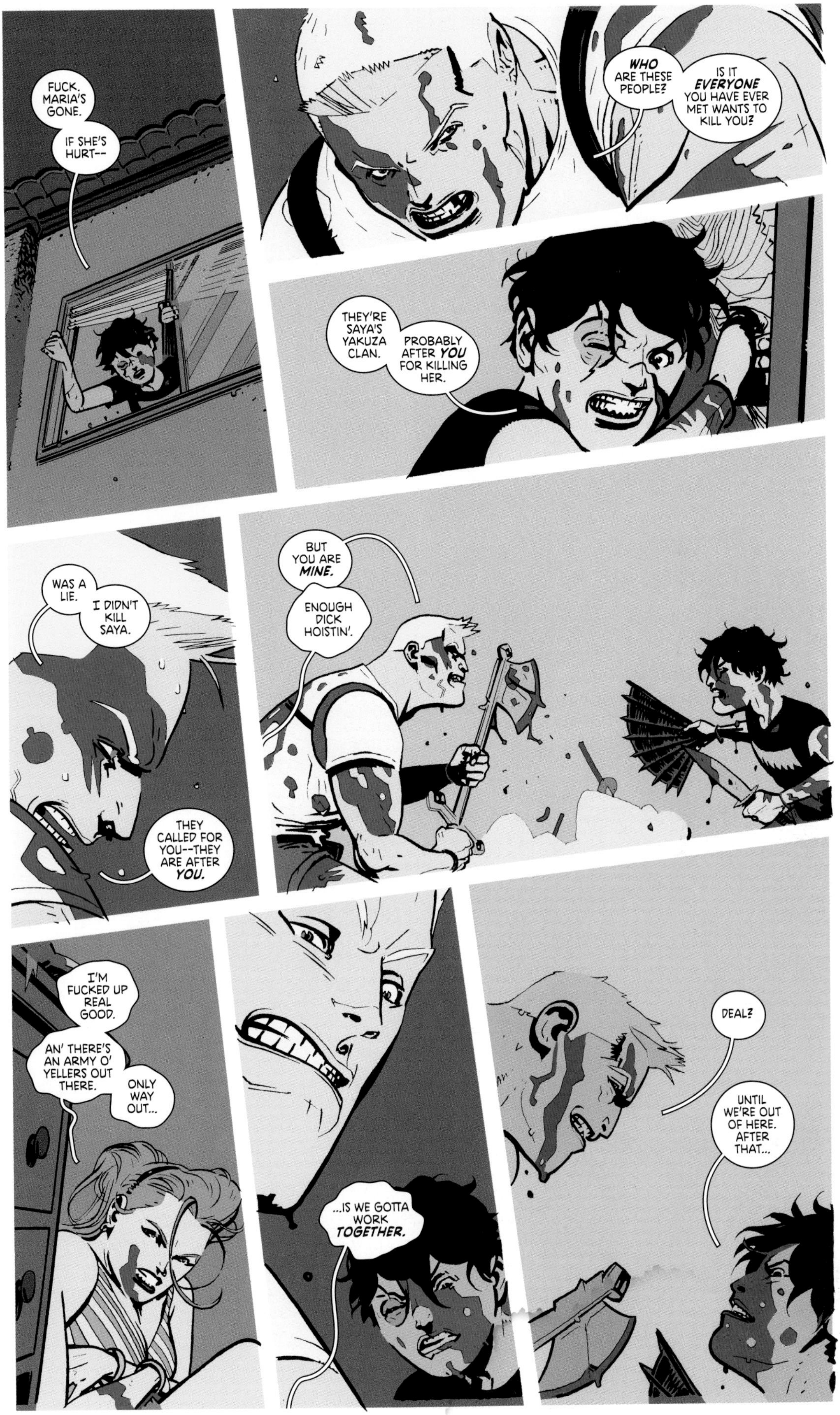
FUCK. MARIA'S GONE.
IF SHE'S HURT--
WHO ARE THESE PEOPLE?
IS IT EVERYONE YOU HAVE EVER MET WANTS TO KILL YOU?
THEY'RE SAYA'S YAKUZA CLAN.
PROBABLY AFTER YOU FOR KILLING HER.
WAS A LIE.
I DIDN'T KILL SAYA.
THEY CALLED FOR YOU--THEY ARE AFTER YOU.
BUT YOU ARE MINE.
ENOUGH DICK HOISTIN'.
I'M FUCKED UP REAL GOOD.
AN' THERE'S AN ARMY O' YELLERS OUT THERE.
ONLY WAY OUT...
...IS WE GOTTA WORK TOGETHER.
DEAL?
UNTIL WE'RE OUT OF HERE. AFTER THAT...

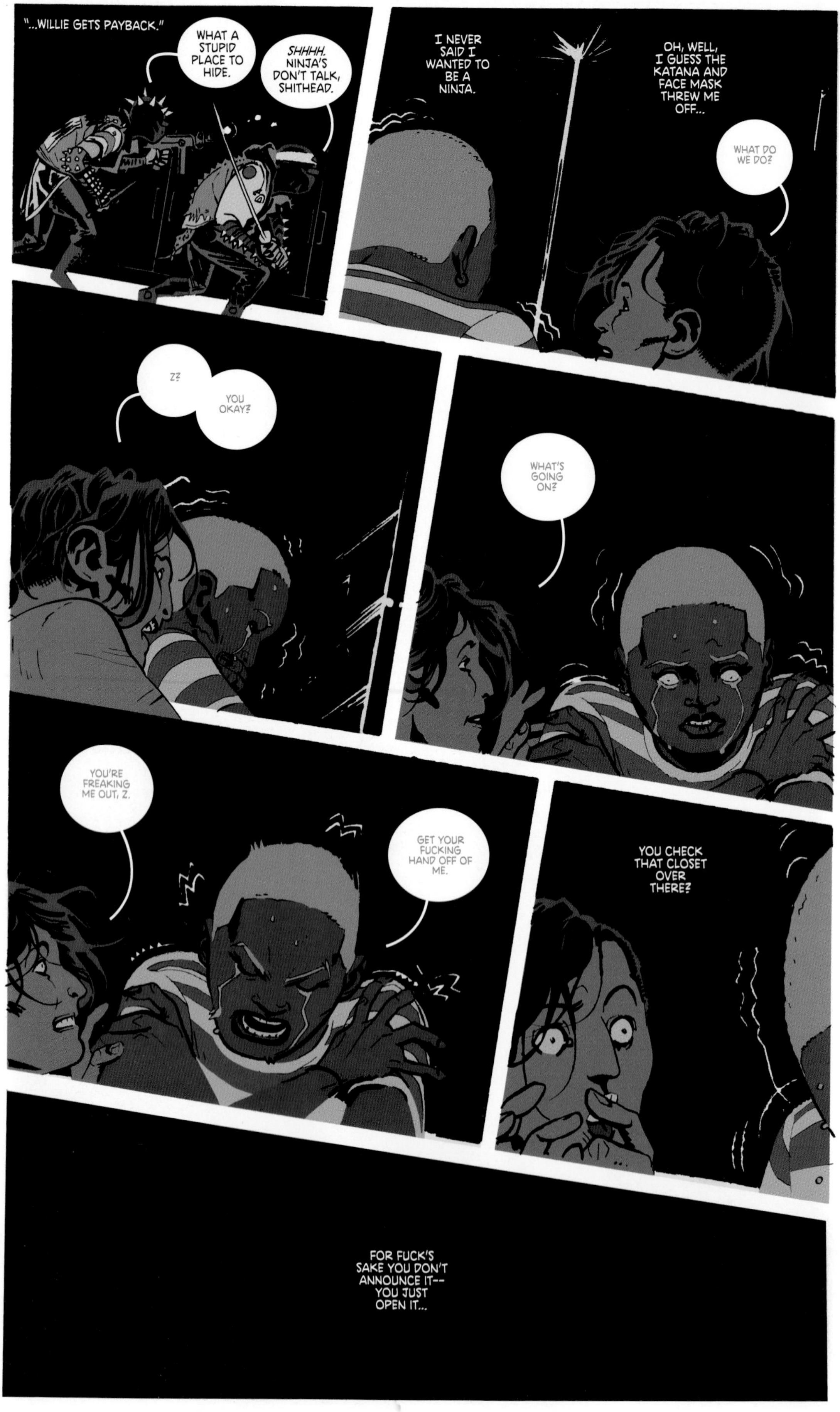
"...WILLIE GETS PAYBACK."
WHAT A STUPID PLACE TO HIDE.
SHHHH. NINJA'S DON'T TALK, SHITHEAD.
I NEVER SAID I WANTED TO BE A NINJA.
OH, WELL, I GUESS THE KATANA AND FACE MASK THREW ME OFF...
WHAT DO WE DO?
Z?
YOU OKAY?
WHAT'S GOING ON?
YOU'RE FREAKING ME OUT, Z.
GET YOUR FUCKING HAND OFF OF ME.
YOU CHECK THAT CLOSET OVER THERE?
FOR FUCK'S SAKE YOU DON'T ANNOUNCE IT-- YOU JUST OPEN IT...

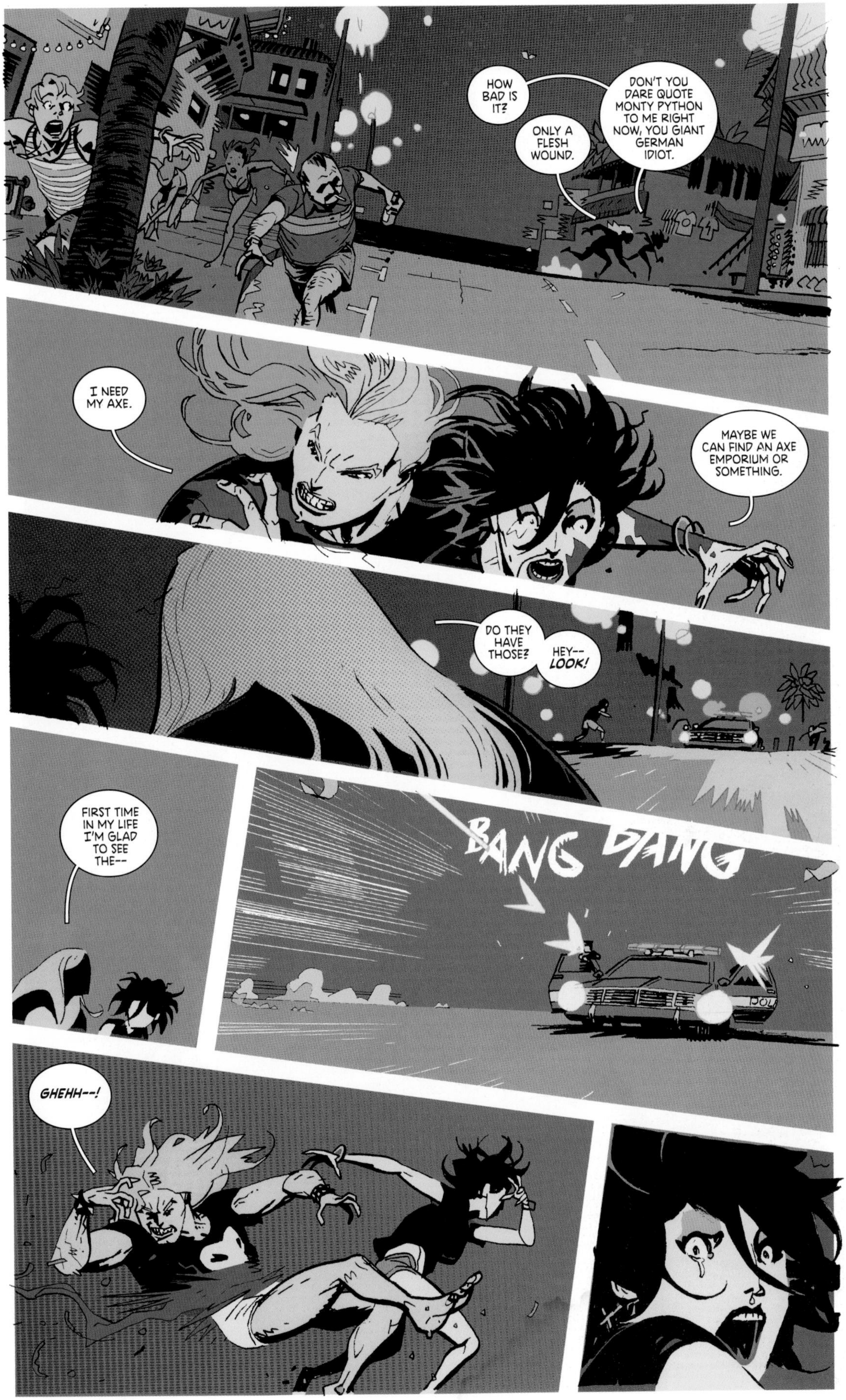
HOW BAD IS IT?
ONLY A FLESH WOUND.
DON'T YOU DARE QUOTE MONTY PYTHON TO ME RIGHT NOW, YOU GIANT GERMAN IDIOT.
I NEED MY AXE.
MAYBE WE CAN FIND AN AXE EMPORIUM OR SOMETHING.
DO THEY HAVE THOSE?
HEY-- LOOK!
FIRST TIME IN MY LIFE I'M GLAD TO SEE THE--
BANG BANG
GHEHH--!

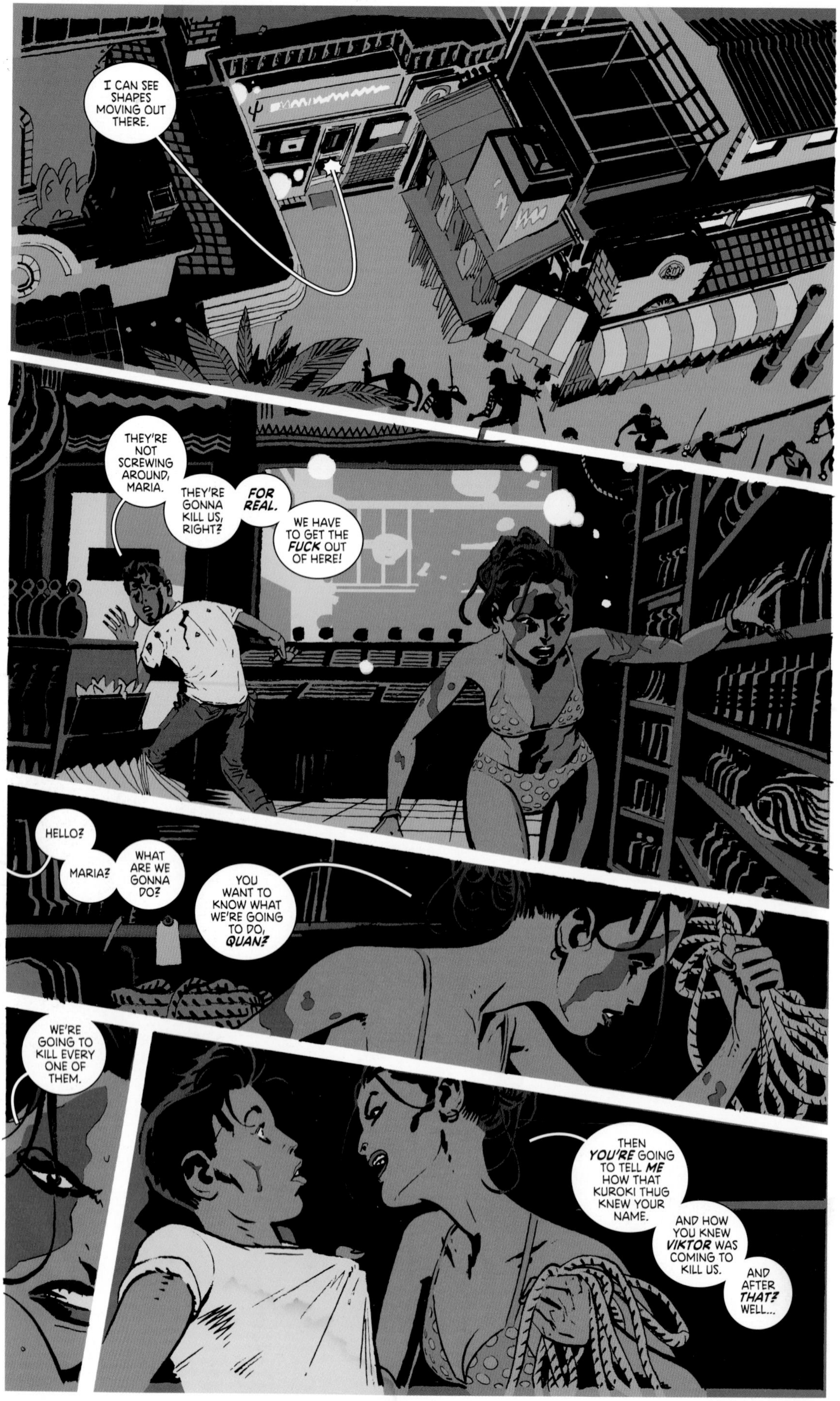
I CAN SEE SHAPES MOVING OUT THERE.
THEY'RE NOT SCREWING AROUND, MARIA.
THEY'RE GONNA KILL US, RIGHT?
FOR REAL.
WE HAVE TO GET THE FUCK OUT OF HERE!
HELLO?
MARIA?
WHAT ARE WE GONNA DO?
YOU WANT TO KNOW WHAT WE'RE GOING TO DO, QUAN?
WE'RE GOING TO KILL EVERY ONE OF THEM.
THEN YOU'RE GOING TO TELL ME HOW THAT KUROKI THUG KNEW YOUR NAME.
AND HOW YOU KNEW VIKTOR WAS COMING TO KILL US.
AND AFTER THAT? WELL...

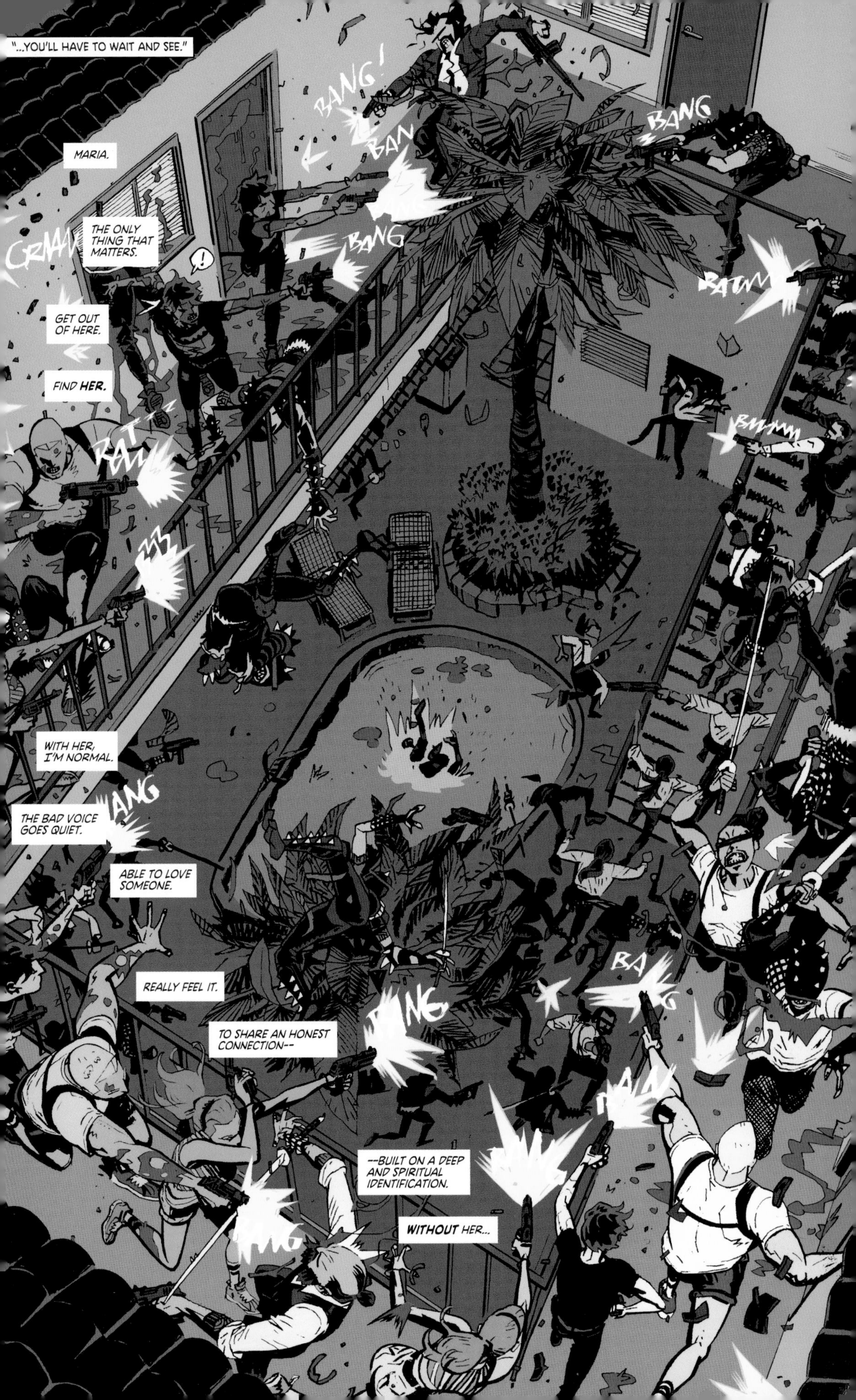
"...YOU'LL HAVE TO WAIT AND SEE."
BANG!
BANG
BAN
BANG
MARIA.
THE ONLY THING THAT MATTERS.
BANG
GET OUT OF HERE.
FIND HER.
WITH HER, I'M NORMAL.
THE BAD VOICE GOES QUIET.
ABLE TO LOVE SOMEONE.
REALLY FEEL IT.
TO SHARE AN HONEST CONNECTION--
--BUILT ON A DEEP AND SPIRITUAL IDENTIFICATION.
WITHOUT HER...

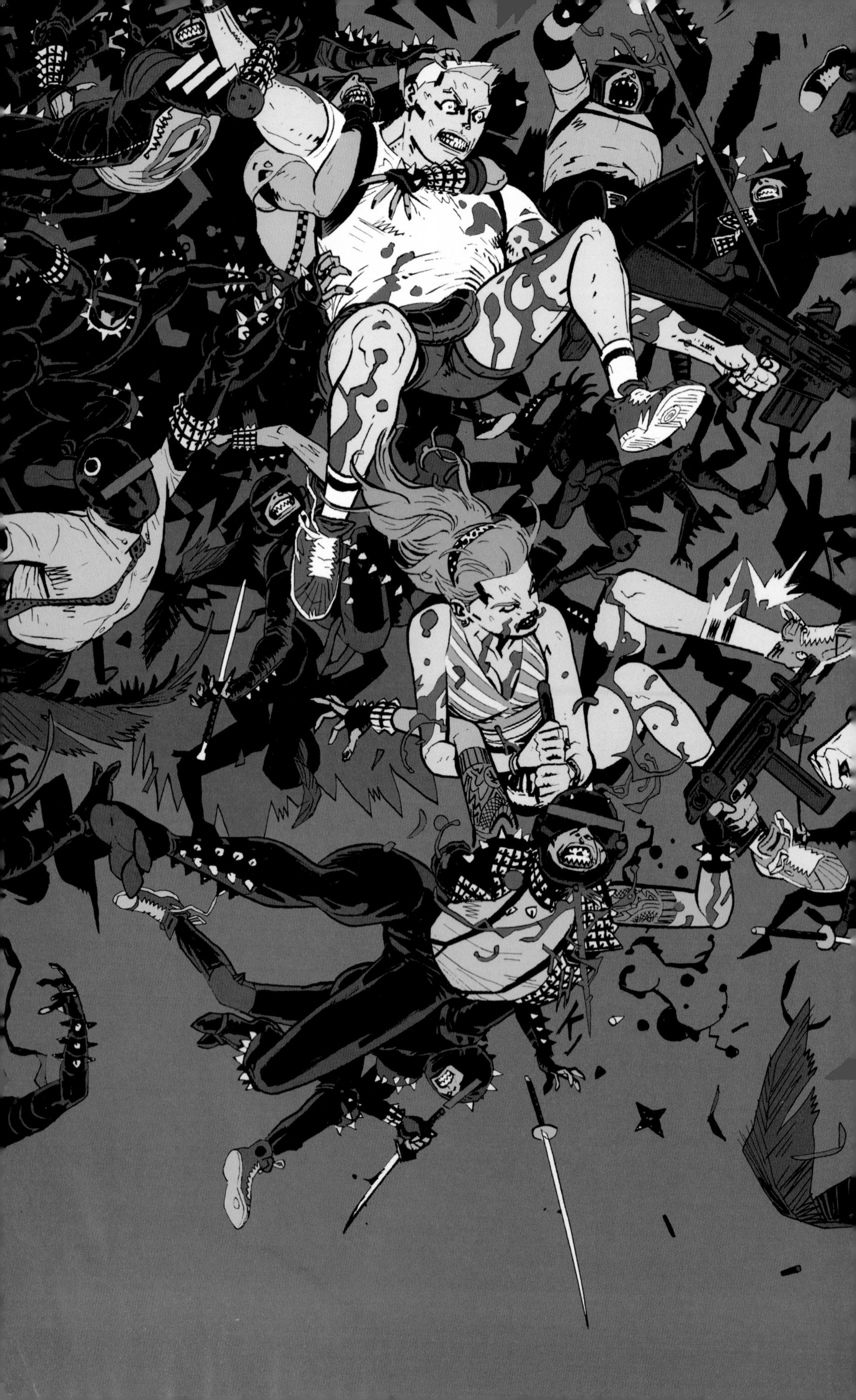

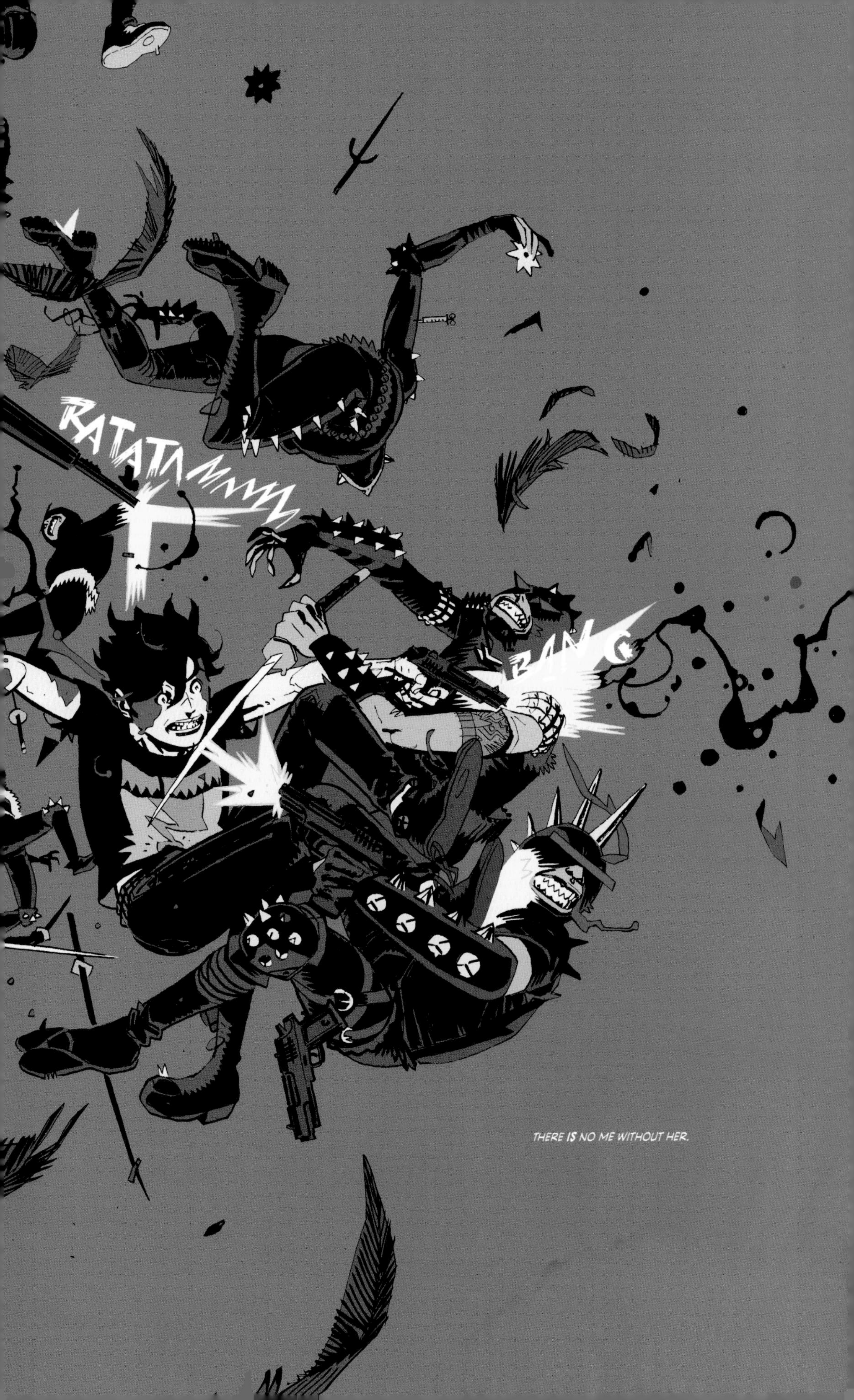
RATATAMMM
BANG
THERE IS NO ME WITHOUT HER.

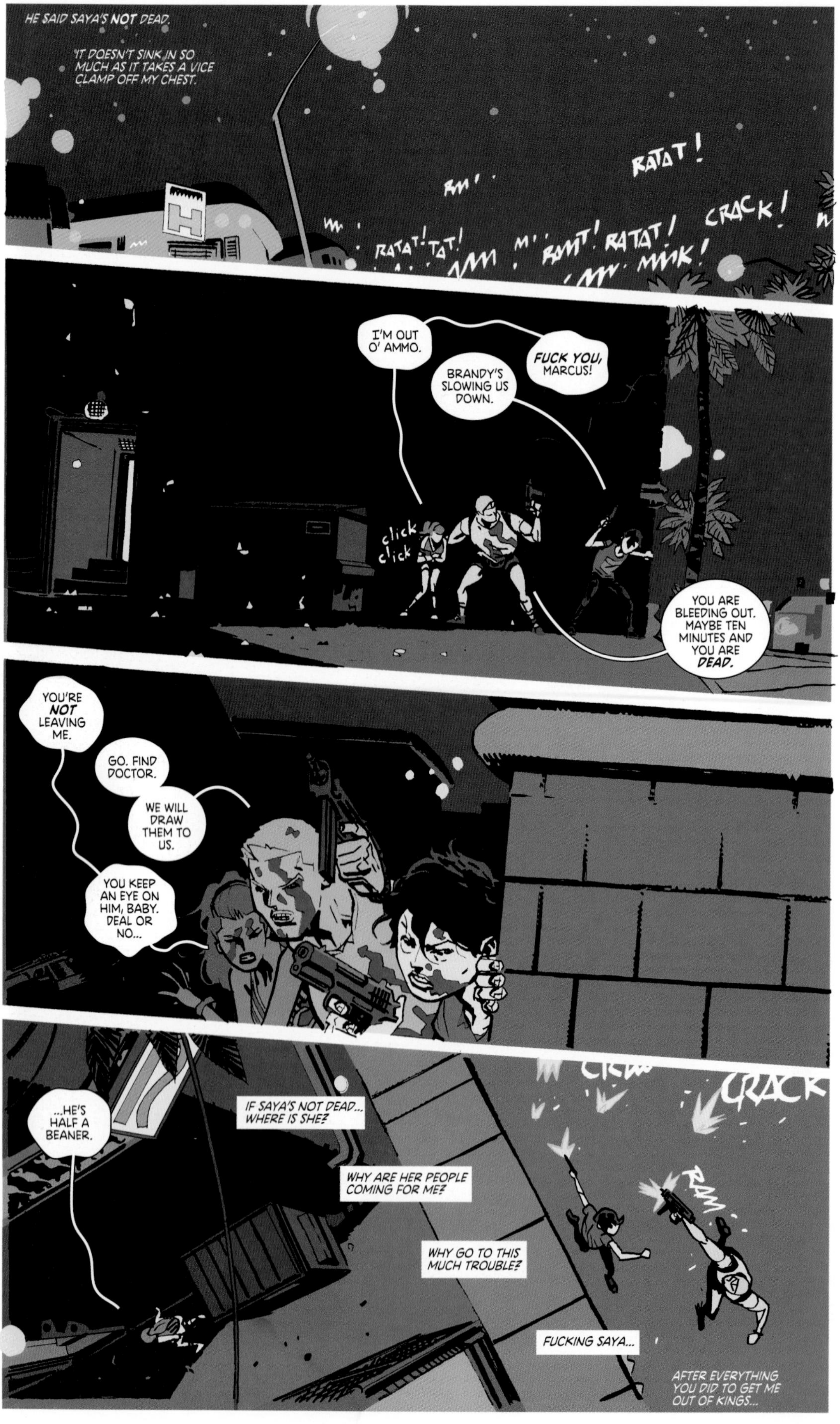
HE SAID SAYA'S NOT DEAD.
IT DOESN'T SINK IN SO MUCH AS IT TAKES A VICE CLAMP OFF MY CHEST.
RATAT!
CRACK!
RATAT! TAT!
RAMT! RATAT!
I'M OUT O' AMMO.
BRANDY'S SLOWING US DOWN.
FUCK YOU, MARCUS!
click click
YOU ARE BLEEDING OUT. MAYBE TEN MINUTES AND YOU ARE DEAD.
YOU'RE NOT LEAVING ME.
GO. FIND DOCTOR.
WE WILL DRAW THEM TO US.
YOU KEEP AN EYE ON HIM, BABY. DEAL OR NO...
...HE'S HALF A BEANER.
IF SAYA'S NOT DEAD... WHERE IS SHE?
CRACK
WHY ARE HER PEOPLE COMING FOR ME?
BLAM
WHY GO TO THIS MUCH TROUBLE?
FUCKING SAYA...
AFTER EVERYTHING YOU DID TO GET ME OUT OF KINGS...

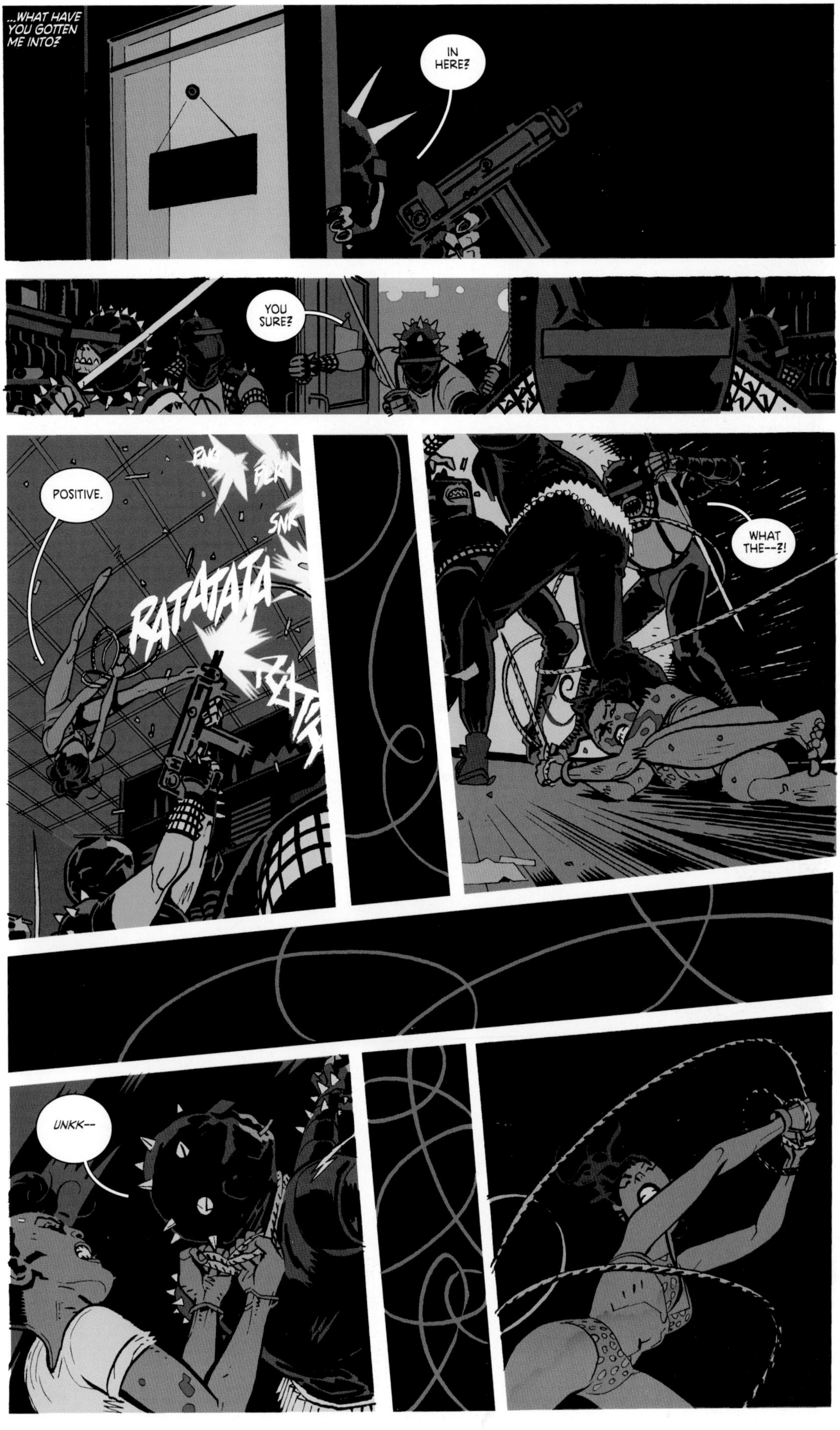
...WHAT HAVE YOU GOTTEN ME INTO?
IN HERE?
YOU SURE?
POSITIVE.
FLK
SNK
RATATATA
WHAT THE--?!
UNKK--

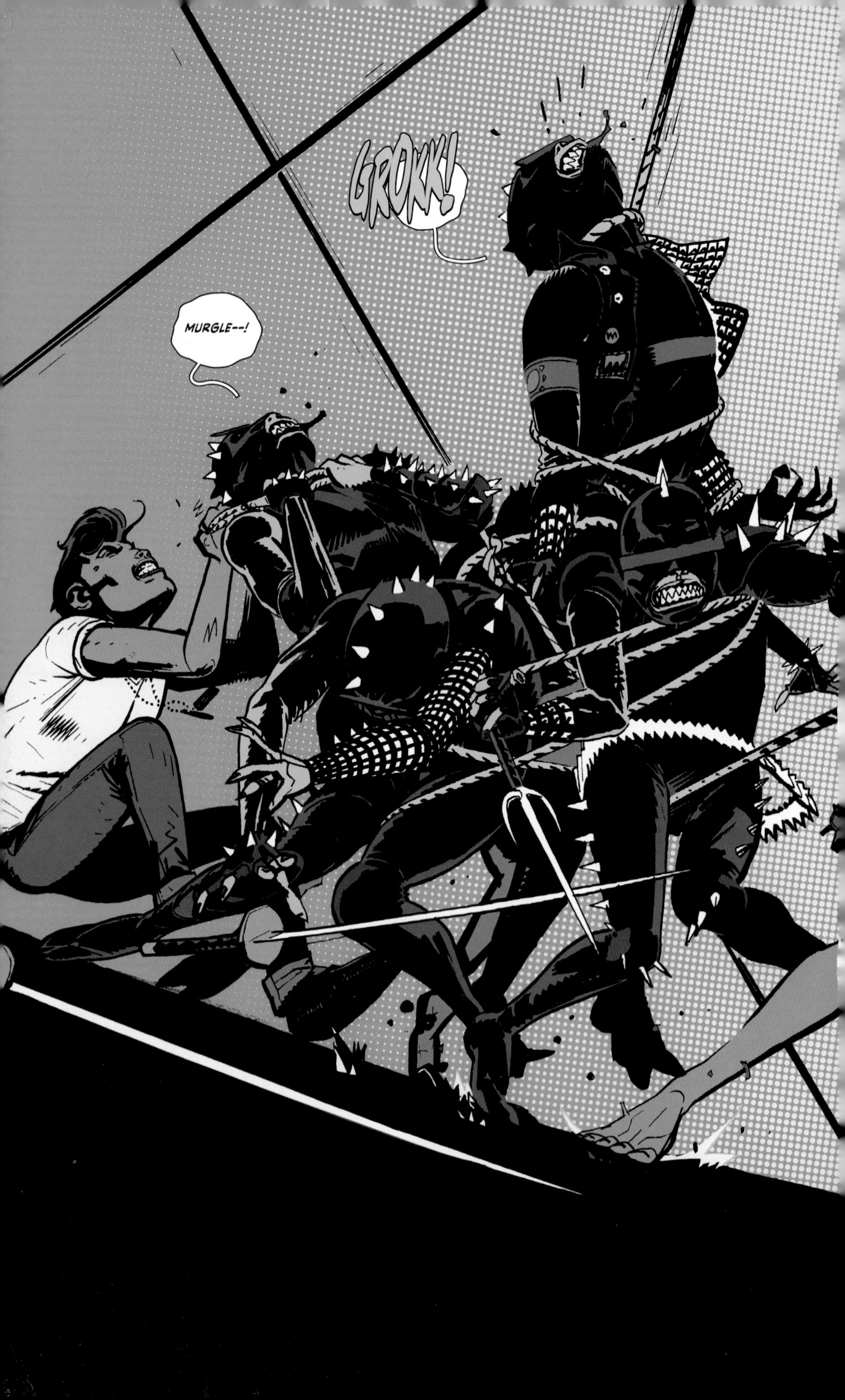
GROKK!
MURGLE--!

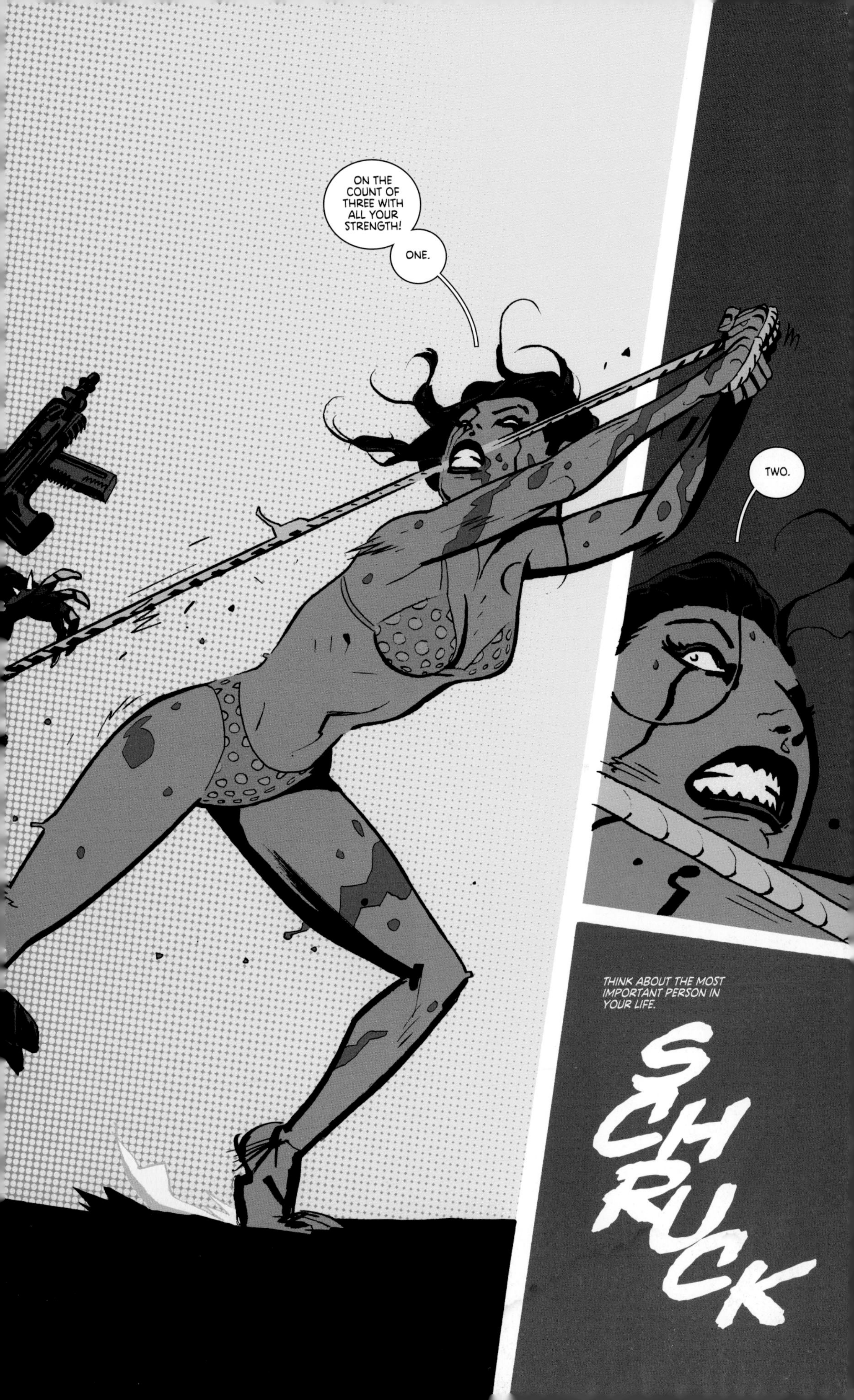

ON THE COUNT OF THREE WITH ALL YOUR STRENGTH!
ONE.
TWO.
THINK ABOUT THE MOST IMPORTANT PERSON IN YOUR LIFE.
SCHRUCK

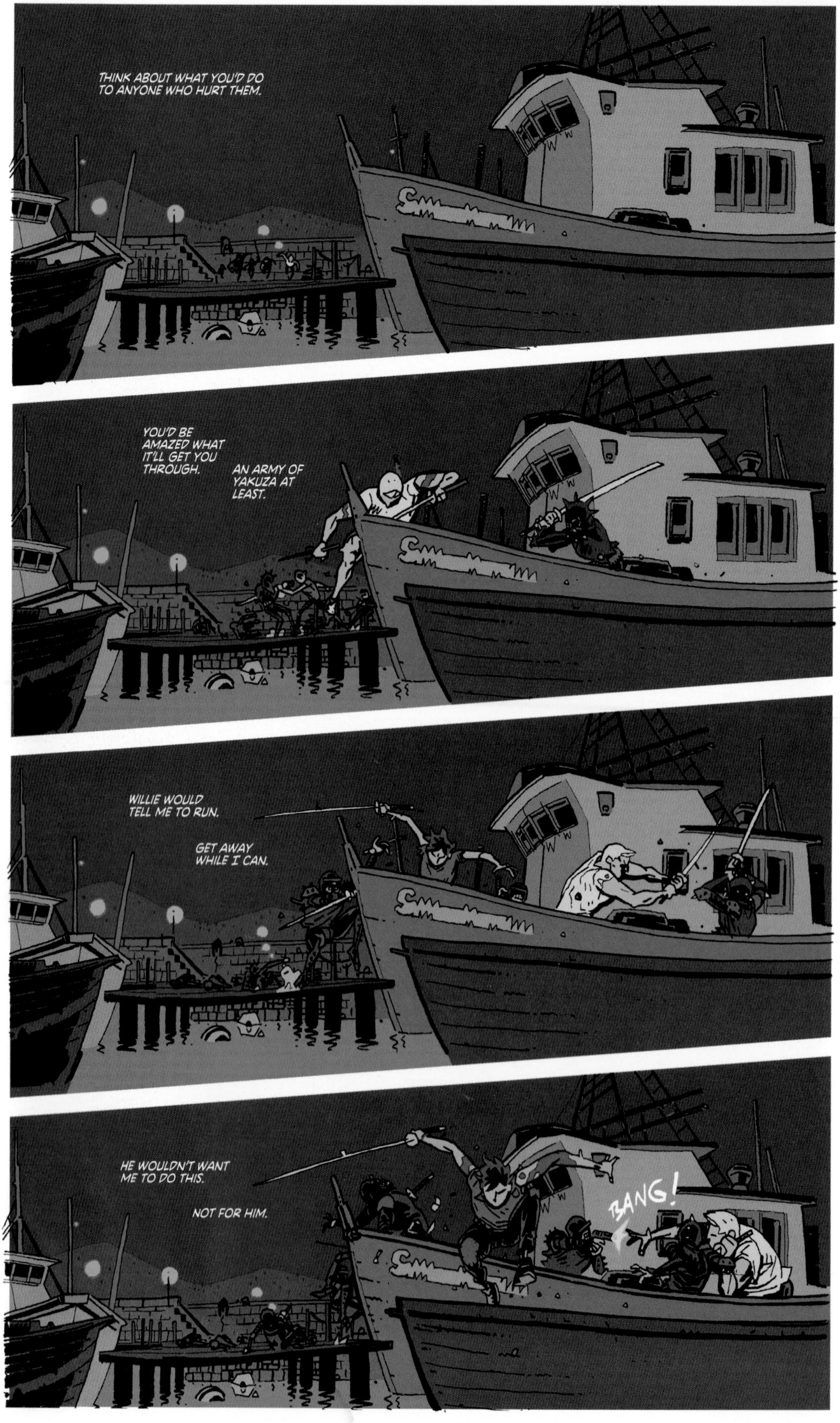
THINK ABOUT WHAT YOU'D DO
TO ANYONE WHO HURT THEM.
YOU'D BE AMAZED WHAT IT'LL GET YOU THROUGH.
AN ARMY OF YAKUZA AT LEAST.
WILLIE WOULD TELL ME TO RUN.
GET AWAY WHILE I CAN.
HE WOULDN'T WANT ME TO DO THIS.
NOT FOR HIM.
BANG!

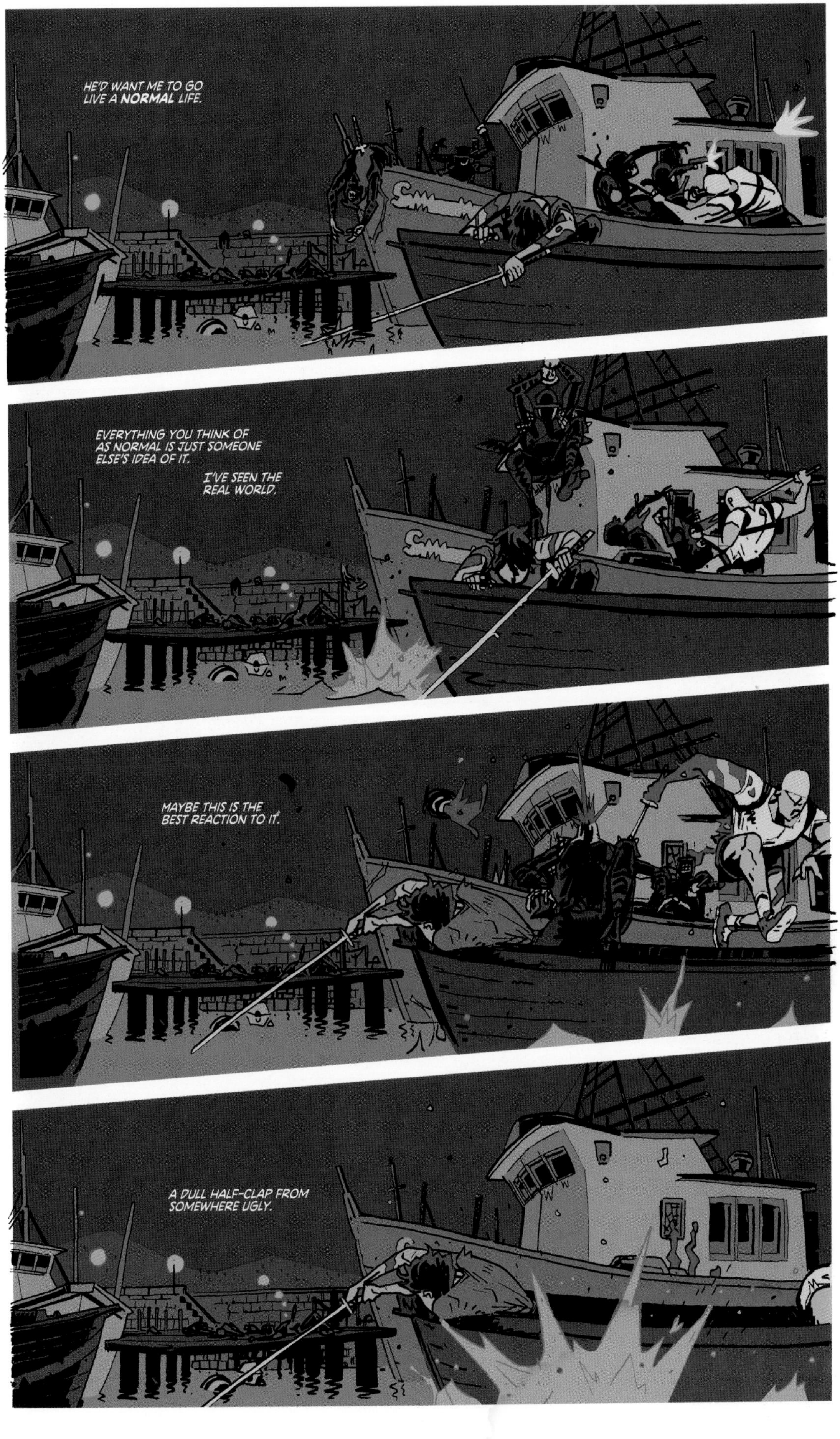
HE'D WANT ME TO GO LIVE A **NORMAL** LIFE.
EVERYTHING YOU THINK OF AS NORMAL IS JUST SOMEONE ELSE'S IDEA OF IT.
I'VE SEEN THE REAL WORLD.
MAYBE THIS IS THE BEST REACTION TO IT.
A DULL HALF-CLAP FROM SOMEWHERE UGLY.

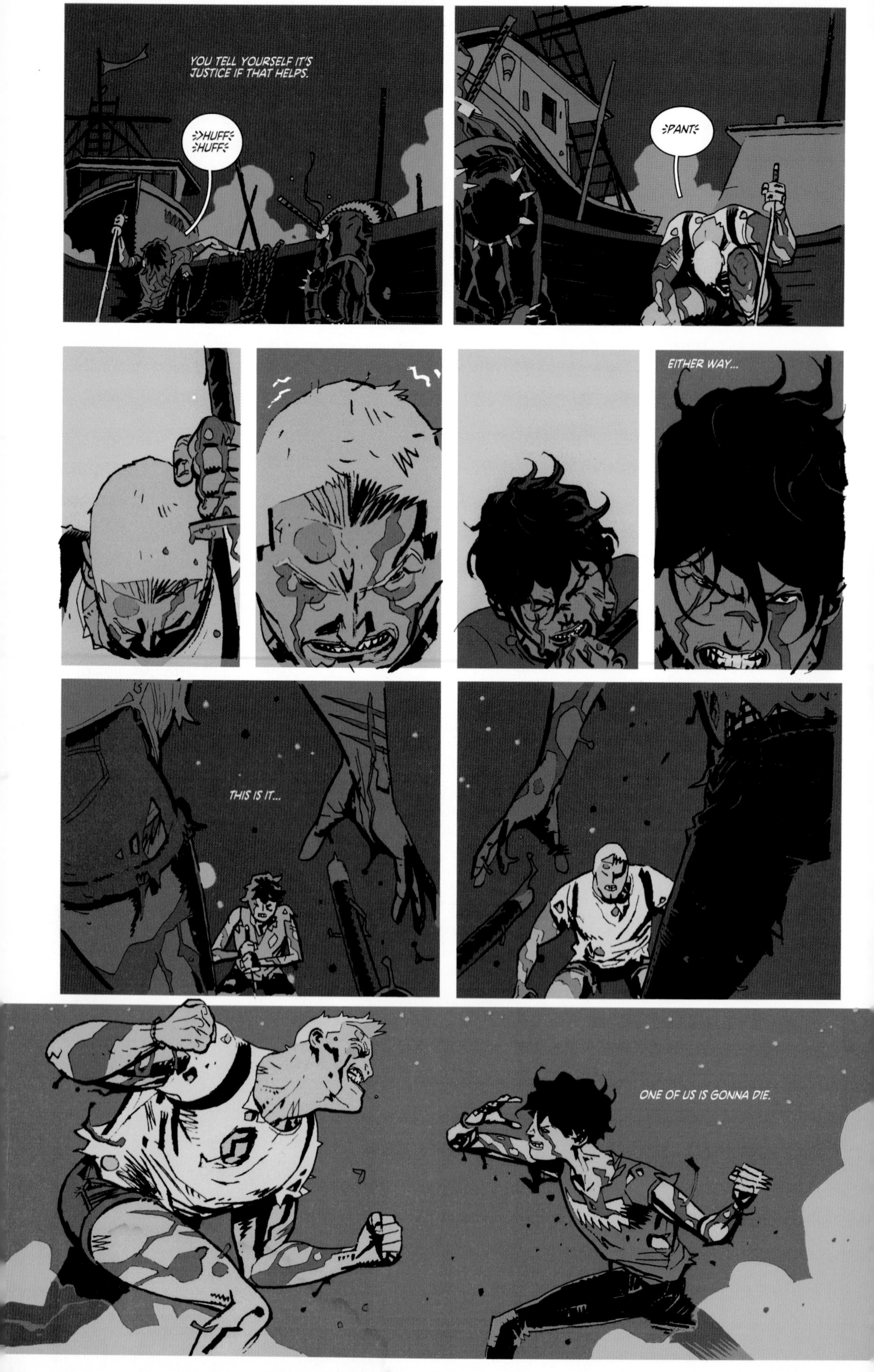
YOU TELL YOURSELF IT'S JUSTICE IF THAT HELPS.
HUFF HUFF
PANT
EITHER WAY...
THIS IS IT...
ONE OF US IS GONNA DIE.

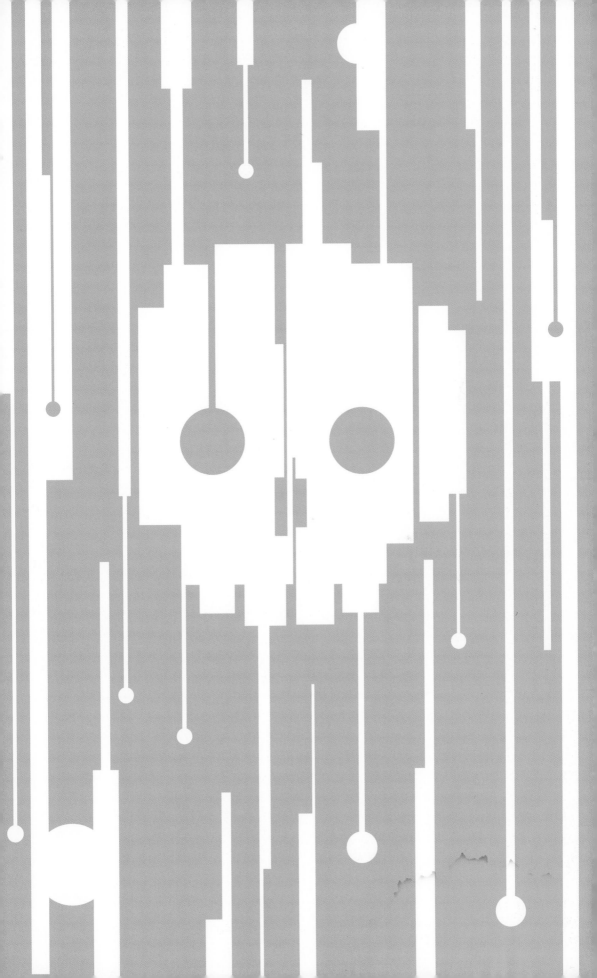

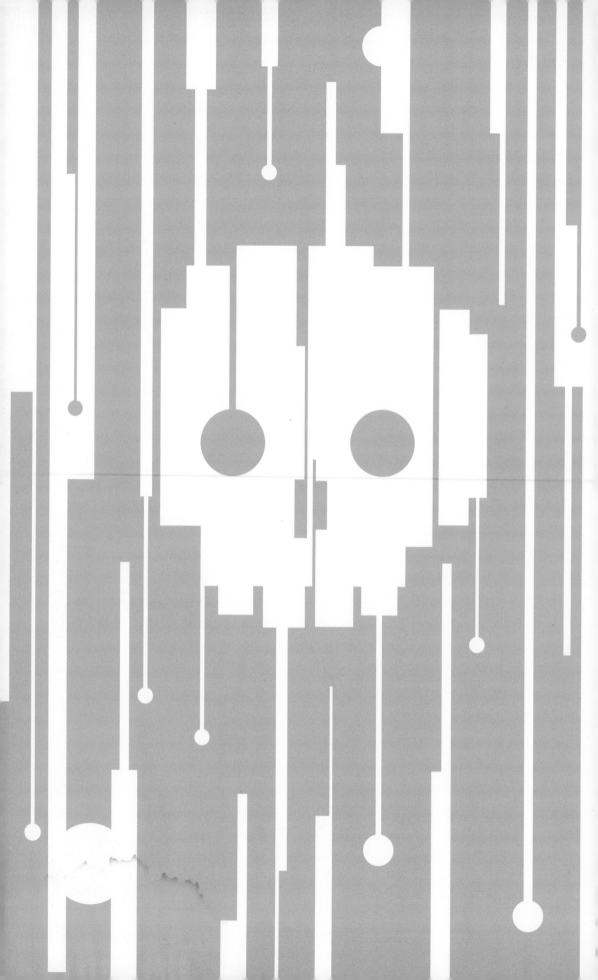

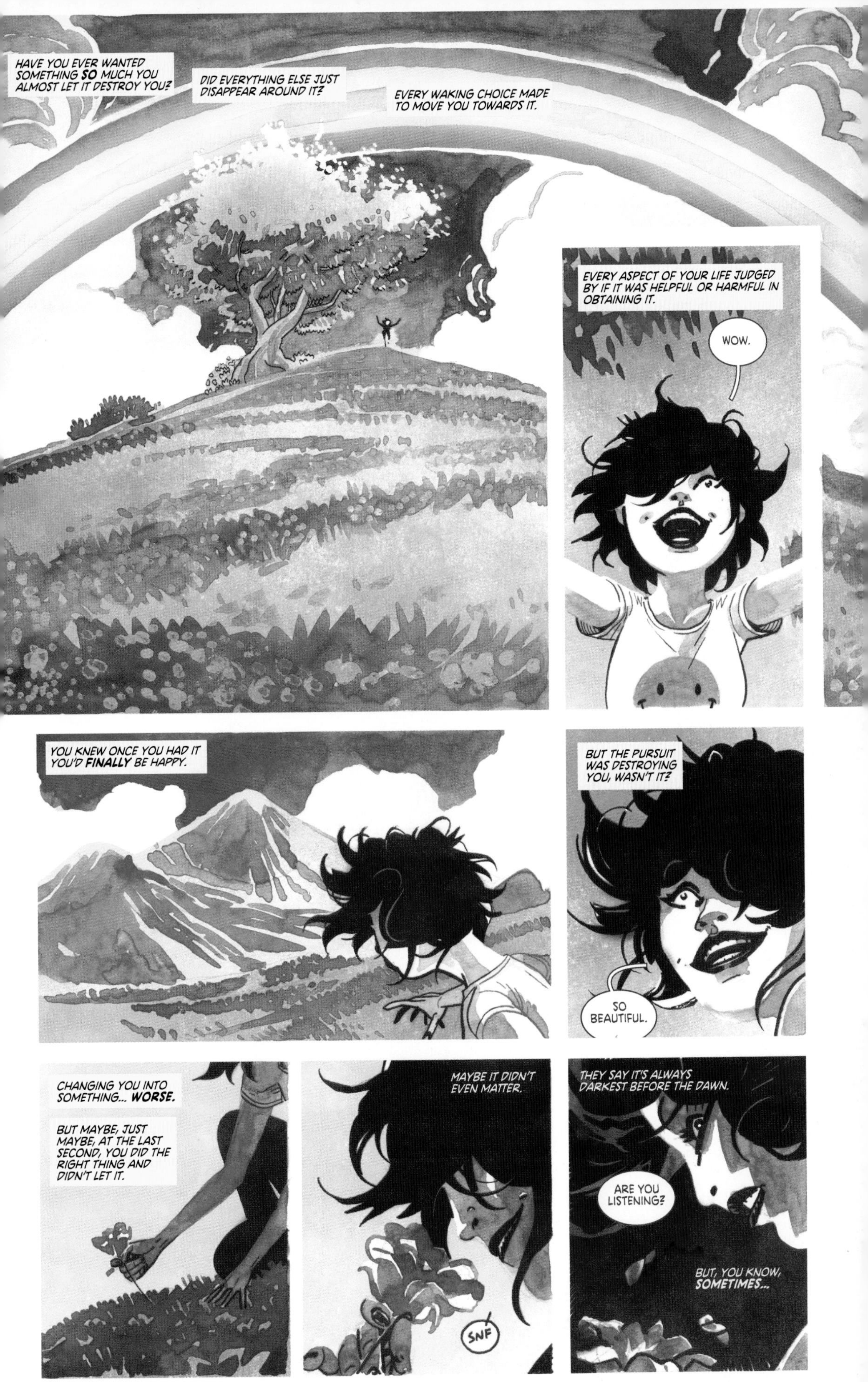
HAVE YOU EVER WANTED SOMETHING **SO** MUCH YOU ALMOST LET IT DESTROY YOU?
DID EVERYTHING ELSE JUST DISAPPEAR AROUND IT?
EVERY WAKING CHOICE MADE TO MOVE YOU TOWARDS IT.
EVERY ASPECT OF YOUR LIFE JUDGED BY IF IT WAS HELPFUL OR HARMFUL IN OBTAINING IT.
WOW.
YOU KNEW ONCE YOU HAD IT YOU'D **FINALLY** BE HAPPY.
BUT THE PURSUIT WAS DESTROYING YOU, WASN'T IT?
SO BEAUTIFUL.
CHANGING YOU INTO SOMETHING... **WORSE.**
BUT MAYBE, JUST MAYBE, AT THE LAST SECOND, YOU DID THE RIGHT THING AND DIDN'T LET IT.
MAYBE IT DIDN'T EVEN MATTER.
SNF
THEY SAY IT'S ALWAYS DARKEST BEFORE THE DAWN.
ARE YOU LISTENING?
BUT, YOU KNOW, **SOMETIMES...**

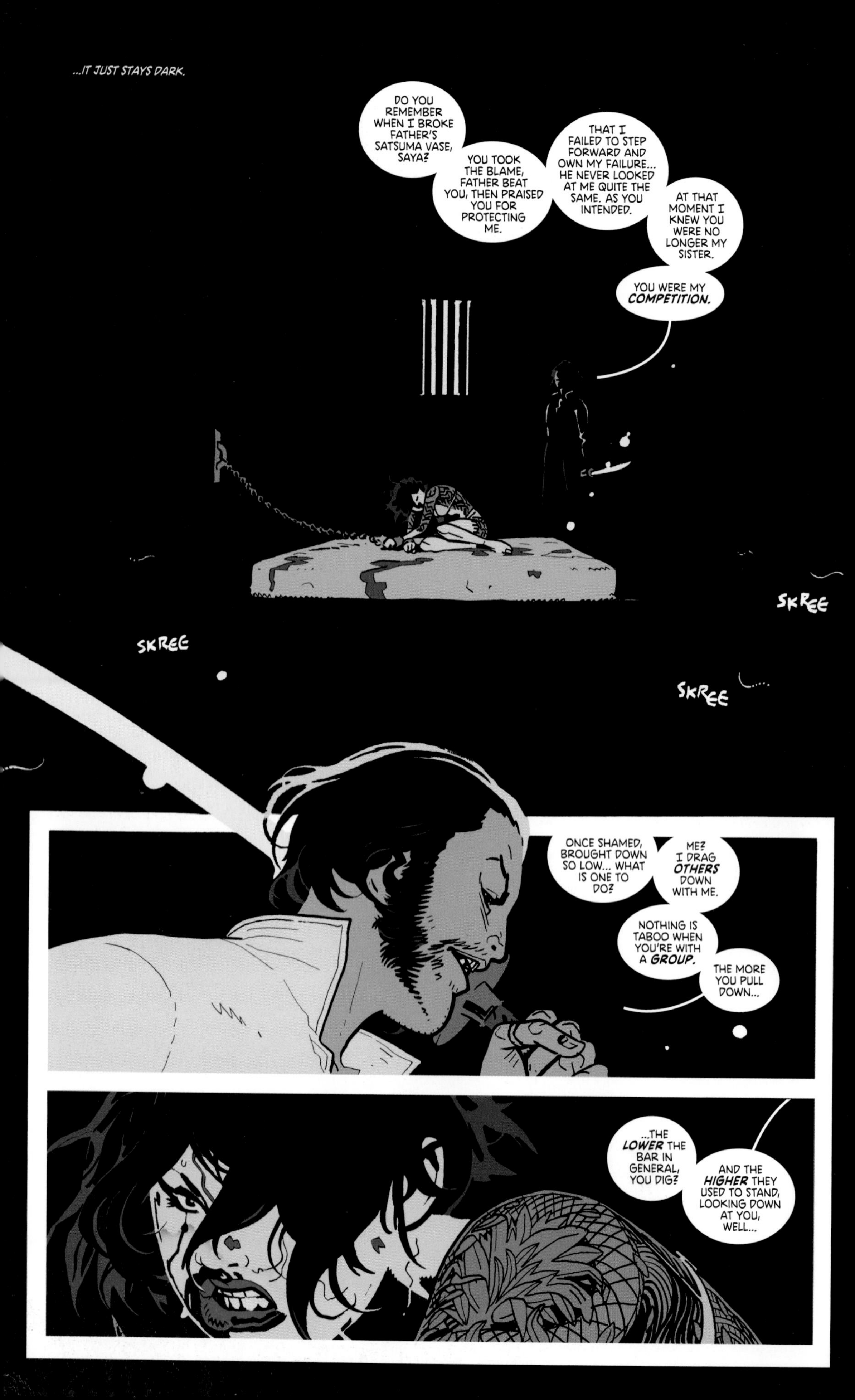
...IT JUST STAYS DARK.
DO YOU REMEMBER WHEN I BROKE FATHER'S SATSUMA VASE, SAYA?
YOU TOOK THE BLAME, FATHER BEAT YOU, THEN PRAISED YOU FOR PROTECTING ME.
THAT I FAILED TO STEP FORWARD AND OWN MY FAILURE... HE NEVER LOOKED AT ME QUITE THE SAME. AS YOU INTENDED.
AT THAT MOMENT I KNEW YOU WERE NO LONGER MY SISTER.
YOU WERE MY COMPETITION.
SKREE
SKREE
SKREE
ONCE SHAMED, BROUGHT DOWN SO LOW... WHAT IS ONE TO DO?
ME? I DRAG OTHERS DOWN WITH ME.
NOTHING IS TABOO WHEN YOU'RE WITH A GROUP.
THE MORE YOU PULL DOWN...
...THE LOWER THE BAR IN GENERAL, YOU DIG?
AND THE HIGHER THEY USED TO STAND, LOOKING DOWN AT YOU, WELL...

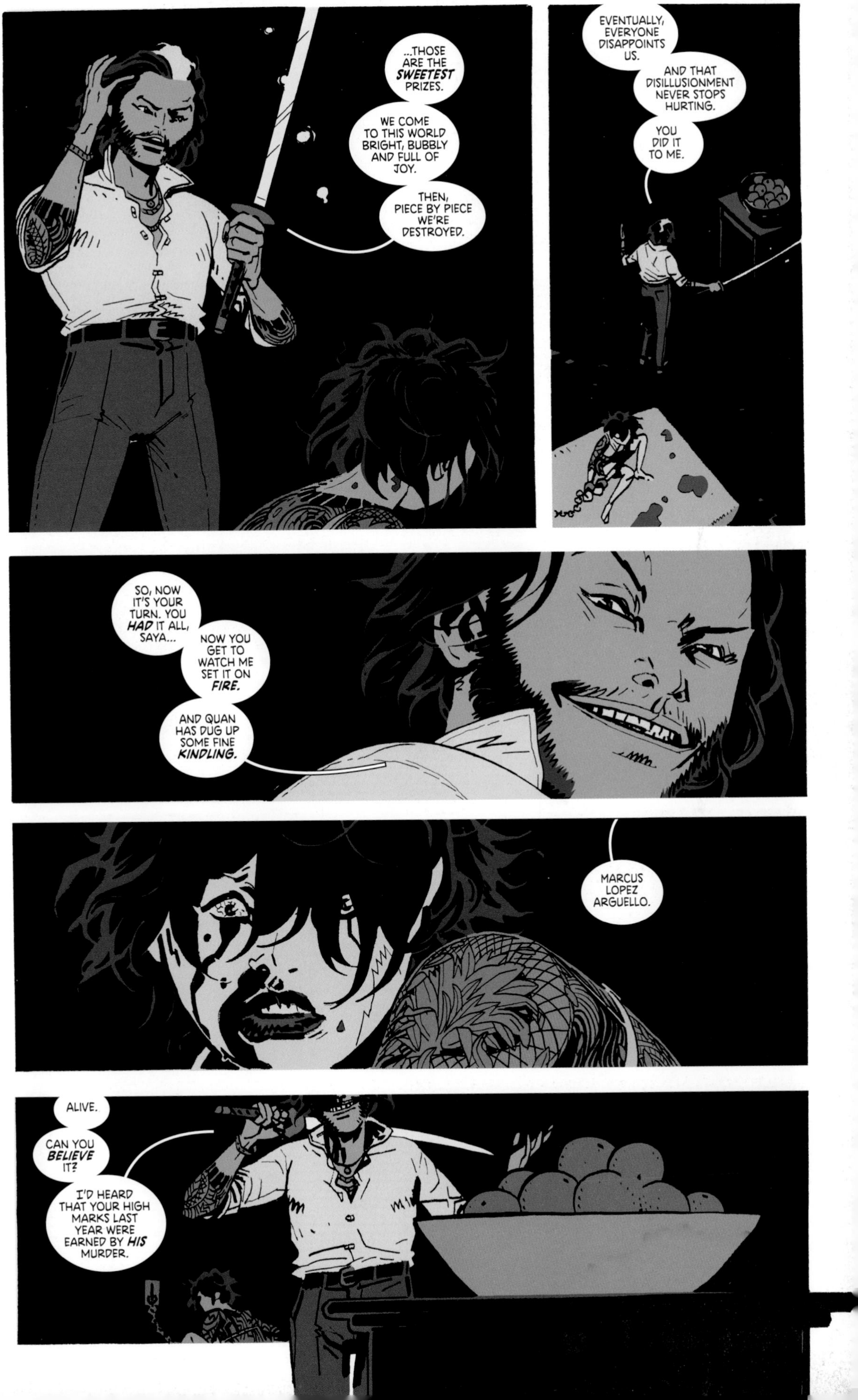

...THOSE ARE THE SWEETEST PRIZES.
WE COME TO THIS WORLD BRIGHT, BUBBLY AND FULL OF JOY.
THEN, PIECE BY PIECE WE'RE DESTROYED.
EVENTUALLY, EVERYONE DISAPPOINTS US.
AND THAT DISILLUSIONMENT NEVER STOPS HURTING.
YOU DID IT TO ME.
SO, NOW IT'S YOUR TURN. YOU HAD IT ALL, SAYA...
NOW YOU GET TO WATCH ME SET IT ON FIRE.
AND QUAN HAS DUG UP SOME FINE KINDLING.
MARCUS LOPEZ ARGUELLO.
ALIVE.
CAN YOU BELIEVE IT?
I'D HEARD THAT YOUR HIGH MARKS LAST YEAR WERE EARNED BY HIS MURDER.

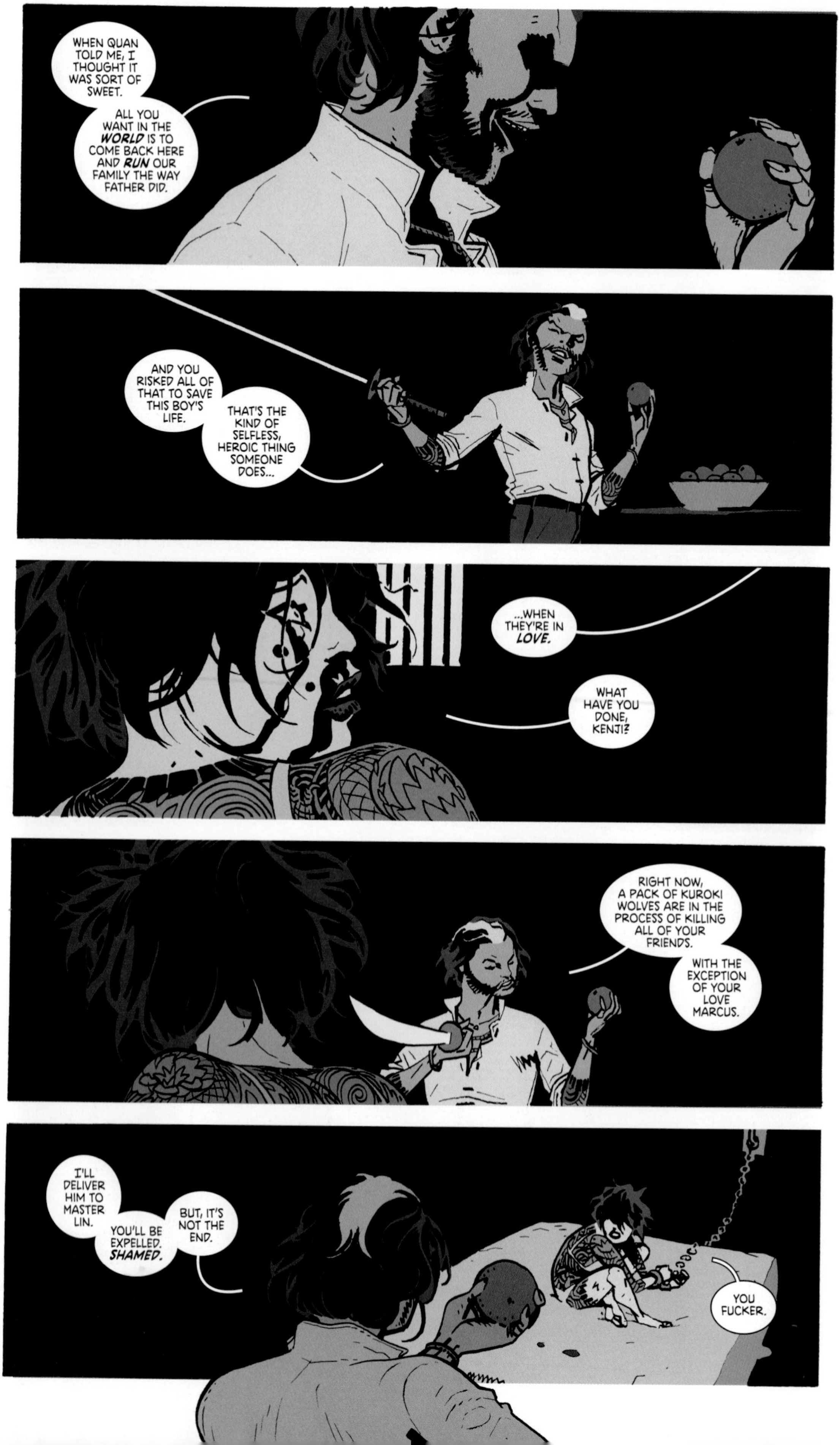
WHEN QUAN TOLD ME, I THOUGHT IT WAS SORT OF SWEET.
ALL YOU WANT IN THE **WORLD** IS TO COME BACK HERE AND **RUN** OUR FAMILY THE WAY FATHER DID.
AND YOU RISKED ALL OF THAT TO SAVE THIS BOY'S LIFE.
THAT'S THE KIND OF SELFLESS, HEROIC THING SOMEONE DOES...
...WHEN THEY'RE IN **LOVE.**
WHAT HAVE YOU DONE, KENJI?
RIGHT NOW, A PACK OF KUROKI WOLVES ARE IN THE PROCESS OF KILLING ALL OF YOUR FRIENDS.
WITH THE EXCEPTION OF YOUR LOVE MARCUS.
I'LL DELIVER HIM TO MASTER LIN.
YOU'LL BE EXPELLED. **SHAMED.**
BUT, IT'S NOT THE END.
YOU FUCKER.

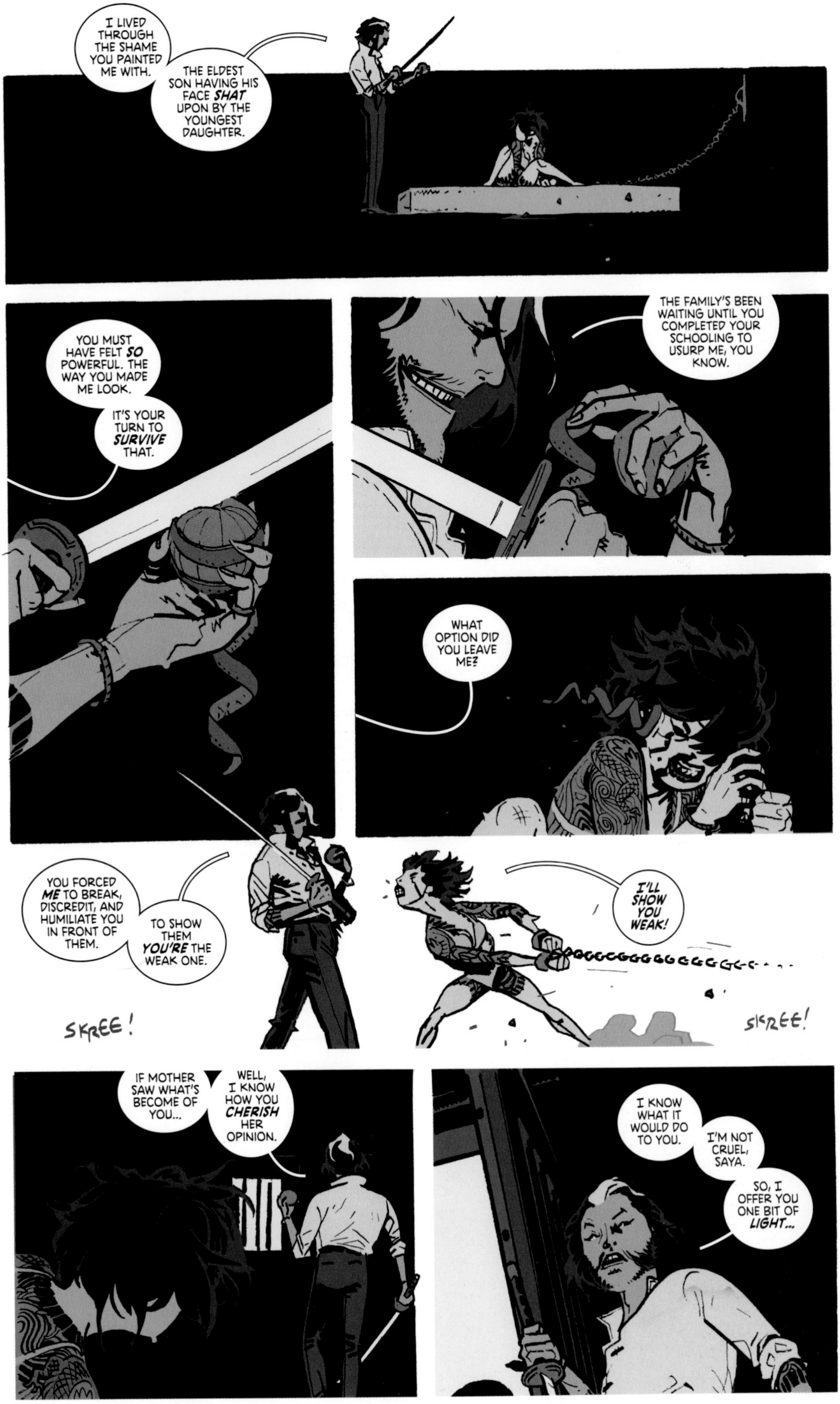
I LIVED THROUGH THE SHAME YOU PAINTED ME WITH.
THE ELDEST SON HAVING HIS FACE SHAT UPON BY THE YOUNGEST DAUGHTER.
YOU MUST HAVE FELT SO POWERFUL. THE WAY YOU MADE ME LOOK.
IT'S YOUR TURN TO SURVIVE THAT.
THE FAMILY'S BEEN WAITING UNTIL YOU COMPLETED YOUR SCHOOLING TO USURP ME, YOU KNOW.
WHAT OPTION DID YOU LEAVE ME?
YOU FORCED ME TO BREAK, DISCREDIT, AND HUMILIATE YOU IN FRONT OF THEM.
TO SHOW THEM YOU'RE THE WEAK ONE.
I'LL SHOW YOU WEAK!
SKREE!
SKREE!
IF MOTHER SAW WHAT'S BECOME OF YOU...
WELL, I KNOW HOW YOU CHERISH HER OPINION.
I KNOW WHAT IT WOULD DO TO YOU.
I'M NOT CRUEL, SAYA.
SO, I OFFER YOU ONE BIT OF LIGHT...

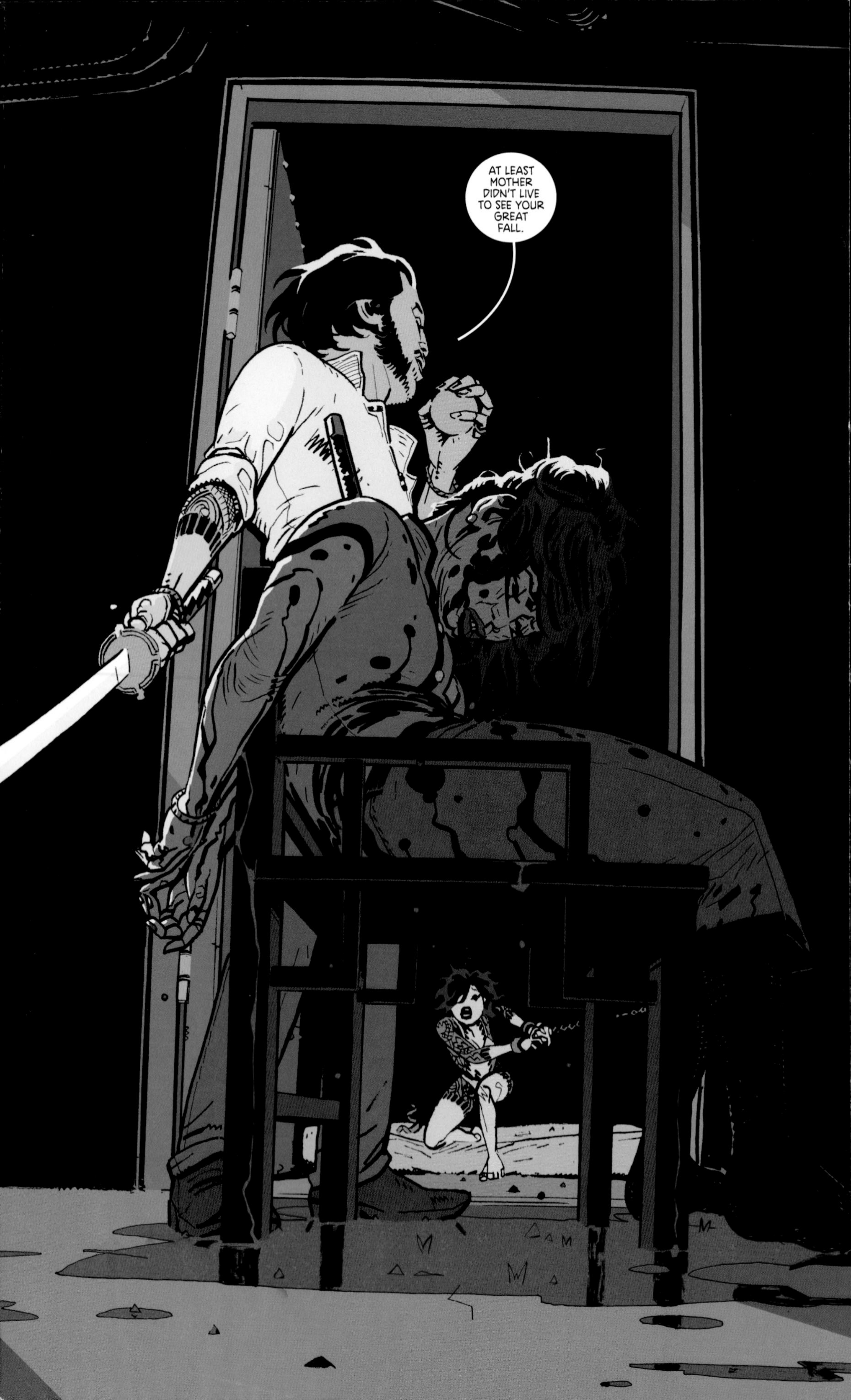
AT LEAST MOTHER DIDN'T LIVE TO SEE YOUR GREAT FALL.

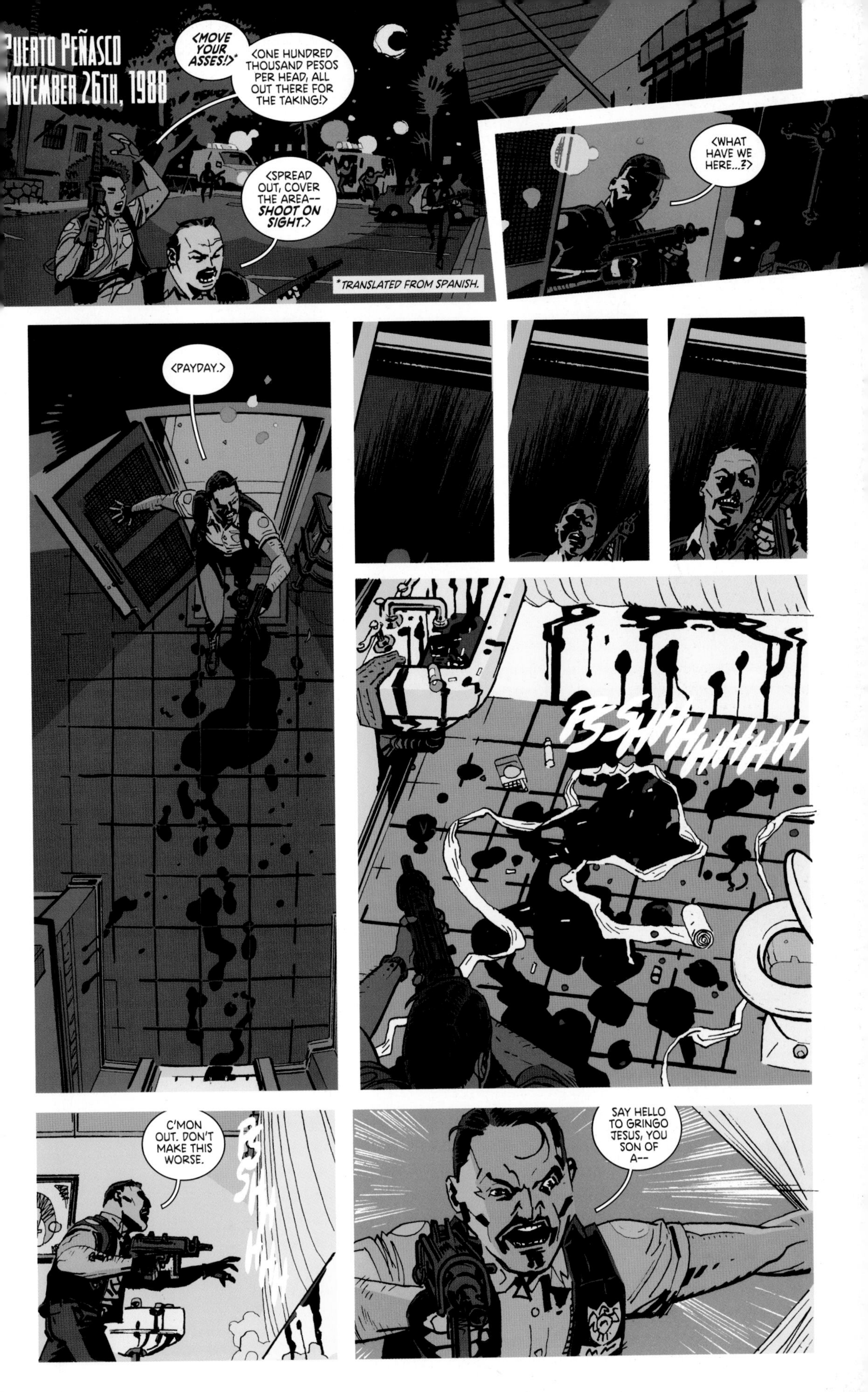
PUERTO PEÑASCO
NOVEMBER 26TH, 1988
<MOVE YOUR ASSES!>*
<ONE HUNDRED THOUSAND PESOS PER HEAD, ALL OUT THERE FOR THE TAKING!>
<SPREAD OUT, COVER THE AREA-- SHOOT ON SIGHT.>
*TRANSLATED FROM SPANISH.
<WHAT HAVE WE HERE...?>
<PAYDAY.>
PSSHHHHHHHH
C'MON OUT. DON'T MAKE THIS WORSE.
PSSHHHHH
SAY HELLO TO GRINGO JESUS, YOU SON OF A--

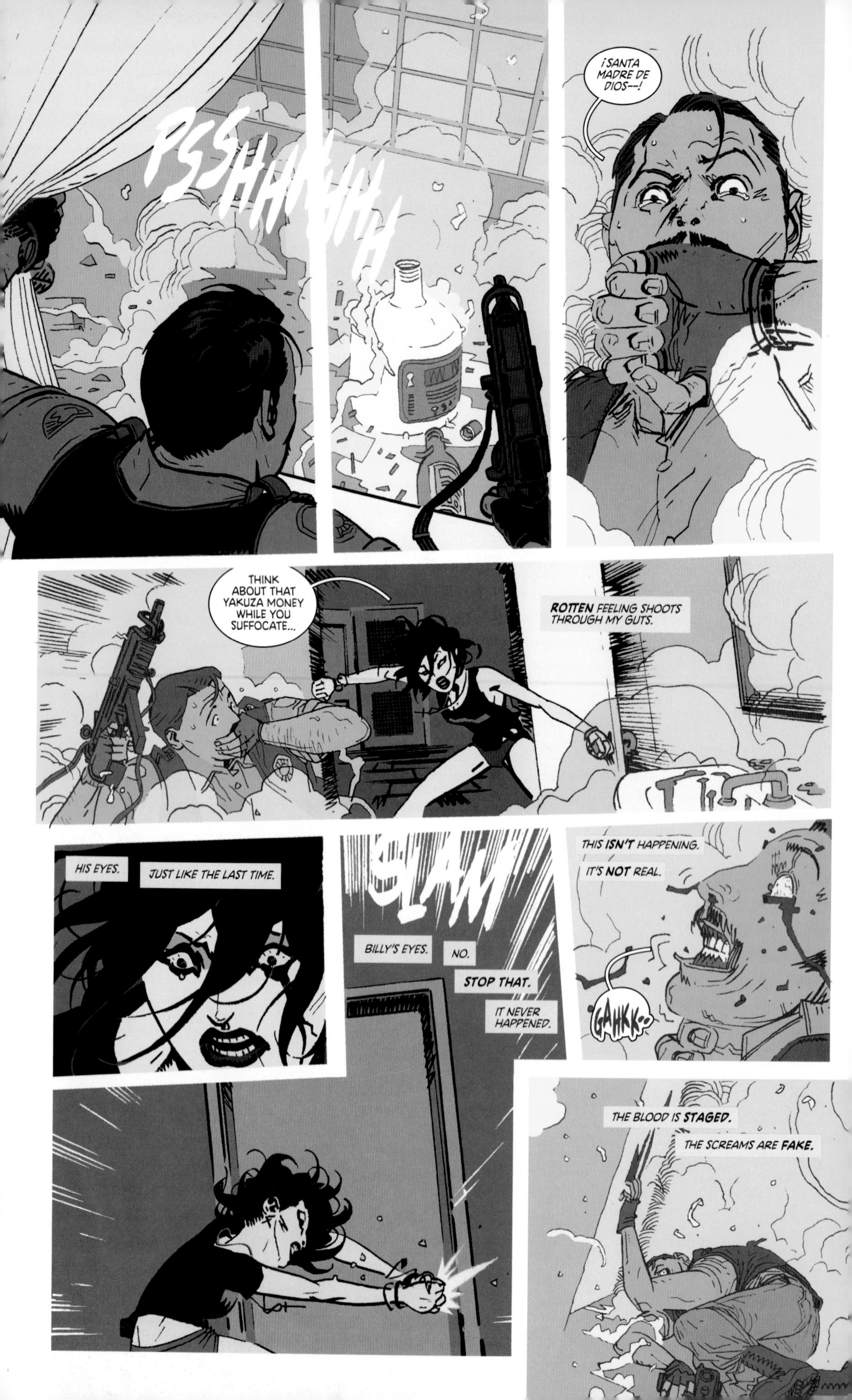
PSSHHHHHH
¡SANTA MADRE DE DIOS--!
THINK ABOUT THAT YAKUZA MONEY WHILE YOU SUFFOCATE...
ROTTEN FEELING SHOOTS THROUGH MY GUTS.
HIS EYES.
JUST LIKE THE LAST TIME.
SLAM
BILLY'S EYES.
NO.
STOP THAT.
IT NEVER HAPPENED.
THIS ISN'T HAPPENING.
IT'S NOT REAL.
GAHKK..
THE BLOOD IS STAGED.
THE SCREAMS ARE FAKE.

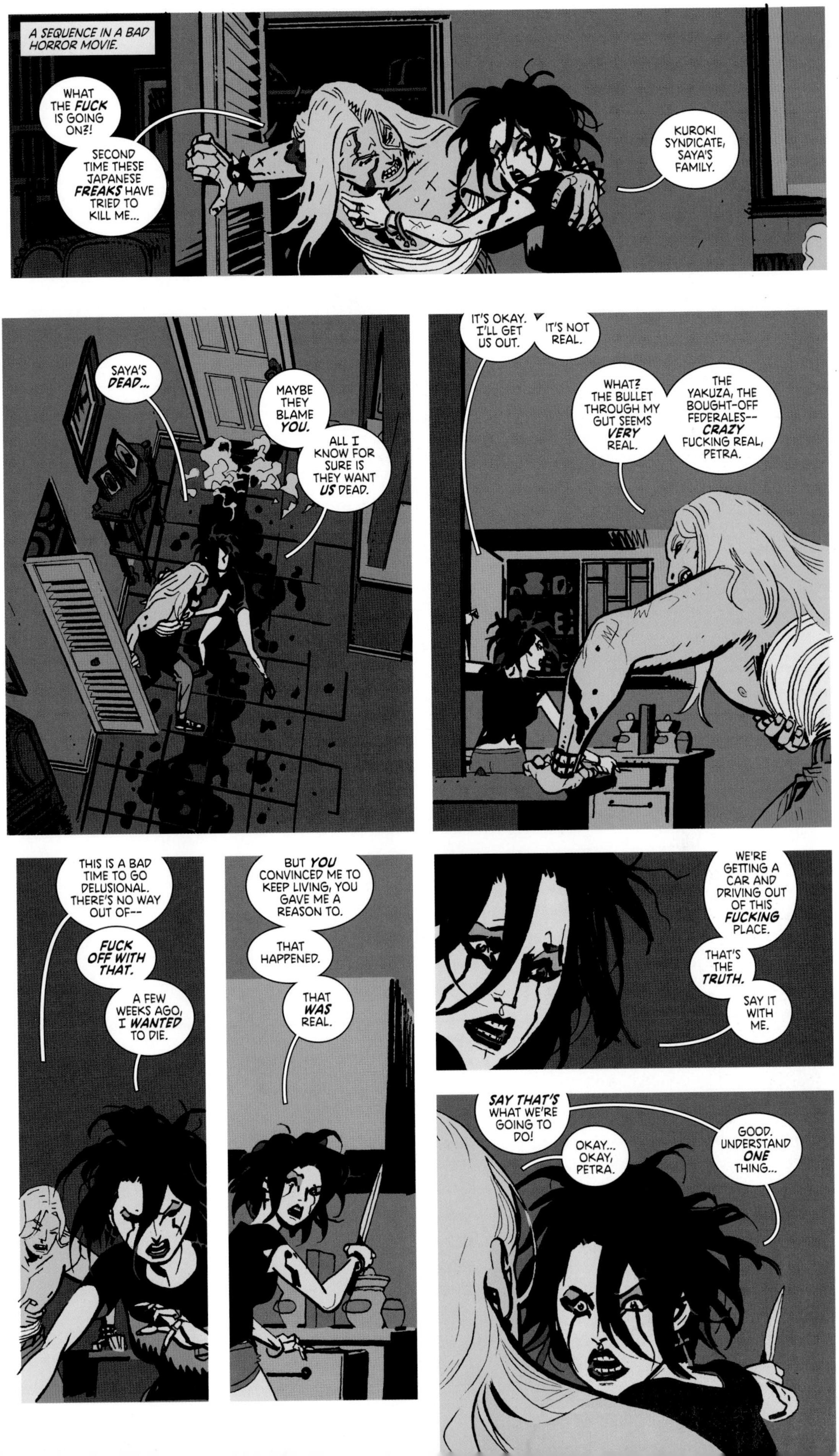
A SEQUENCE IN A BAD HORROR MOVIE.
WHAT THE FUCK IS GOING ON?!
SECOND TIME THESE JAPANESE FREAKS HAVE TRIED TO KILL ME...
KUROKI SYNDICATE, SAYA'S FAMILY.
SAYA'S DEAD...
MAYBE THEY BLAME YOU.
ALL I KNOW FOR SURE IS THEY WANT US DEAD.
IT'S OKAY. I'LL GET US OUT.
IT'S NOT REAL.
WHAT? THE BULLET THROUGH MY GUT SEEMS VERY REAL.
THE YAKUZA, THE BOUGHT-OFF FEDERALES-- CRAZY FUCKING REAL, PETRA.
THIS IS A BAD TIME TO GO DELUSIONAL. THERE'S NO WAY OUT OF--
FUCK OFF WITH THAT.
A FEW WEEKS AGO, I WANTED TO DIE.
BUT YOU CONVINCED ME TO KEEP LIVING, YOU GAVE ME A REASON TO.
THAT HAPPENED.
THAT WAS REAL.
WE'RE GETTING A CAR AND DRIVING OUT OF THIS FUCKING PLACE.
THAT'S THE TRUTH.
SAY IT WITH ME.
SAY THAT'S WHAT WE'RE GOING TO DO!
OKAY... OKAY, PETRA.
GOOD. UNDERSTAND ONE THING...

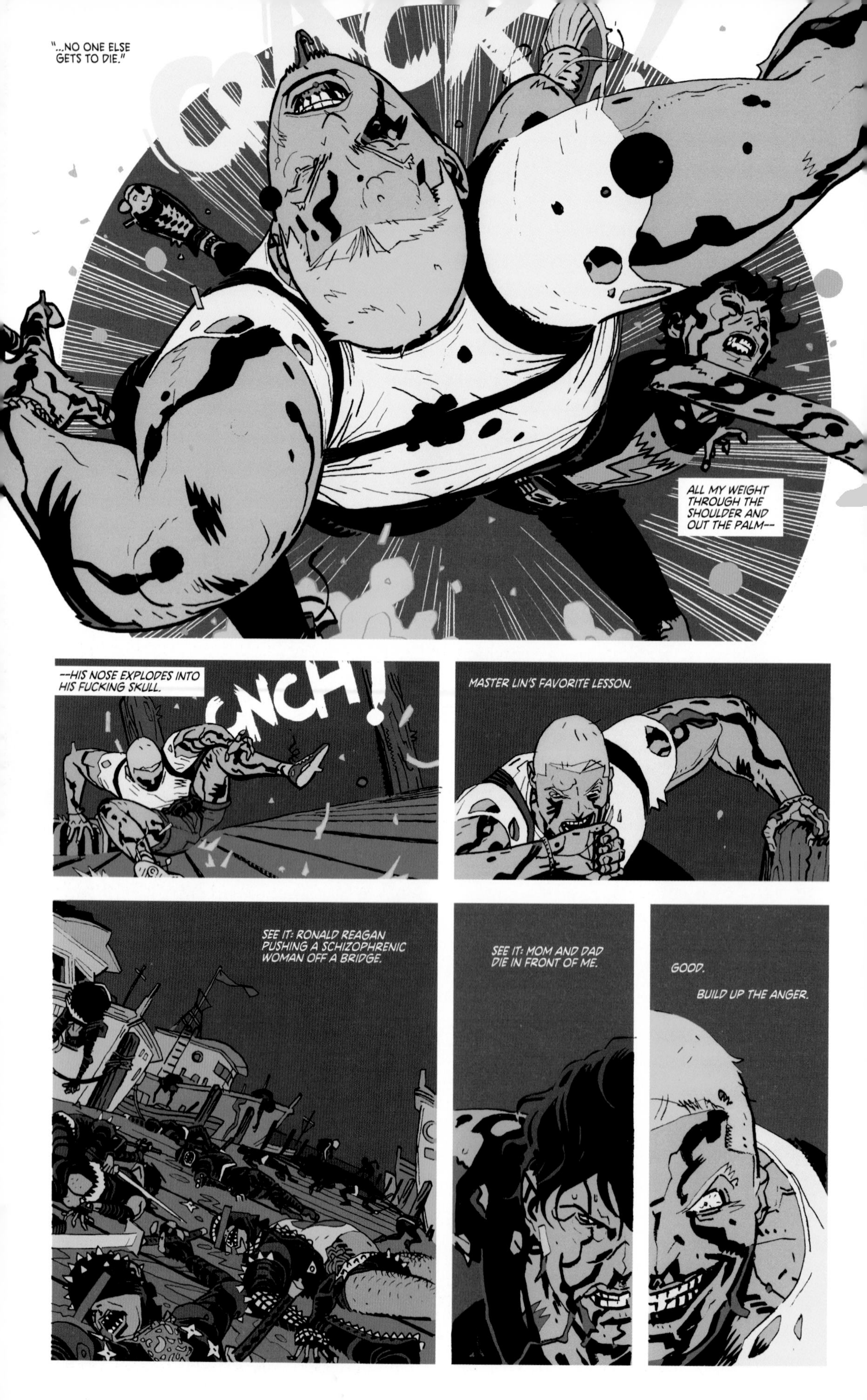
"...NO ONE ELSE GETS TO DIE."
CRACK!
ALL MY WEIGHT THROUGH THE SHOULDER AND OUT THE PALM--
--HIS NOSE EXPLODES INTO HIS FUCKING SKULL.
NCH!
MASTER LIN'S FAVORITE LESSON.
SEE IT: RONALD REAGAN PUSHING A SCHIZOPHRENIC WOMAN OFF A BRIDGE.
SEE IT: MOM AND DAD DIE IN FRONT OF ME.
GOOD.
BUILD UP THE ANGER.

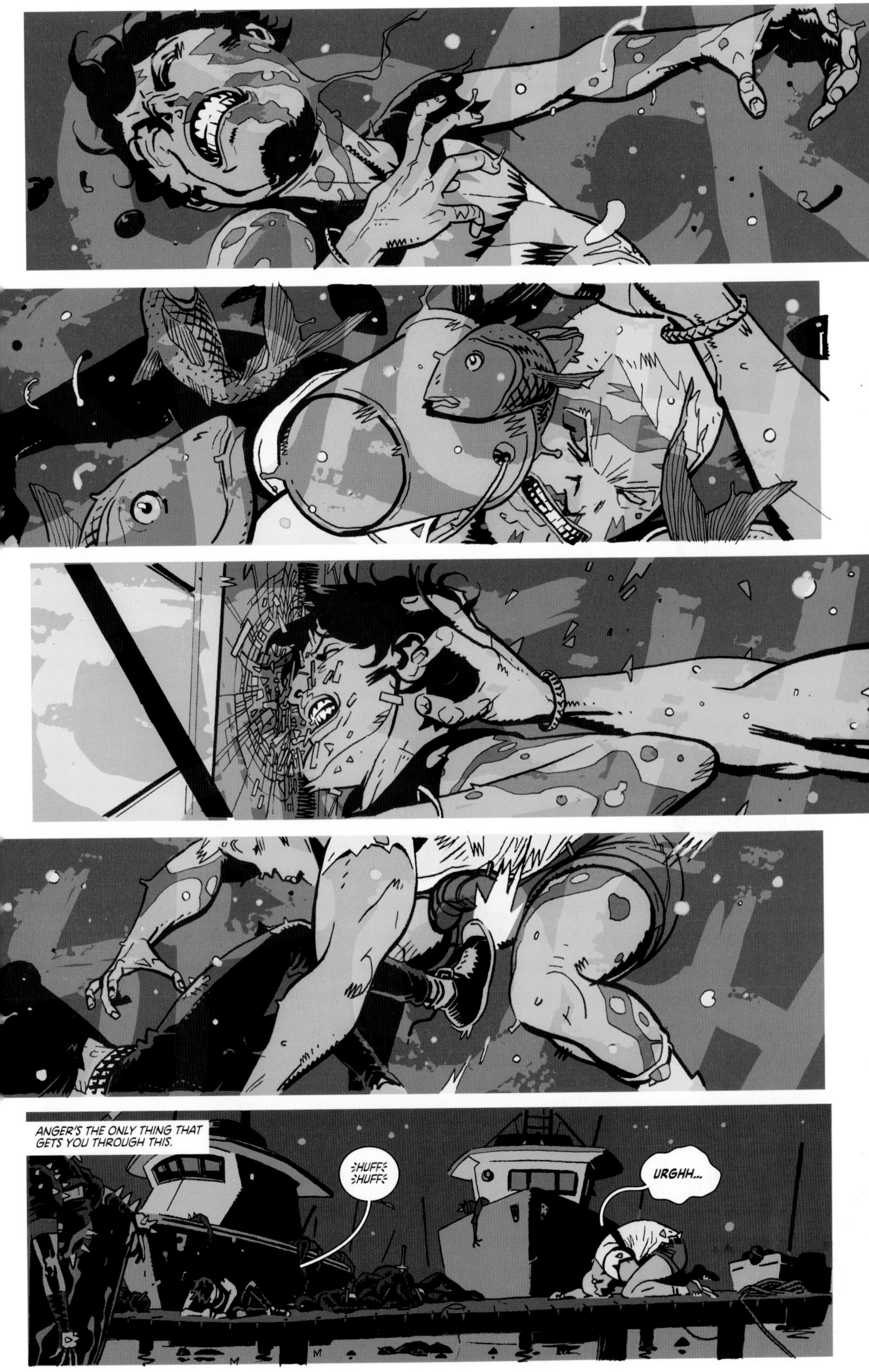
ANGER'S THE ONLY THING THAT GETS YOU THROUGH THIS.
HUFF HUFF
URGHH...

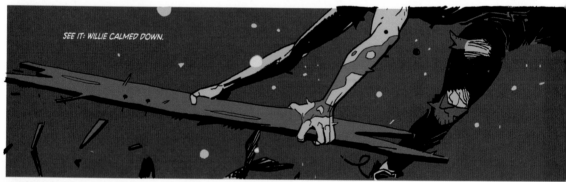

SEE IT: WILLIE CALMED DOWN.

SEE HIM: READY TO RUN AWAY WITH ME.

REMEMBER.

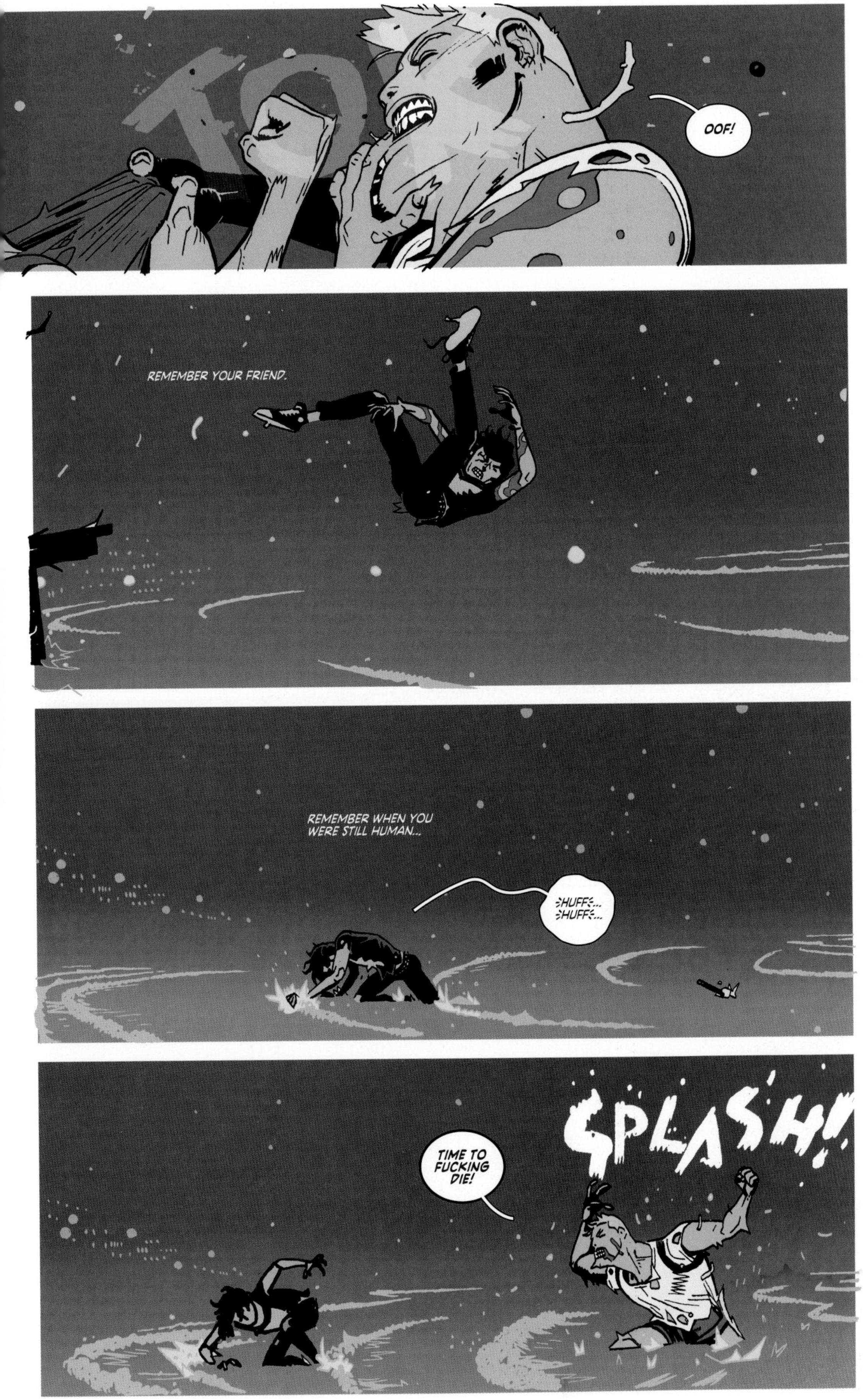
OOF!
REMEMBER YOUR FRIEND.
REMEMBER WHEN YOU WERE STILL HUMAN...
HUFF...
HUFF...
TIME TO FUCKING DIE!
SPLASH!

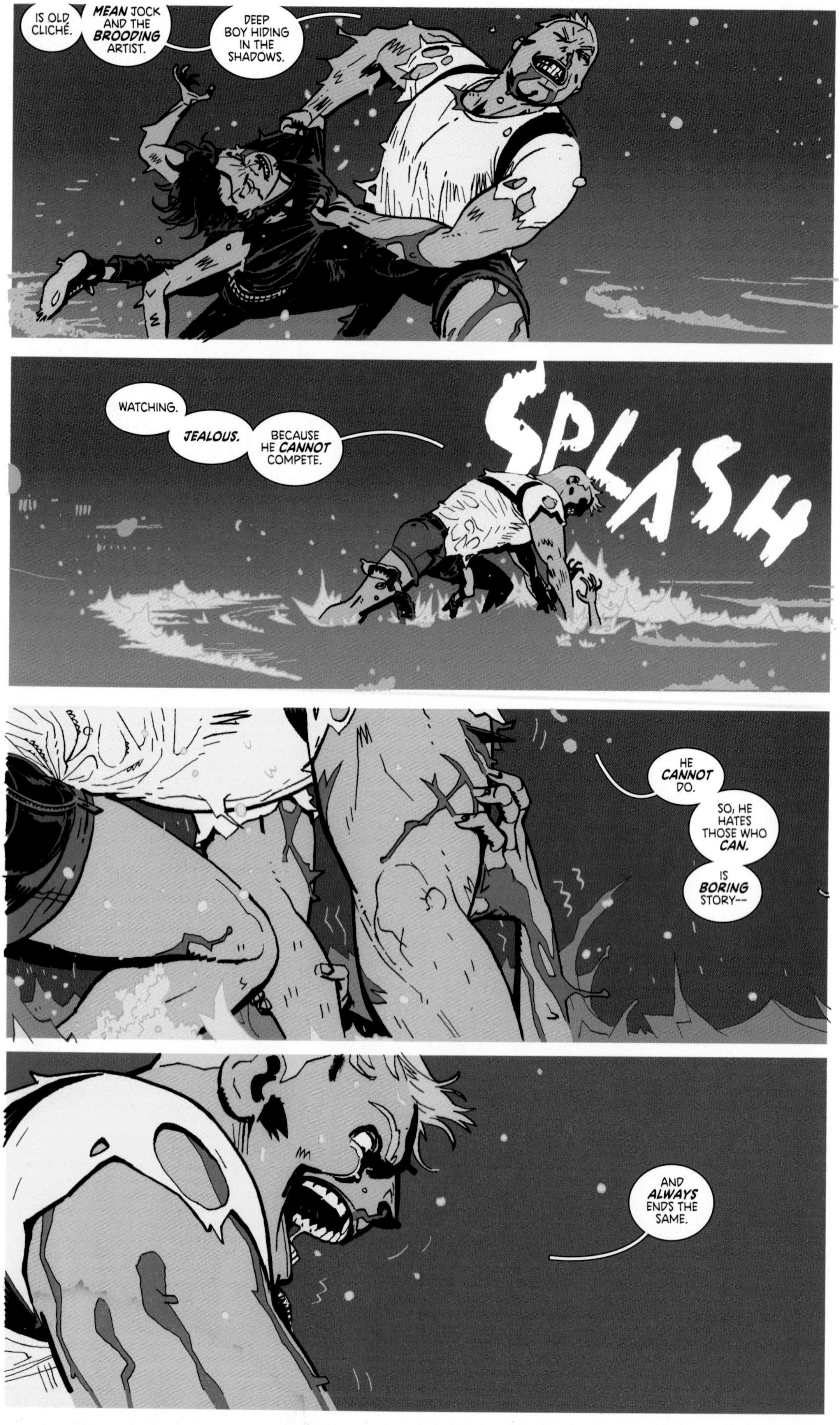
IS OLD CLICHÉ.
MEAN JOCK AND THE BROODING ARTIST.
DEEP BOY HIDING IN THE SHADOWS.
WATCHING.
JEALOUS.
BECAUSE HE CANNOT COMPETE.
SPLASH
HE CANNOT DO.
SO, HE HATES THOSE WHO CAN.
IS BORING STORY--
AND ALWAYS ENDS THE SAME.

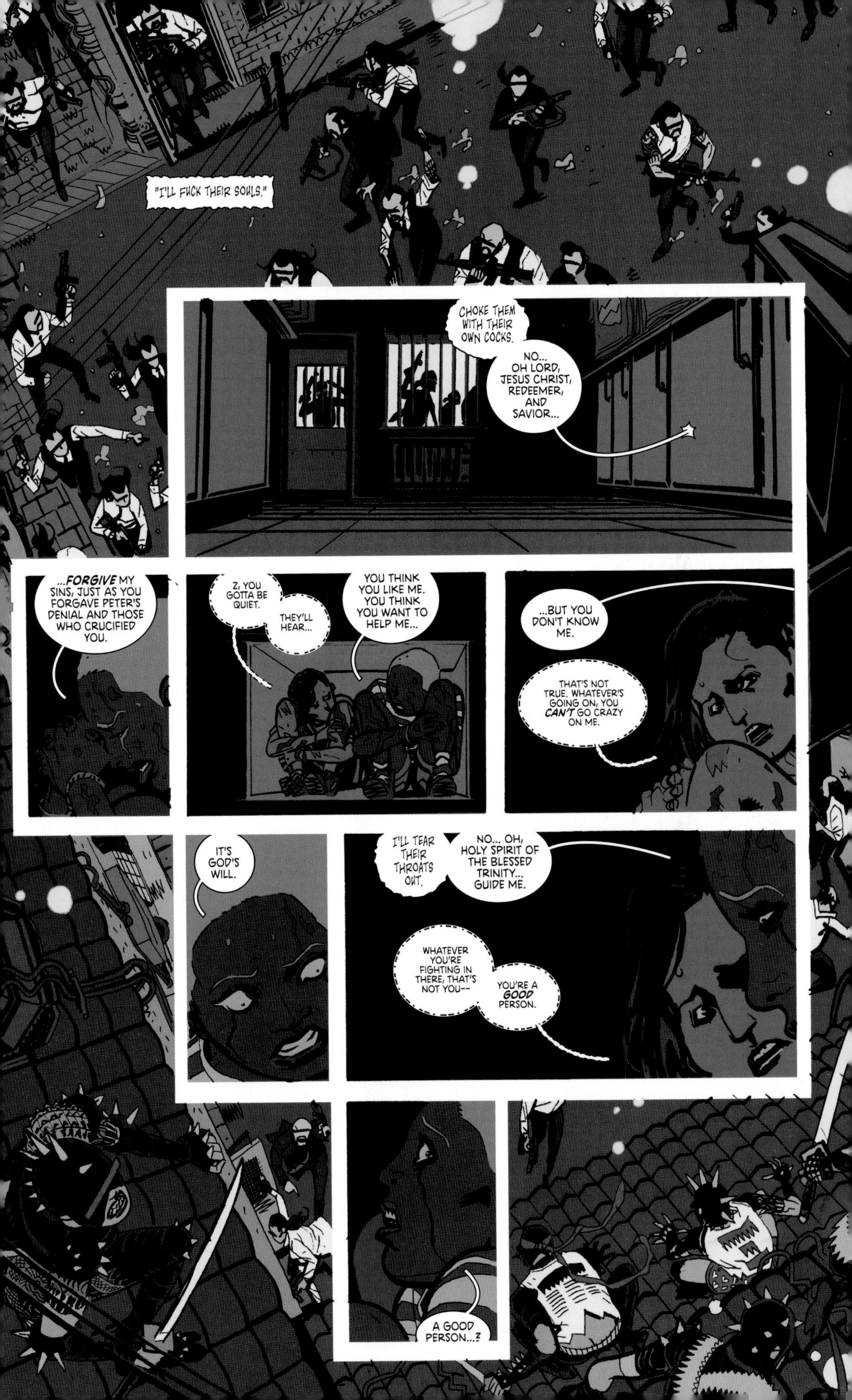
"I'LL FUCK THEIR SOULS."
CHOKE THEM WITH THEIR OWN COCKS.
NO... OH LORD, JESUS CHRIST, REDEEMER, AND SAVIOR...
...FORGIVE MY SINS, JUST AS YOU FORGAVE PETER'S DENIAL AND THOSE WHO CRUCIFIED YOU.
Z, YOU GOTTA BE QUIET.
THEY'LL HEAR...
YOU THINK YOU LIKE ME. YOU THINK YOU WANT TO HELP ME...
...BUT YOU DON'T KNOW ME.
THAT'S NOT TRUE. WHATEVER'S GOING ON, YOU CAN'T GO CRAZY ON ME.
IT'S GOD'S WILL.
I'LL TEAR THEIR THROATS OUT.
NO... OH, HOLY SPIRIT OF THE BLESSED TRINITY... GUIDE ME.
WHATEVER YOU'RE FIGHTING IN THERE, THAT'S NOT YOU--
YOU'RE A GOOD PERSON.
A GOOD PERSON...?

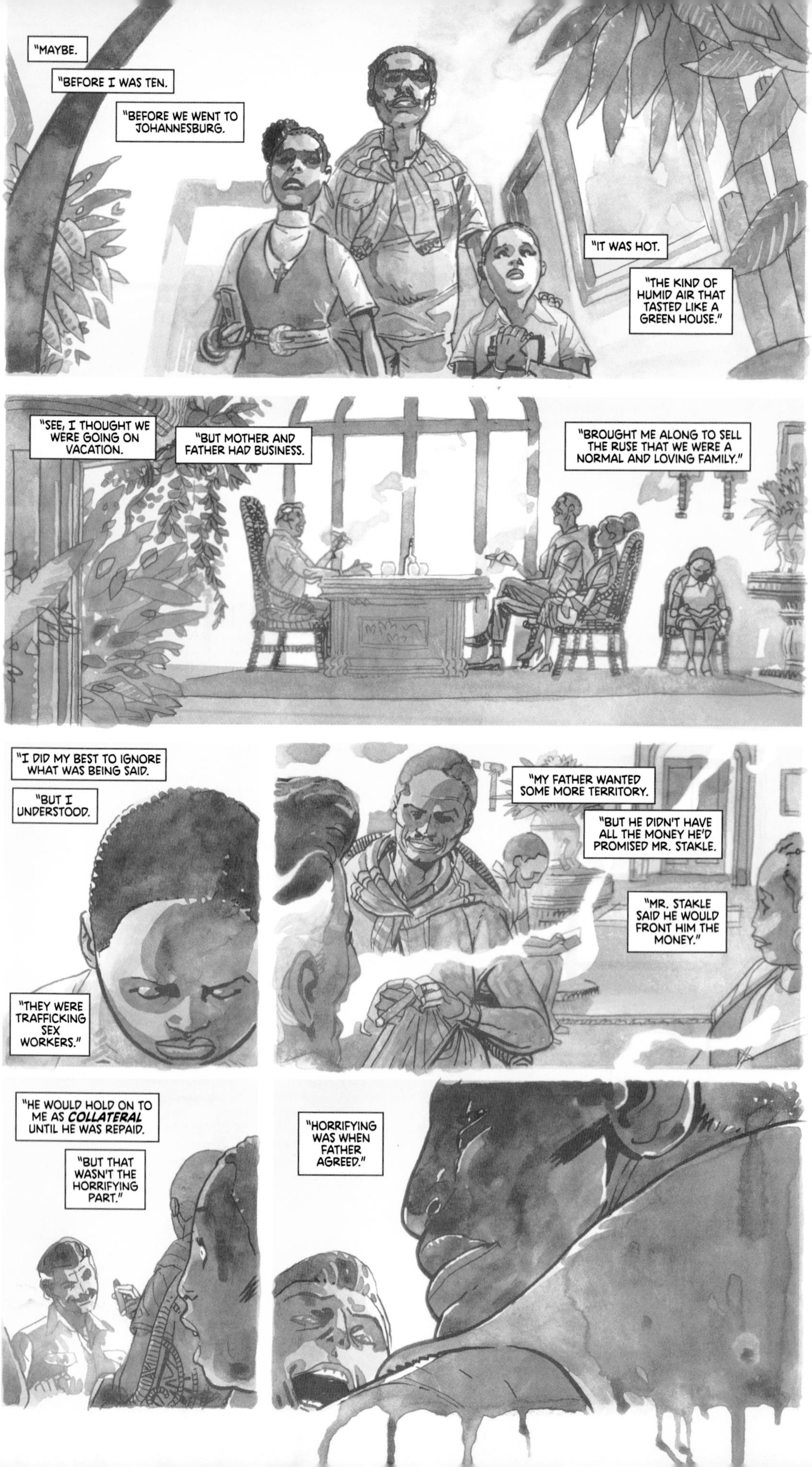
"MAYBE.
"BEFORE I WAS TEN.
"BEFORE WE WENT TO JOHANNESBURG.
"IT WAS HOT.
"THE KIND OF HUMID AIR THAT TASTED LIKE A GREEN HOUSE."
"SEE, I THOUGHT WE WERE GOING ON VACATION.
"BUT MOTHER AND FATHER HAD BUSINESS.
"BROUGHT ME ALONG TO SELL THE RUSE THAT WE WERE A NORMAL AND LOVING FAMILY."
"I DID MY BEST TO IGNORE WHAT WAS BEING SAID.
"BUT I UNDERSTOOD.
"THEY WERE TRAFFICKING SEX WORKERS."
"MY FATHER WANTED SOME MORE TERRITORY.
"BUT HE DIDN'T HAVE ALL THE MONEY HE'D PROMISED MR. STAKLE.
"MR. STAKLE SAID HE WOULD FRONT HIM THE MONEY."
"HE WOULD HOLD ON TO ME AS COLLATERAL UNTIL HE WAS REPAID.
"BUT THAT WASN'T THE HORRIFYING PART."
"HORRIFYING WAS WHEN FATHER AGREED."

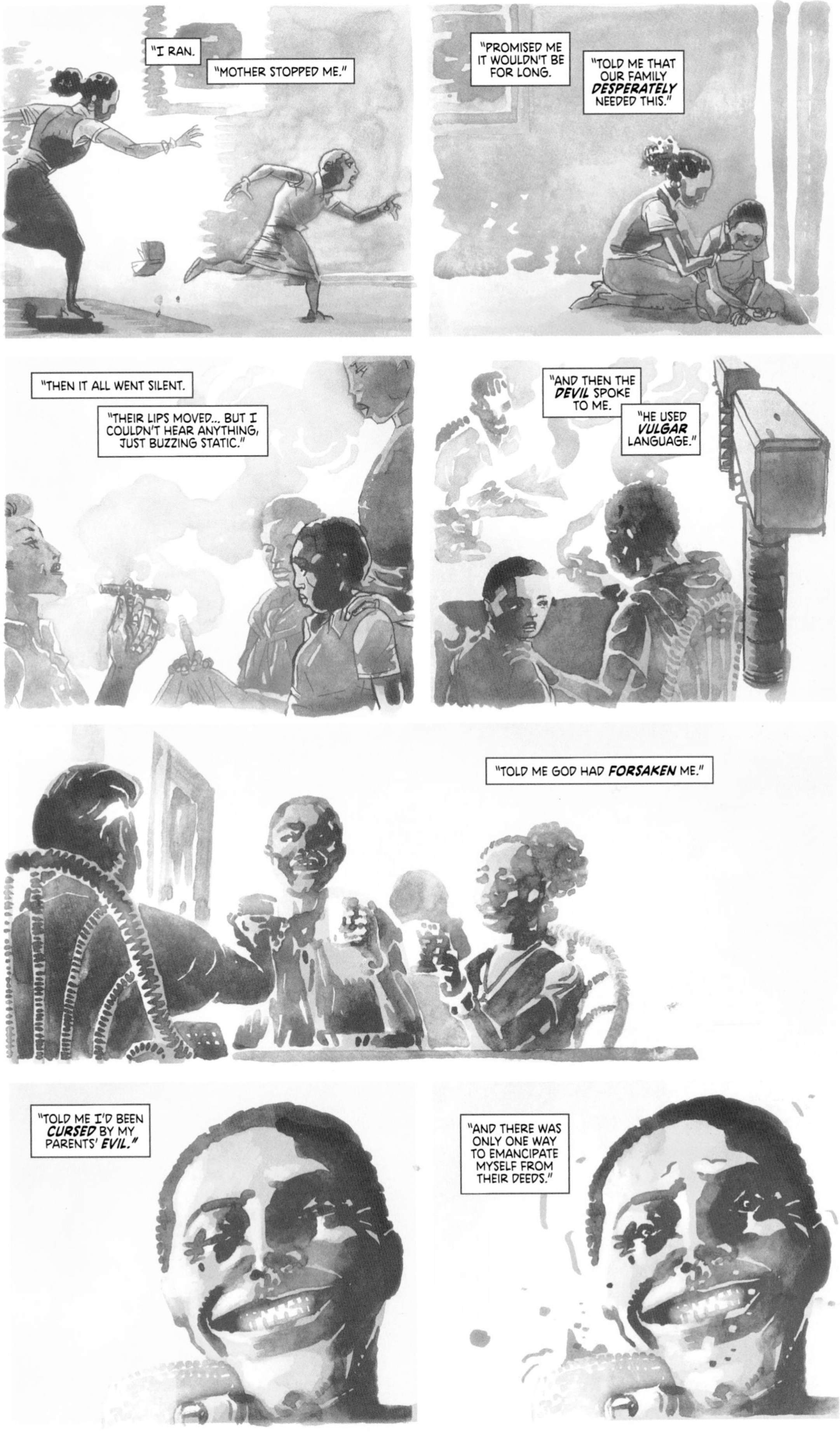
"I RAN.
"MOTHER STOPPED ME."
"PROMISED ME IT WOULDN'T BE FOR LONG.
"TOLD ME THAT OUR FAMILY DESPERATELY NEEDED THIS."
"THEN IT ALL WENT SILENT.
"THEIR LIPS MOVED... BUT I COULDN'T HEAR ANYTHING, JUST BUZZING STATIC."
"AND THEN THE DEVIL SPOKE TO ME.
"HE USED VULGAR LANGUAGE."
"TOLD ME GOD HAD FORSAKEN ME."
"TOLD ME I'D BEEN CURSED BY MY PARENTS' EVIL."
"AND THERE WAS ONLY ONE WAY TO EMANCIPATE MYSELF FROM THEIR DEEDS."

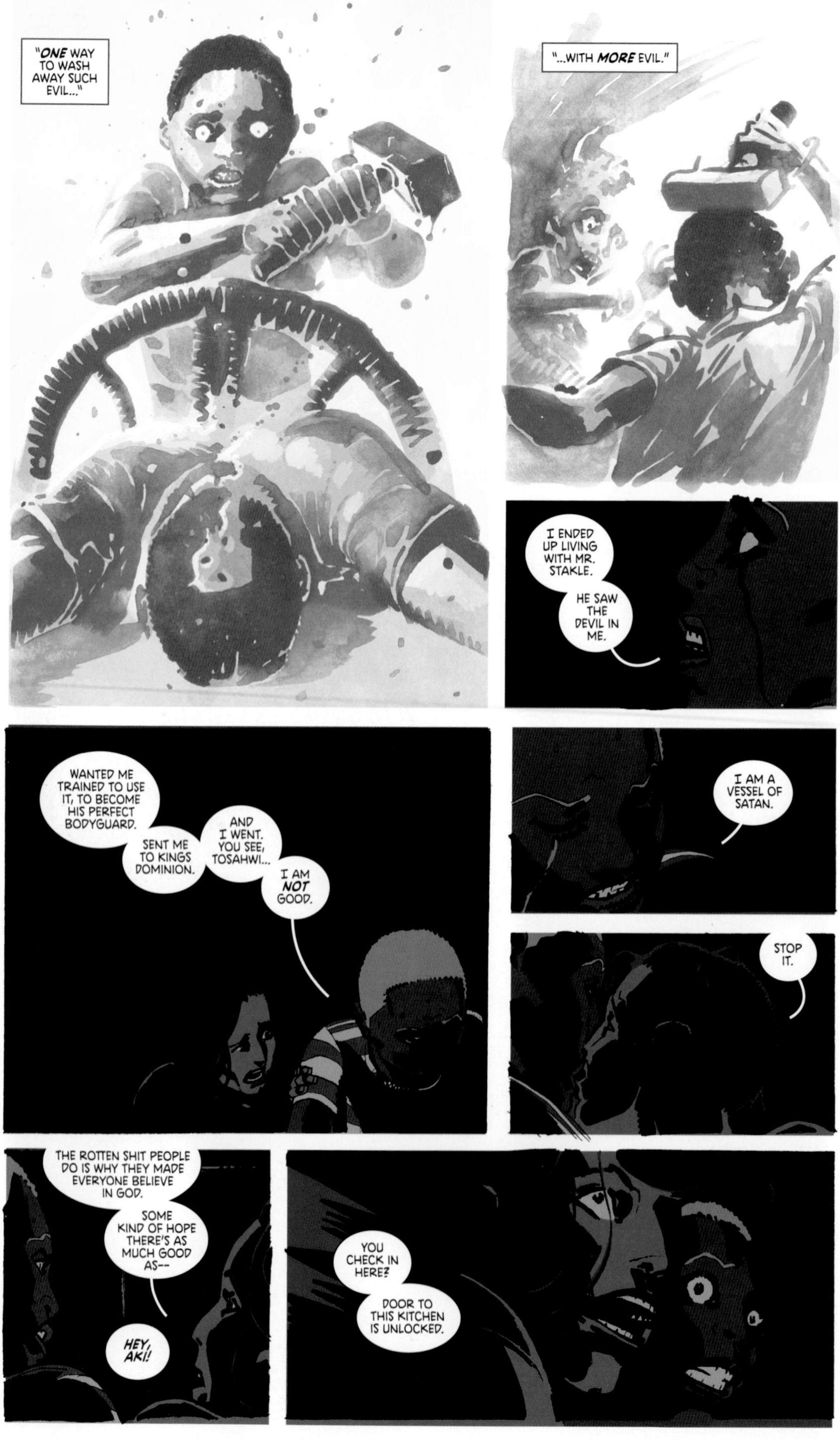
"ONE WAY TO WASH AWAY SUCH EVIL..."
"...WITH MORE EVIL."
I ENDED UP LIVING WITH MR. STAKLE.
HE SAW THE DEVIL IN ME.
WANTED ME TRAINED TO USE IT, TO BECOME HIS PERFECT BODYGUARD.
SENT ME TO KINGS DOMINION.
AND I WENT. YOU SEE, TOSAHWI...
I AM NOT GOOD.
I AM A VESSEL OF SATAN.
STOP IT.
THE ROTTEN SHIT PEOPLE DO IS WHY THEY MADE EVERYONE BELIEVE IN GOD.
SOME KIND OF HOPE THERE'S AS MUCH GOOD AS--
HEY, AKI!
YOU CHECK IN HERE?
DOOR TO THIS KITCHEN IS UNLOCKED.

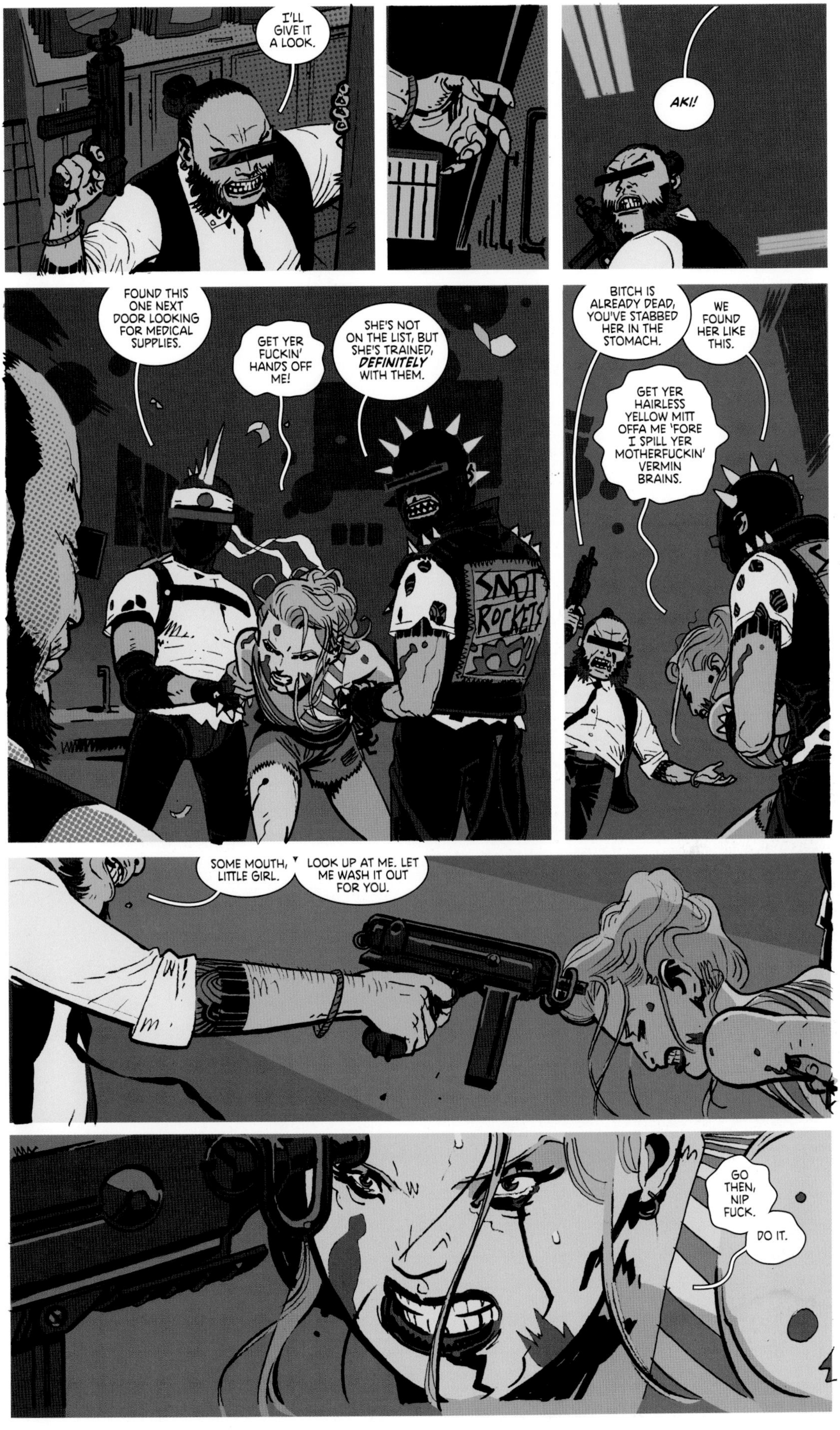
I'LL GIVE IT A LOOK.
AKI!
FOUND THIS ONE NEXT DOOR LOOKING FOR MEDICAL SUPPLIES.
GET YER FUCKIN' HANDS OFF ME!
SHE'S NOT ON THE LIST, BUT SHE'S TRAINED, ***DEFINITELY*** WITH THEM.
SNOT ROCKETS
BITCH IS ALREADY DEAD, YOU'VE STABBED HER IN THE STOMACH.
WE FOUND HER LIKE THIS.
GET YER HAIRLESS YELLOW MITT OFFA ME 'FORE I SPILL YER MOTHERFUCKIN' VERMIN BRAINS.
SOME MOUTH, LITTLE GIRL.
LOOK UP AT ME. LET ME WASH IT OUT FOR YOU.
GO THEN, NIP FUCK.
DO IT.

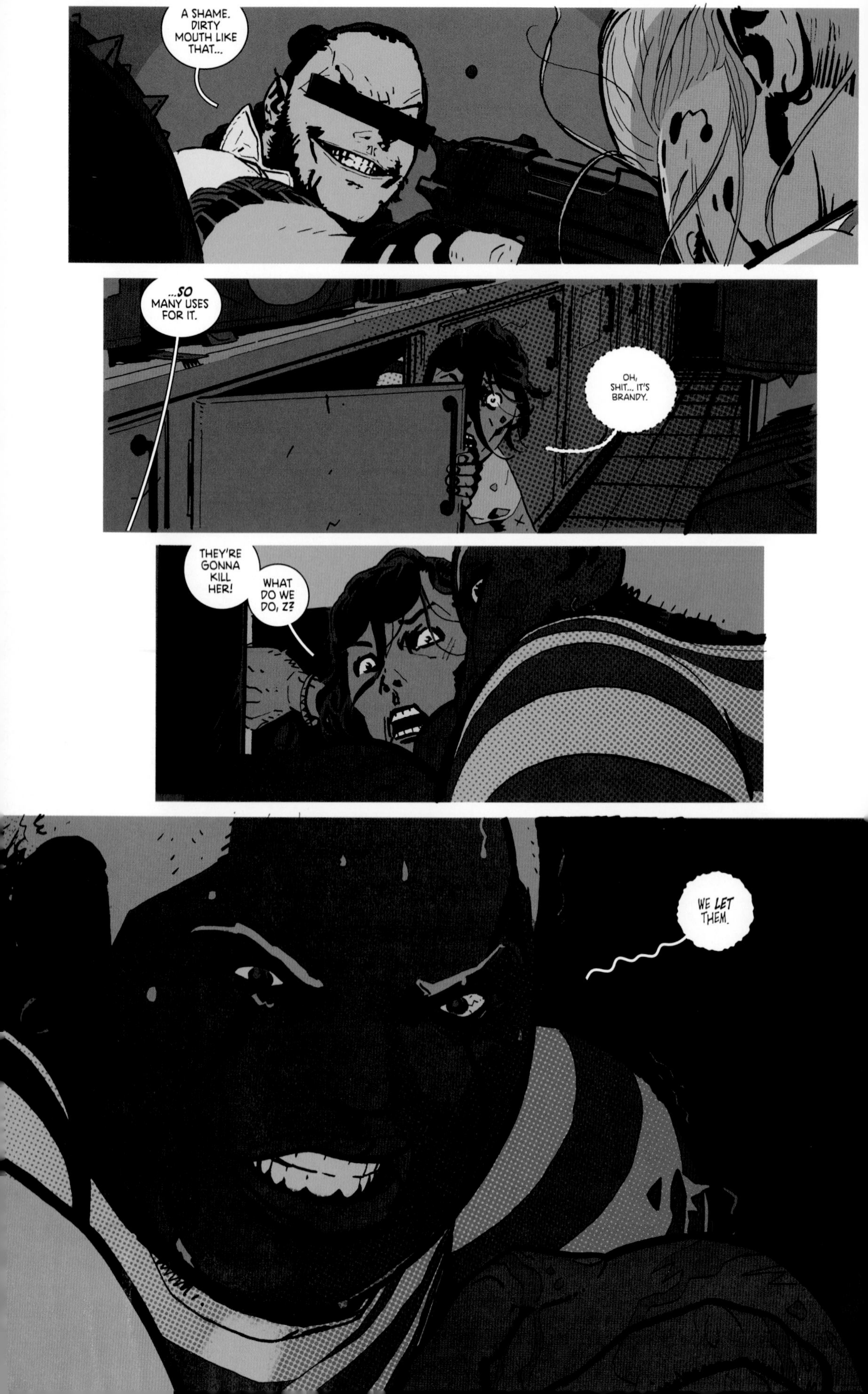
A SHAME. DIRTY MOUTH LIKE THAT...
...SO MANY USES FOR IT.
OH, SHIT... IT'S BRANDY.
THEY'RE GONNA KILL HER!
WHAT DO WE DO, Z?
WE LET THEM.

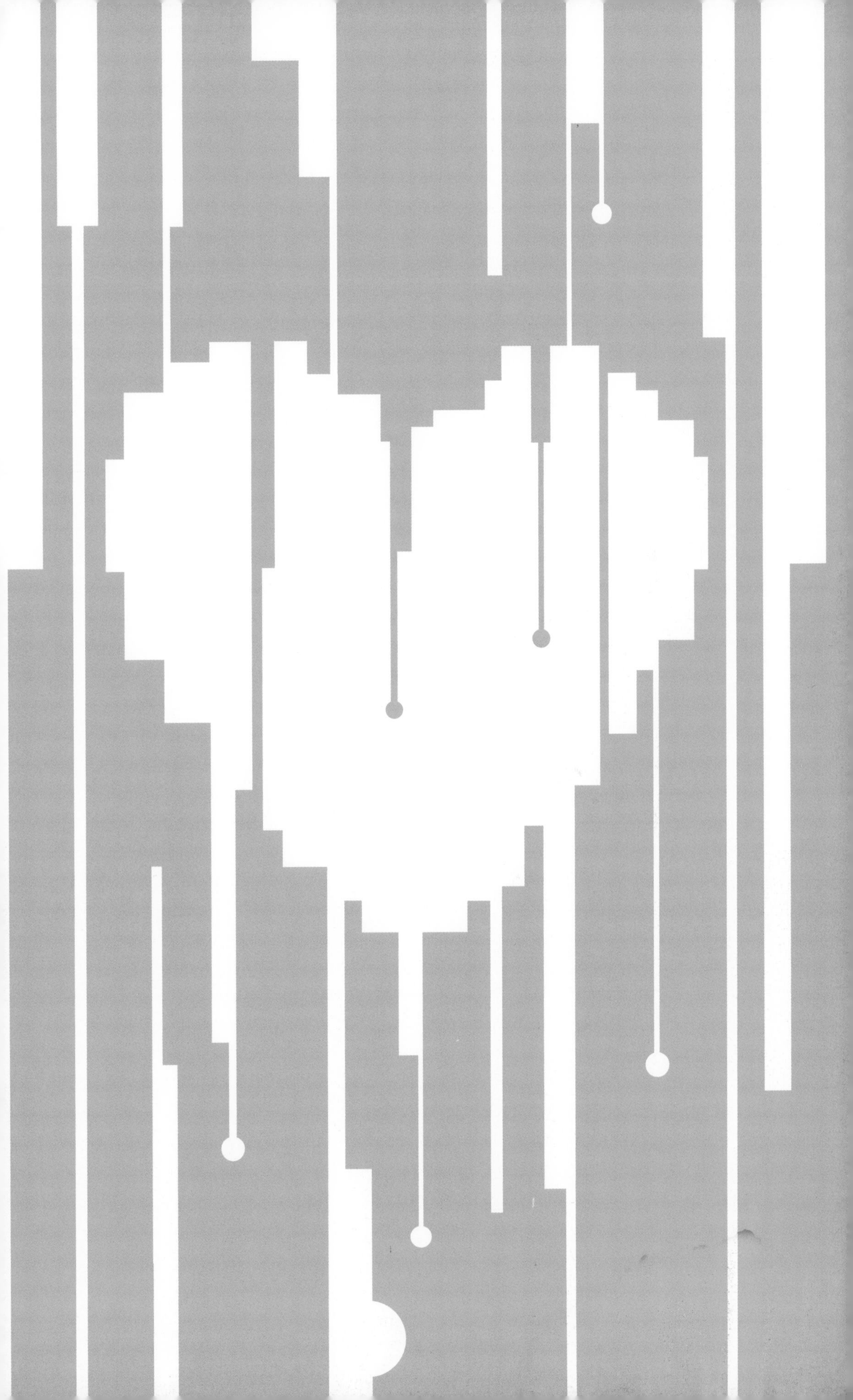

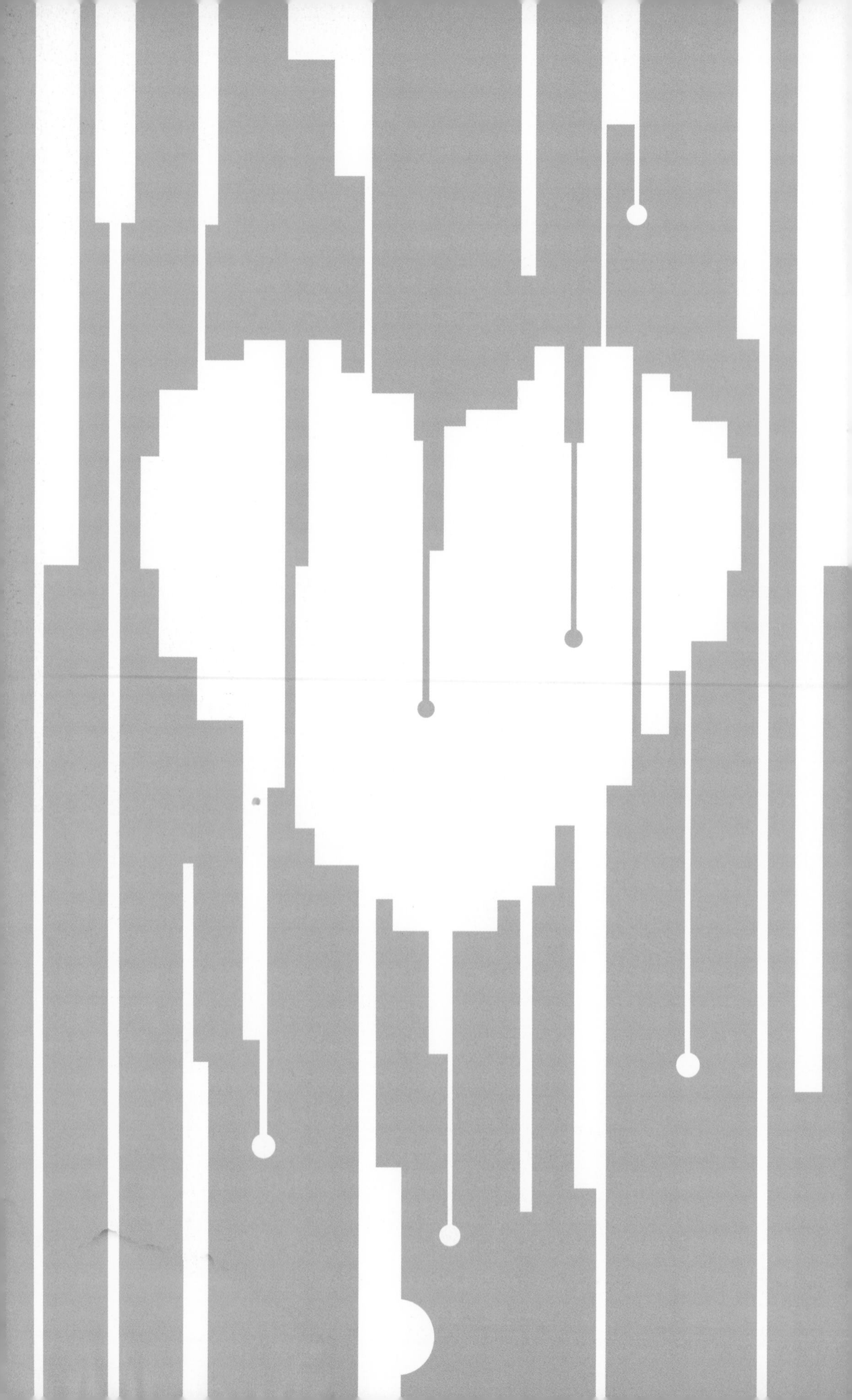

FUCK. WE'RE SO FUCKED.

THEY'RE ALL OVER THE PLACE--I MEAN EVERYWHERE.

THIS FIGHT--IT'S NOT MY THING--

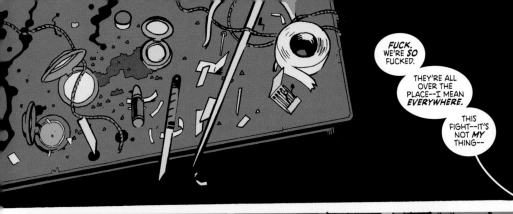

I JUST, DON'T WANT ANY PART OF THIS.

I'M NO TOUGH GUY.

SHITTY IN CLASS, TERRIBLE EVEN, DON'T PAY ATTENTION.

THEN WHY GO TO KINGS?

MY, UH, MY DAD. HE RAN HORSE OUTTA VIETNAM... WANTED ME TO BECOME FAMILY MUSCLE.

WHY DO THE KUROKI KNOW YOUR NAME?

WHAT? THE FUCK DO I KNOW?

MAYBE THEY WANT US TO TURN ON EACH OTHER. PROBABLY. RIGHT?

PLEASE, MARIA.

JUST... JUST GET US OUT OF HERE.

I'M HAVING A BAD TIME.

I-I'M NOT CUT OUT FOR THIS.

THAT MUCH IS OBVIOUS.

THE QUESTION IS...

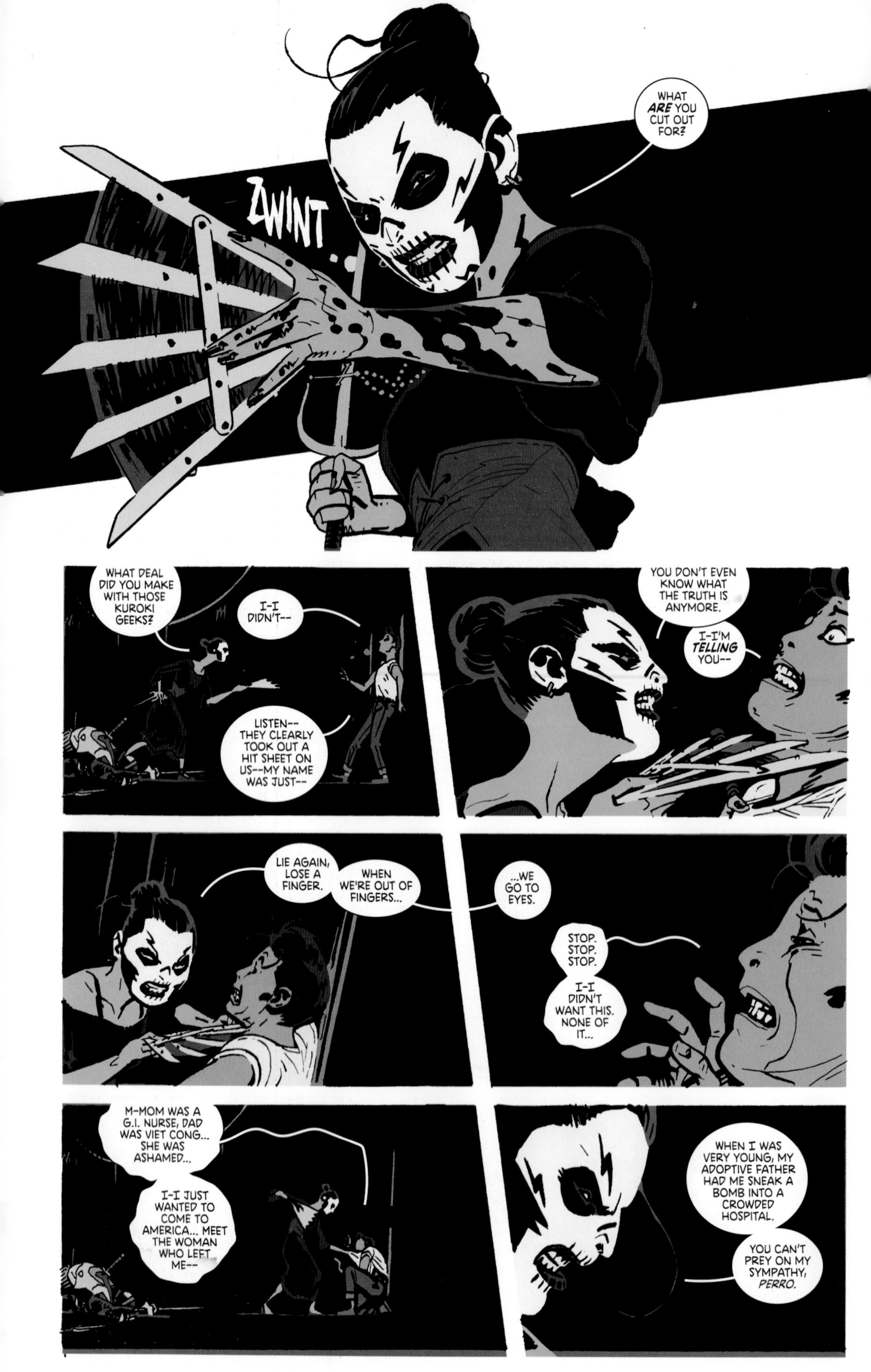
ZWINT
WHAT *ARE* YOU CUT OUT FOR?
WHAT DEAL DID YOU MAKE WITH THOSE KUROKI GEEKS?
I-I DIDN'T--
LISTEN-- THEY CLEARLY TOOK OUT A HIT SHEET ON US--MY NAME WAS JUST--
YOU DON'T EVEN KNOW WHAT THE TRUTH IS ANYMORE.
I-I'M *TELLING* YOU--
LIE AGAIN, LOSE A FINGER.
WHEN WE'RE OUT OF FINGERS...
...WE GO TO EYES.
STOP. STOP. STOP.
I-I DIDN'T WANT THIS. NONE OF IT...
M-MOM WAS A G.I. NURSE, DAD WAS VIET CONG... SHE WAS ASHAMED...
I-I JUST WANTED TO COME TO AMERICA... MEET THE WOMAN WHO LEFT ME--
WHEN I WAS VERY YOUNG, MY ADOPTIVE FATHER HAD ME SNEAK A BOMB INTO A CROWDED HOSPITAL.
YOU CAN'T PREY ON MY SYMPATHY, *PERRO.*

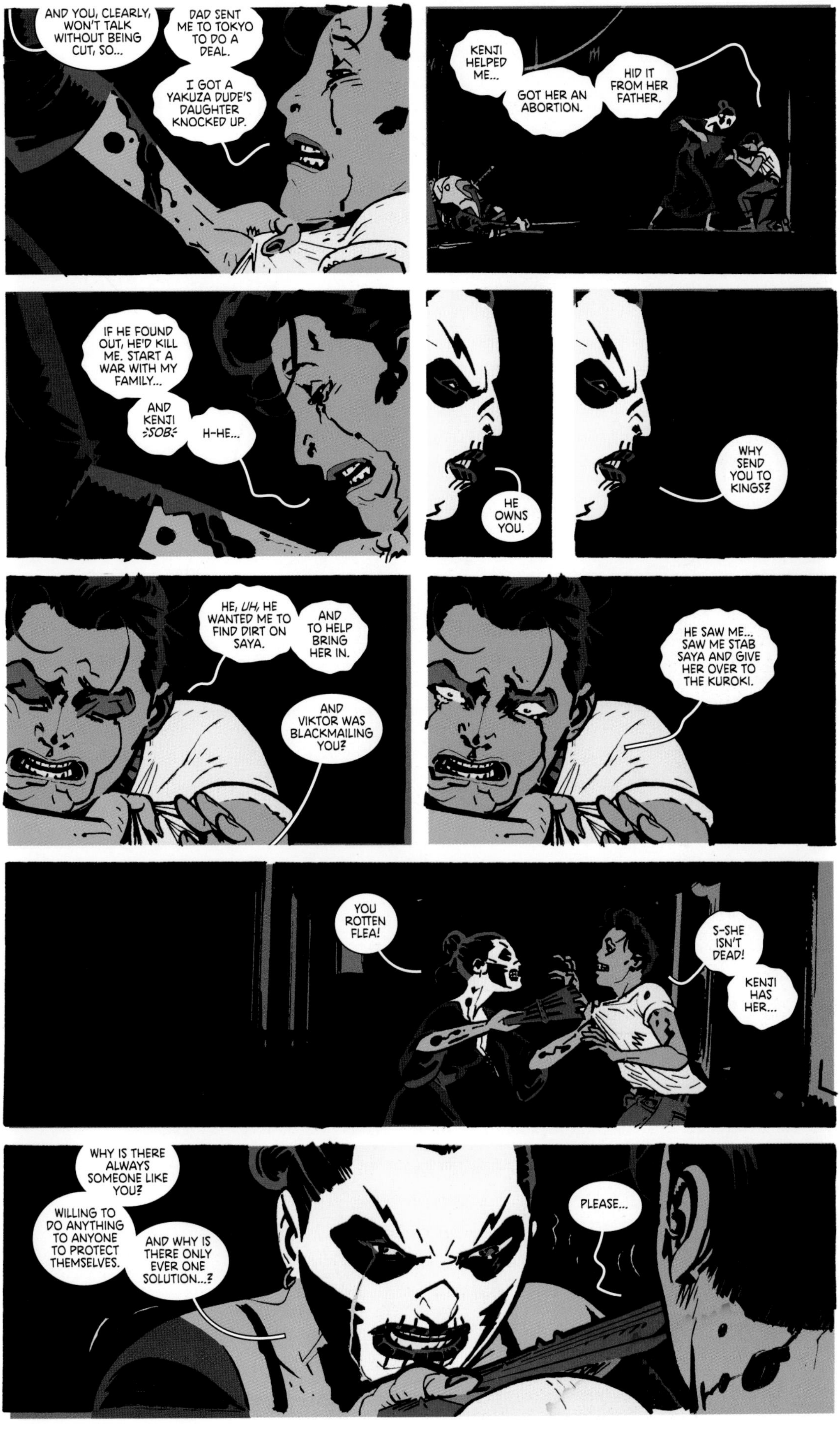
AND YOU, CLEARLY, WON'T TALK WITHOUT BEING CUT, SO...
DAD SENT ME TO TOKYO TO DO A DEAL.
I GOT A YAKUZA DUDE'S DAUGHTER KNOCKED UP.
KENJI HELPED ME...
GOT HER AN ABORTION.
HID IT FROM HER FATHER.
IF HE FOUND OUT, HE'D KILL ME. START A WAR WITH MY FAMILY...
AND KENJI *SOB*
H-HE...
HE OWNS YOU.
WHY SEND YOU TO KINGS?
HE, *UH*, HE WANTED ME TO FIND DIRT ON SAYA.
AND TO HELP BRING HER IN.
AND VIKTOR WAS BLACKMAILING YOU?
HE SAW ME... SAW ME STAB SAYA AND GIVE HER OVER TO THE KUROKI.
YOU ROTTEN FLEA!
S-SHE ISN'T DEAD!
KENJI HAS HER...
WHY IS THERE ALWAYS SOMEONE LIKE YOU?
WILLING TO DO ANYTHING TO ANYONE TO PROTECT THEMSELVES.
AND WHY IS THERE ONLY EVER ONE SOLUTION...?
PLEASE...

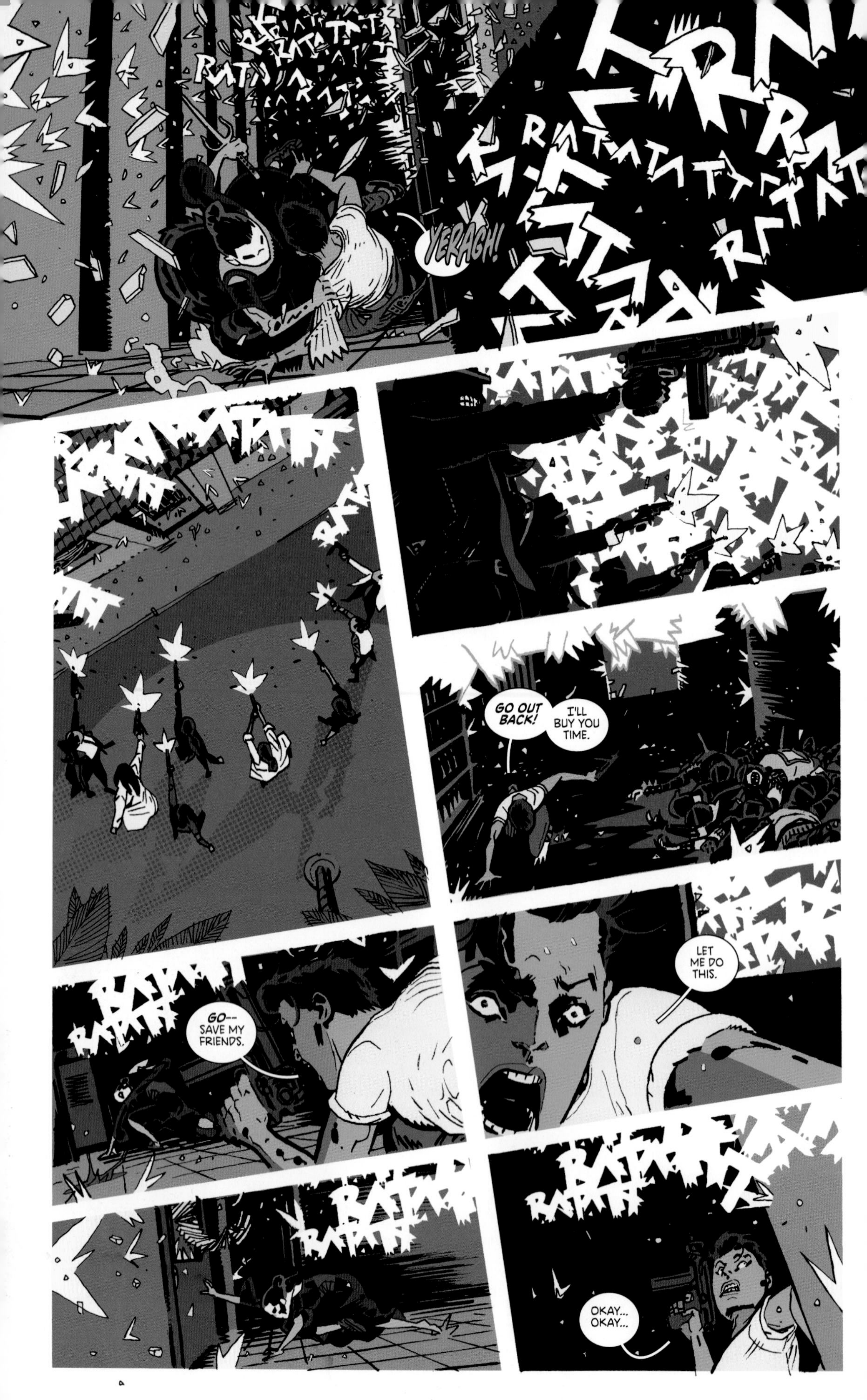
YERAGH!
GO OUT BACK!
I'LL BUY YOU TIME.
GO-- SAVE MY FRIENDS.
LET ME DO THIS.
OKAY... OKAY...

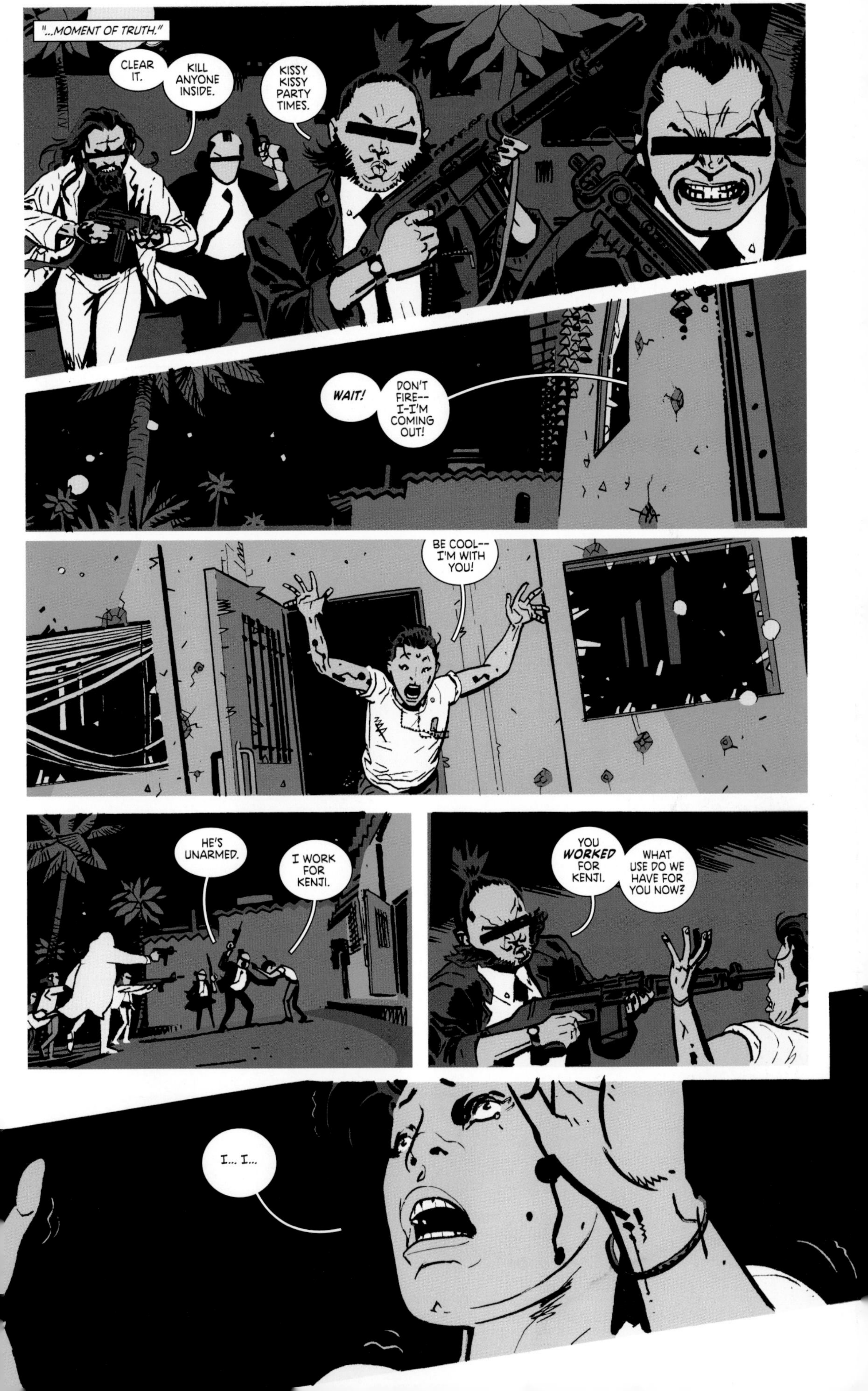
"...MOMENT OF TRUTH."
CLEAR IT.
KILL ANYONE INSIDE.
KISSY KISSY PARTY TIMES.
WAIT!
DON'T FIRE-- I-I'M COMING OUT!
BE COOL-- I'M WITH YOU!
HE'S UNARMED.
I WORK FOR KENJI.
YOU WORKED FOR KENJI.
WHAT USE DO WE HAVE FOR YOU NOW?
I... I...

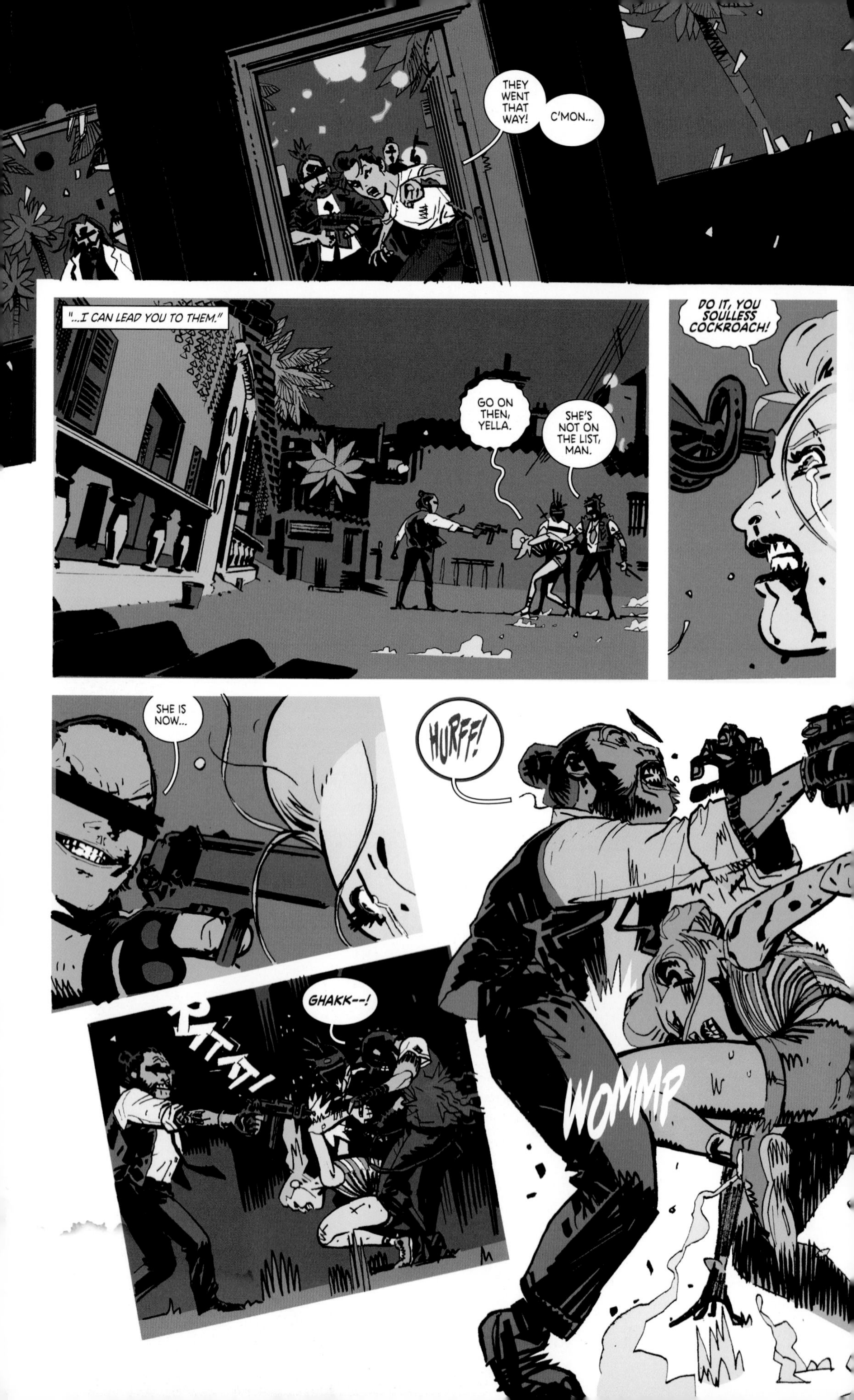
THEY WENT THAT WAY!
C'MON...
"...I CAN LEAD YOU TO THEM."
GO ON THEN, YELLA.
SHE'S NOT ON THE LIST, MAN.
DO IT, YOU SOULLESS COCKROACH!
SHE IS NOW...
RATATI
GHAKK--!
HURFF!
WOMMP

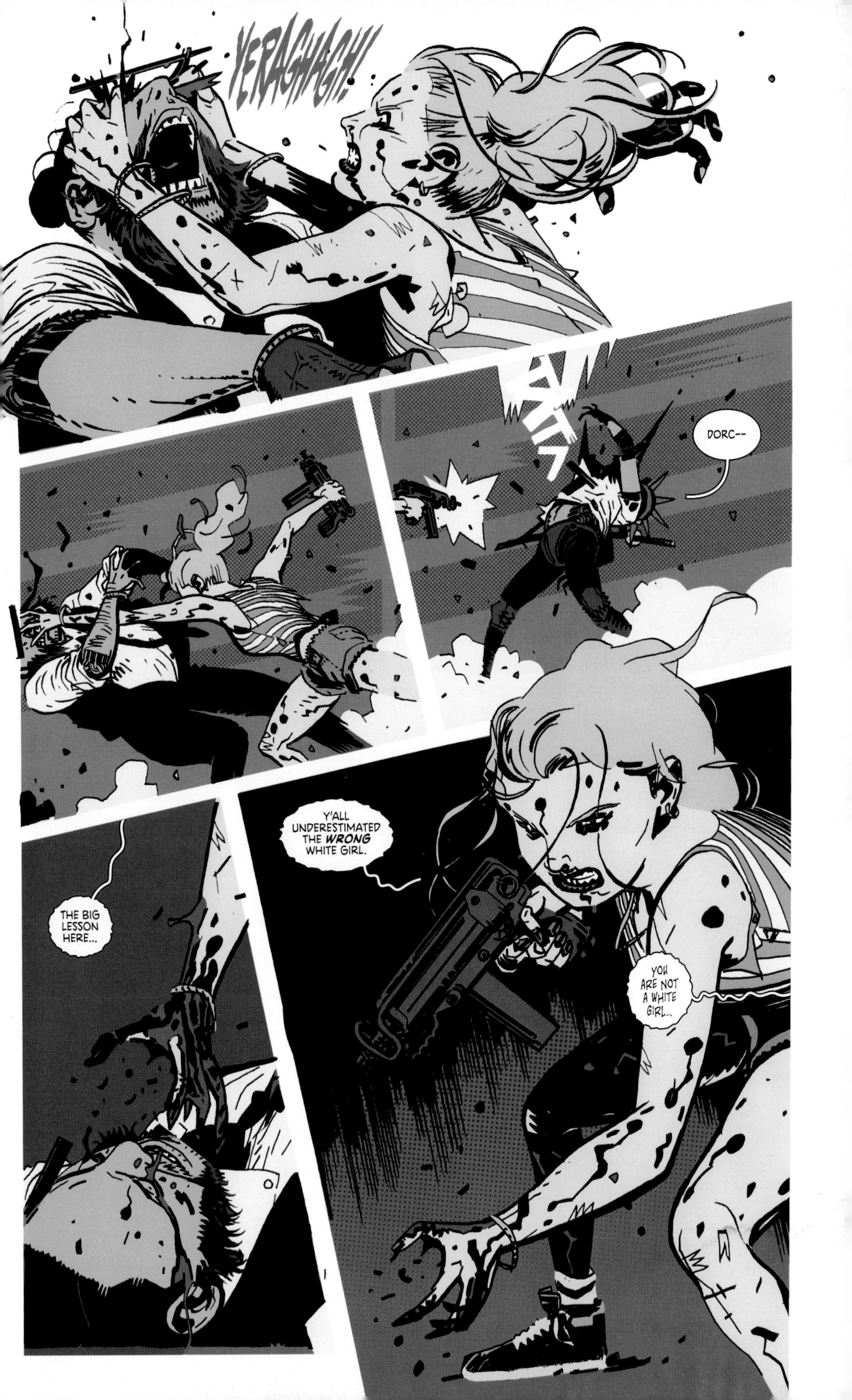
YERAGHAGH!
DORC--
THE BIG LESSON HERE...
Y'ALL UNDERESTIMATED THE *WRONG* WHITE GIRL.
YOU ARE NOT A WHITE GIRL...

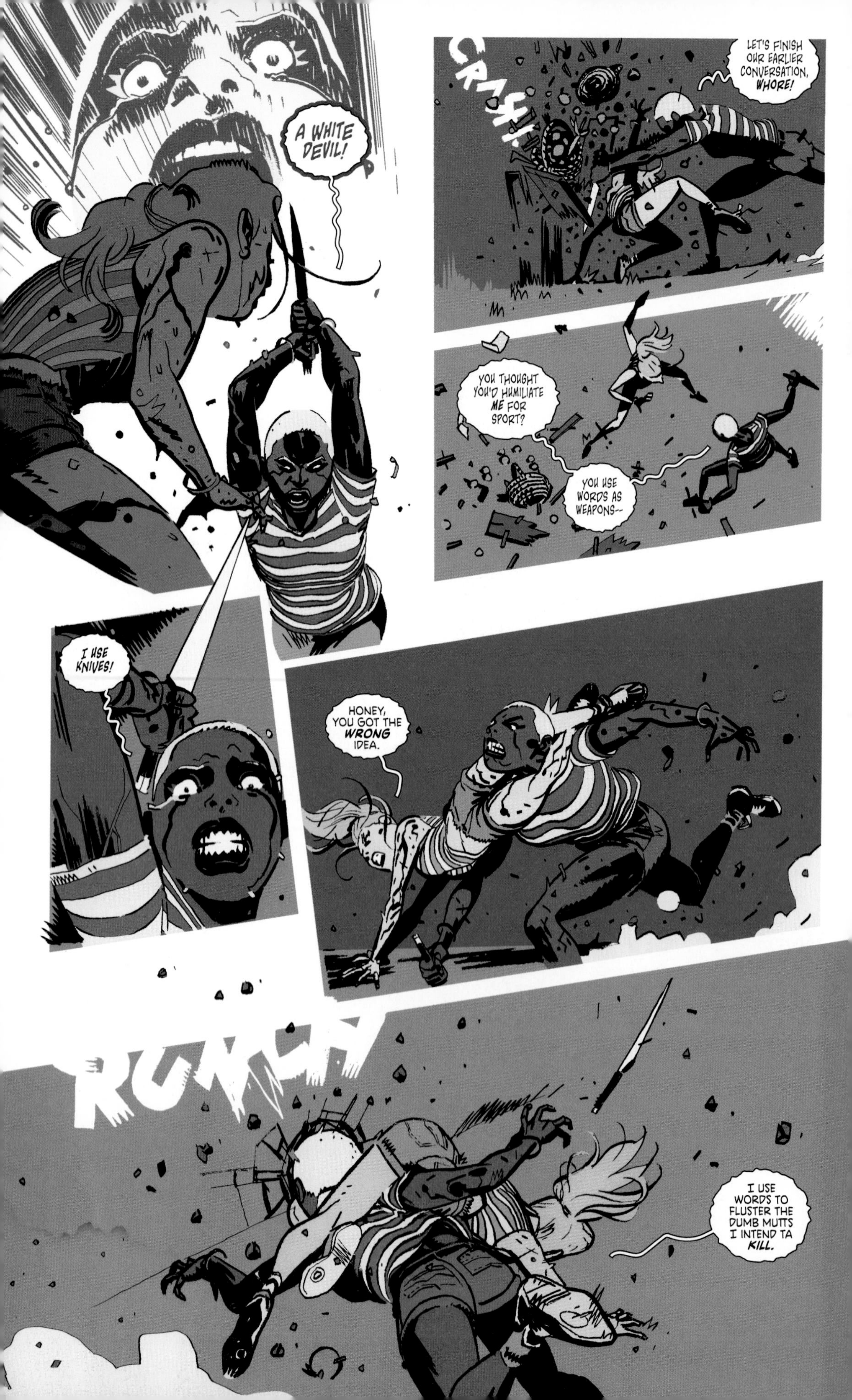
A WHITE DEVIL!
CRASH!
LET'S FINISH OUR EARLIER CONVERSATION, WHORE!
YOU THOUGHT YOU'D HUMILIATE ME FOR SPORT?
YOU USE WORDS AS WEAPONS--
I USE KNIVES!
HONEY, YOU GOT THE WRONG IDEA.
I USE WORDS TO FLUSTER THE DUMB MUTTS I INTEND TA KILL.

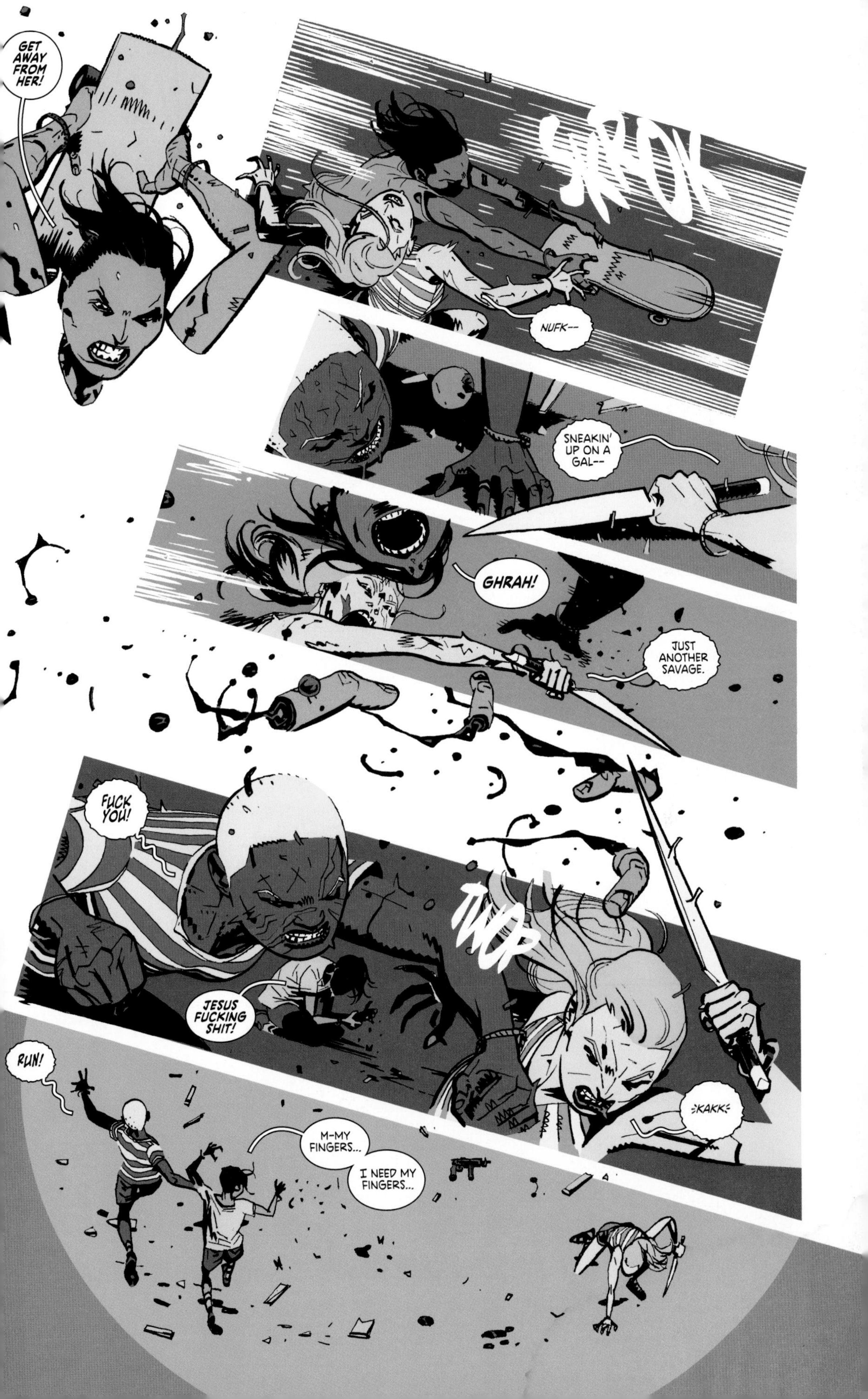
GET AWAY FROM HER!
SKROK
NUFK--
SNEAKIN' UP ON A GAL--
GHRAH!
JUST ANOTHER SAVAGE.
FUCK YOU!
TWOK
JESUS FUCKING SHIT!
KAKK
RUN!
M-MY FINGERS...
I NEED MY FINGERS...

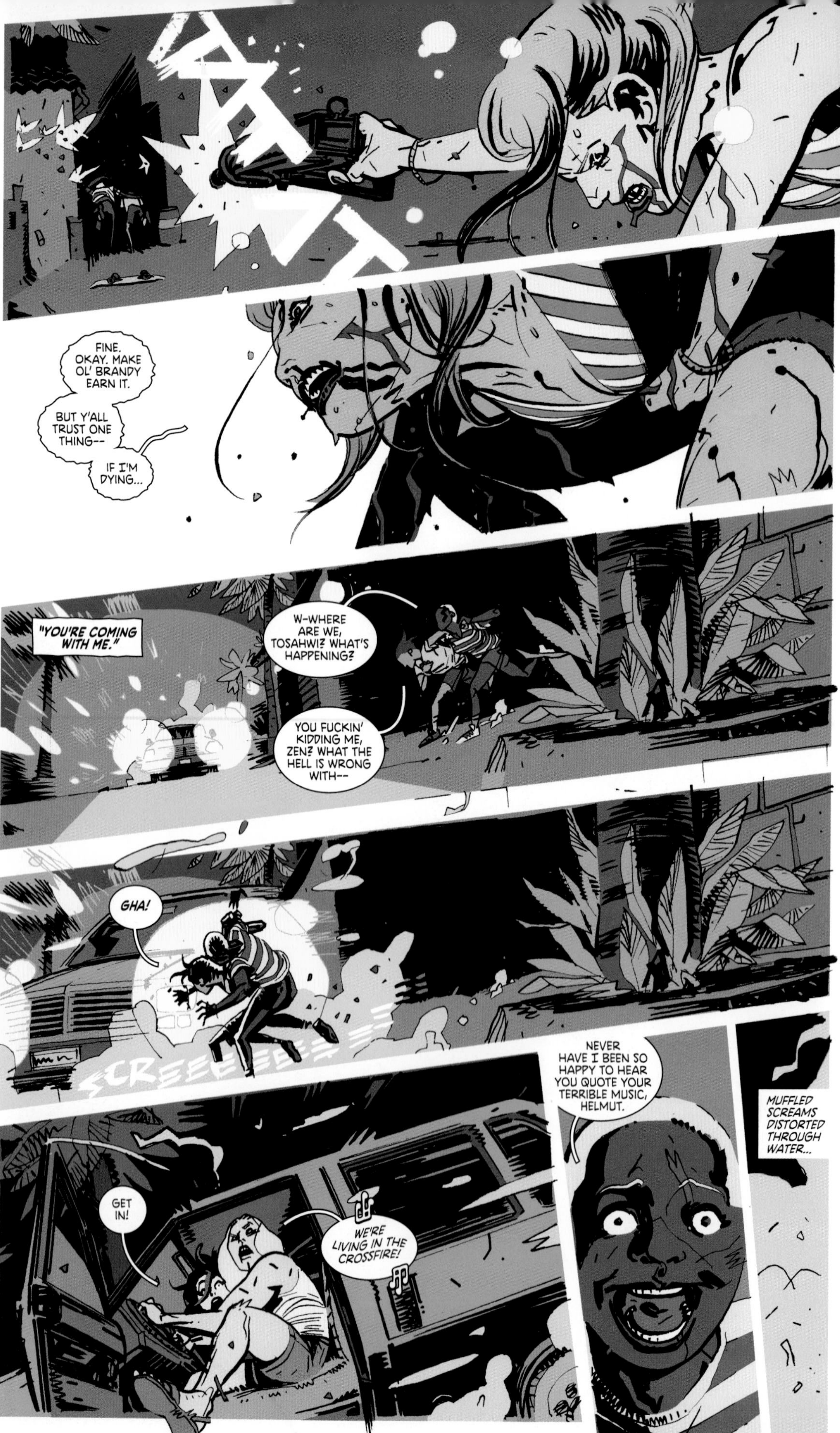
FINE. OKAY. MAKE OL' BRANDY EARN IT.
BUT Y'ALL TRUST ONE THING--
IF I'M DYING...
"YOU'RE COMING WITH ME."
W-WHERE ARE WE, TOSAHWI? WHAT'S HAPPENING?
YOU FUCKIN' KIDDING ME, ZEN? WHAT THE HELL IS WRONG WITH--
GHA!
SCREEEEEEEEE
GET IN!
WE'RE LIVING IN THE CROSSFIRE!
NEVER HAVE I BEEN SO HAPPY TO HEAR YOU QUOTE YOUR TERRIBLE MUSIC, HELMUT.
MUFFLED SCREAMS DISTORTED THROUGH WATER...

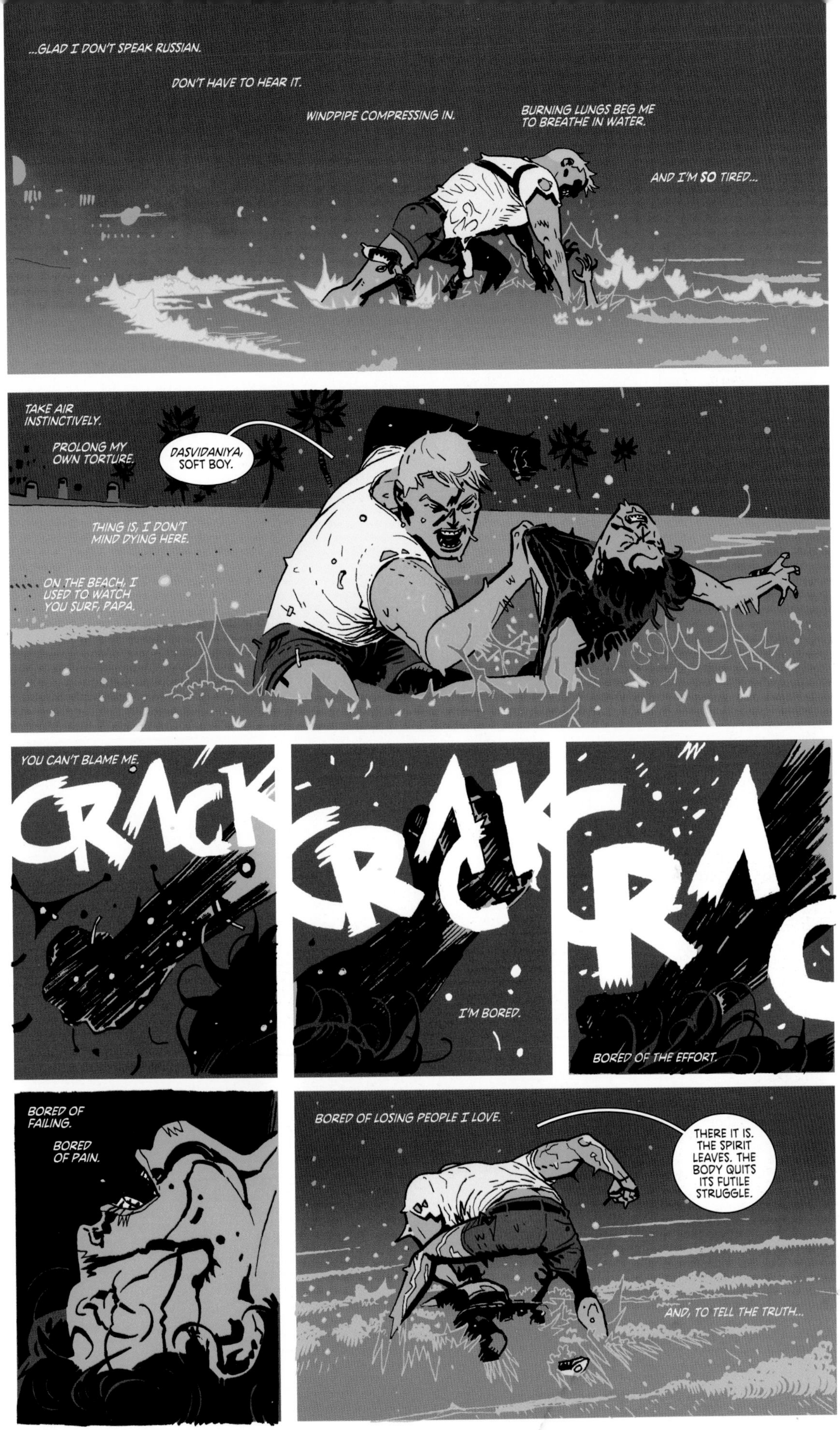
...GLAD I DON'T SPEAK RUSSIAN.
DON'T HAVE TO HEAR IT.
WINDPIPE COMPRESSING IN.
BURNING LUNGS BEG ME TO BREATHE IN WATER.
AND I'M SO TIRED...
TAKE AIR INSTINCTIVELY.
PROLONG MY OWN TORTURE.
DASVIDANIYA, SOFT BOY.
THING IS, I DON'T MIND DYING HERE.
ON THE BEACH, I USED TO WATCH YOU SURF, PAPA.
YOU CAN'T BLAME ME.
CRACK
CRACK
CRA
I'M BORED.
BORED OF THE EFFORT.
BORED OF FAILING.
BORED OF PAIN.
BORED OF LOSING PEOPLE I LOVE.
THERE IT IS. THE SPIRIT LEAVES. THE BODY QUITS ITS FUTILE STRUGGLE.
AND, TO TELL THE TRUTH...

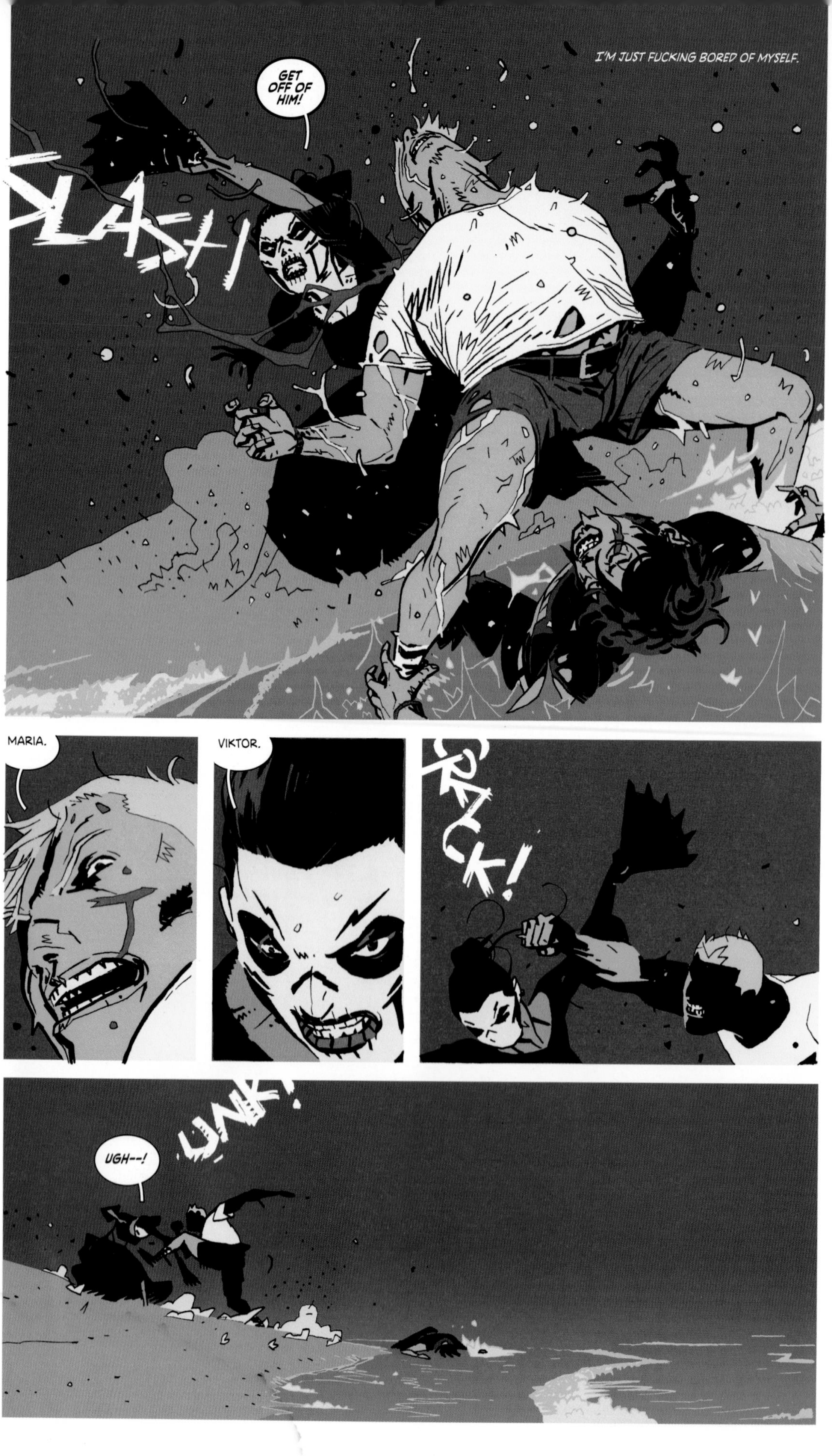
I'M JUST FUCKING BORED OF MYSELF.
GET OFF OF HIM!
LASH!
MARIA.
VIKTOR.
CRACK!
UNK!
UGH--!

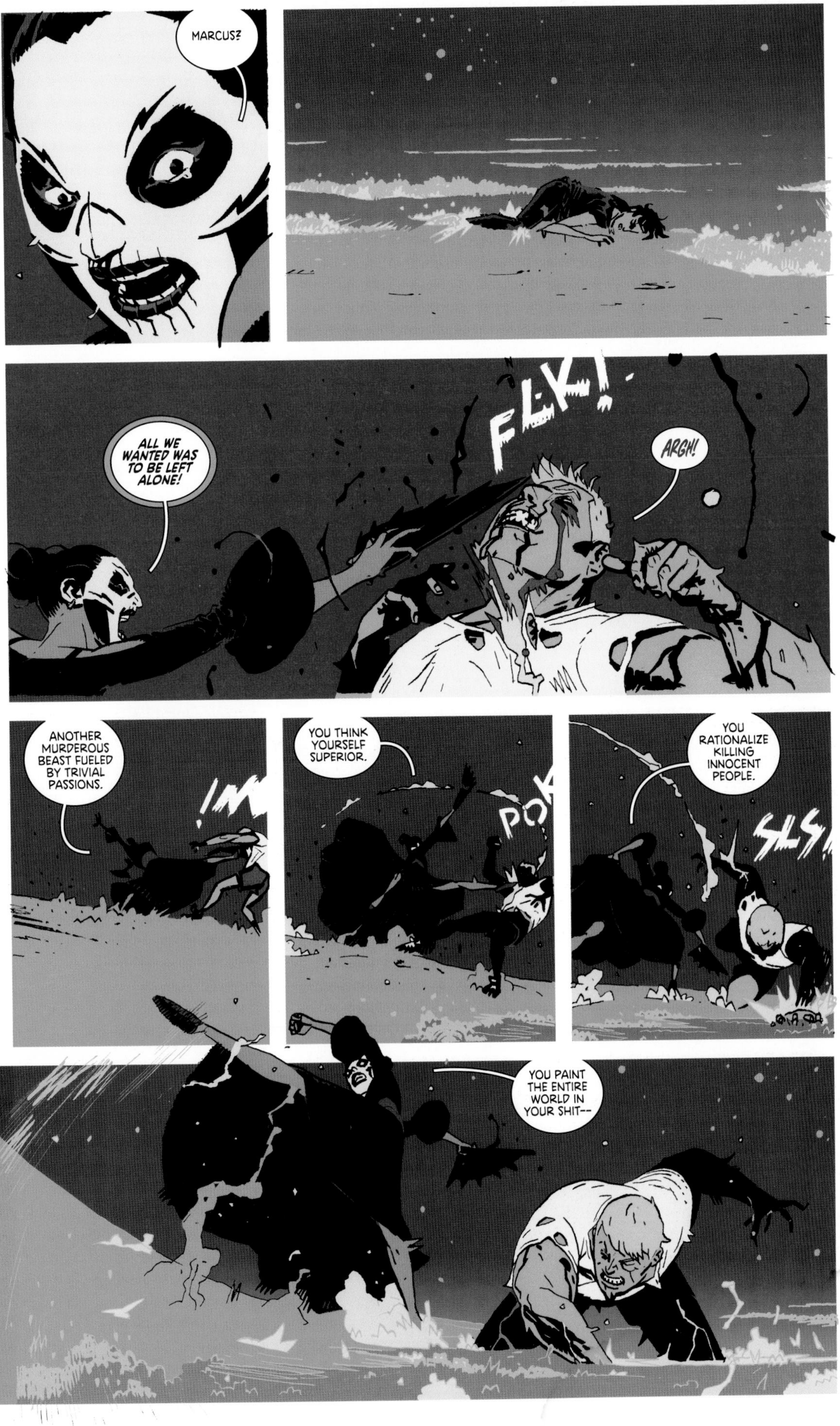
MARCUS?
ALL WE WANTED WAS TO BE LEFT ALONE!
FLK!
ARGH!
ANOTHER MURDEROUS BEAST FUELED BY TRIVIAL PASSIONS.
YOU THINK YOURSELF SUPERIOR.
POK
YOU RATIONALIZE KILLING INNOCENT PEOPLE.
YOU PAINT THE ENTIRE WORLD IN YOUR SHIT--

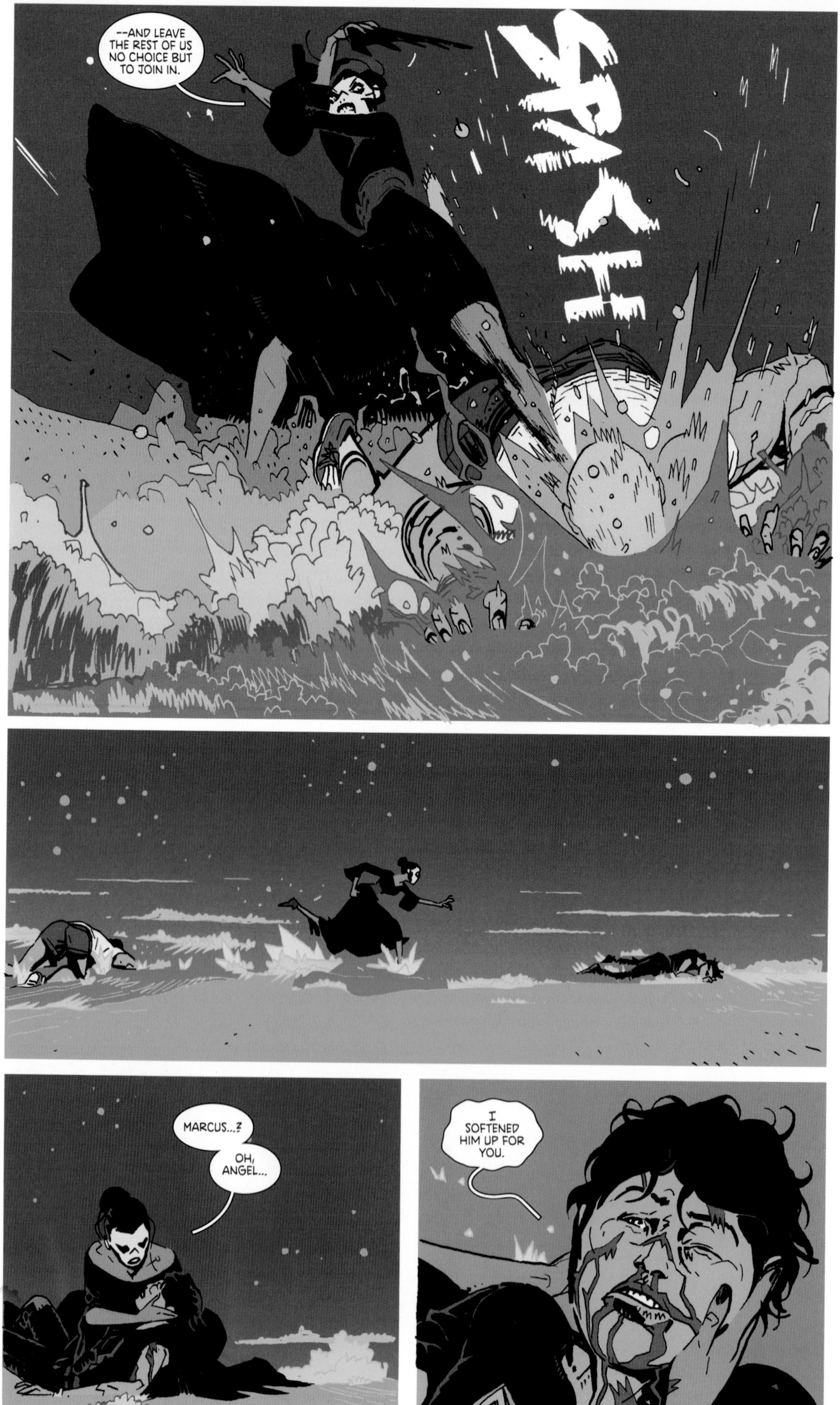
--AND LEAVE THE REST OF US NO CHOICE BUT TO JOIN IN.
SPLASH
MARCUS...?
OH, ANGEL...
I SOFTENED HIM UP FOR YOU.

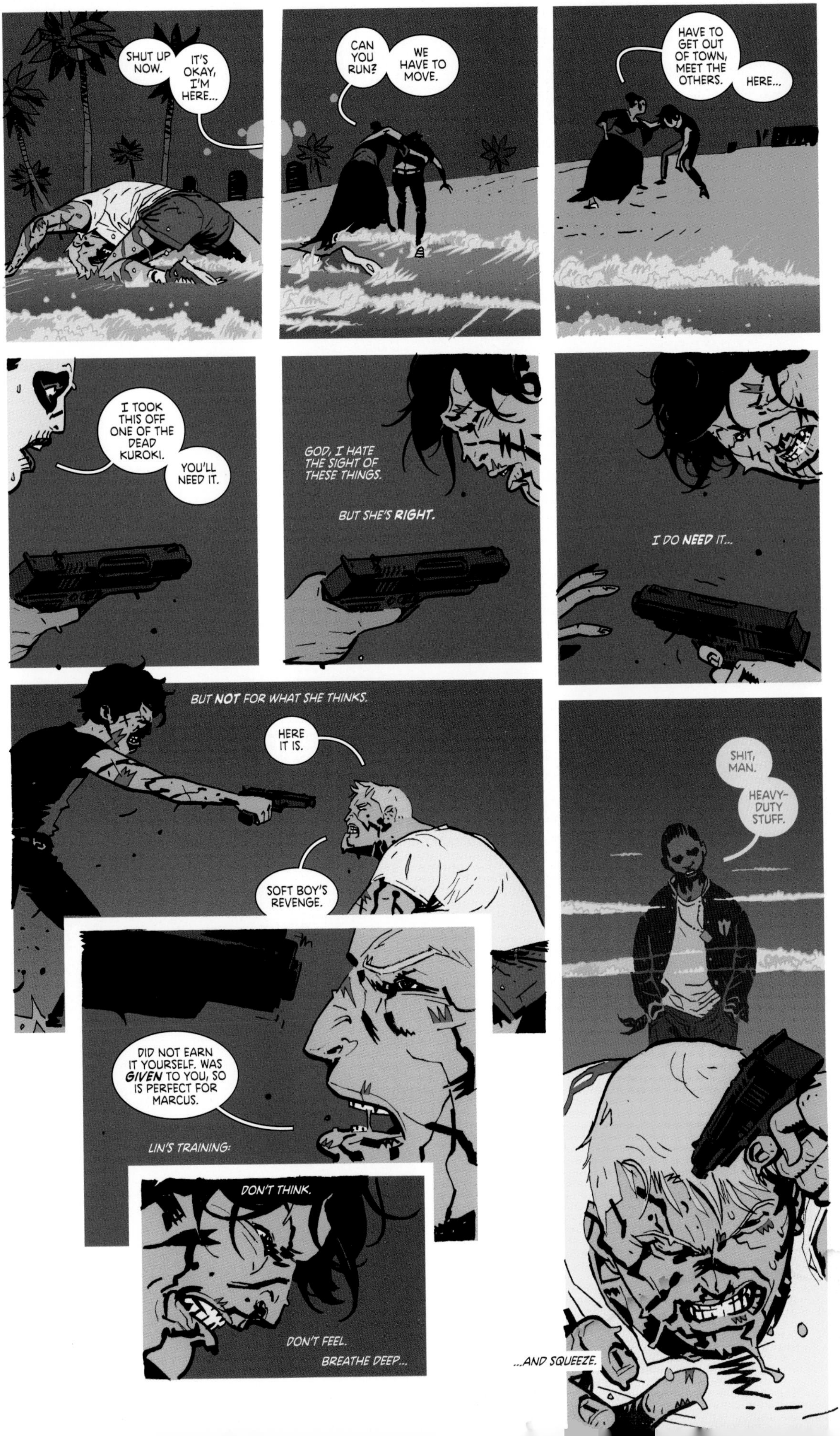
SHUT UP NOW.
IT'S OKAY, I'M HERE...
CAN YOU RUN?
WE HAVE TO MOVE.
HAVE TO GET OUT OF TOWN, MEET THE OTHERS.
HERE...
I TOOK THIS OFF ONE OF THE DEAD KUROKI.
YOU'LL NEED IT.
GOD, I HATE THE SIGHT OF THESE THINGS.
BUT SHE'S RIGHT.
I DO NEED IT...
BUT NOT FOR WHAT SHE THINKS.
HERE IT IS.
SOFT BOY'S REVENGE.
DID NOT EARN IT YOURSELF. WAS GIVEN TO YOU, SO IS PERFECT FOR MARCUS.
LIN'S TRAINING:
DON'T THINK.
DON'T FEEL.
BREATHE DEEP...
SHIT, MAN.
HEAVY-DUTY STUFF.
...AND SQUEEZE.

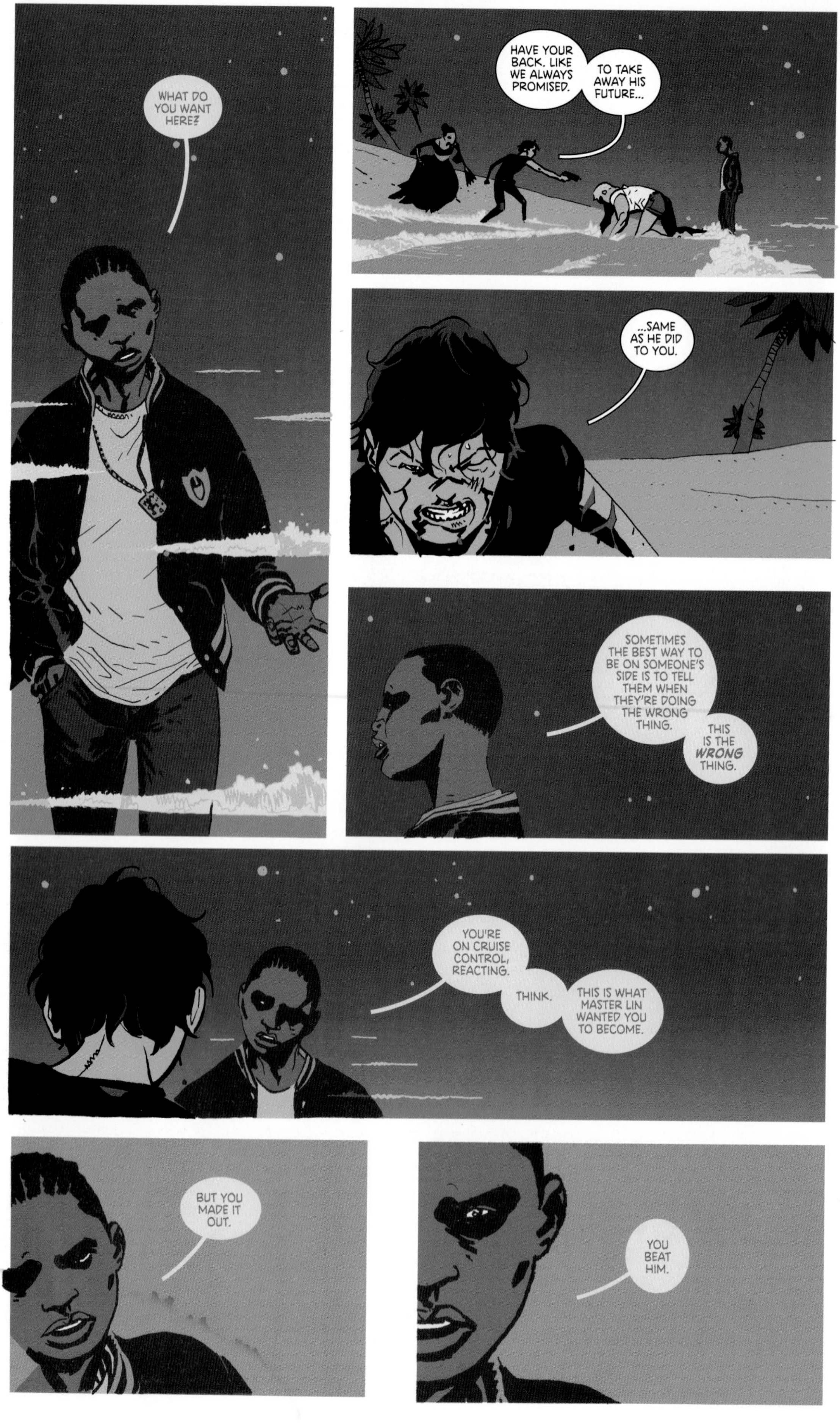
WHAT DO YOU WANT HERE?
HAVE YOUR BACK. LIKE WE ALWAYS PROMISED.
TO TAKE AWAY HIS FUTURE...
...SAME AS HE DID TO YOU.
SOMETIMES THE BEST WAY TO BE ON SOMEONE'S SIDE IS TO TELL THEM WHEN THEY'RE DOING THE WRONG THING.
THIS IS THE WRONG THING.
YOU'RE ON CRUISE CONTROL, REACTING.
THINK.
THIS IS WHAT MASTER LIN WANTED YOU TO BECOME.
BUT YOU MADE IT OUT.
YOU BEAT HIM.

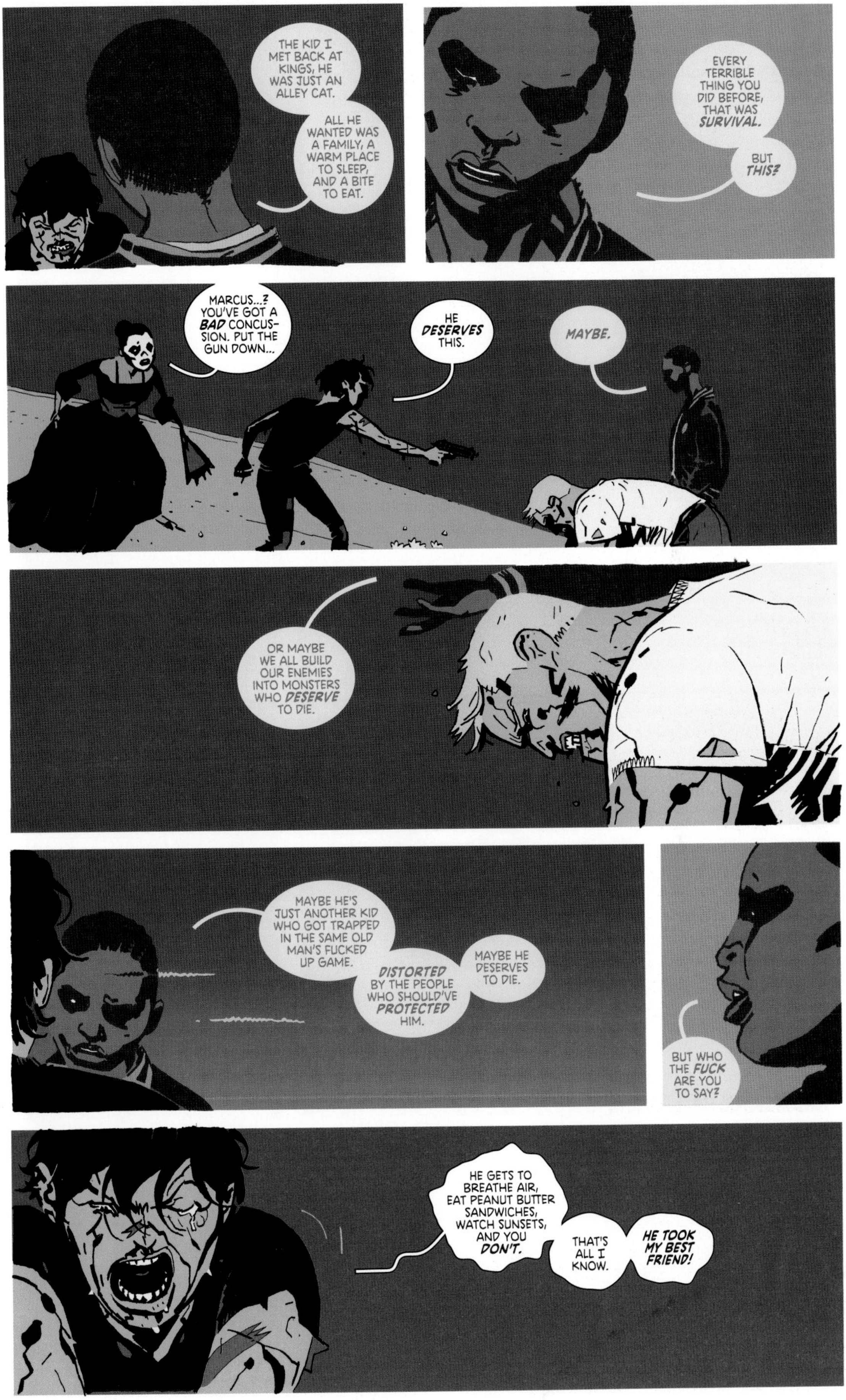

THE KID I MET BACK AT KINGS, HE WAS JUST AN ALLEY CAT.
ALL HE WANTED WAS A FAMILY, A WARM PLACE TO SLEEP, AND A BITE TO EAT.
EVERY TERRIBLE THING YOU DID BEFORE, THAT WAS SURVIVAL.
BUT THIS?
MARCUS...? YOU'VE GOT A BAD CONCUSSION. PUT THE GUN DOWN...
HE DESERVES THIS.
MAYBE.
OR MAYBE WE ALL BUILD OUR ENEMIES INTO MONSTERS WHO DESERVE TO DIE.
MAYBE HE'S JUST ANOTHER KID WHO GOT TRAPPED IN THE SAME OLD MAN'S FUCKED UP GAME.
DISTORTED BY THE PEOPLE WHO SHOULD'VE PROTECTED HIM.
MAYBE HE DESERVES TO DIE.
BUT WHO THE FUCK ARE YOU TO SAY?
HE GETS TO BREATHE AIR, EAT PEANUT BUTTER SANDWICHES, WATCH SUNSETS, AND YOU DON'T.
THAT'S ALL I KNOW.
HE TOOK MY BEST FRIEND!

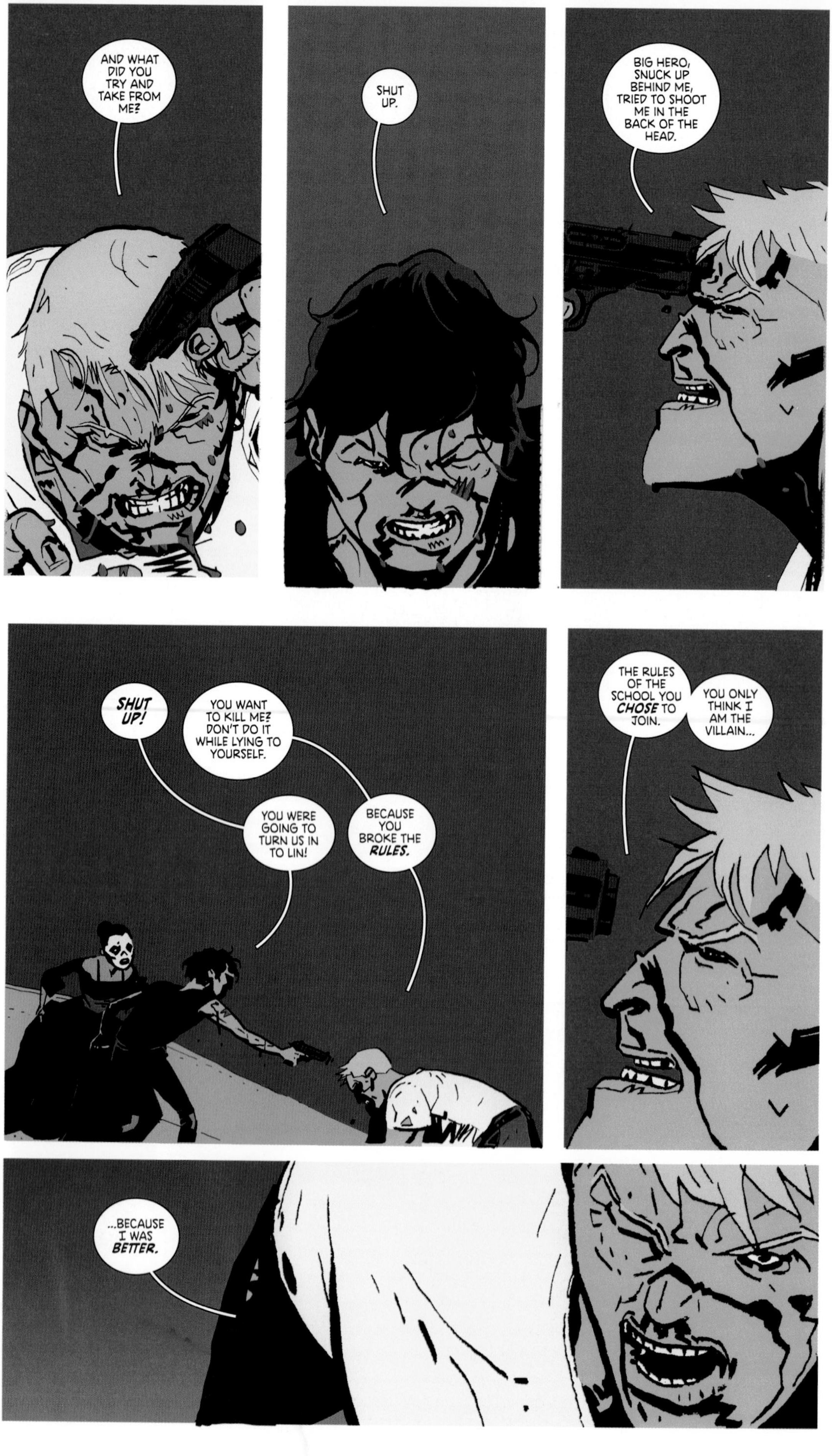
AND WHAT DID YOU TRY AND TAKE FROM ME?
SHUT UP.
BIG HERO, SNUCK UP BEHIND ME, TRIED TO SHOOT ME IN THE BACK OF THE HEAD.
SHUT UP!
YOU WANT TO KILL ME? DON'T DO IT WHILE LYING TO YOURSELF.
YOU WERE GOING TO TURN US IN TO LIN!
BECAUSE YOU BROKE THE RULES.
THE RULES OF THE SCHOOL YOU CHOSE TO JOIN.
YOU ONLY THINK I AM THE VILLAIN...
...BECAUSE I WAS BETTER.

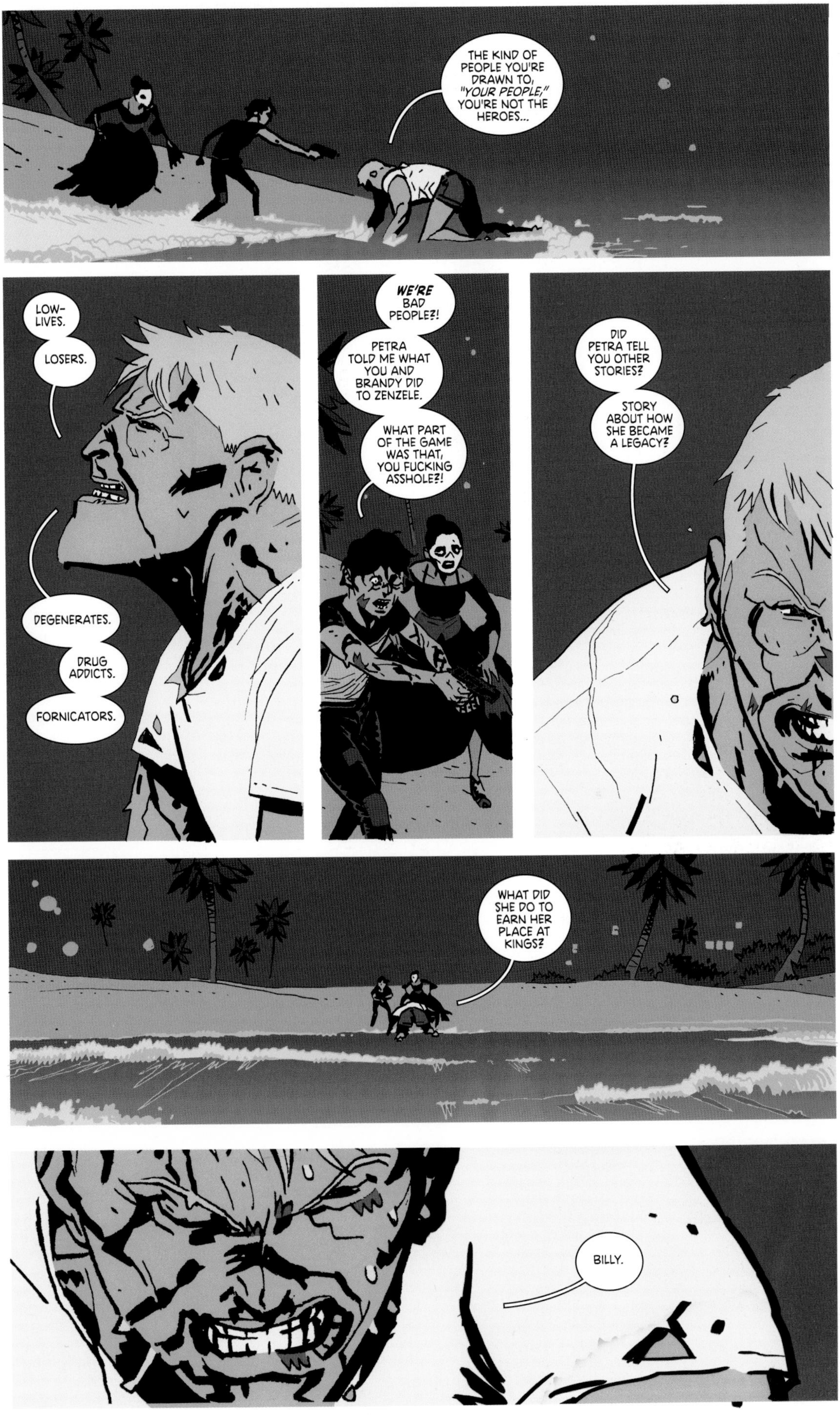
THE KIND OF PEOPLE YOU'RE DRAWN TO, *"YOUR PEOPLE,"* YOU'RE NOT THE HEROES...
LOW-LIVES.
LOSERS.
DEGENERATES.
DRUG ADDICTS.
FORNICATORS.
WE'RE BAD PEOPLE?!
PETRA TOLD ME WHAT YOU AND BRANDY DID TO ZENZELE.
WHAT PART OF THE GAME WAS THAT, YOU FUCKING ASSHOLE?!
DID PETRA TELL YOU OTHER STORIES?
STORY ABOUT HOW SHE BECAME A LEGACY?
WHAT DID SHE DO TO EARN HER PLACE AT KINGS?
BILLY.

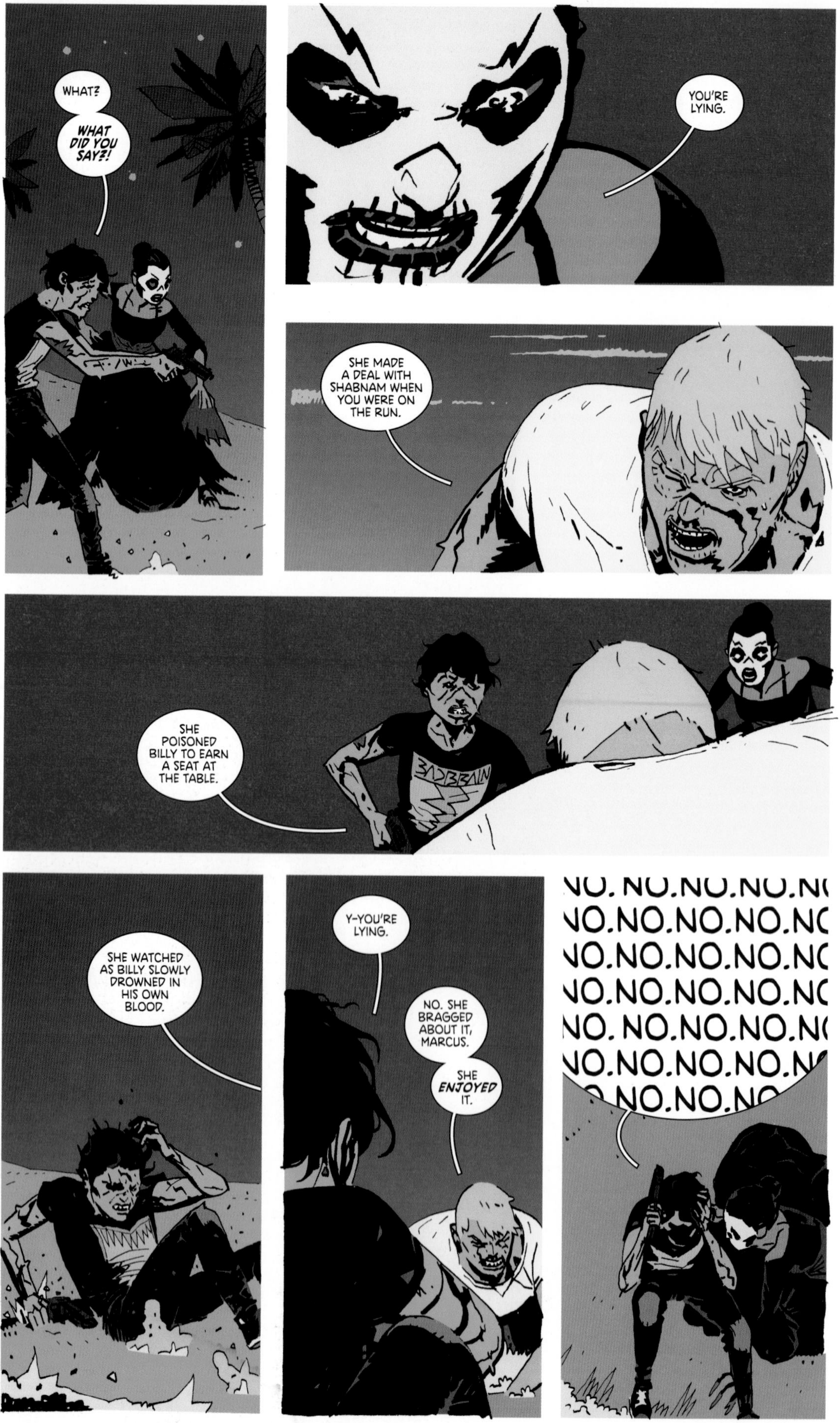
WHAT?
WHAT DID YOU SAY?!
YOU'RE LYING.
SHE MADE A DEAL WITH SHABNAM WHEN YOU WERE ON THE RUN.
SHE POISONED BILLY TO EARN A SEAT AT THE TABLE.
SHE WATCHED AS BILLY SLOWLY DROWNED IN HIS OWN BLOOD.
Y-YOU'RE LYING.
NO. SHE BRAGGED ABOUT IT, MARCUS.
SHE ENJOYED IT.
NO. NO.NO.NO.NO.
NO.NO.NO.NO.NO.
NO.NO.NO.NO.NO.
NO.NO.NO.NO.NO.
NO. NO.NO.NO.NO.
NO.NO.NO.NO.
NO.NO.NO.

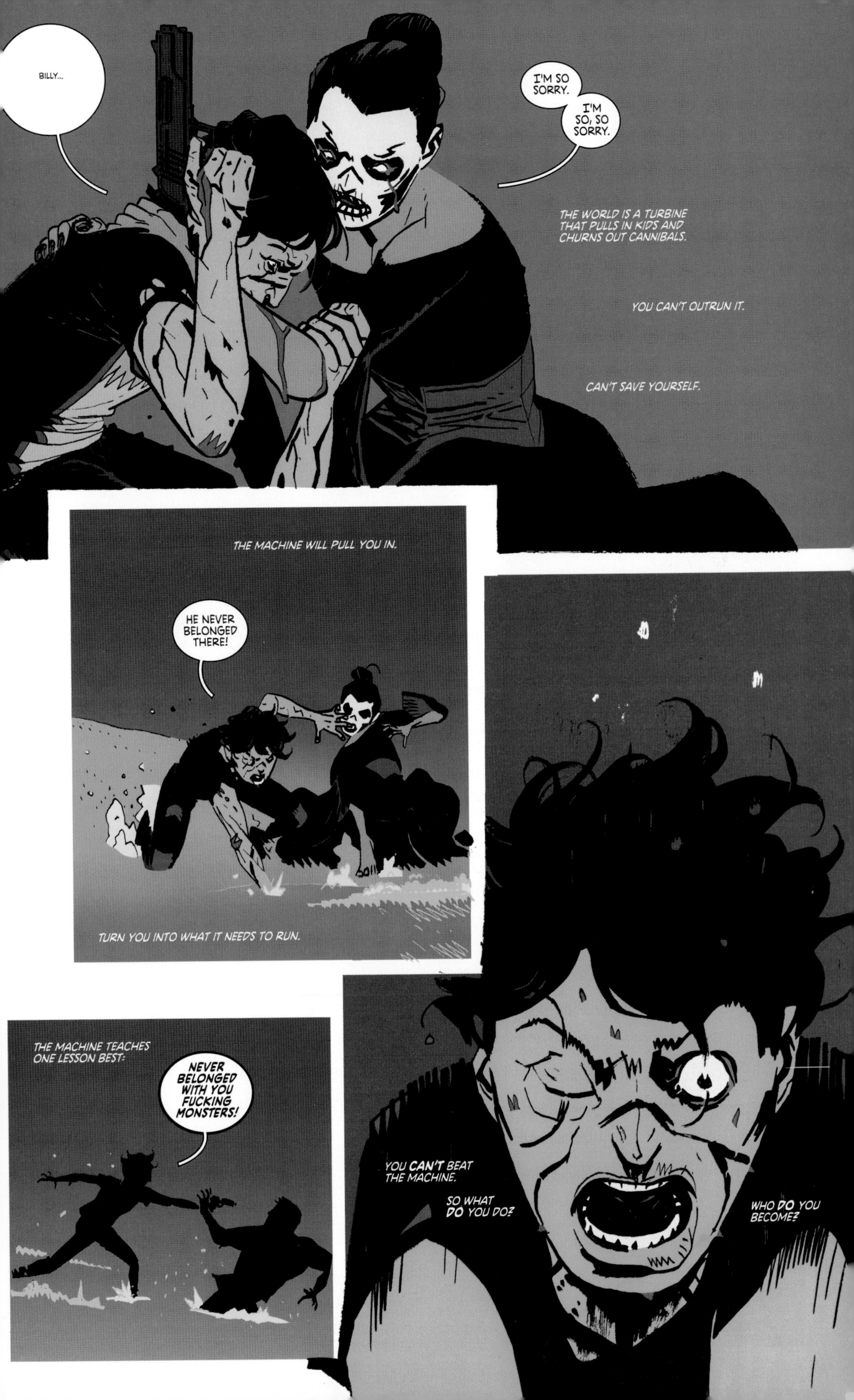
BILLY...
I'M SO SORRY.
I'M SO, SO SORRY.
THE WORLD IS A TURBINE THAT PULLS IN KIDS AND CHURNS OUT CANNIBALS.
YOU CAN'T OUTRUN IT.
CAN'T SAVE YOURSELF.
THE MACHINE WILL PULL YOU IN.
HE NEVER BELONGED THERE!
TURN YOU INTO WHAT IT NEEDS TO RUN.
THE MACHINE TEACHES ONE LESSON BEST:
NEVER BELONGED WITH YOU FUCKING MONSTERS!
YOU CAN'T BEAT THE MACHINE.
SO WHAT DO YOU DO?
WHO DO YOU BECOME?

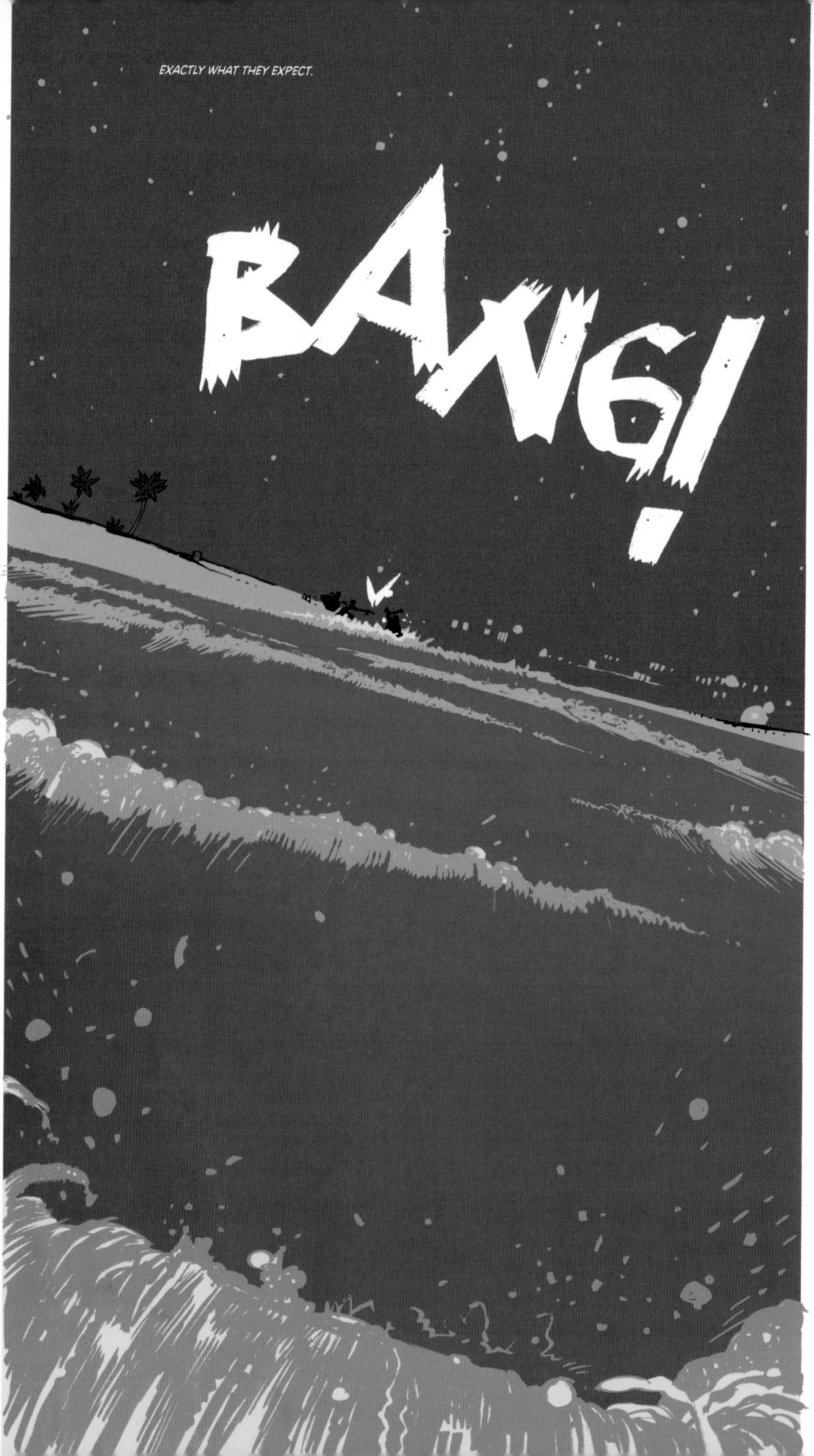
EXACTLY WHAT THEY EXPECT.
BANG!

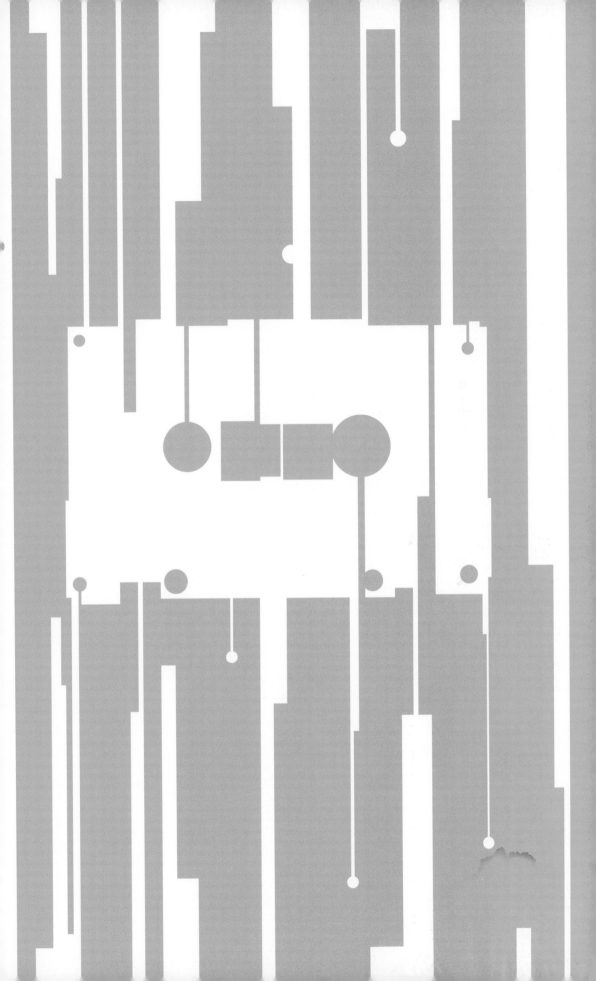

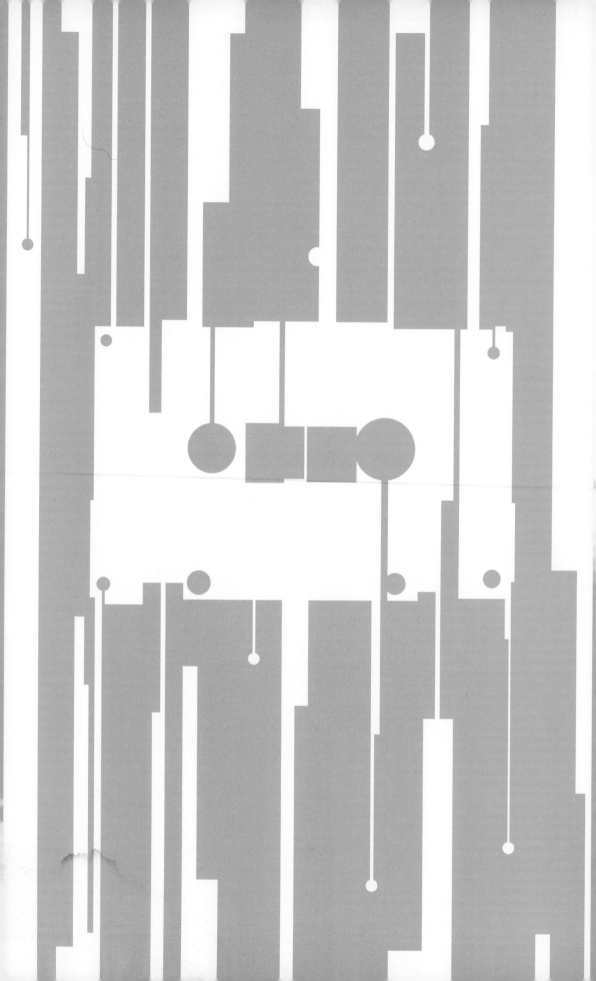

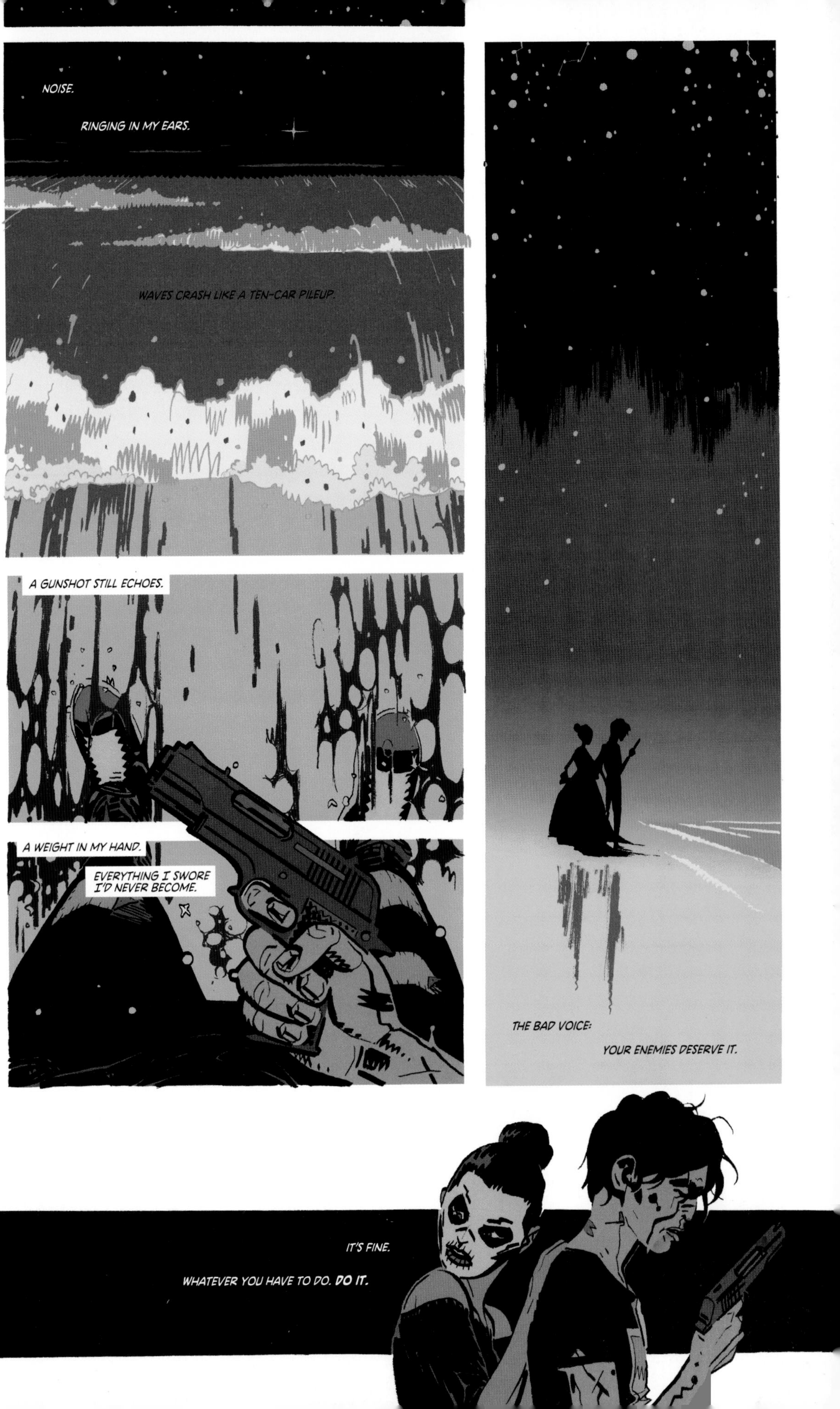
NOISE.
RINGING IN MY EARS.
WAVES CRASH LIKE A TEN-CAR PILEUP.
A GUNSHOT STILL ECHOES.
A WEIGHT IN MY HAND.
EVERYTHING I SWORE I'D NEVER BECOME.
THE BAD VOICE:
YOUR ENEMIES DESERVE IT.
IT'S FINE.
WHATEVER YOU HAVE TO DO. **DO IT.**

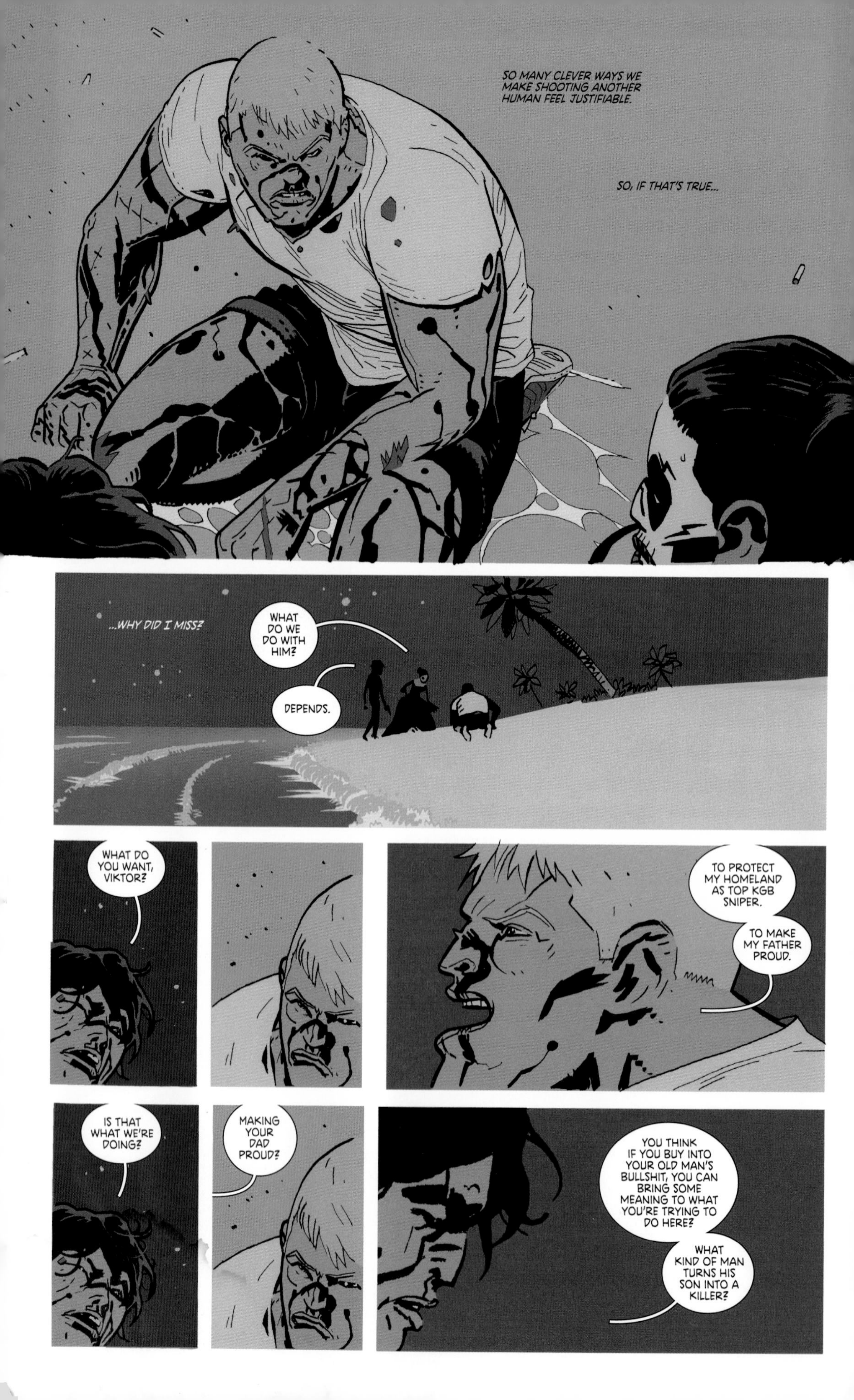
SO MANY CLEVER WAYS WE MAKE SHOOTING ANOTHER HUMAN FEEL JUSTIFIABLE.
SO, IF THAT'S TRUE...
...WHY DID I MISS?
WHAT DO WE DO WITH HIM?
DEPENDS.
WHAT DO YOU WANT, VIKTOR?
TO PROTECT MY HOMELAND AS TOP KGB SNIPER.
TO MAKE MY FATHER PROUD.
IS THAT WHAT WE'RE DOING?
MAKING YOUR DAD PROUD?
YOU THINK IF YOU BUY INTO YOUR OLD MAN'S BULLSHIT, YOU CAN BRING SOME MEANING TO WHAT YOU'RE TRYING TO DO HERE?
WHAT KIND OF MAN TURNS HIS SON INTO A KILLER?

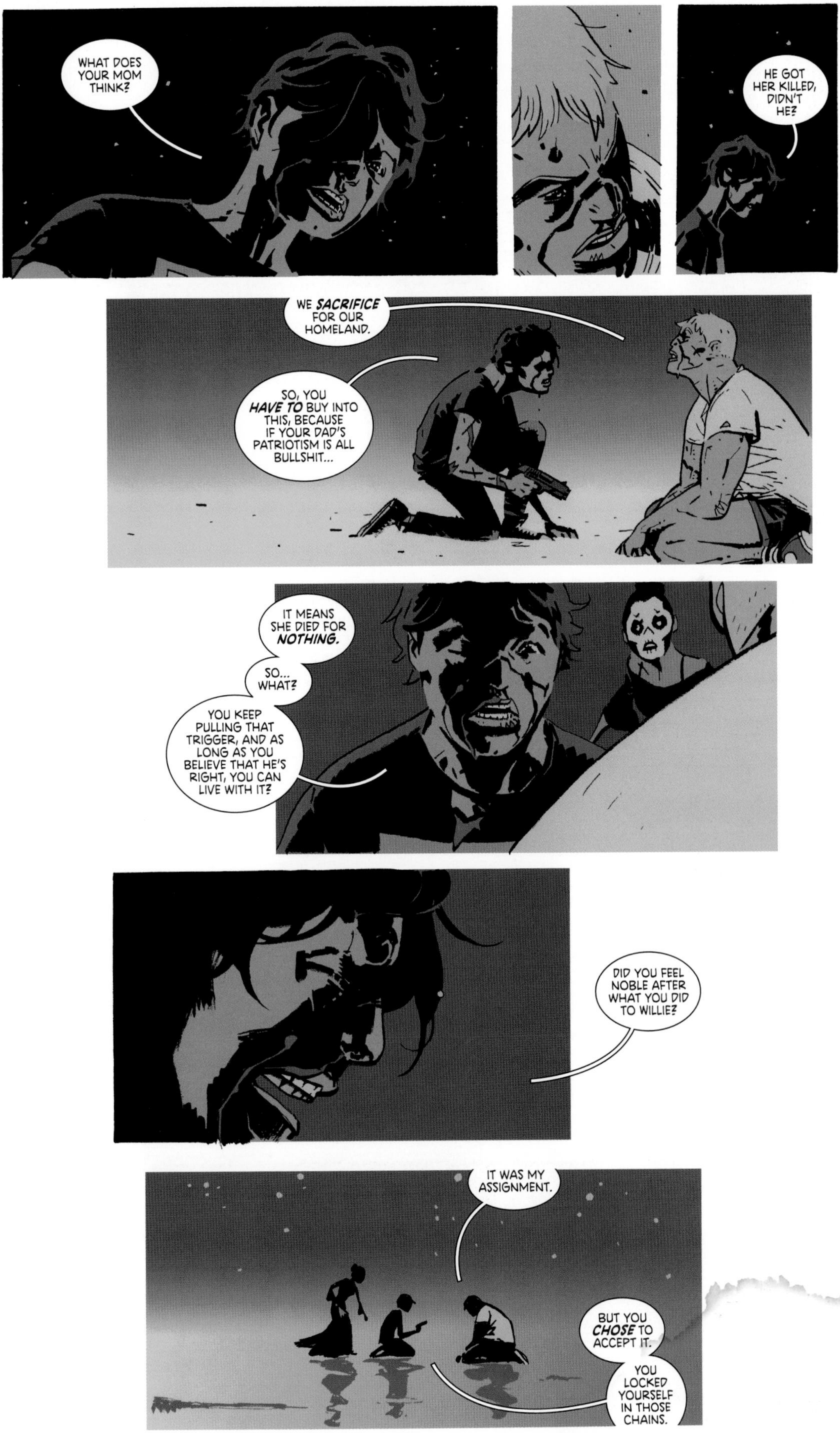
WHAT DOES YOUR MOM THINK?
HE GOT HER KILLED, DIDN'T HE?
WE SACRIFICE FOR OUR HOMELAND.
SO, YOU HAVE TO BUY INTO THIS, BECAUSE IF YOUR DAD'S PATRIOTISM IS ALL BULLSHIT...
IT MEANS SHE DIED FOR NOTHING.
SO... WHAT?
YOU KEEP PULLING THAT TRIGGER, AND AS LONG AS YOU BELIEVE THAT HE'S RIGHT, YOU CAN LIVE WITH IT?
DID YOU FEEL NOBLE AFTER WHAT YOU DID TO WILLIE?
IT WAS MY ASSIGNMENT.
BUT YOU CHOSE TO ACCEPT IT.
YOU LOCKED YOURSELF IN THOSE CHAINS.

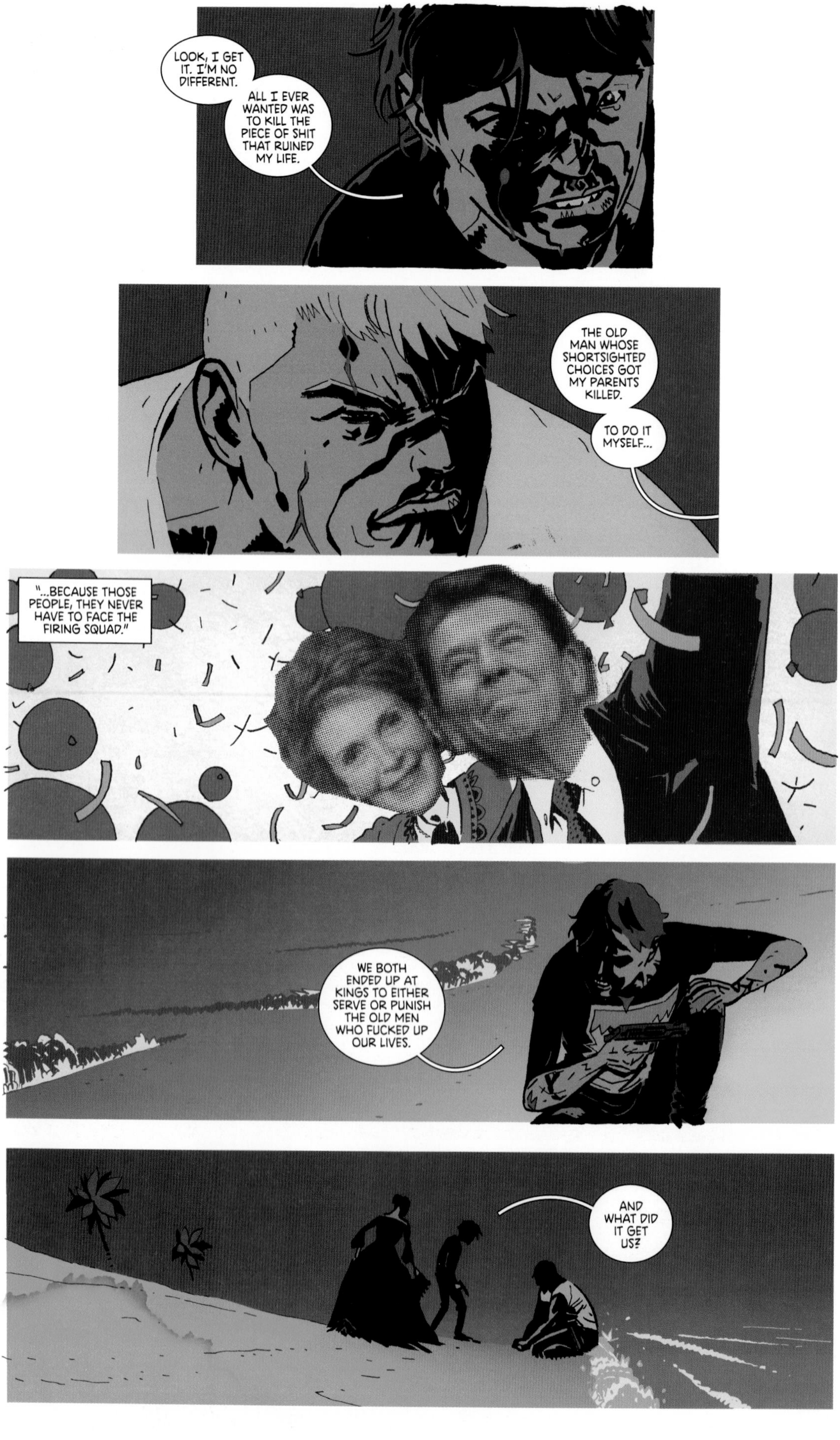
LOOK, I GET IT. I'M NO DIFFERENT.
ALL I EVER WANTED WAS TO KILL THE PIECE OF SHIT THAT RUINED MY LIFE.
THE OLD MAN WHOSE SHORTSIGHTED CHOICES GOT MY PARENTS KILLED.
TO DO IT MYSELF...
"...BECAUSE THOSE PEOPLE, THEY NEVER HAVE TO FACE THE FIRING SQUAD."
WE BOTH ENDED UP AT KINGS TO EITHER SERVE OR PUNISH THE OLD MEN WHO FUCKED UP OUR LIVES.
AND WHAT DID IT GET US?

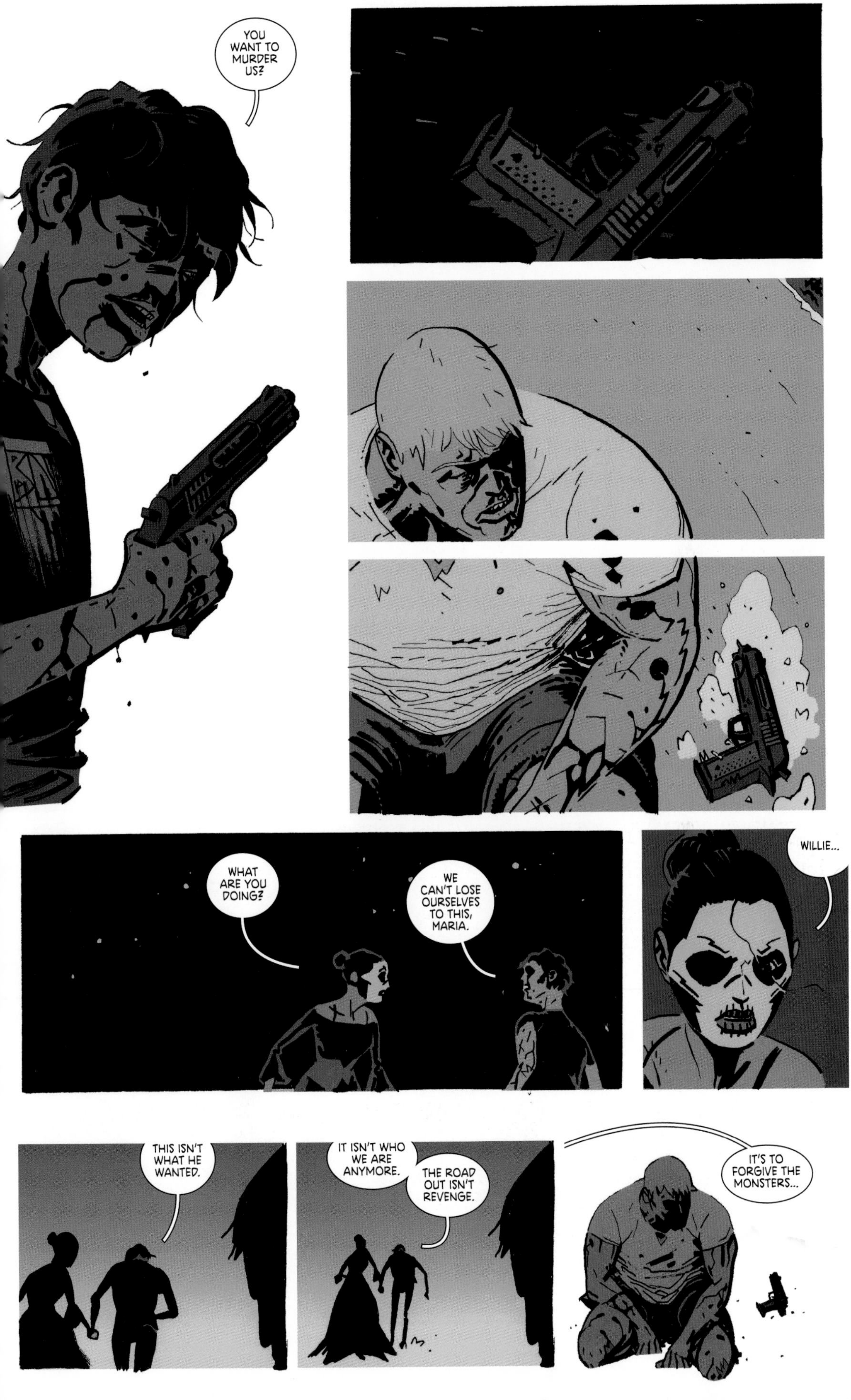
YOU WANT TO MURDER US?
WHAT ARE YOU DOING?
WE CAN'T LOSE OURSELVES TO THIS, MARIA.
WILLIE...
THIS ISN'T WHAT HE WANTED.
IT ISN'T WHO WE ARE ANYMORE.
THE ROAD OUT ISN'T REVENGE.
IT'S TO FORGIVE THE MONSTERS...

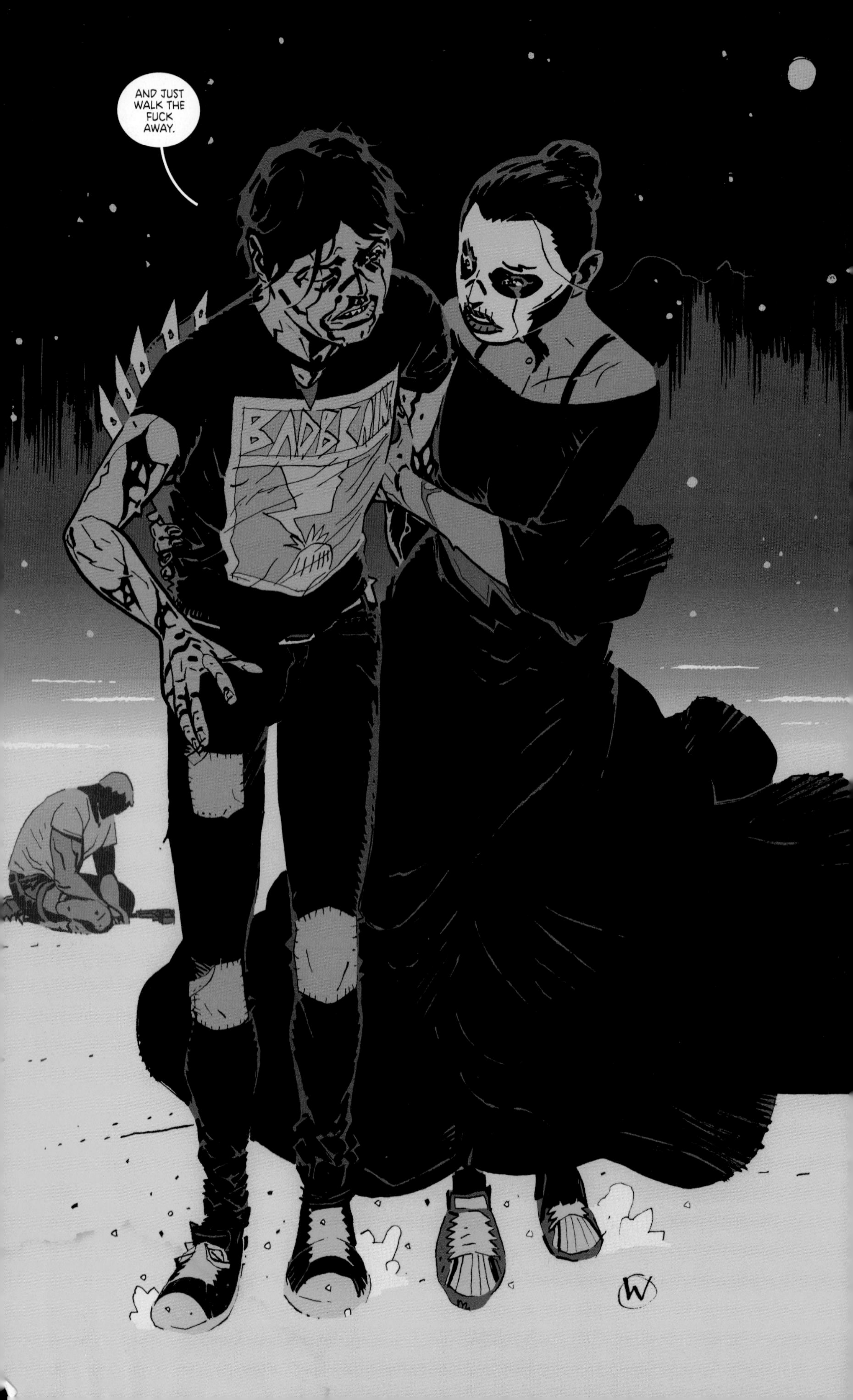
AND JUST WALK THE FUCK AWAY.
BADBRAINS

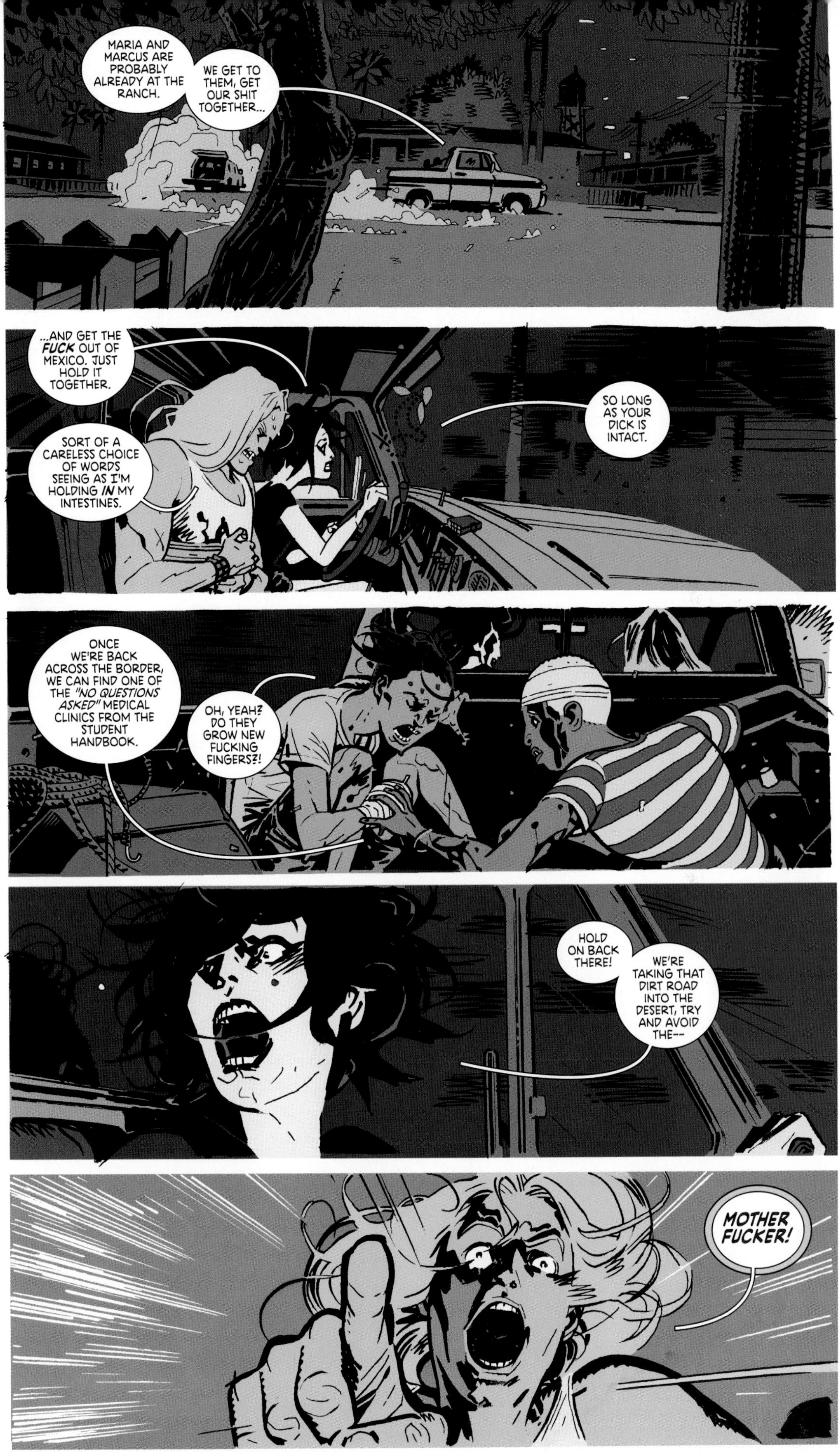
MARIA AND MARCUS ARE PROBABLY ALREADY AT THE RANCH.
WE GET TO THEM, GET OUR SHIT TOGETHER...
...AND GET THE FUCK OUT OF MEXICO. JUST HOLD IT TOGETHER.
SORT OF A CARELESS CHOICE OF WORDS SEEING AS I'M HOLDING IN MY INTESTINES.
SO LONG AS YOUR DICK IS INTACT.
ONCE WE'RE BACK ACROSS THE BORDER, WE CAN FIND ONE OF THE "NO QUESTIONS ASKED" MEDICAL CLINICS FROM THE STUDENT HANDBOOK.
OH, YEAH? DO THEY GROW NEW FUCKING FINGERS?!
HOLD ON BACK THERE!
WE'RE TAKING THAT DIRT ROAD INTO THE DESERT, TRY AND AVOID THE--
MOTHER FUCKER!

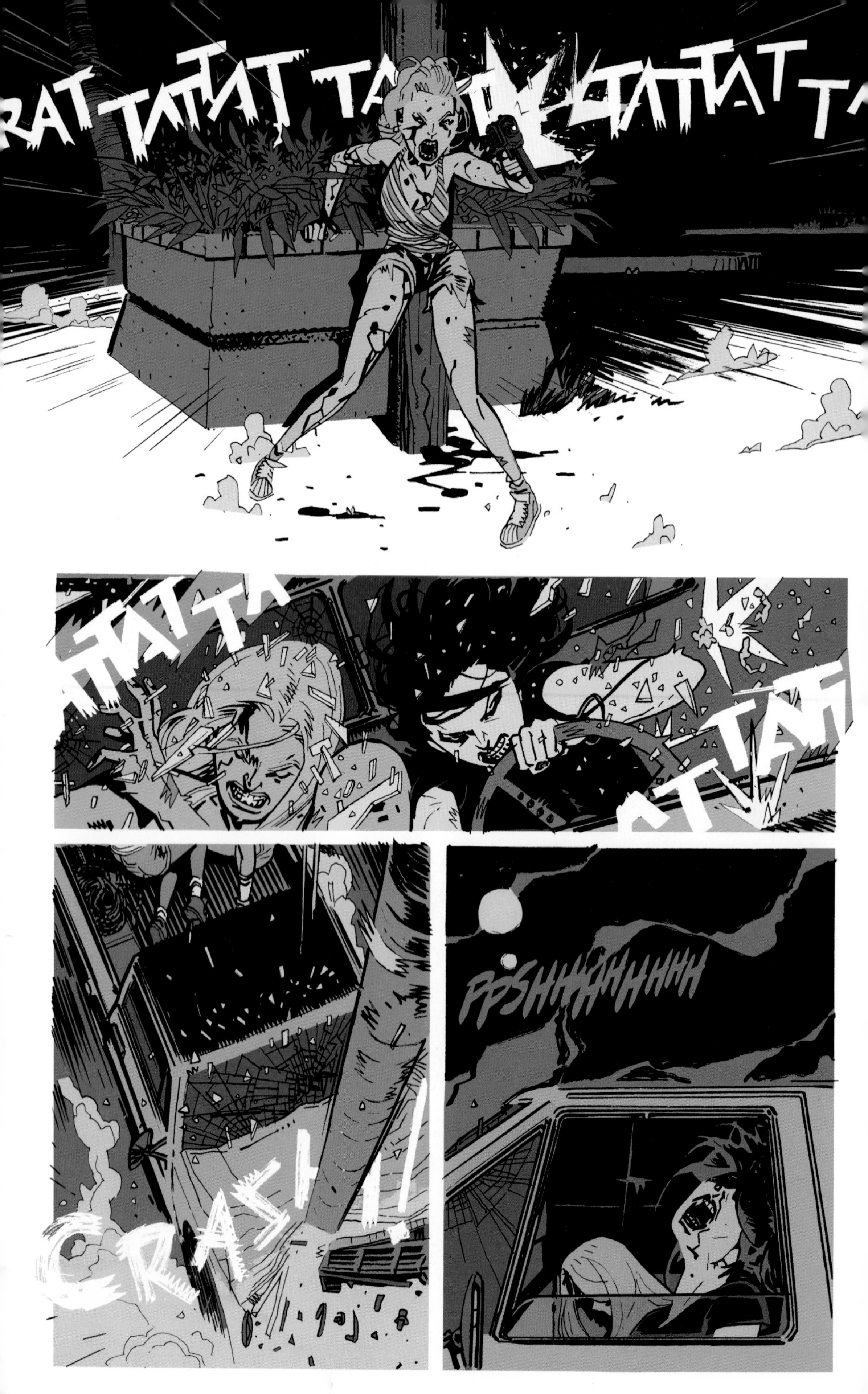
RAT-TATATAT TA
TATATAT TA
TATATA
TAT
CRASH!!
PPSHHHHHHHHH

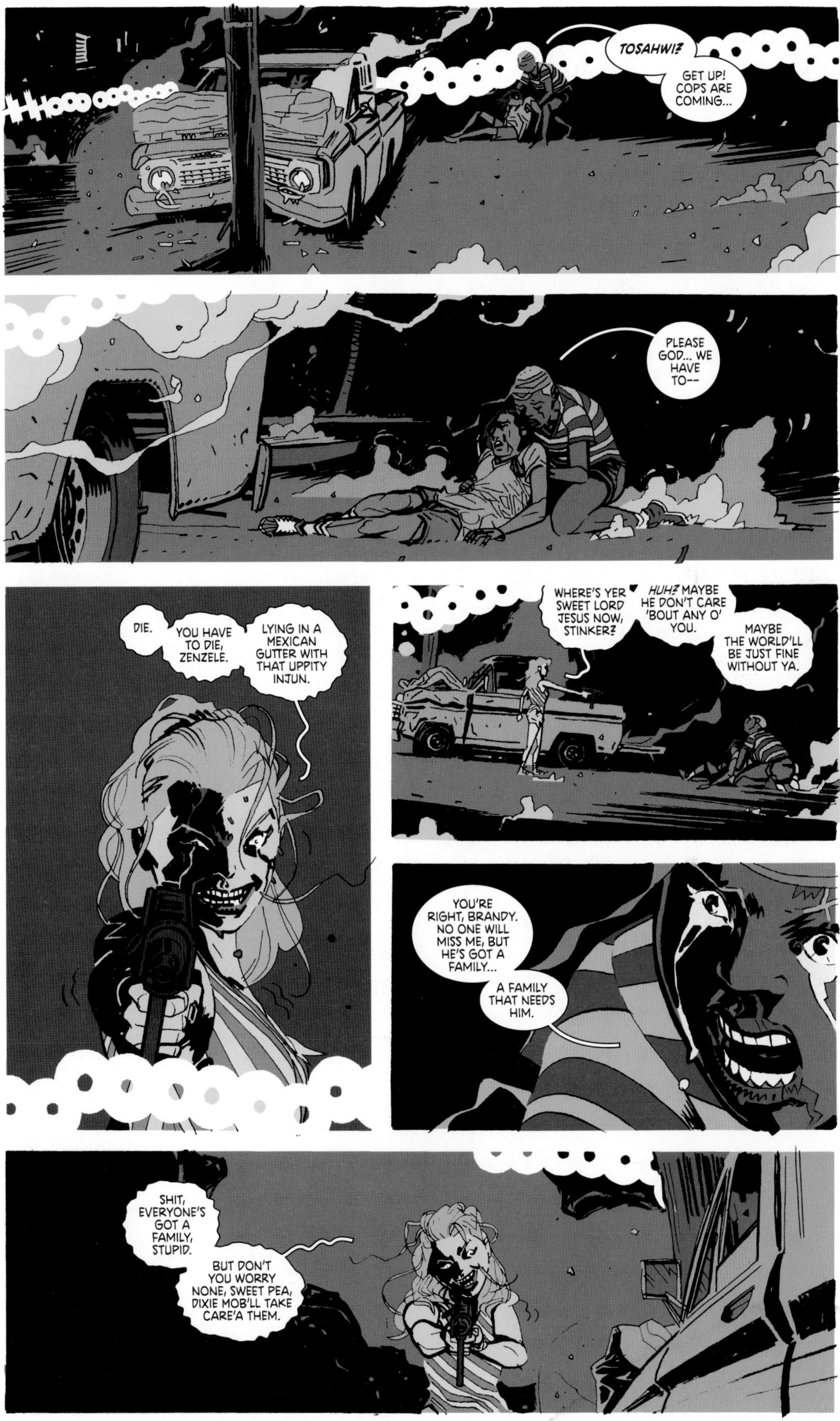

TOSAHWI?
GET UP! COPS ARE COMING...
PLEASE GOD... WE HAVE TO--
DIE.
YOU HAVE TO DIE, ZENZELE.
LYING IN A MEXICAN GUTTER WITH THAT UPPITY INJUN.
WHERE'S YER SWEET LORD JESUS NOW, STINKER?
HUH? MAYBE HE DON'T CARE 'BOUT ANY O' YOU.
MAYBE THE WORLD'LL BE JUST FINE WITHOUT YA.
YOU'RE RIGHT, BRANDY. NO ONE WILL MISS ME, BUT HE'S GOT A FAMILY...
A FAMILY THAT NEEDS HIM.
SHIT, EVERYONE'S GOT A FAMILY, STUPID.
BUT DON'T YOU WORRY NONE, SWEET PEA, DIXIE MOB'LL TAKE CARE'A THEM.

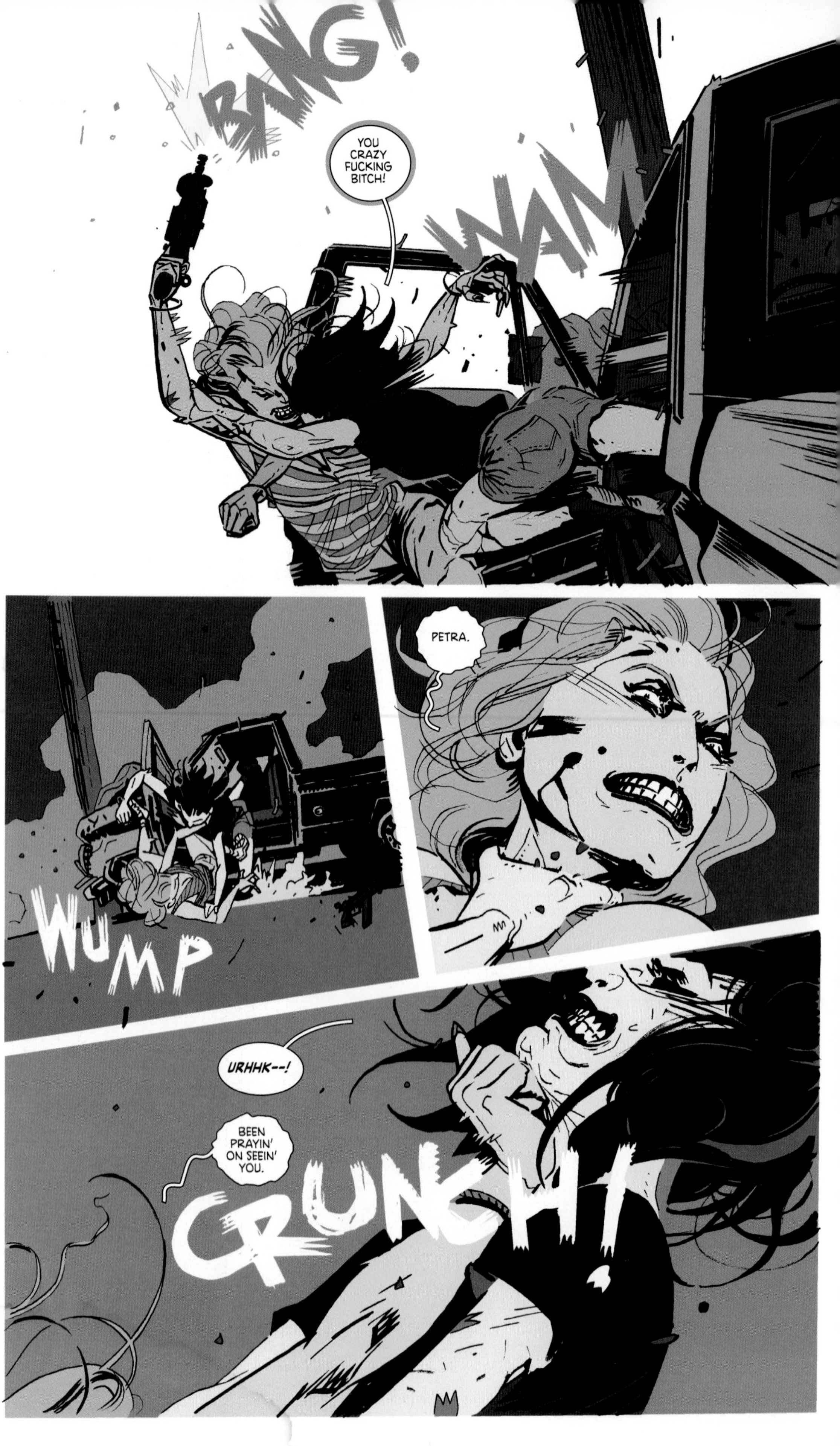
BANG!
YOU CRAZY FUCKING BITCH!
WAM
WUMP
PETRA.
URHHK--!
BEEN PRAYIN' ON SEEIN' YOU.
CRUNCH!

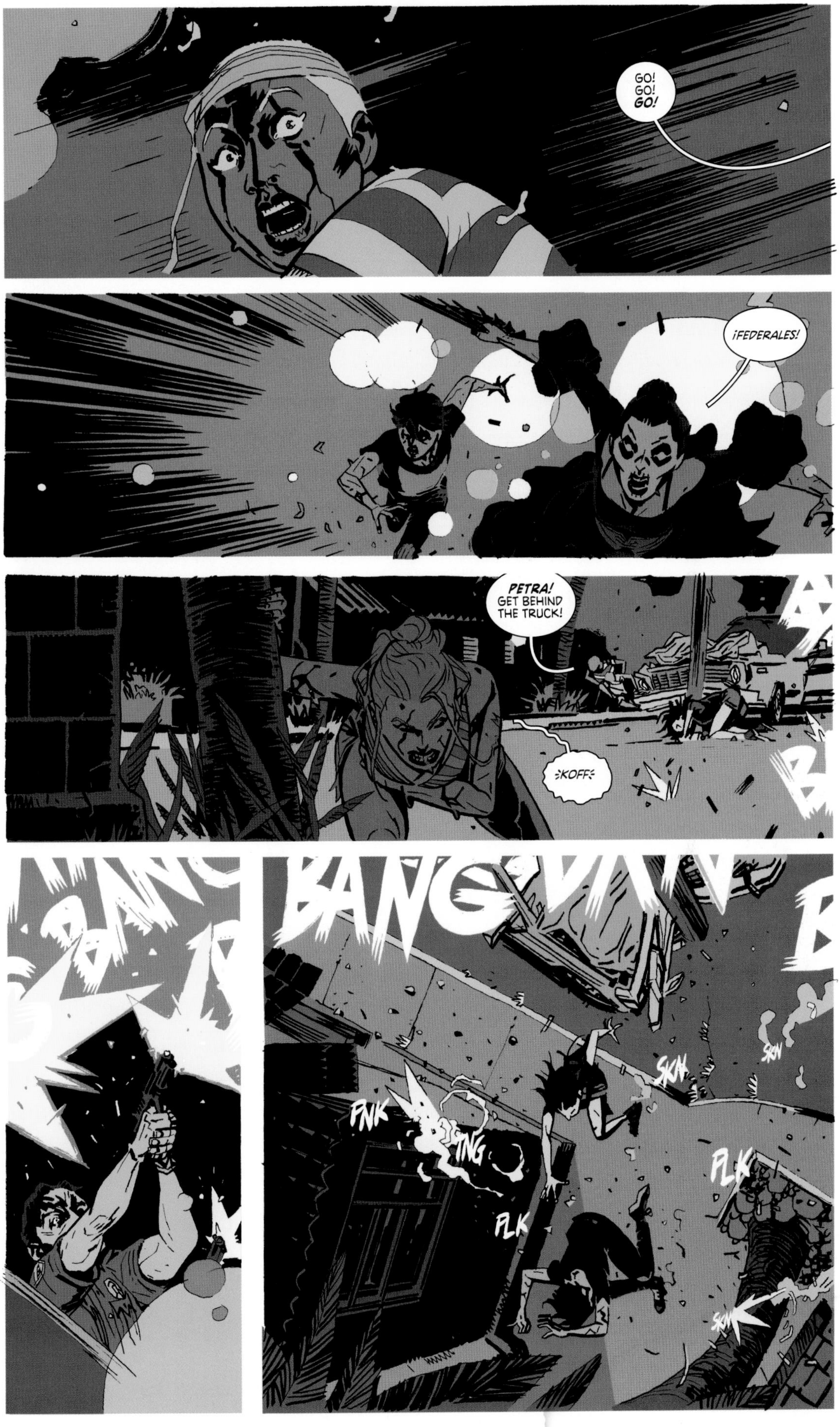
GO! GO! GO!
¡FEDERALES!
PETRA! GET BEHIND THE TRUCK!
KOFF
BANG
PNK
PLK
PLK

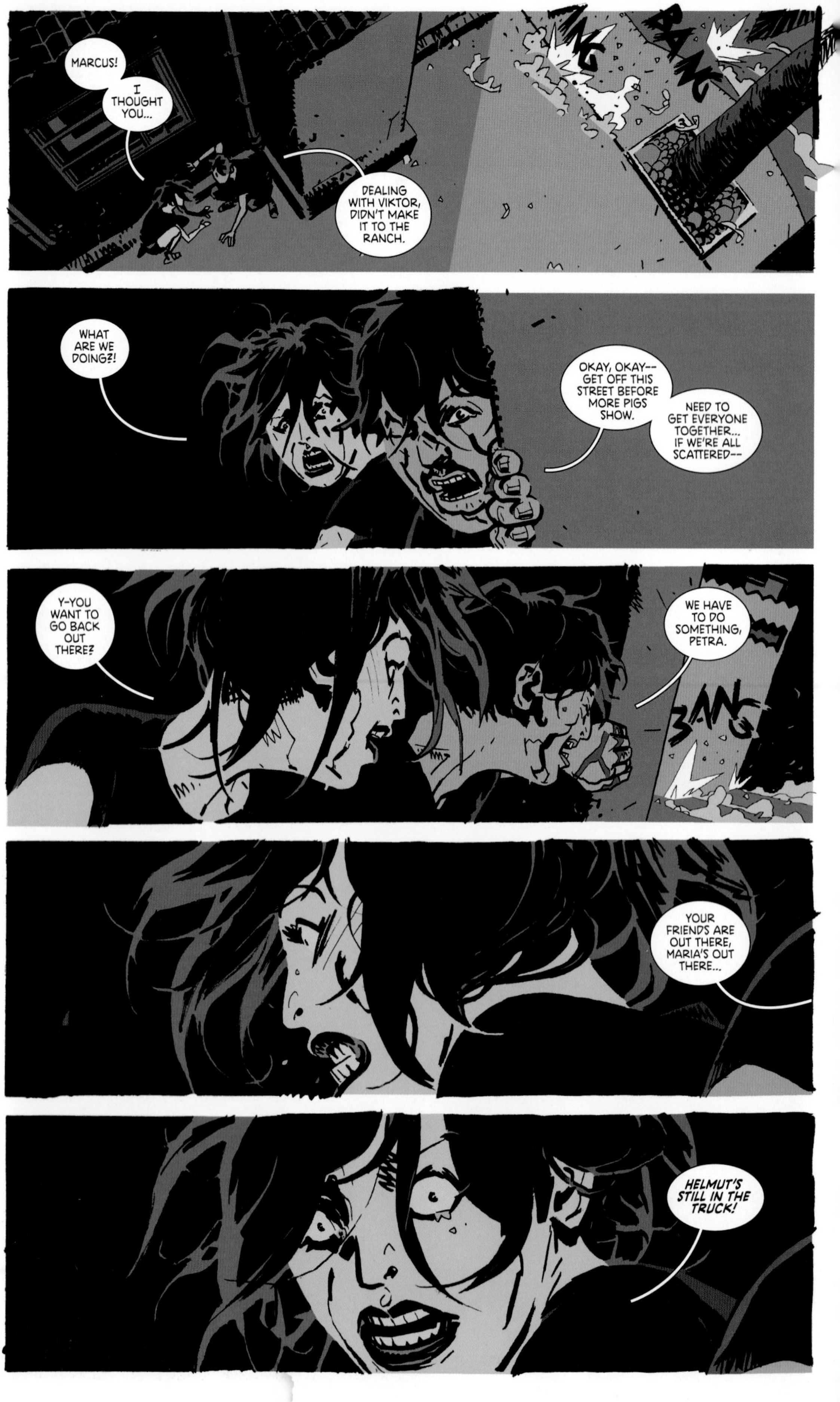

BANG
BANG
MARCUS!
I THOUGHT YOU...
DEALING WITH VIKTOR, DIDN'T MAKE IT TO THE RANCH.
WHAT ARE WE DOING?!
OKAY, OKAY-- GET OFF THIS STREET BEFORE MORE PIGS SHOW.
NEED TO GET EVERYONE TOGETHER... IF WE'RE ALL SCATTERED--
Y-YOU WANT TO GO BACK OUT THERE?
WE HAVE TO DO SOMETHING, PETRA.
BANG
YOUR FRIENDS ARE OUT THERE, MARIA'S OUT THERE...
HELMUT'S STILL IN THE TRUCK!

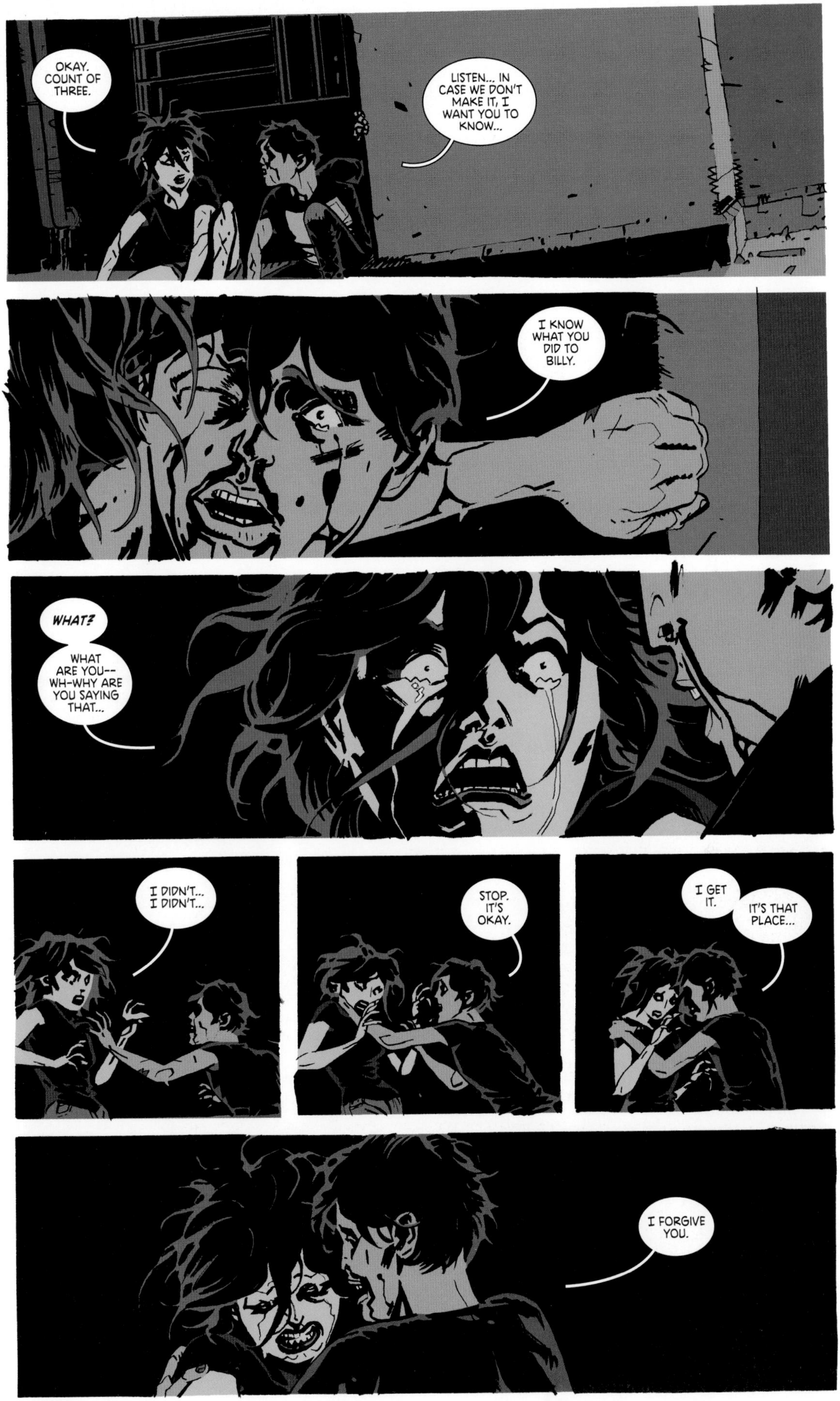
OKAY. COUNT OF THREE.
LISTEN... IN CASE WE DON'T MAKE IT, I WANT YOU TO KNOW...
I KNOW WHAT YOU DID TO BILLY.
WHAT?
WHAT ARE YOU-- WH-WHY ARE YOU SAYING THAT...
I DIDN'T... I DIDN'T...
STOP. IT'S OKAY.
I GET IT.
IT'S THAT PLACE...
I FORGIVE YOU.

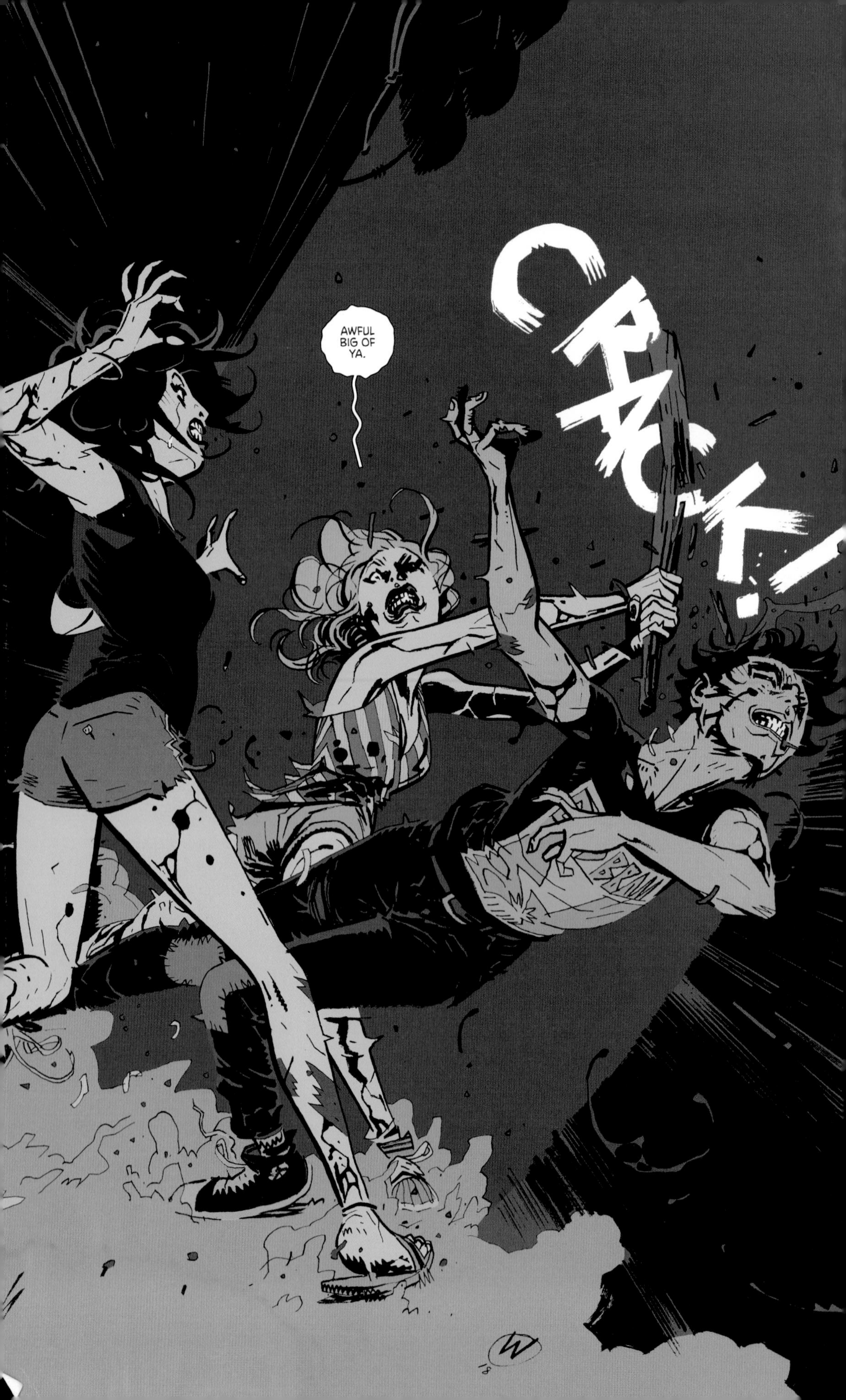
AWFUL BIG OF YA.
CRACK!

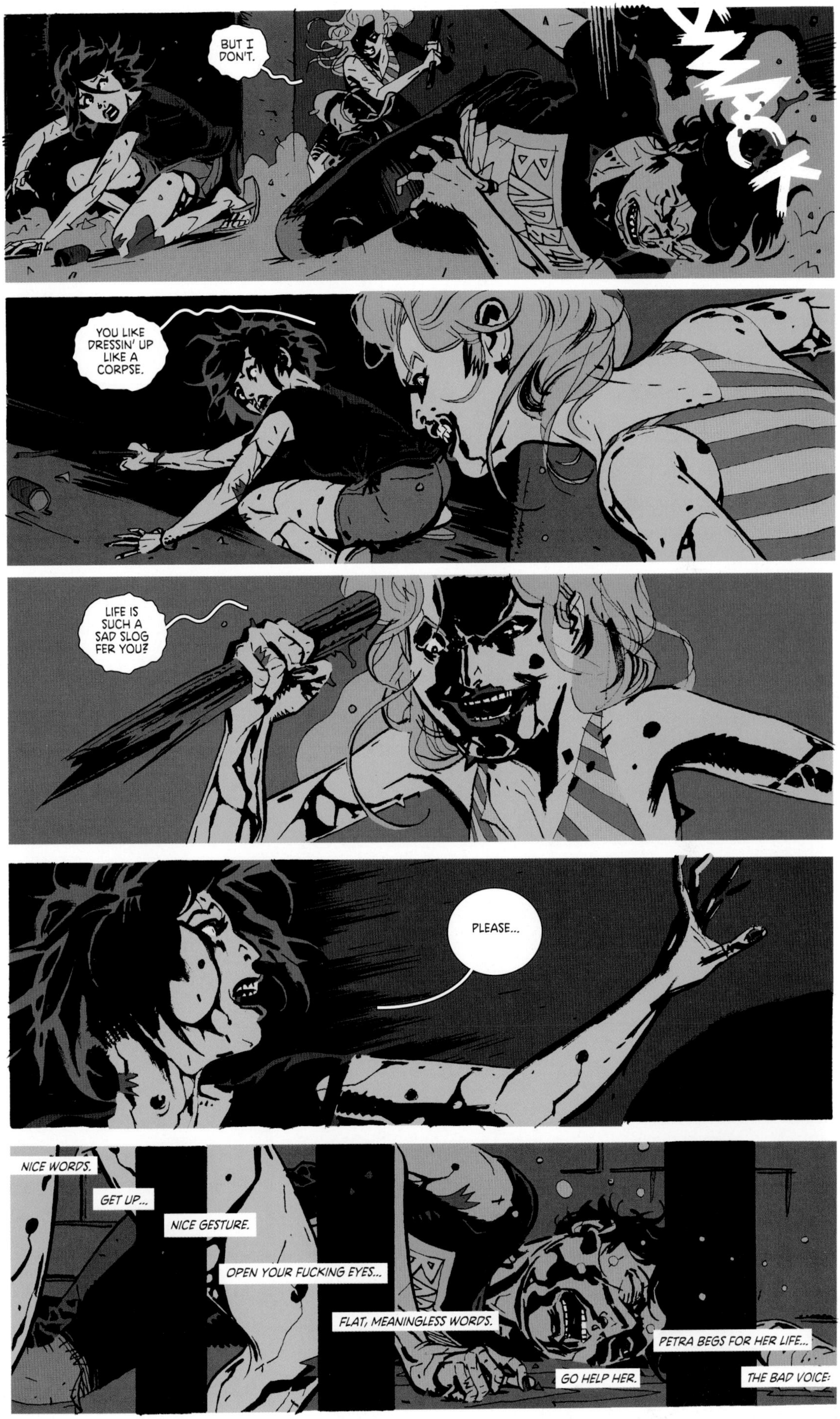
BUT I DON'T.
YOU LIKE DRESSIN' UP LIKE A CORPSE.
LIFE IS SUCH A SAD SLOG FER YOU?
PLEASE...
NICE WORDS.
GET UP...
NICE GESTURE.
OPEN YOUR FUCKING EYES...
FLAT, MEANINGLESS WORDS.
PETRA BEGS FOR HER LIFE...
GO HELP HER.
THE BAD VOICE:

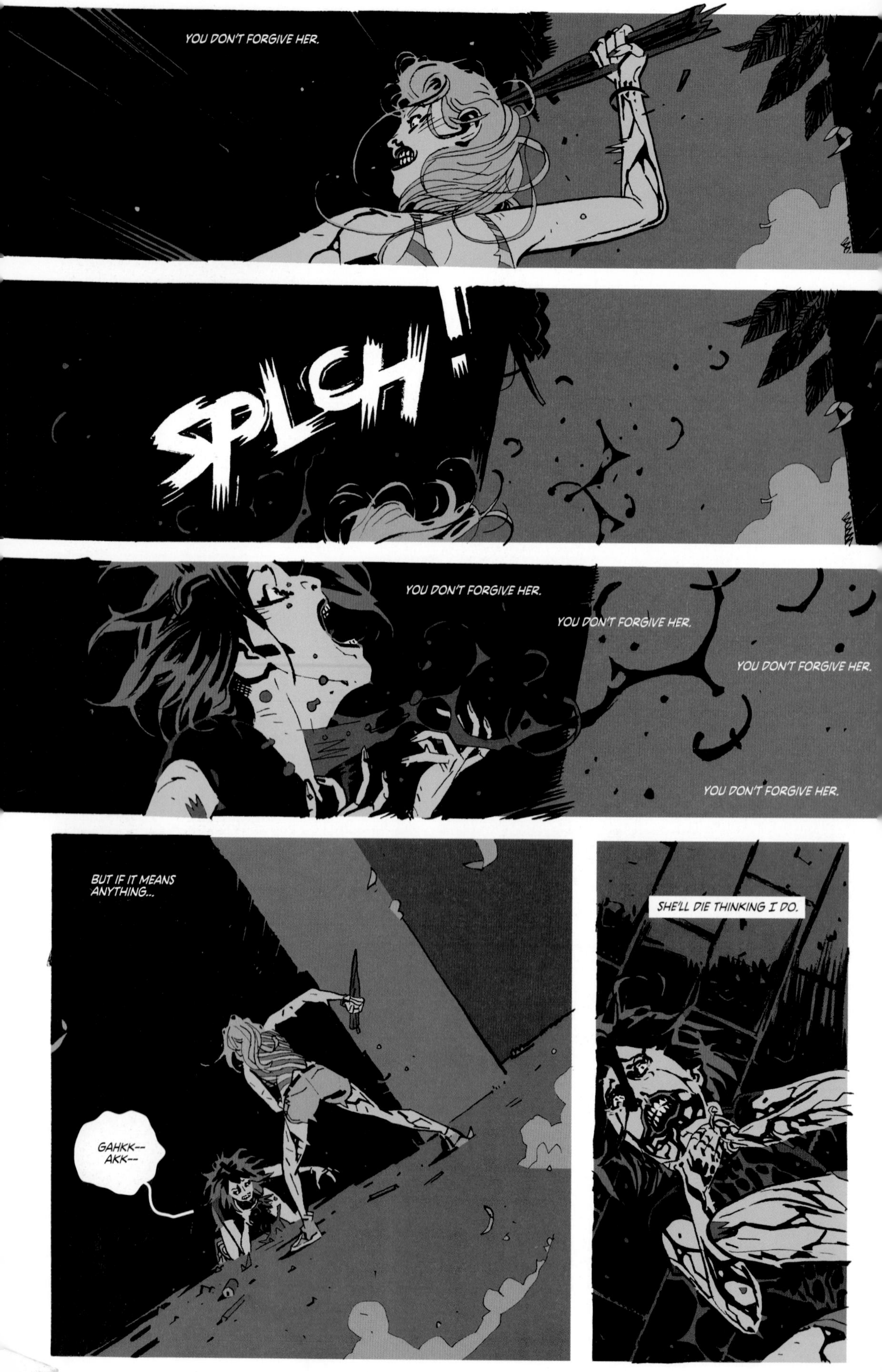
YOU DON'T FORGIVE HER.
SPLCH!
YOU DON'T FORGIVE HER.
YOU DON'T FORGIVE HER.
YOU DON'T FORGIVE HER.
YOU DON'T FORGIVE HER.
BUT IF IT MEANS ANYTHING...
GAHKK-- AKK--
SHE'LL DIE THINKING I DO.

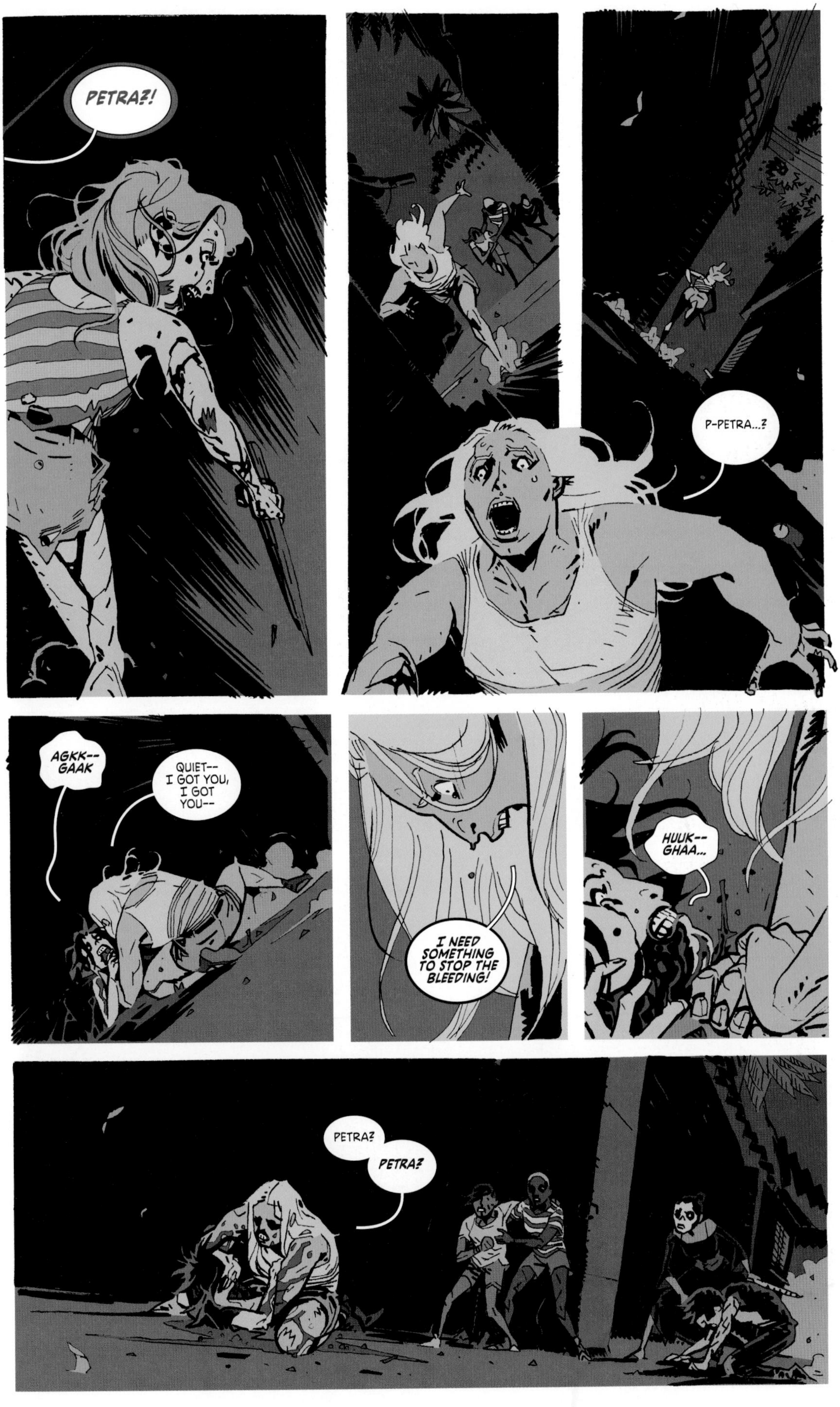
PETRA?!
P-PETRA...?
AGKK--GAAK
QUIET-- I GOT YOU, I GOT YOU--
I NEED SOMETHING TO STOP THE BLEEDING!
HUUK--GHAA...
PETRA?
PETRA?

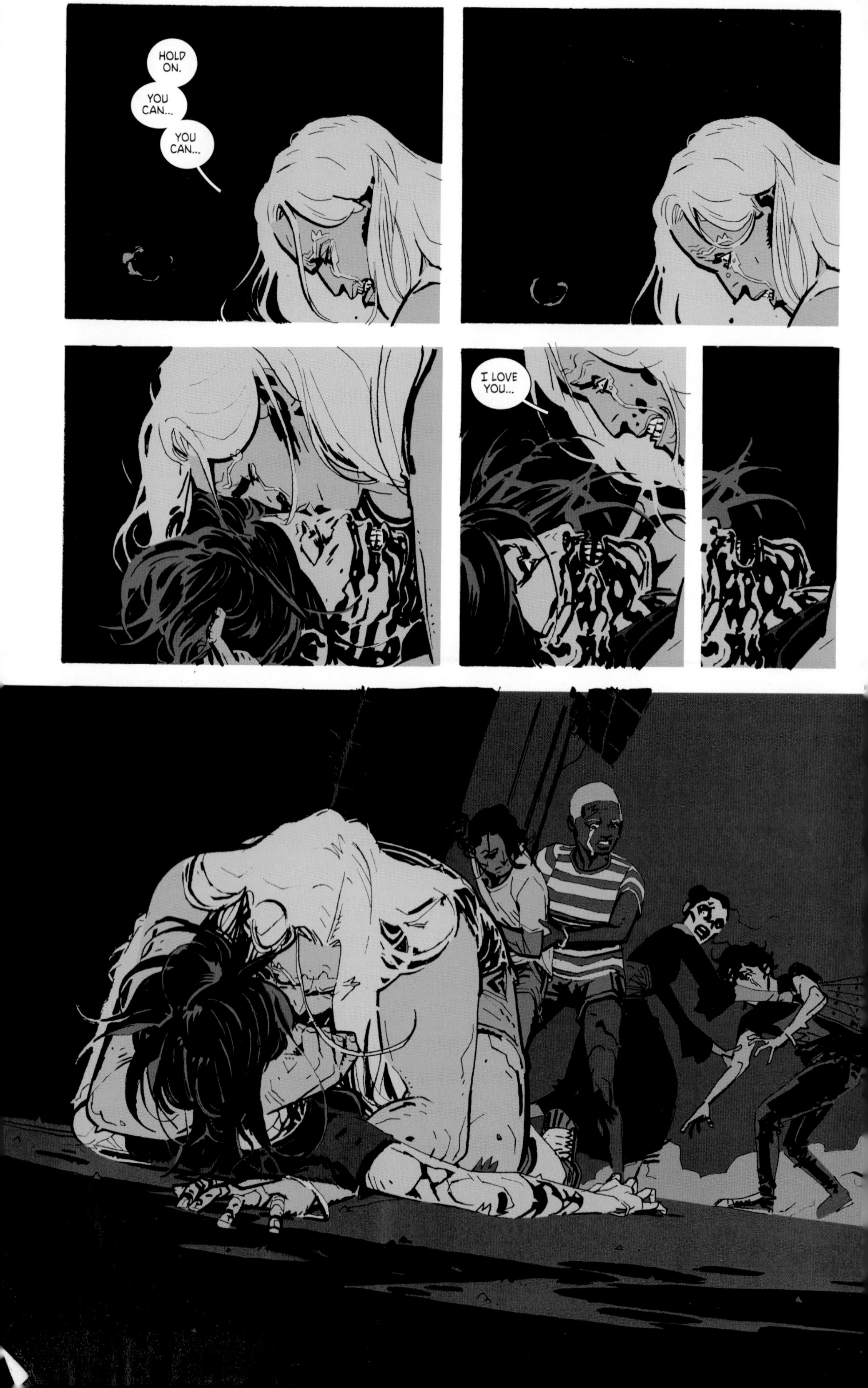
HOLD ON.
YOU CAN...
YOU CAN...
I LOVE YOU...

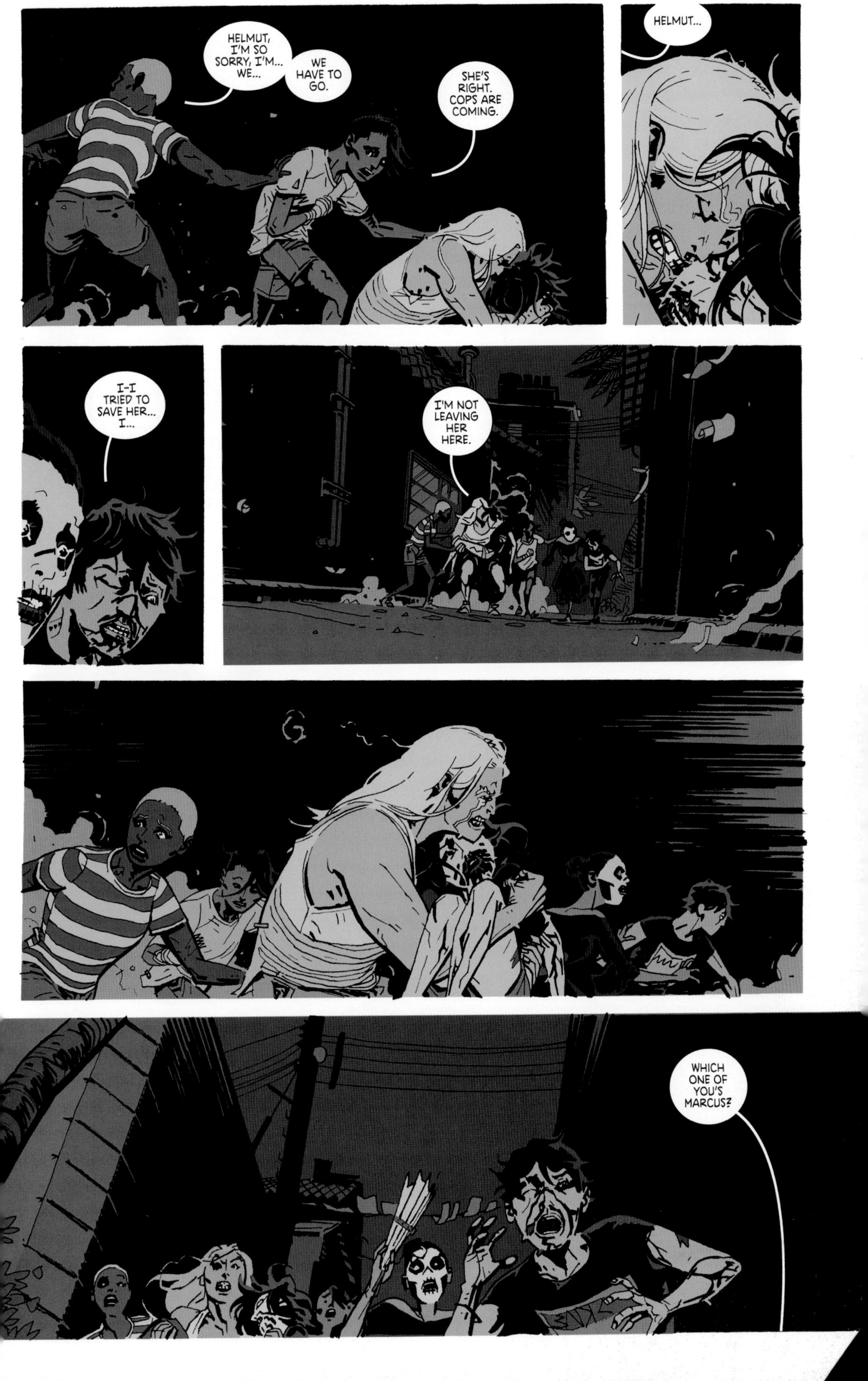
HELMUT, I'M SO SORRY, I'M... WE...
WE HAVE TO GO.
SHE'S RIGHT. COPS ARE COMING.
HELMUT...
I-I TRIED TO SAVE HER... I...
I'M NOT LEAVING HER HERE.
WHICH ONE OF YOU'S MARCUS?

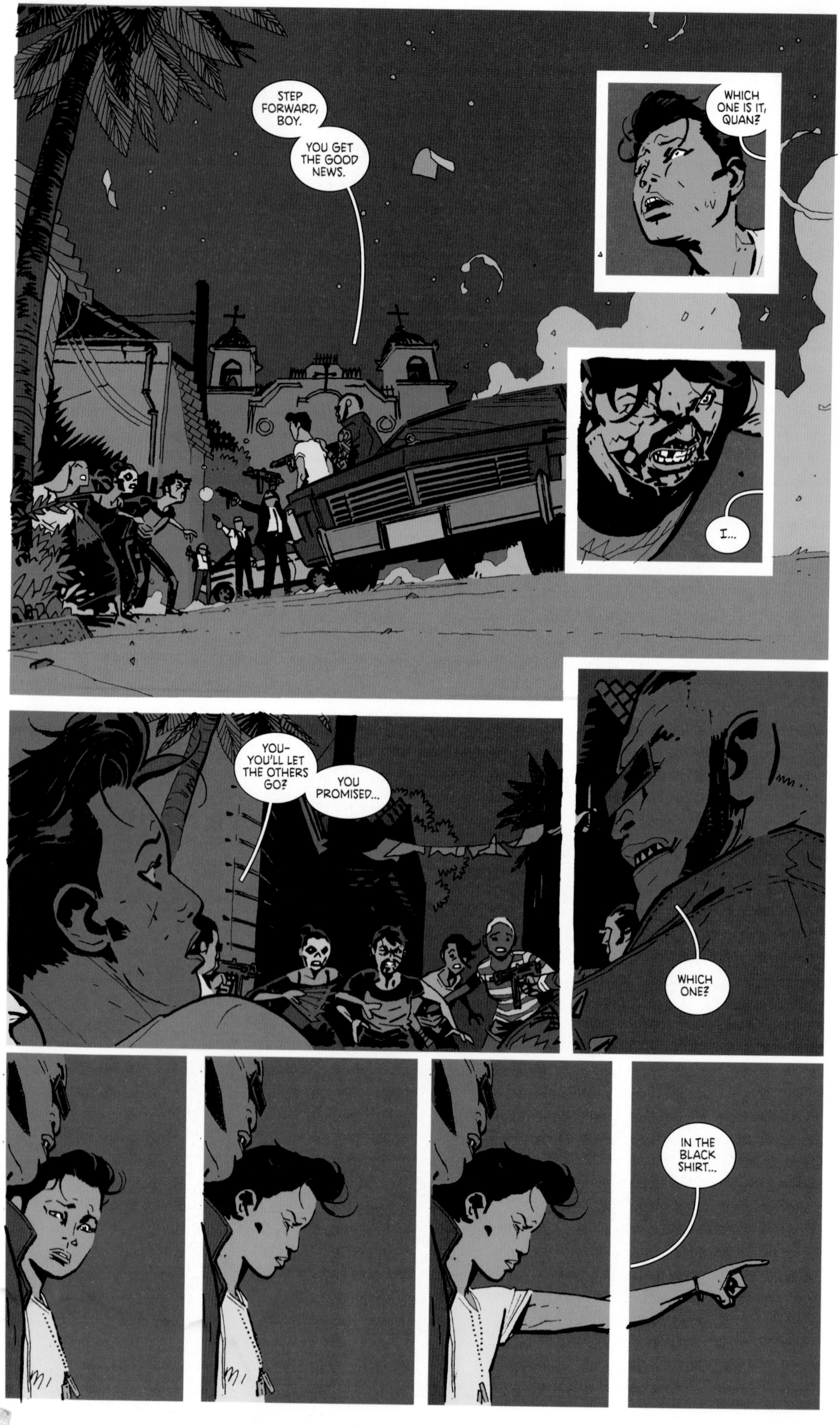
STEP FORWARD, BOY.
YOU GET THE GOOD NEWS.
WHICH ONE IS IT, QUAN?
I...
YOU- YOU'LL LET THE OTHERS GO?
YOU PROMISED...
WHICH ONE?
IN THE BLACK SHIRT...

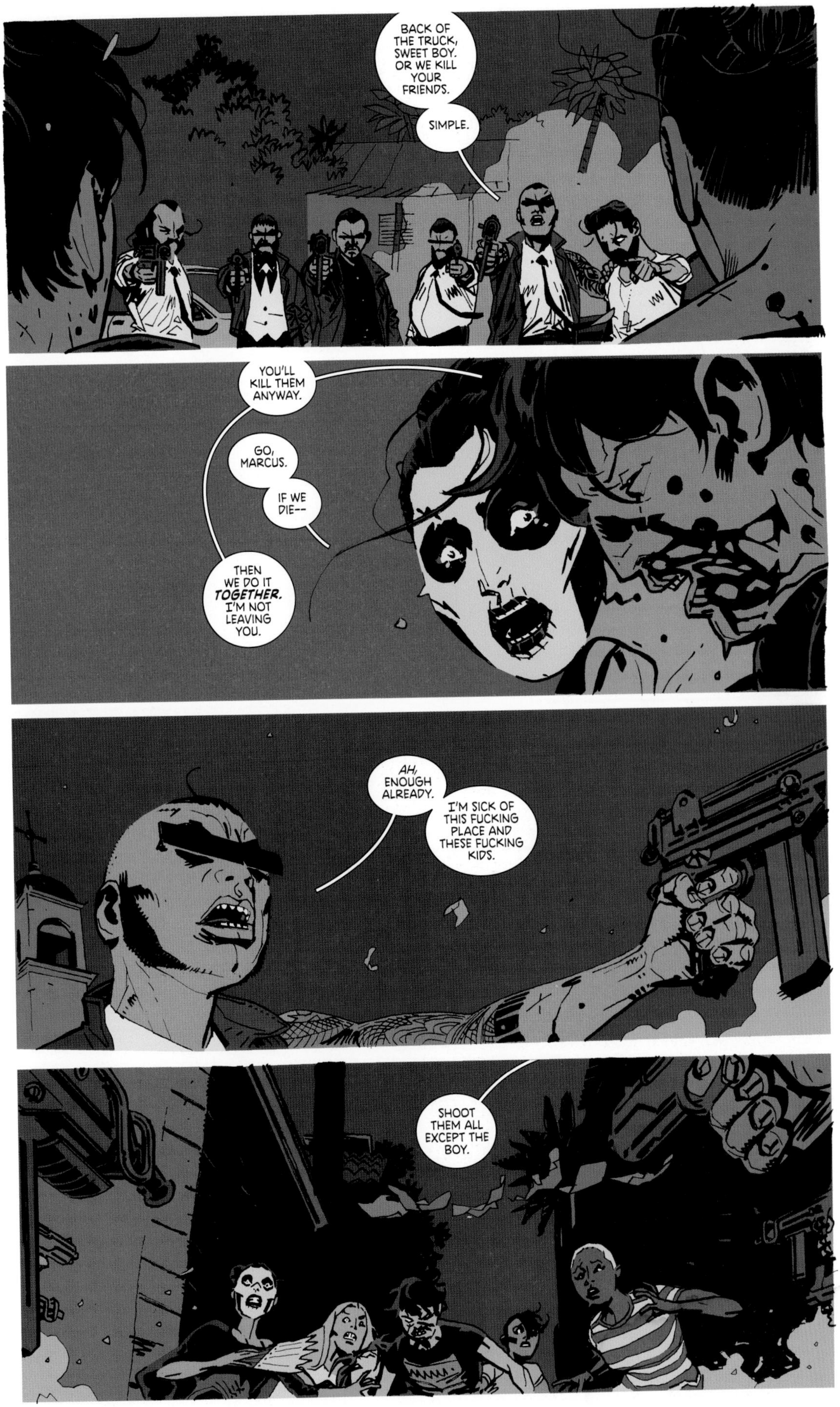
BACK OF THE TRUCK, SWEET BOY. OR WE KILL YOUR FRIENDS.
SIMPLE.
YOU'LL KILL THEM ANYWAY.
GO, MARCUS.
IF WE DIE--
THEN WE DO IT *TOGETHER.* I'M NOT LEAVING YOU.
AH, ENOUGH ALREADY.
I'M SICK OF THIS FUCKING PLACE AND THESE FUCKING KIDS.
SHOOT THEM ALL EXCEPT THE BOY.

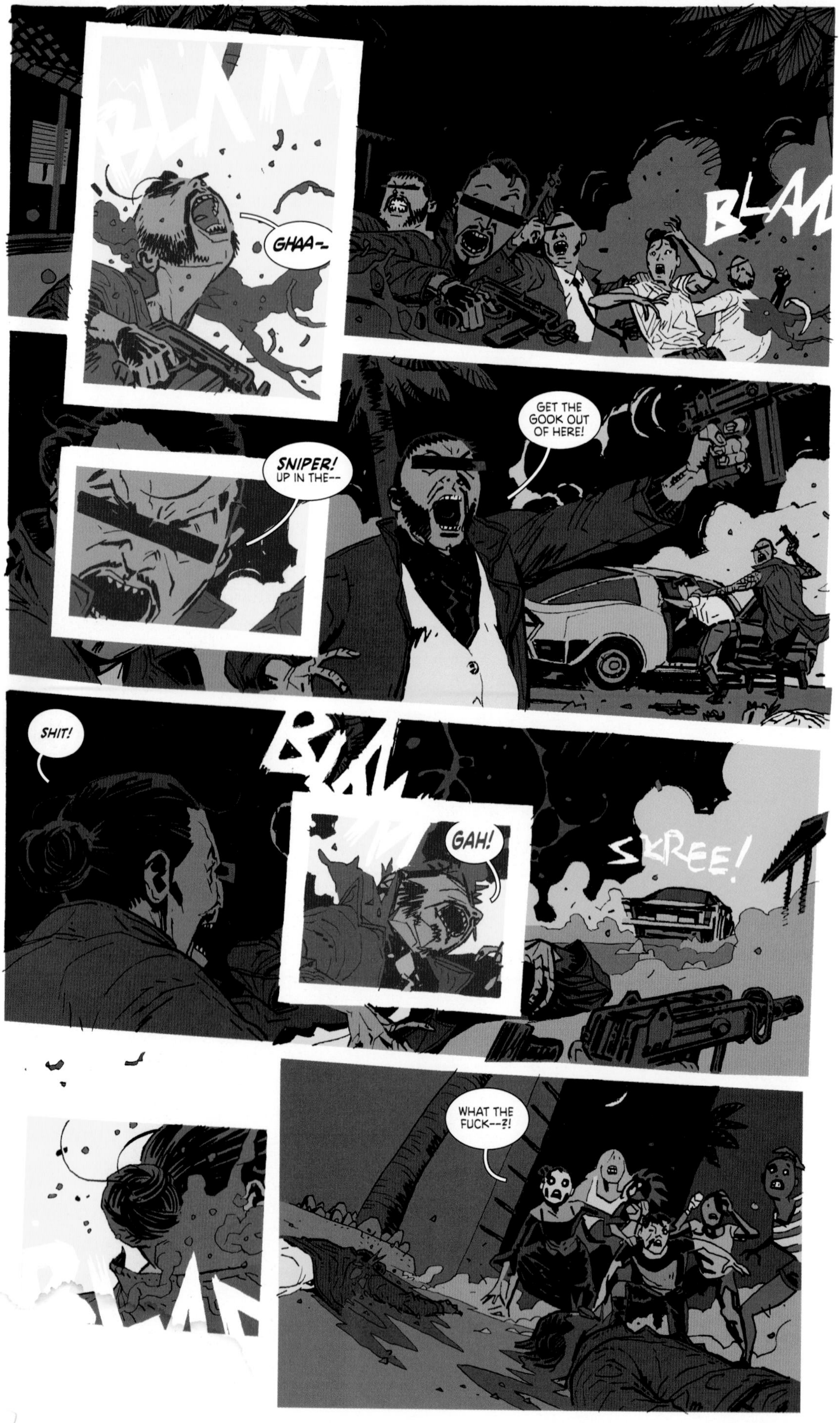
GHAA--
SNIPER! UP IN THE--
GET THE GOOK OUT OF HERE!
SHIT!
GAH!
SKREE!
WHAT THE FUCK--?!

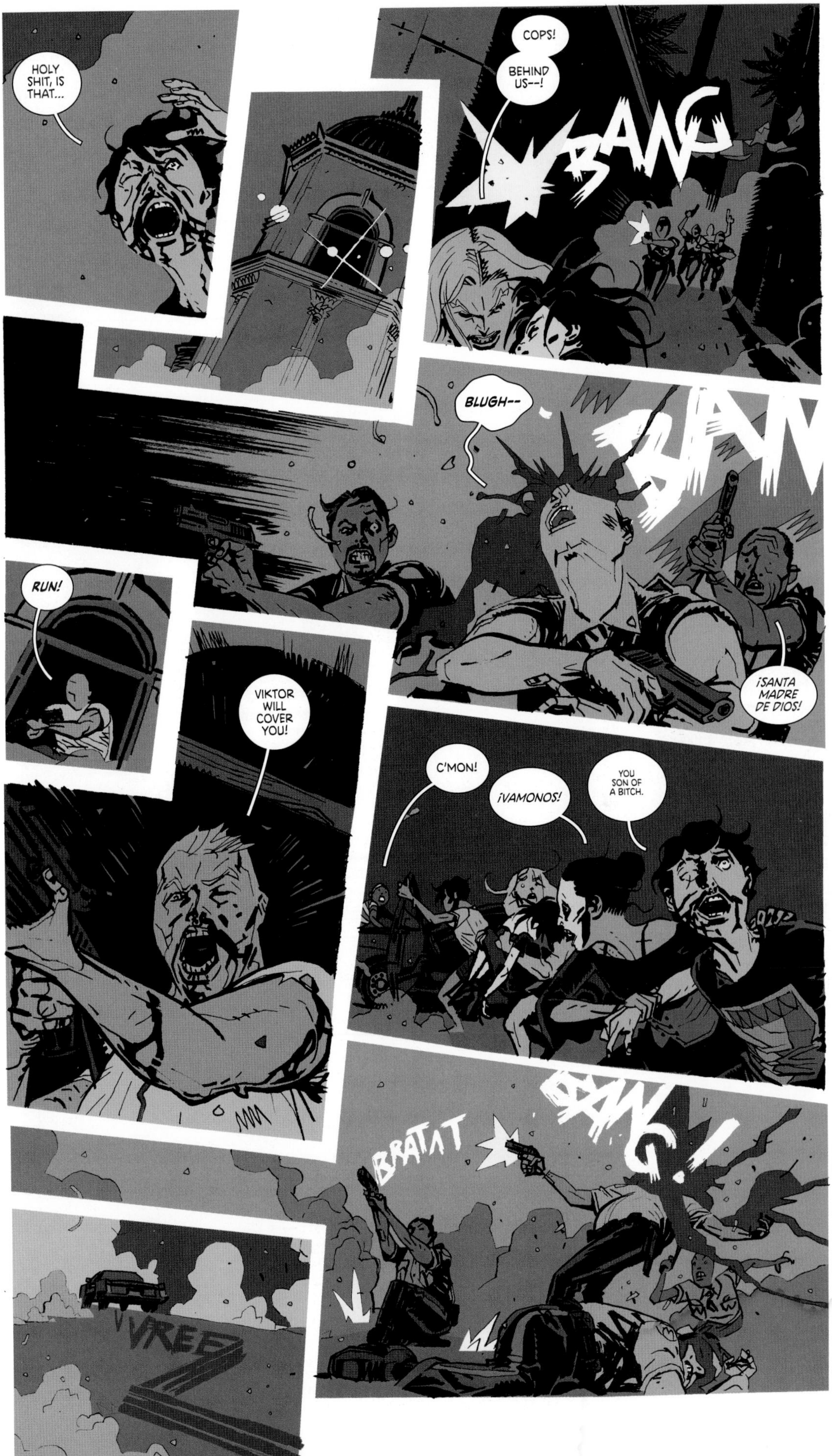
HOLY SHIT, IS THAT...
COPS!
BEHIND US--!
BANG
BLUGH--
RUN!
¡SANTA MADRE DE DIOS!
VIKTOR WILL COVER YOU!
C'MON!
¡VAMONOS!
YOU SON OF A BITCH.
BRATAT
VREE

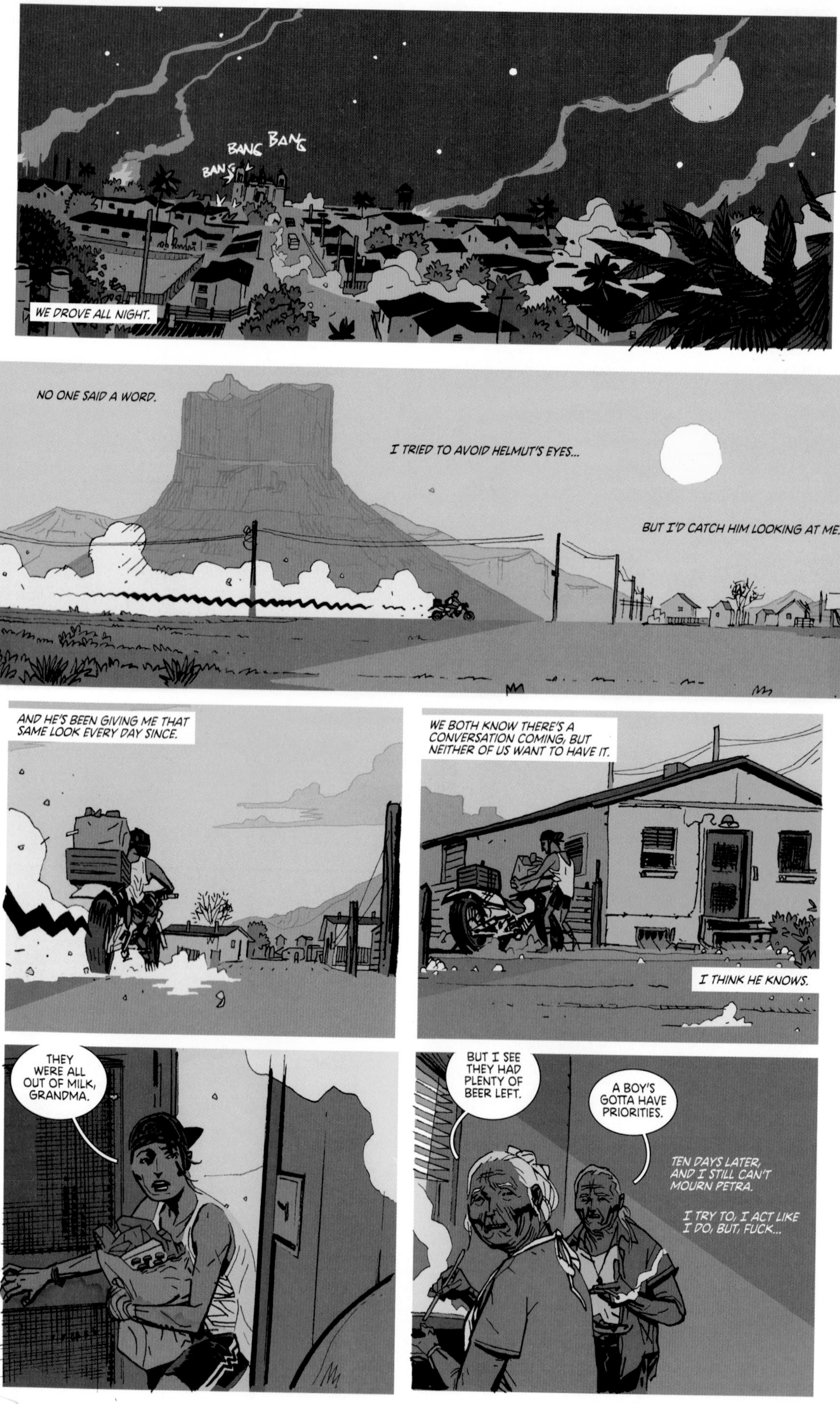
BANG
BANG
BANG
WE DROVE ALL NIGHT.
NO ONE SAID A WORD.
I TRIED TO AVOID HELMUT'S EYES...
BUT I'D CATCH HIM LOOKING AT ME.
AND HE'S BEEN GIVING ME THAT SAME LOOK EVERY DAY SINCE.
WE BOTH KNOW THERE'S A CONVERSATION COMING, BUT NEITHER OF US WANT TO HAVE IT.
I THINK HE KNOWS.
THEY WERE ALL OUT OF MILK, GRANDMA.
BUT I SEE THEY HAD PLENTY OF BEER LEFT.
A BOY'S GOTTA HAVE PRIORITIES.
TEN DAYS LATER, AND I STILL CAN'T MOURN PETRA.
I TRY TO, I ACT LIKE I DO, BUT, FUCK...

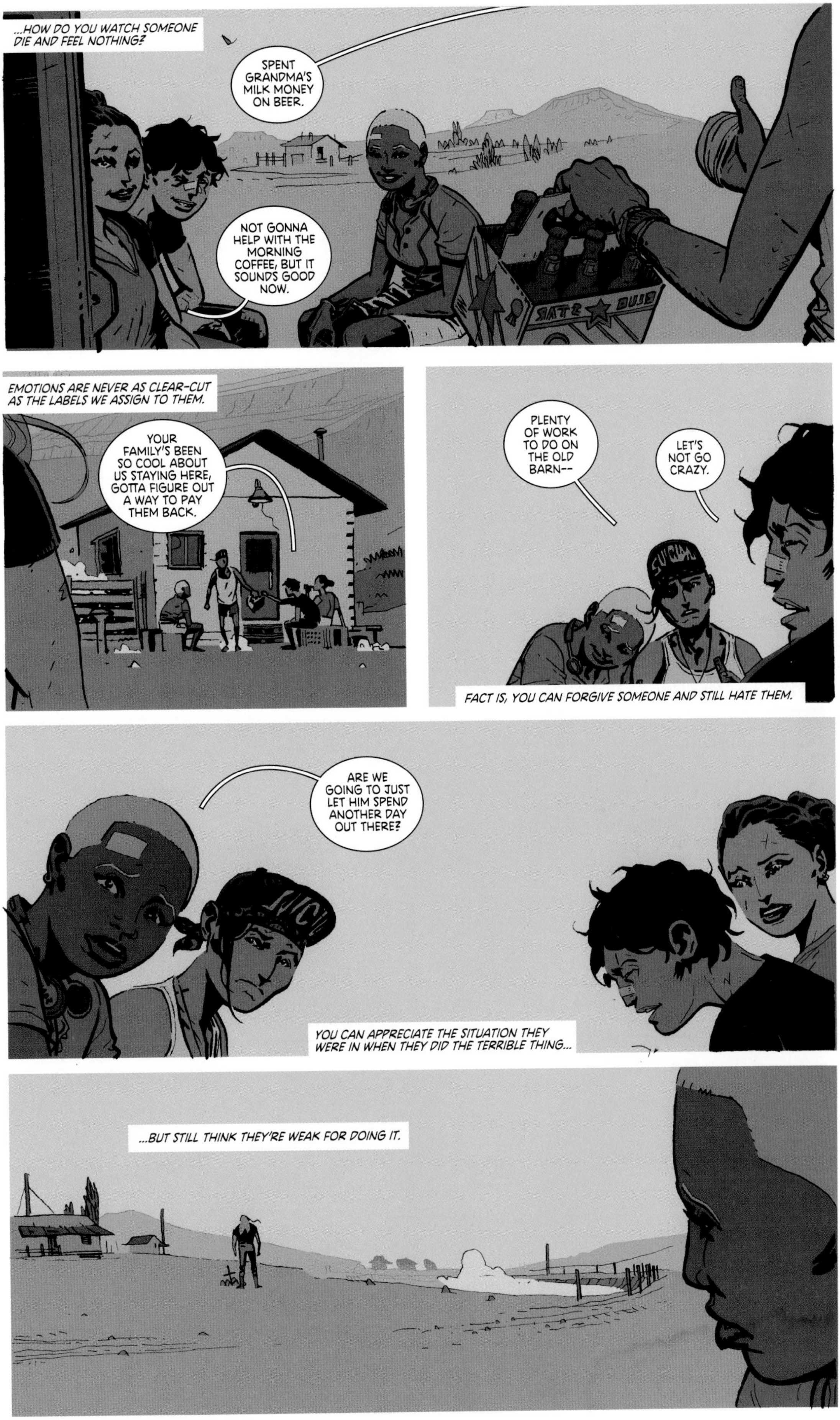
...HOW DO YOU WATCH SOMEONE DIE AND FEEL NOTHING?
SPENT GRANDMA'S MILK MONEY ON BEER.
NOT GONNA HELP WITH THE MORNING COFFEE, BUT IT SOUNDS GOOD NOW.
EMOTIONS ARE NEVER AS CLEAR-CUT AS THE LABELS WE ASSIGN TO THEM.
YOUR FAMILY'S BEEN SO COOL ABOUT US STAYING HERE, GOTTA FIGURE OUT A WAY TO PAY THEM BACK.
PLENTY OF WORK TO DO ON THE OLD BARN--
LET'S NOT GO CRAZY.
FACT IS, YOU CAN FORGIVE SOMEONE AND STILL HATE THEM.
ARE WE GOING TO JUST LET HIM SPEND ANOTHER DAY OUT THERE?
YOU CAN APPRECIATE THE SITUATION THEY WERE IN WHEN THEY DID THE TERRIBLE THING...
...BUT STILL THINK THEY'RE WEAK FOR DOING IT.

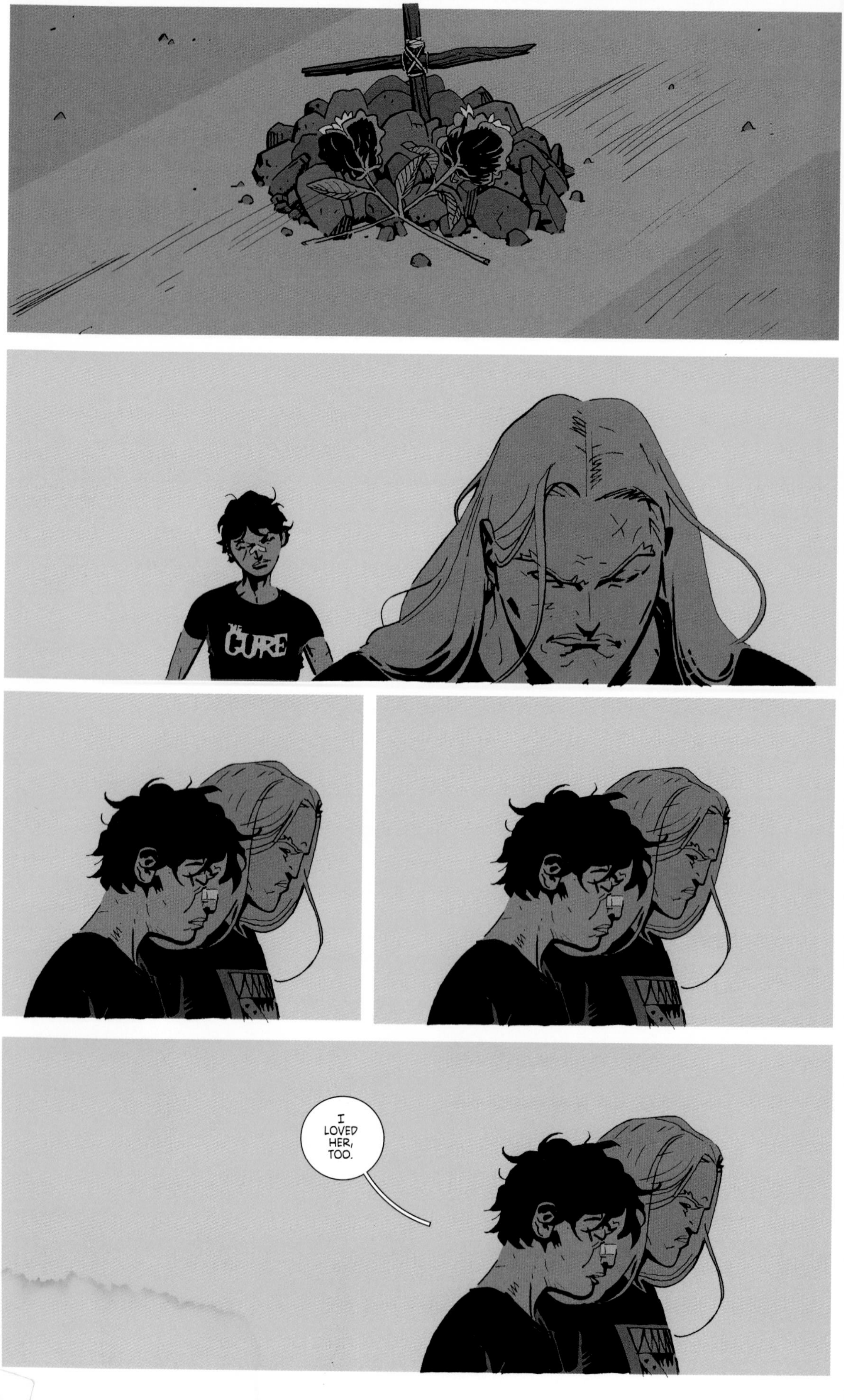
THE CURE
I LOVED HER, TOO.

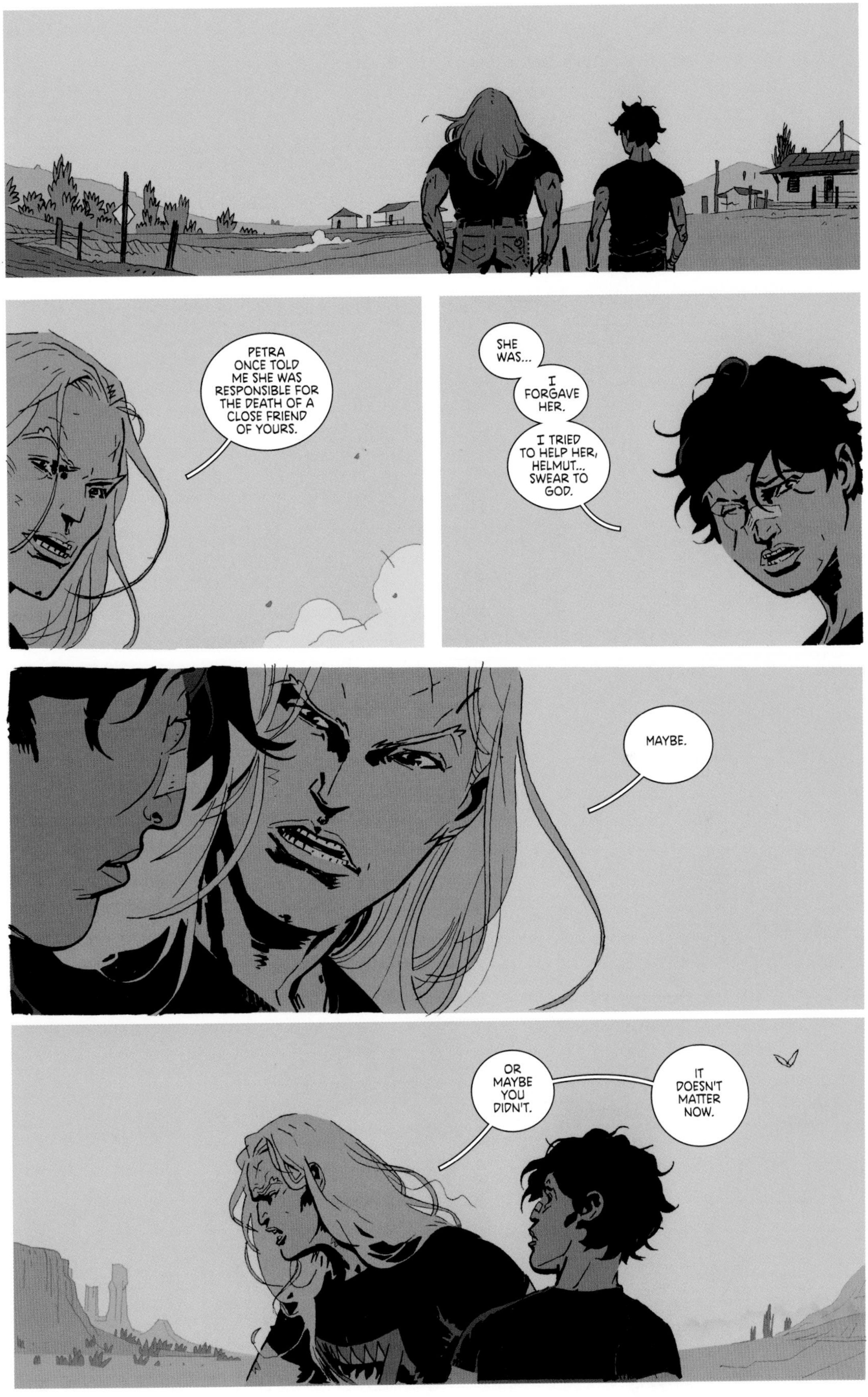
PETRA ONCE TOLD ME SHE WAS RESPONSIBLE FOR THE DEATH OF A CLOSE FRIEND OF YOURS.
SHE WAS...
I FORGAVE HER.
I TRIED TO HELP HER, HELMUT... SWEAR TO GOD.
MAYBE.
OR MAYBE YOU DIDN'T.
IT DOESN'T MATTER NOW.

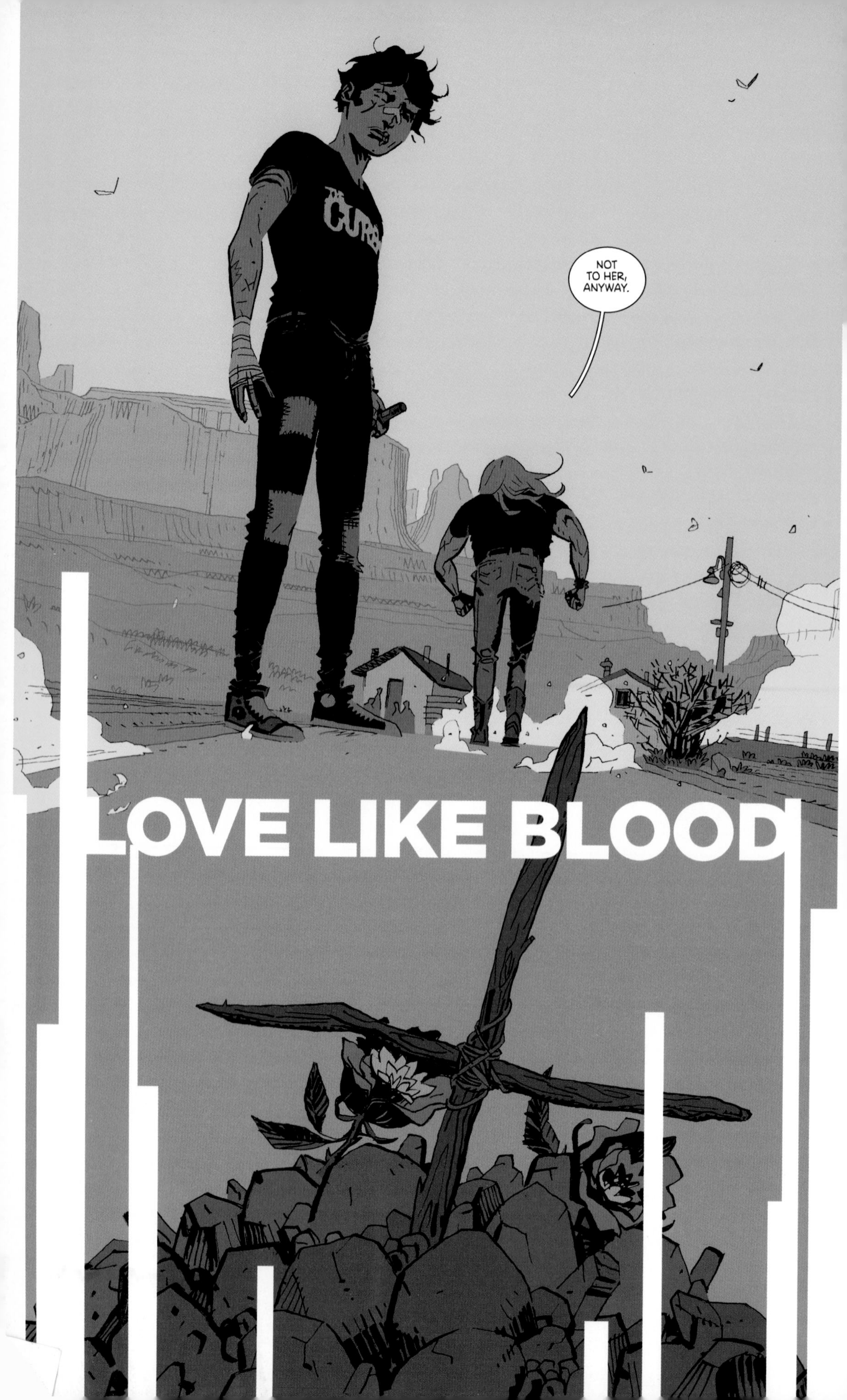
NOT TO HER, ANYWAY.
LOVE LIKE BLOOD

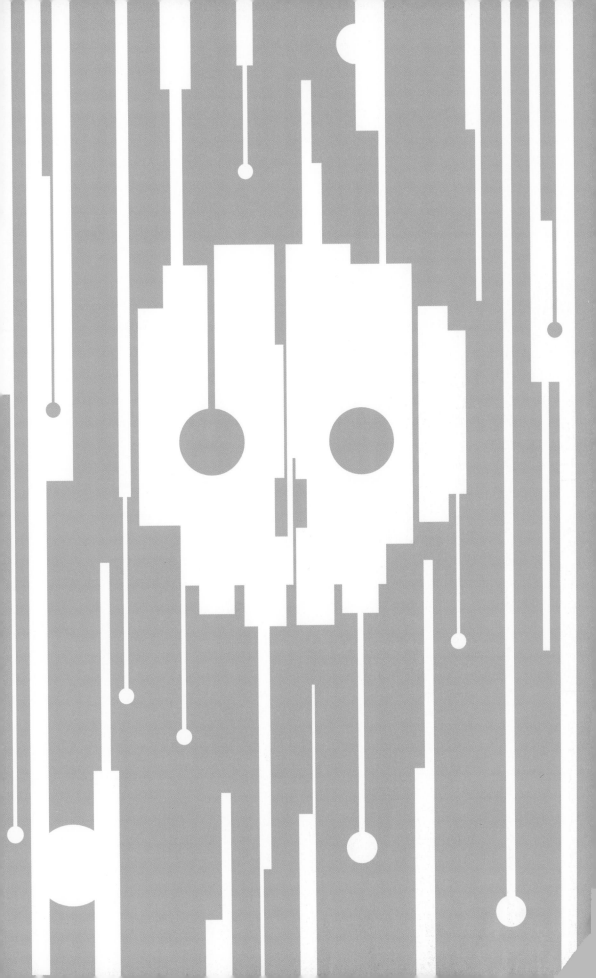

COVER GALLERY

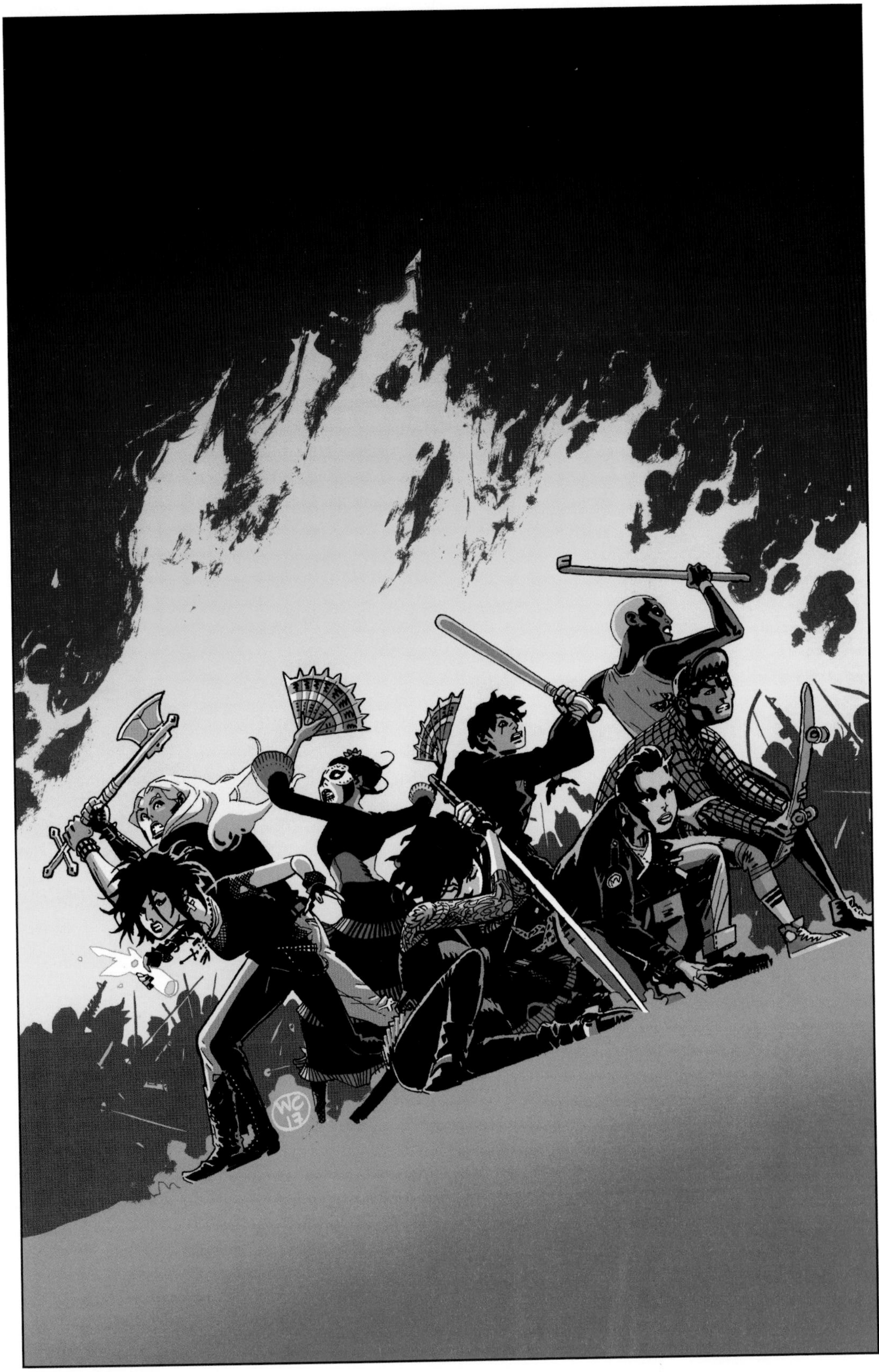

#32 COVER BY **WES CRAIG**

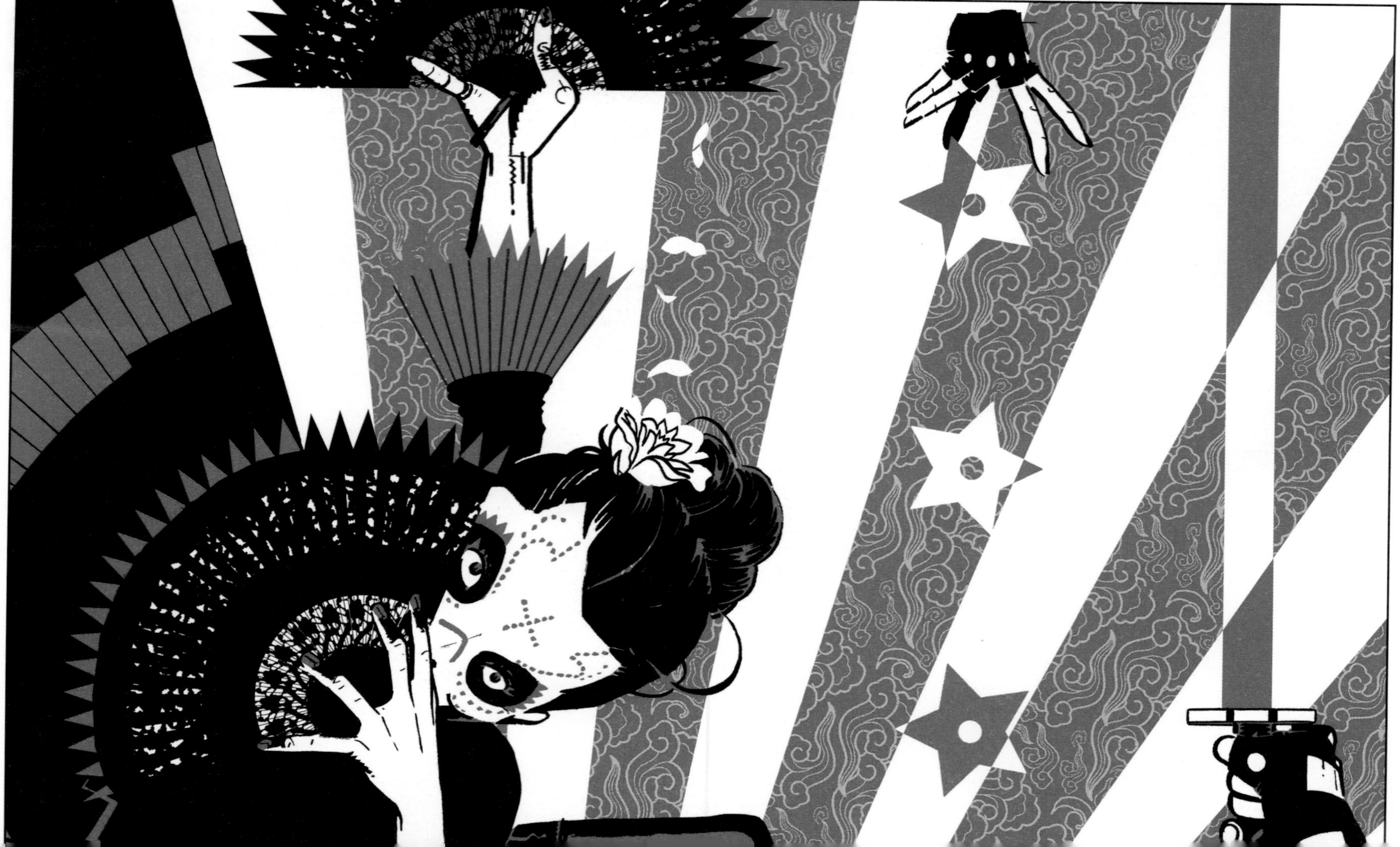

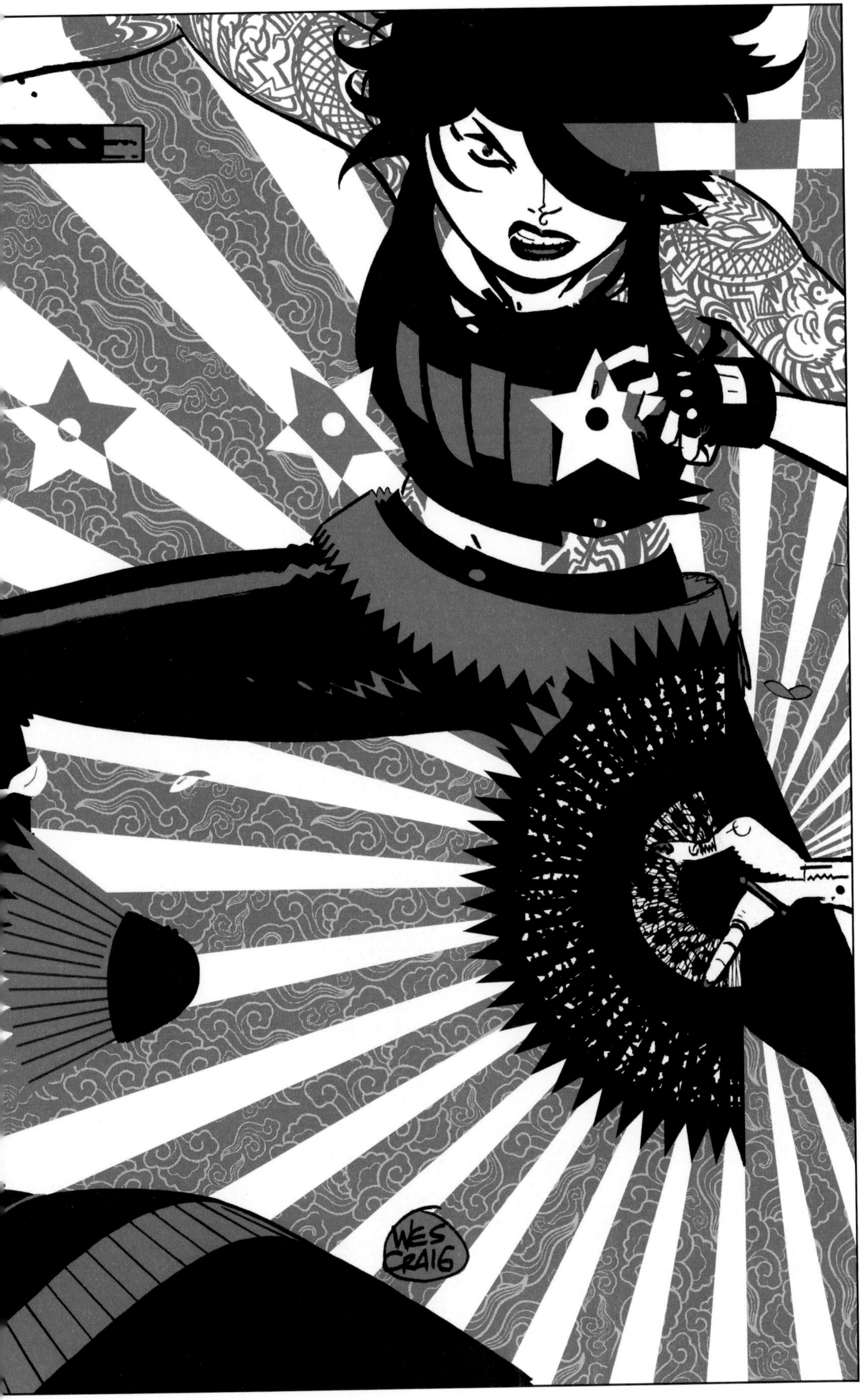
WES
CRAIG

#32 VARIANT BY **JASON SHAWN ALEXANDER**

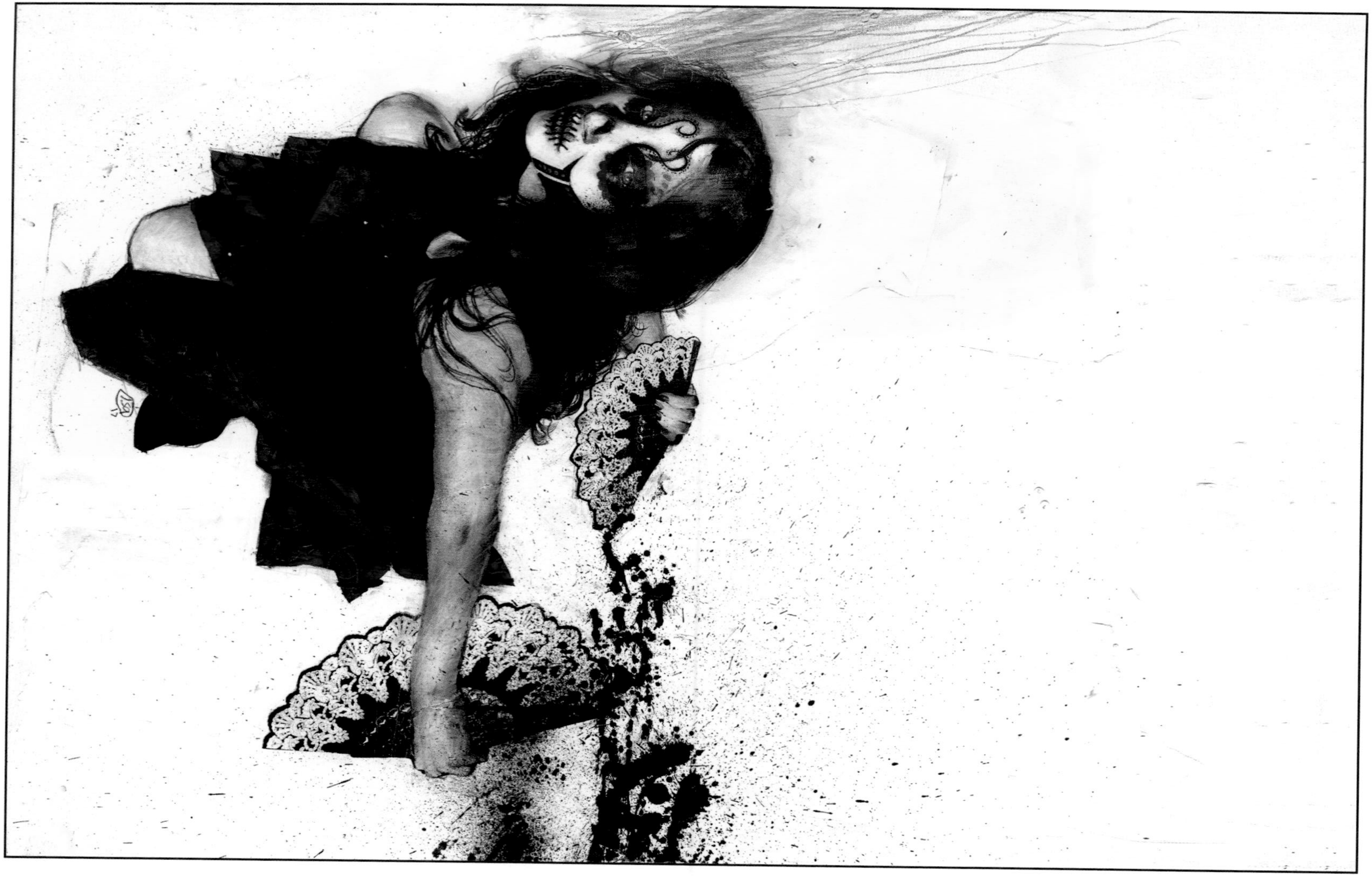

#33 COVER BY **WES CRAIG**

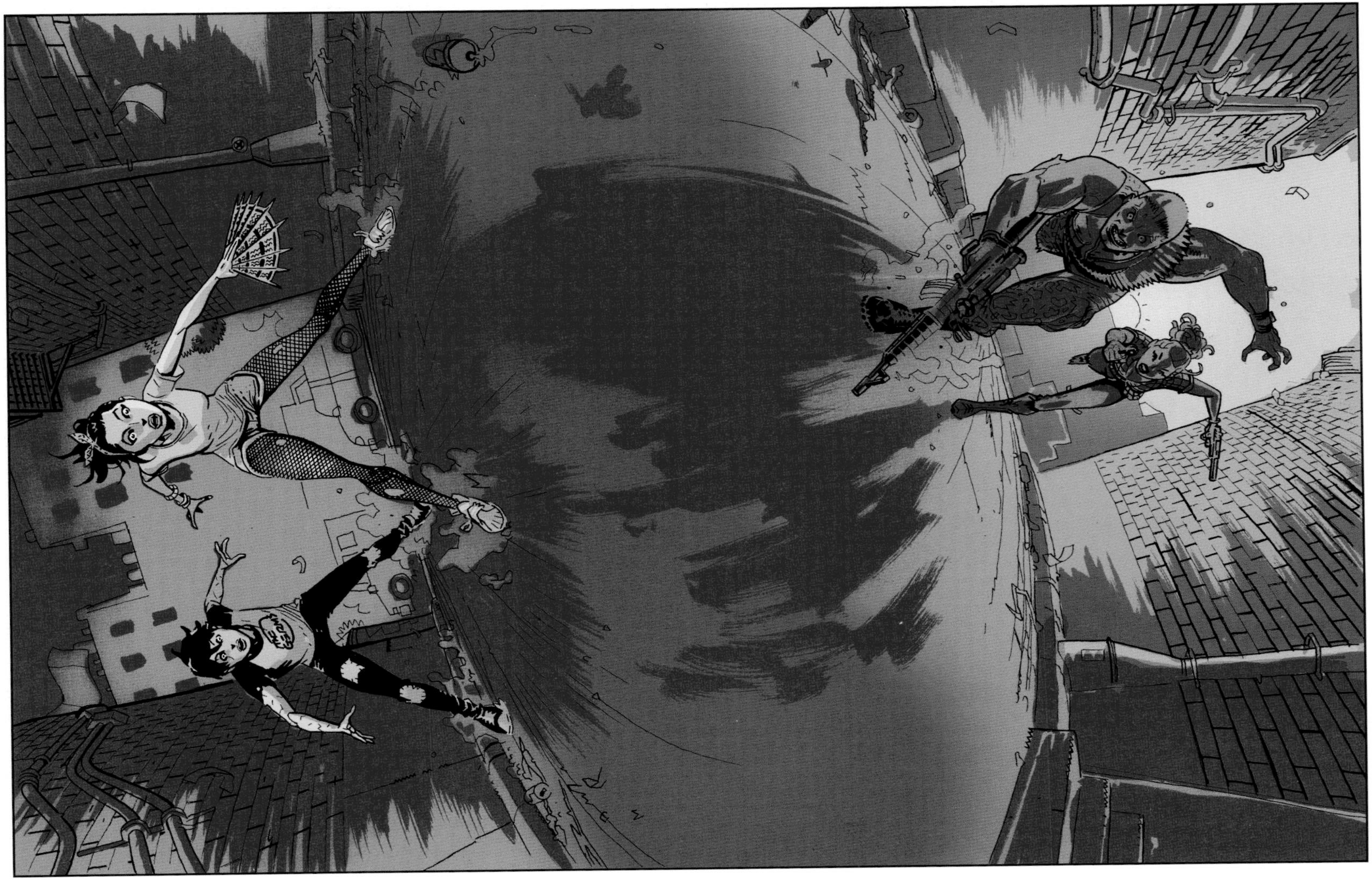

#33 VARIANT BY **JEFF STOKLEY**

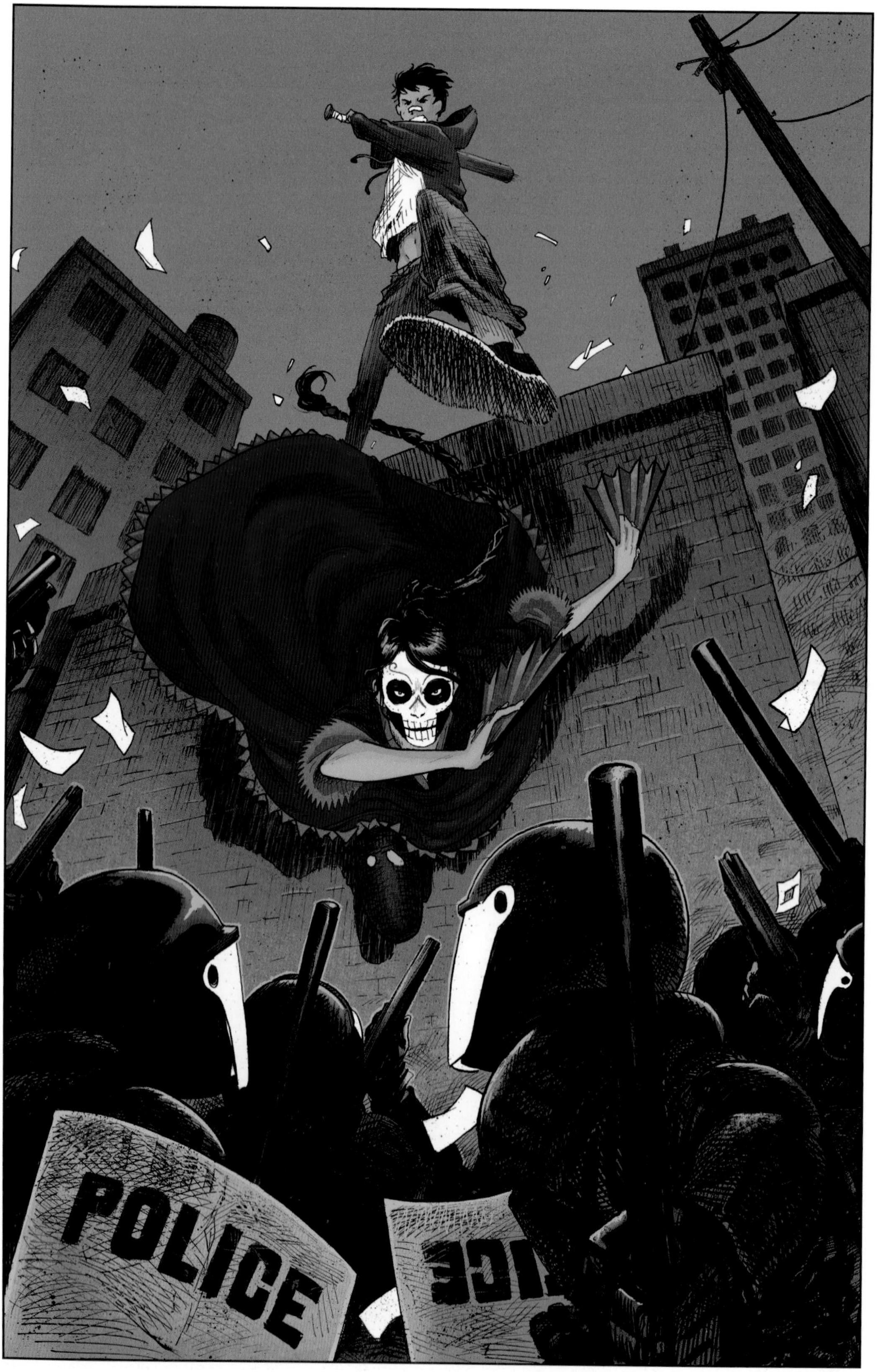
POLICE

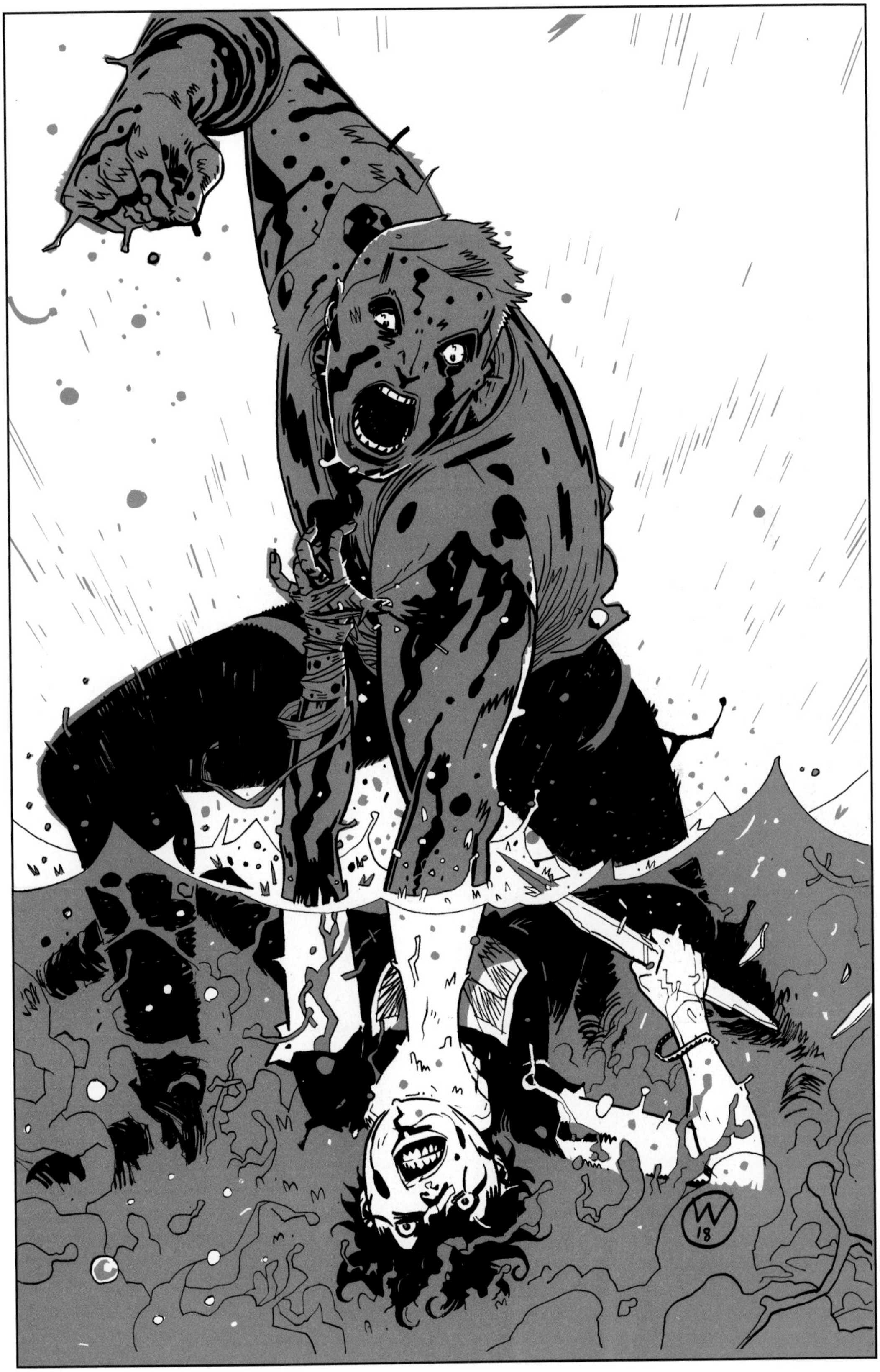

#34 COVER BY **WES CRAIG**

#34 VARIANT BY **RORY HENSLEY**

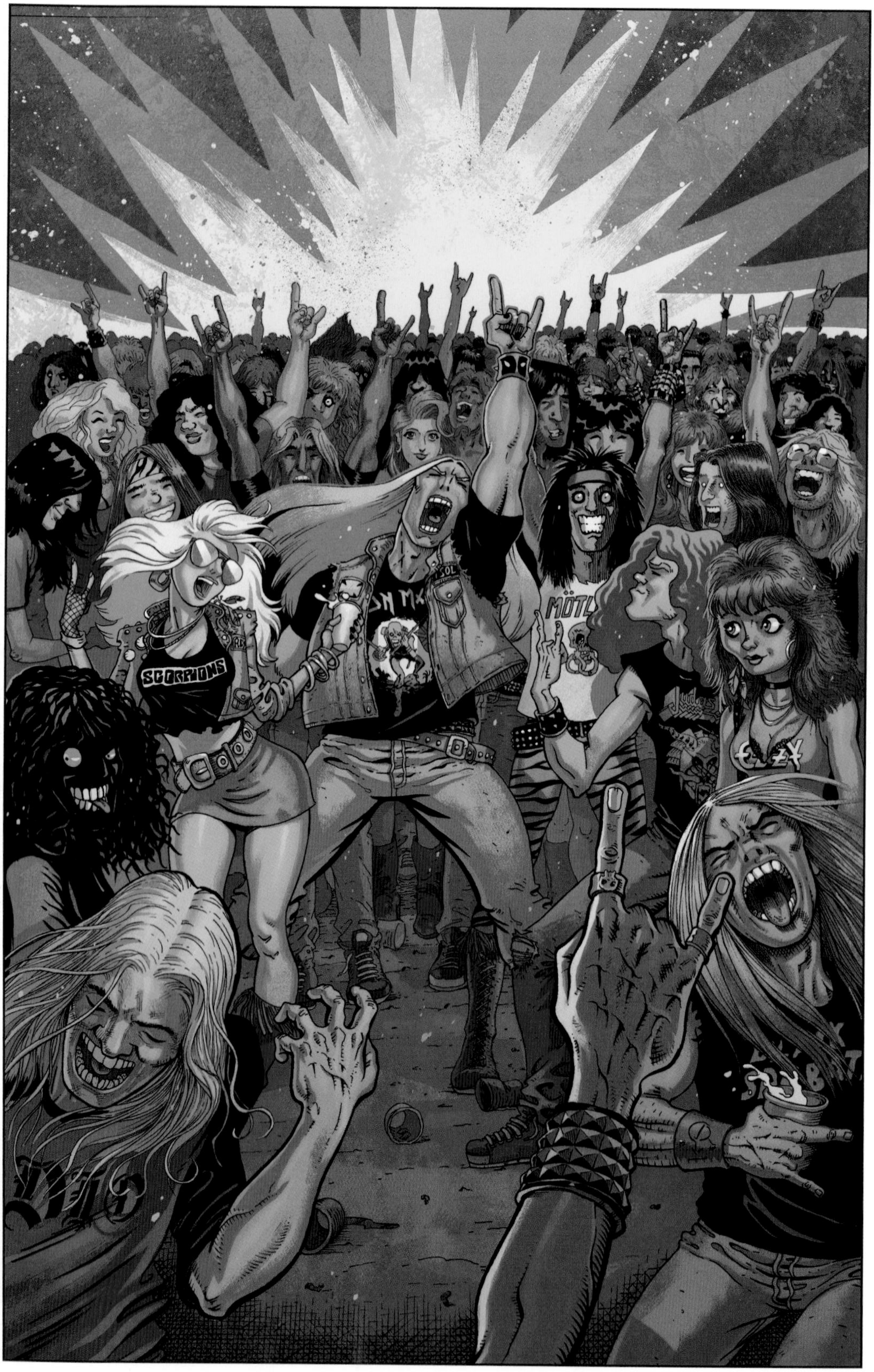
SCORPIONS

#35 COVER BY **WES CRAIG**

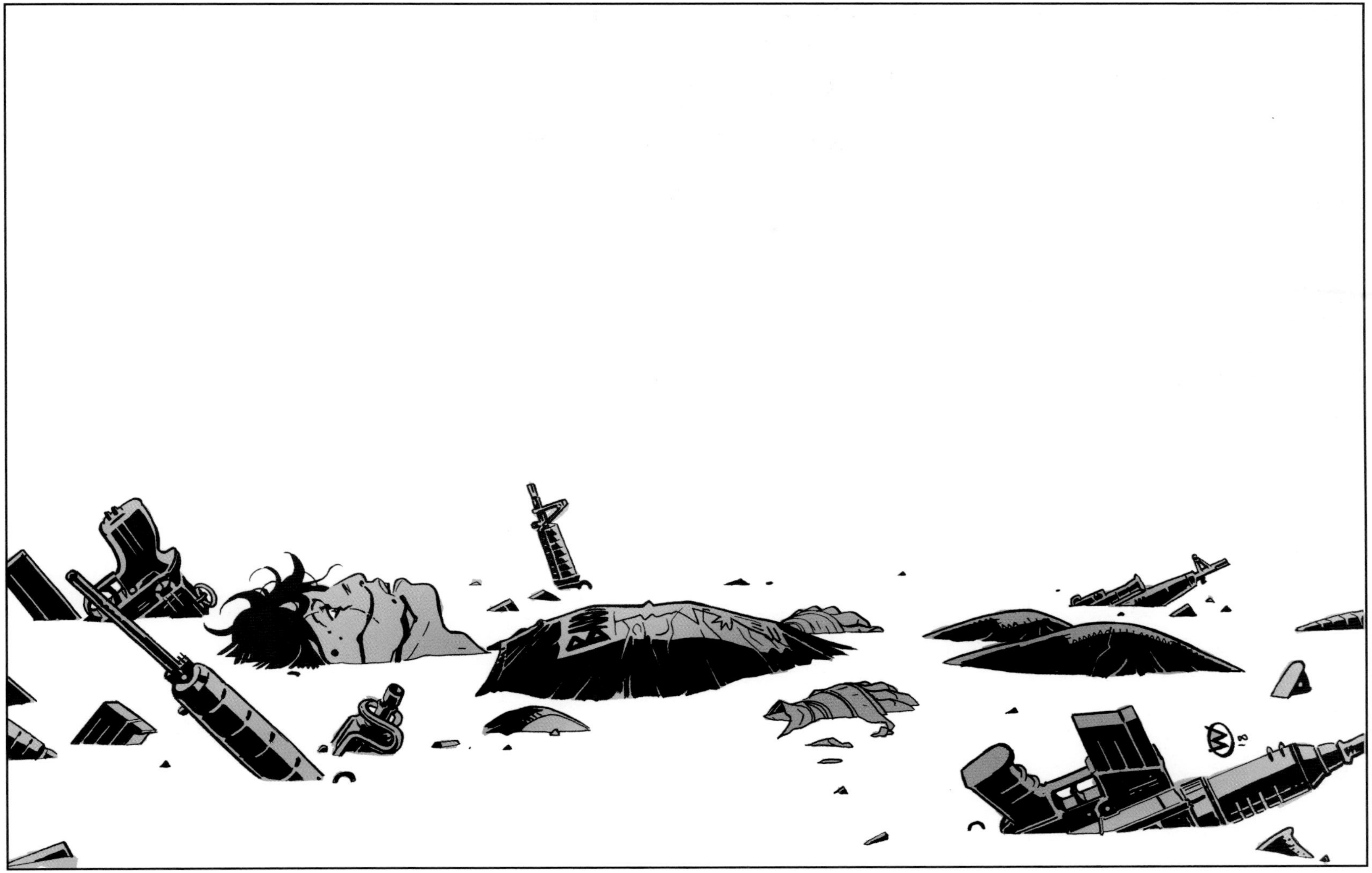

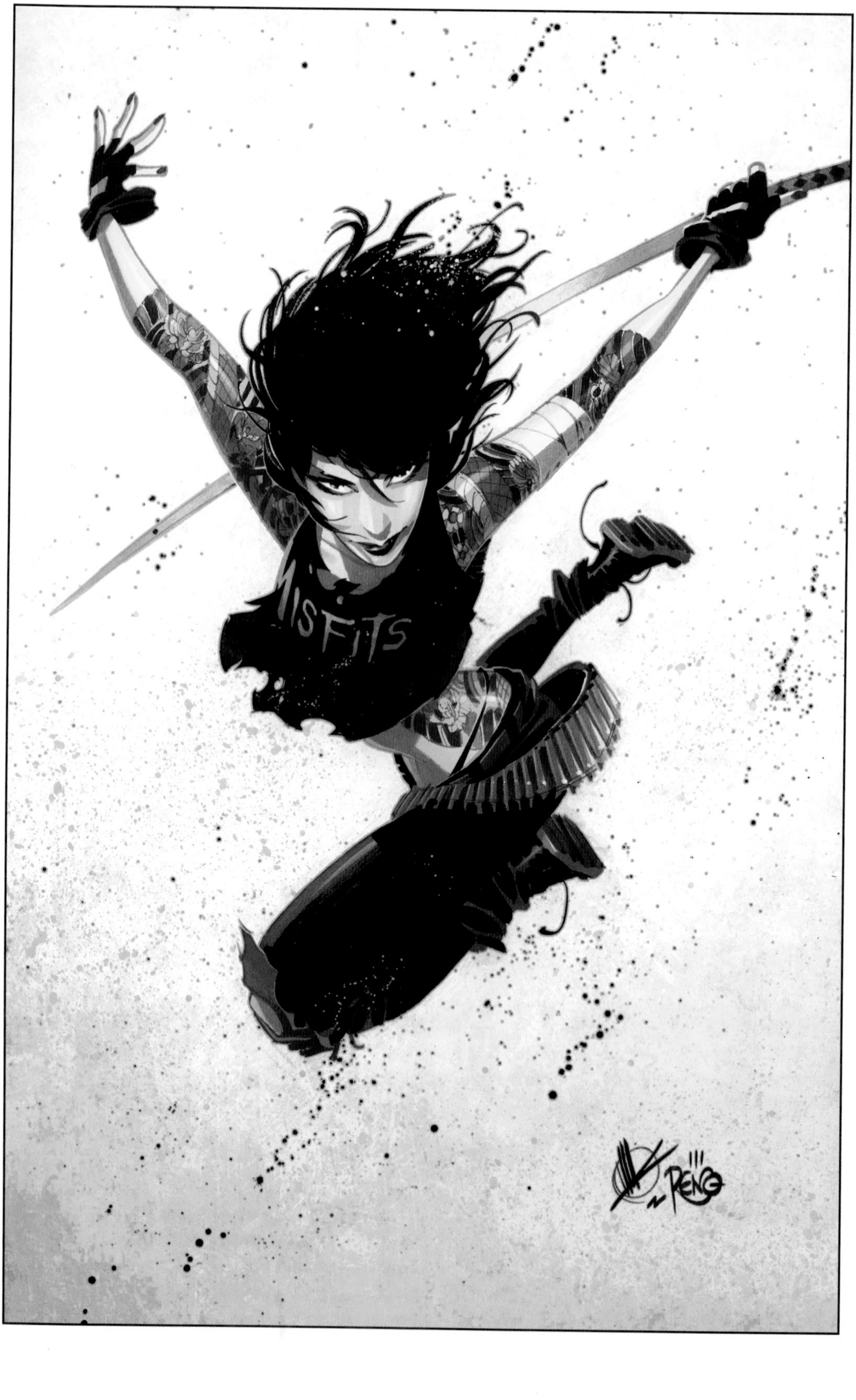
MISFITS

#35 VARIANT BY **MATTEO SCALERA & MORENO DINISIO**

#32 INTERIOR ROUGHS BY **WES CRAIG**

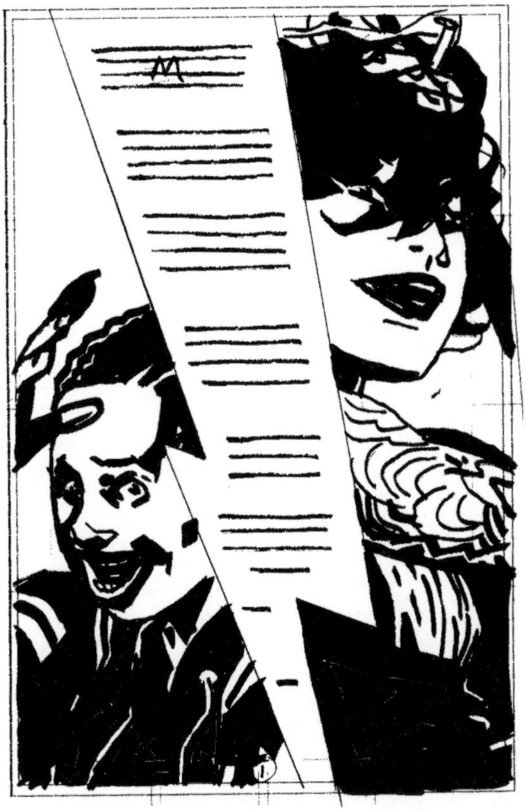
M

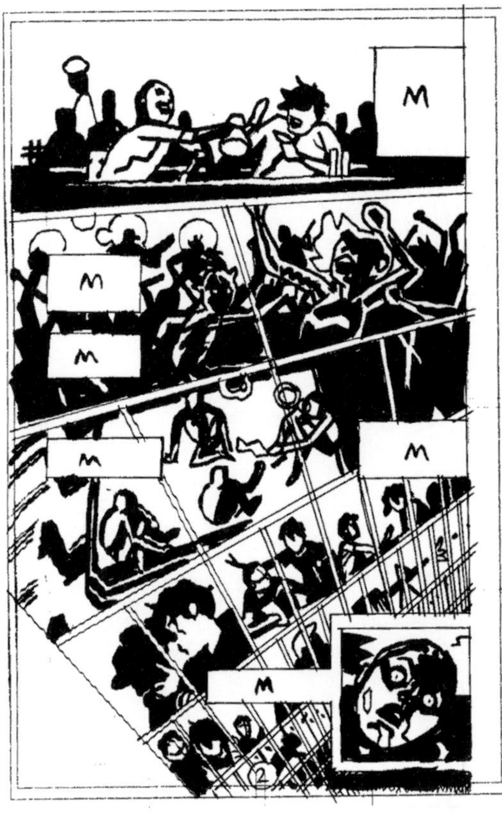
M
M
M
M
M
M
M

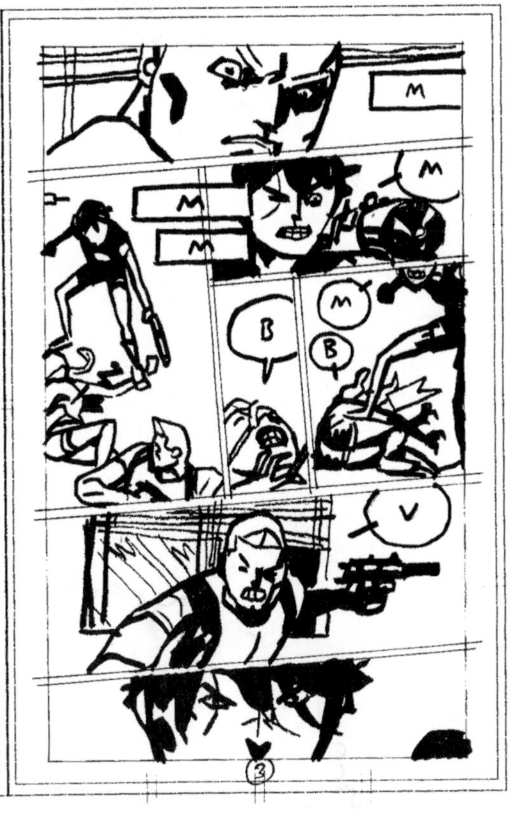
M
M
M
M
B
M
B
V

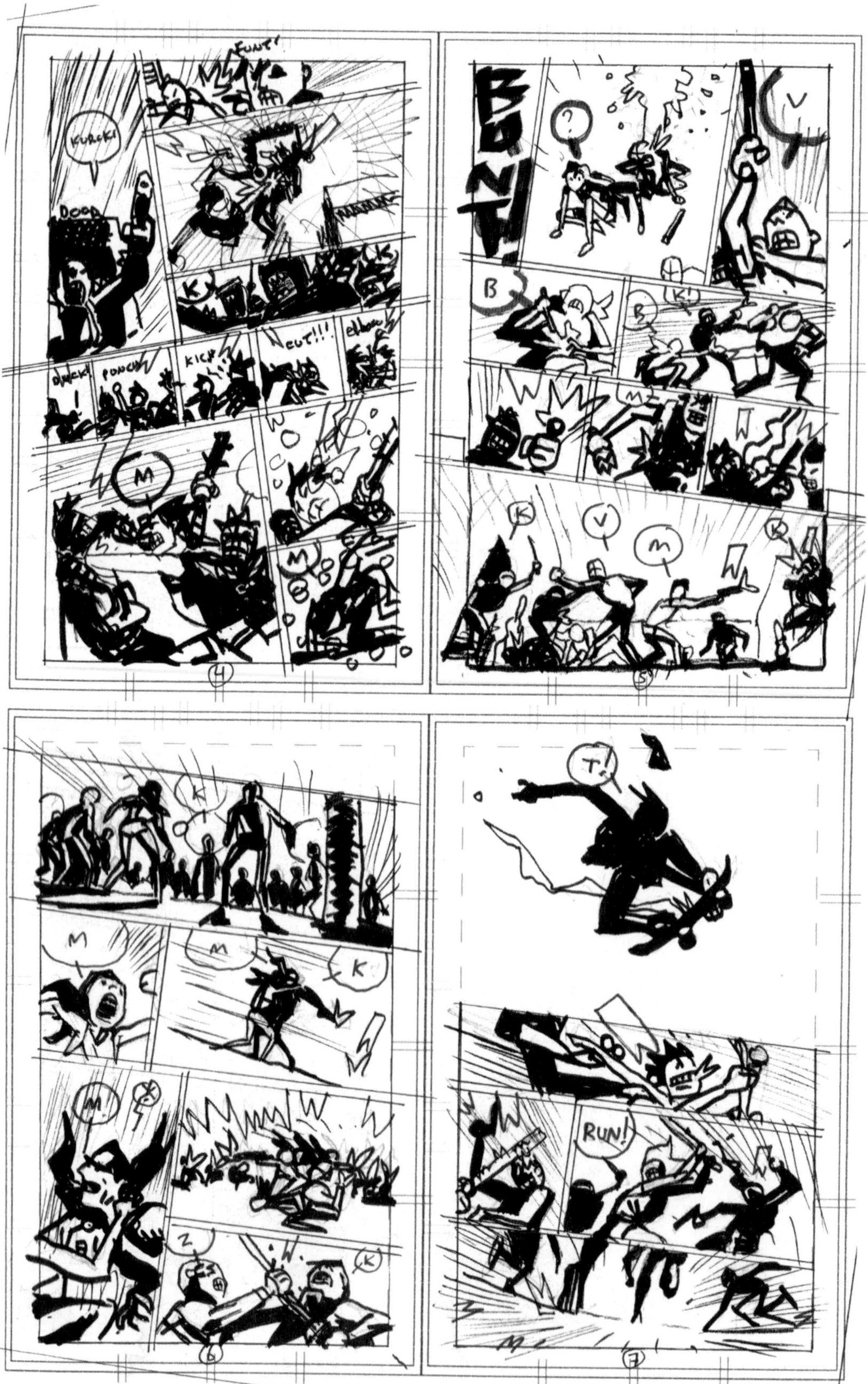

KURCK!
DOOD
KICK
CUT!!!
RUN!

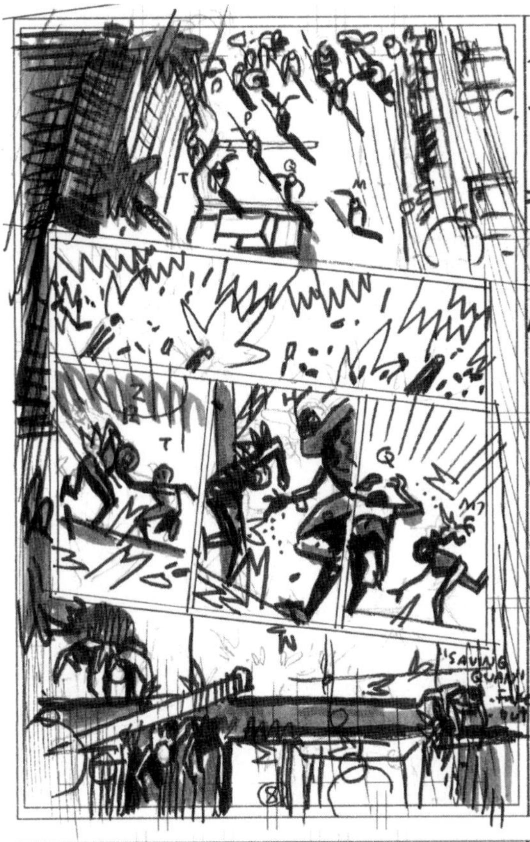
'SAVING
8

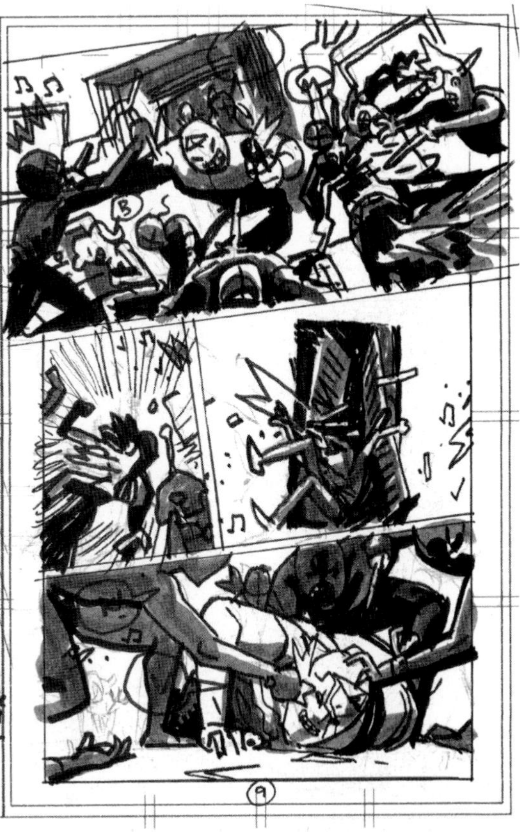
9

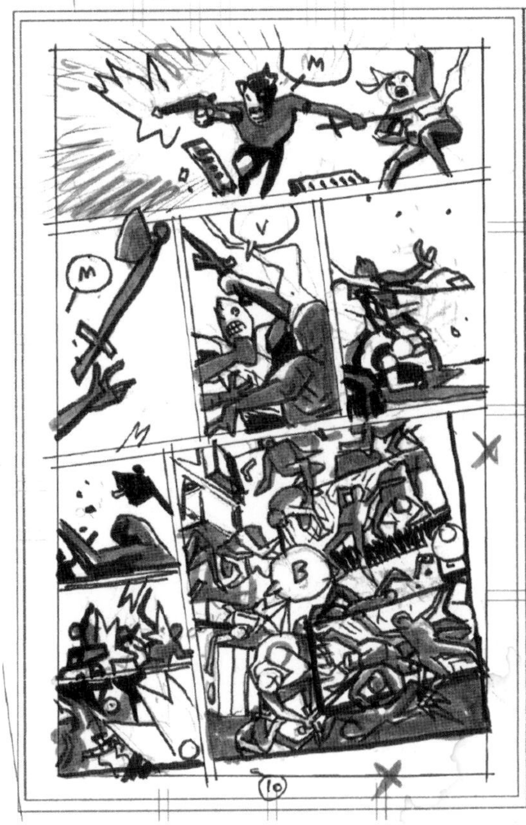
M
V
M
B
10

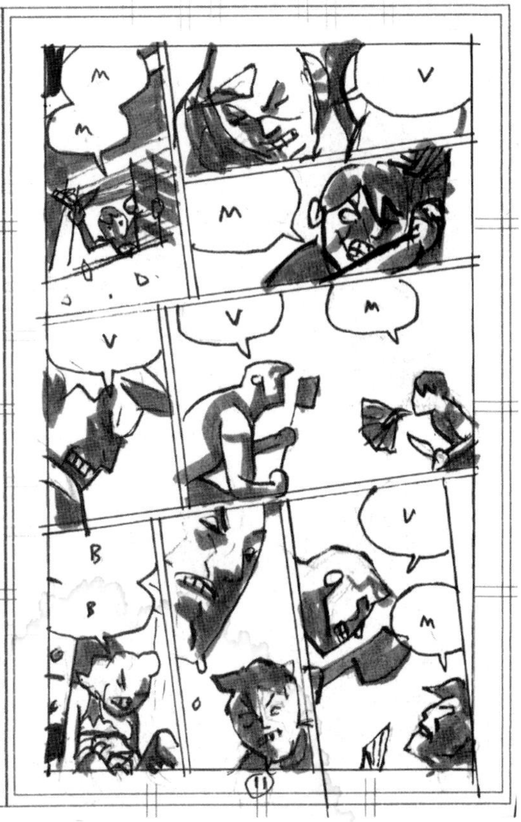
M
M
V
M
V
V
M
B
B
V
M
11

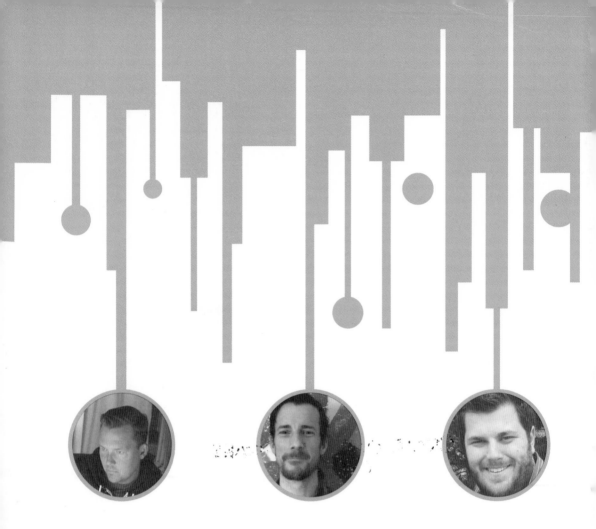

RICK REMENDER is the writer/ co-creator of comics such as *Deadly Class*, *Fear Agent*, *Black Science*, *Seven to Eternity*, and *Death or Glory*. During his years at Marvel, he wrote *Captain America*, *Uncanny X-Force*, and *Venom* and created *The Uncanny Avengers*. Outside of comics, he served as lead writer on EA's *Bulletstorm* game and the hit game *Dead Space*. Prior to this, he ran a satellite of Wild Brain animation, worked on films such as *The Iron Giant* and *Anastasia*, and taught sequential art and animation at San Francisco's Academy of Art University.

He currently curates his own publishing imprint, Giant Generator, at Image Comics while serving as lead writer/ co-showrunner on SyFy's adaption of his co-creation *Deadly Class*.

WES CRAIG is the artist and co-creator of *Deadly Class* with Rick Remender; the writer, co-creator, and cover artist of *The Gravediggers Union* with Toby Cypress; and the writer-artist of *Blackhand Comics*, published by Image. Working out of Montreal, Quebec, he has been drawing comic books professionally since 2004 on such titles as *Guardians of the Galaxy*, *Batman*, and *The Flash*.

Despite nearly flunking kindergarten for his exclusive use of black crayons, **JORDAN BOYD** has moved on to become an increasingly prolific comic book colorist, including work on *Astonishing Ant-Man* and *All-New Wolverine* for Marvel; *Invisible Republic*, *Evolution*, and *Deadly Class* for Image; *Devolution* at Dynamite; and *Suiciders: Kings of HelL.A.* from DC/Vertigo. He and his wife, kids, dogs, hedgehogs, and fish currently live in Norman, OK.